THE DAISY

R. E. Garber, Jr.

authorHOUSE®

AuthorHouse™
1663 Liberty Drive
Bloomington, IN 47403
www.authorhouse.com
Phone: 1-800-839-8640

Published by AuthorHouse 1/4/2013

ISBN: 978-1-4772-9856-5 (sc)
ISBN: 978-1-4772-9854-1 (hc)
ISBN: 978-1-4772-9855-8 (e)

Library of Congress Control Number: 2012923406

Table of Contents

Acknowledgement

If I could point to one person who has made this work possible, it would be the late Miss Ester Eloise Schneider. As my 9th grade English teacher, she soon discovered my reading skills were sorely lacking. She used her extensive skills involving speed reading techniques, which not only greatly increased my ability to read, but also developed a deep and lifelong love of reading, which extended into writing. Her early interest and efforts in me will always be remembered with deep gratitude.

I also wish to express my sincere appreciation to Diane Albertsen. Her knowledge, research, encouragement and dedication were invaluable in assisting with editing, bringing *The Daisy* to fruition. Any errors that may still be evident are the result of my bull-headed opposition to her recommendations.

And finally, I owe a great deal of thanks to my family; my wife for blindly allowing uninterrupted time to devote to this effort, never asking what *The Daisy* is about. I guess after 51 years, she already knew.

Special thanks to my grandson Josh Garber, for providing the cover reference sketch.

Foreword

The basketball game ended with a loss, and he was feeling down until he found her waiting at the door of the school. He had showered and most had already left to go home, but she waited for him to walk her home. It wasn't a very long walk from the school to her house; even the light mist that was not really falling, but more like hovering around everything, did not seem to bother them as they walked slowly, hand in hand. Was it really damp? Did it really matter? Her hand in his was warm and snug, but it seemed they arrived at her house way too soon. She was in the eighth grade, he in the seventh; would that make a difference in this great feeling he had for her? Was she more experienced than he in this new experience he was now feeling with her?

Soon they were standing on her back porch, and the light was so glaringly bright. For a moment they stood there gazing into one another's eyes; the situation was static and uncomfortable. Abruptly she opened the door, and went inside. Oh no!!! Is this how it is going to end? She didn't even say goodnight! The light was extinguished along with his hopes, but wait~~~she returned, took his hand and pulled him closer to her. He could see her eyes in the dim illumination the street light provided, and what he saw he had never seen before, but years later knew exactly what it meant; he was soon to discover what it meant now, for this moment. He felt their faces drawing closer and somehow, some way, their lips met. For one glorious moment the world stopped, his head was spinning, and his knees were suddenly weak. What if he should fall? How long it lasted, he will never know. There was no movement that he could remember. There was only the feel of her lips soft upon his, the feel of her breath from her nostrils on his cheek, the scent of her perfume filling his nostrils, and the feeling he had died and was in Paradise.

And quickly as it began, it was over. She pulled away slowly, but there was a tiny string of saliva keeping them united. He wondered where that came from, as his lips and mouth were so dry. She smiled at him, squeezed his hand and said, her voice soft and exciting, "Good night." She then turned and went back into the house. He stood there transfixed for what seemed an eternity, wondering what had just happened to him.

Slowly, he went down the steps and started his walk home, not remembering the steps he took to get there, or how the mist had turned to a light rain. He floated home, no longer thinking of the humiliating loss of the basketball game. Instead, his only thoughts were of this new feeling that was sweeping over him, and if it could be this thing called love. Somehow he found his way home and to bed, but sleep evaded him. The feel of her lips on his was still there, unlike anything he had ever felt in his young life.

His last thoughts before finally drifting off to sleep were~~~would she look different to him in the morning? Would he look different to her? Would he ever be the same again?

REG 1968

Chapter I
The First Daisy

Late September 2007

The late September morning air provided a hint of much colder weather that would soon find its way from the northern stretches of Canada. The sun never quite made it through the overcast to burn off the low hanging early fog, leaving patches of limited visibility. It was a dank, dismal day that previously had been nice fall weather for Midland, Michigan.

A sudden crisp breeze swept red and gold leaves across the gravel road, as the lead car of the procession slowly turned into the cemetery, followed closely by the hearse carrying his body.

The line slowly filled in around the site where a tent had been erected around the freshly opened grave, except for one vehicle off at a distant part of the cemetery occupied by a lone observer. A military contingent approached the rear of the hearse waiting for the funeral director to open the door to remove the casket and move it toward the receptacle. While family and friends gathered in and around the tent, several gentlemen helped position a wheelchair carrying the widow of the deceased near the head end of the receptacle as the casket was being placed.

The preacher proceeded with the simple ceremony, ending it with a conventional Christian prayer. Behind and off to the side of the tent, three volleys of seven shots rang out from an honor guard of veterans, while others lifted the flag over the casket and neatly folded it in the customary triangle, before presenting it to the widow and her daughter. Slowly, the family stood up and began to leave, some taking a single flower with them from the many baskets and sprays of flowers that had been placed around the grave site. Julie embraced her mother, holding her hand as the wheelchair was carefully maneuvered through the soft soil back to their car.

After the procession left the cemetery, the casket was lowered into the vault, followed by the lid and the soil, filling in the grave. The remaining funeral sprays and bouquets were arranged on top of the grave; the custodians gathered their tools and departed. All had left now, except for the lone observer in the vehicle that was parked some distance away.

The driver's door opened and a small figure emerged and slowly approached the grave site. If the tan jacket the figure was wearing failed to reveal the fact that the shape was feminine, the small hand carrying the single daisy certainly did not. Her hand was trembling as she lowered the daisy onto the grave amidst the other flowers that were there, followed by a tear that fell onto the ground beside them. She stood there for countless minutes, weeping quietly, and then brushed away her tears, turned and walked away.

One Year Later, 2008

It was midmorning when Julie entered the cemetery, parked her car and approached the grave with a fresh bouquet of flowers for her dad's grave, and a small utility bag that contained a small grass trimmer, some glass cleaner and some paper towels. She noticed a single fresh daisy already on the grave, thought it strange and wondered how it came to be there, but quickly brushed the question aside and added it to her bouquet. She had intended to tidy up the grave a bit, but noticed that it appeared neatly trimmed and was in good shape. Satisfied that the cemetery custodians were taking good care of the gravesite, she sat a while quietly talking to her father in words that one wonders if anyone really hears. Finally she dabbed her eyes with a tissue, slowly rose and departed.

Two Years Later, 2009

It was the second anniversary of her father's passing, as Julie returned to the cemetery with a handful of flowers she had picked from her own garden. Again, she found a neatly trimmed and orderly grave with a single daisy carefully placed near the headstone, which had been freshly cleaned. Observing the other graves, she noticed that they had not recently been trimmed or weeded; the headstones had dried bird droppings on them and were obviously dirty. She was bewildered, as clearly someone had been taking care of her father's grave and leaving a single daisy. What she had dismissed last year without much thought, she now found wildly curious and wondered who was doing this; more importantly~~~why?

She resolved to come to the cemetery a day or two earlier next year; keep an eye on the gravesite from a distance, and perhaps then she could meet the unknown person who was pruning her father's grave. As she left the cemetery, questions swirled around inside her head. "Why just a single daisy?" she wondered.

Three Years Later, 2010

Julie nearly forgot the pledge she made to herself the year before, to visit the cemetery a few days before the anniversary of her father's death. She dropped what she was doing, packed a small lunch, grabbed a light jacket, and drove out to the cemetery.

After arriving and casually walking past the grave, it was clear to her no one had been there for quite some time. "Good, I'm not too late. Now all I have to do is find a place very inconspicuous to keep an eye on dad's grave", she mumbled to herself, as she moved her car around a curve where she could park and still see the grave clearly. She felt a rush as she thought of herself a detective on a stake out, smiling as she contemplated how exciting this could be.

Soon the sun started to set and no one had entered the cemetery. The rush she had felt earlier was now turning to doubt; perhaps she was too early, or maybe the secret visitor was not going to make an appearance anymore. As darkness started to creep in around her and the cool evening breeze sent a chill down her spine, she started the engine and made her way home.

The next morning the sun rose around 6:45 and Julie was already on her way to the cemetery. If that daisy was already there and she missed the event, she would scream so loudly she would be heard in town. Certainly no one comes out here in the dark of night to place a daisy and clean up a grave. She knew she could not do that, as it would be too spooky.

But again, it was evident that no one had been there. Settling in at her chosen spot some distance away to observe the grave, she soon began to feel frustration start edging in as she was rapidly running out of patience.

This detective stuff was quickly losing its luster and excitement. As the sun started setting in the west, she gathered herself together to leave.

Before leaving, she stopped her car and walked over to the grave. As she stared down at the headstone, a frown creased her brow and said, "Don't worry Dad. I'll find out who is doing this if it is the last thing I do." Then, as an afterthought she turned, walked back to the grave and said, "Do you~~~already know?" As she walked back to her car, she wondered.

Julie dragged herself out of bed before sunrise the next morning, pulled on a pair of faded jeans and an old sweat shirt. Grabbing a jacket as she left the house, she mumbled to herself, "Dammit, I'm going to be comfortable this time." Her patience was wearing pretty thin now and the thought that the visitor might never return was playing heavily on her mind. Nearing the cemetery, she noticed the car that she had been following, turned into the gate ahead of her. Her spirits soared as she noticed the car stopping near her father's grave. Julie continued past the car, over to the far side where she had been staking out the site the past two days. She noticed her heart pounding and her hand shaking as she cut the engine to see what would happen. She didn't have long to wait. The car door opened and a petite lady slowly and carefully made her way to the grave~~~carrying what appeared to be a small bag in one hand, and a single flower in the other. Was it a daisy? Julie could not tell from this distance, but she was about to find out.

She started the car and slowly made her way over to where the woman had parked her car, stopping in front of it. She killed the engine, took a deep breath and opened the door. As she walked toward her father's grave, she kept going over in her head what she would say to this strange lady. The stranger looked up as Julie approached, appearing very nervous at the sight of her.

"Hello. Were you a friend of the man who is buried here?" Julie asked, her voice quivering slightly.

"Yes, I knew him many years ago~~~we were school mates."

Julie noticed the stranger's voice also seemed tight and nervous. "Oh, high school class mates?"

"No~~~it was before high school, actually."

"Do you live around here?" Julie noticed that the lady was slow to answer and that she again seemed very nervous.

"Yes," she paused and then continued, "well~~~no, not anymore. I was born here, but moved away some time ago."

A frown creased Julie's forehead before asking, "Did you know him well?" nodding toward the headstone.

The stranger averted Julie's eyes, looking first at the headstone on the grave and then to the ground. As she slowly raised her face, Julie thought she saw tears in her eyes as she replied, "Not too well; we~~~we were very young;" she paused and stammered, "I really must be going."

"Oh no, please~~~I don't mean to run you off. I come out here every year to tidy up the grave, but someone always beats me to it. Was that you?"

"Oh~~~no, it must have been someone else."

"Really, well that's funny. That someone always left a single daisy on the grave, just like the one you have in your hand. What is your name?"

Julie failed to note how accusatory her questions seemed until the lady appeared very agitated and extremely nervous.

"I'm sorry Julie, but I really must go," she said firmly, as she turned to walk away.

Julie was astounded by what she had just heard."Wait! How did you know my name? I didn't tell you my name. Who are you?"

The stranger stopped and paused for what seemed like an eternity to Julie, before turning around to face her.

"My name is Elizabeth~~~Elizabeth Callaway. Yes, it was I who left the daisy and tended the grave earlier. I didn't mean any harm."

"No, no, I'm sorry. I didn't mean that you did anything wrong. I just wondered why. Why have you done this the past two years? What was my father to you and how did you know my name?"

"Oh Julie, it's a long story. One I don't think you would understand or even believe."

"Well, I'd sure like to hear it. I know my dad was always full of surprises, but I must admit this really has me intrigued."

Elizabeth turned back to the grave, stared at it for what seemed a very long time before facing Julie again. Yes, there were tears in her eyes, as Julie could plainly see. "What is it? Who is this woman, and what was she to my dad?" Julie thought to herself as she looked in Elizabeth's eyes.

"I have an idea. Why don't we tidy up the grave together and you can tell me what you knew about my dad while we work? What do you think? Do you have some tools in that bag?" Julie asked.

"Yes, I have a small clipper, some towels, cleaner and gloves in the bag. But, I don't know what I could tell you about your dad or where I would even start."

"Well, why not start with how you knew my name?"

Elizabeth chuckled a little before she said, "Ohhh that would not be a good place to start. We will have to go back more than 50 years. I think I was in the 8th grade; your dad was in the 7th. We shared a study hall, the only time we were ever in the same room in school. I felt him staring at me from behind, as his seat was behind and to my left. Sometimes I would turn and look back at him, and he would blush and turn his eyes away. He was very shy, but cute."

Julie sensed that Elizabeth seemed more relaxed now and did not want to upset her again,

"My dad was cute?" Julie chuckled as she picked up the trimmer and started clipping the grass.

Elizabeth then knelt down and pulled up a small section of crab grass as she said, "Yes, he was cute and very shy. Of course I was shy too, so it was difficult to start a conversation. Your dad was on the basketball team and my girl friends and I would wait outside the school for the guys to come out after they showered; some of them would walk us home. Your dad walked me home this one particular night, reached down and took my hand without saying a word. We walked like that to my house without a word."

"My dad was speechless? Are you sure it was my dad?" Julie said as she laughed. She was enjoying this conversation with this new found friend of her father.

"Yes, it was your dad", she said with a smile, "and he didn't say a word later on my back porch when he bent down and kissed me. It was my first kiss and later I found out that it was also his first kiss. It was a very special moment, tender and sweet." She paused and was silent for a moment before continuing, "I've never forgotten that moment." Julie noticed a tear running down Elizabeth's cheek, falling to the ground, but could not find the words to speak as she thought, "Clearly, there is more to this story than this one kiss."

They were both silent now for what seemed an eternity before Elizabeth spoke again. "I went in the house afterward and into the bathroom to get ready for bed. I remember looking in the mirror to see if my mouth looked any different. I don't know why, but I felt different and thought I might look different. But of course, I didn't," she said with a sob in her voice.

Julie's mind was reeling. These were just two kids. How could this possibly have such an emotional effect on this woman after all these years from just one kiss? Julie looked down at her father's grave and thought to herself, "All right Dad, what have you done to this woman? What do I not know about you?"

Soon the grave looked neat and tidy and the headstone glistened in the morning sun. Julie looked at Elizabeth and said, "Have you had any breakfast? I know a great place that serves terrific omelets."

"No, I've just had a cup of coffee. An omelet sounds really good; I haven't had one in years."

"Good! Let's pack up and follow me. You still haven't told me how you knew my name."

CHAPTER II
Young Love

Julie took the lead into town and soon arrived at the restaurant with Elizabeth close behind. Her mind was racing with a thousand questions she had for this woman, this Elizabeth, not the least of which was how she knew her name. Where did she come from? How could a kiss a half a century ago bring this woman to her dad's grave? Why were there tears in her eyes?

"Well, here we are," Julie remarked as she pulled into the parking lot. "Are you hungry?" she asked with a cute little smile that her dad loved so much.

"No, not really~~~I don't eat much these days," she replied.

They entered the restaurant and were soon seated. Both ordering small omelets, Julie with tea, Elizabeth requested decaf coffee, black. As the waitress left with their order, Julie sat back and said, "Now, how did you know my name?"

Beth folded her hands and placed them in front of her on the table, took a deep breath and responded."Ben~~~can I call your dad Ben?"

"Of course, that was his name." Julie said with a chuckle.

"Well then, Ben and I happened to meet about 5 years ago quite by accident on Facebook. The changes in technology since Ben and I were young are amazing! It is so easy now to connect with long lost friends and to meet new ones. Ben and I would never have found each other without the Internet." Elizabeth's eyes lit up now, as Julie sensed the excitement in her voice.

"Ben had an ongoing conversation with an old classmate, who also knew and connected with my sister, Lynn. Lynn had never married and was still going by her maiden name. Ben happened to see that name and sent her a message asking if she could per chance be the same Lynn who has a sister, Elizabeth. He mentioned to Lynn that I was the first girl he had ever kissed," she said with a cute chuckle. "Lynn forwarded it to me as a 'blast from the past'. We both sent Ben a reply. He then sent me an email and soon we were emailing back and forth, filling each other in on where our lives had taken us and what we were doing now. We sent pictures back and forth and that is how I not only knew your name, but what you looked like, as well."

"Oh~~~that is so neat! Do you live around here? What do you do?"

"No, I live in Ohio~~~Columbus. I am a pediatrician. I've thought of retiring, but I would miss the children too much. I have greatly reduced my hours, though."

"That is quite a distance to travel just to place a flower on Dad's grave. Should I call you doctor?"

"No, you can call me Beth; that is what Ben called me. It's not really that far to travel. Besides, I love to travel."

Their omelets arrived, and Julie quietly and slowly digested not only the omelet, but also what she had learned so far. Something is missing here. Surely there must be more to this than what Beth has told her. The waitress returned to top off Beth's cup, but she waved her off, then looked at Julie and said, "Julie, I must be heading back," then glancing at her watch, "It's getting late."

"Surely you aren't going to start driving back to Columbus now! It's too late."

"No, the car is a rental, I flew here. I don't like driving very far anymore."

"What airline? I can fix it so you can stay another day."

"Why would you want me to stay? I really have to get back."

Julie shifted nervously in her chair. There was still so much she wanted to learn about this strange relationship this woman had with her father. She had to find a way to keep her here and yet not scare her off.

Smiling at Beth with a smile her father had told her could win any argument, she said, "I have to know how a kiss caused such a bond that would have you come all this way to tidy up Dad's grave and place a single daisy. What happened after that kiss when you were kids?"

Beth did not miss the smile and remembered Ben telling her about how Julie could charm him with that smile to get most anything she wanted. She felt the same charm Ben must have felt all those years when this young woman was growing up.

"Oh, there were some other ones, too." Beth said with a chuckle. Julie noticed that she had a cute, tantalizing chuckle. "Very nice ones, actually; we were an item for a while, but we were too young to take things any farther than kisses, as neither one of us knew enough about all those other things. Sexual mores were quite different back then."

"Yes, quite! Well, what happened? How did the two of you drift apart?" Julie asked impatiently.

There was a long pause. Beth looked down at the table, then across to the wall behind Julie. Julie thought she detected a tear forming in her eyes before she spoke again.

"One night there was an after game party at my house in the basement. There were a lot of kids there. I was just returning from upstairs when this guy that I barely knew, grabbed me and kissed me. I didn't like him very much before that and even less afterward. Ben was coming toward the stairs and saw the kiss, but not how it started. I could see the hurt and anger on his face~~~and in his eyes. I tried to stop him as he went up the stairs to leave, but I couldn't catch him. I went up to my room crying, not knowing what to do. I never went back down to the party."

Beth again paused, and looked up to the ceiling as though to collect herself. Julie sensed that she was having trouble talking about this and was about to speak when Beth continued.

"For days Ben avoided me. If he saw me in the halls, he would look away as if he didn't see me. I tried to call to him, but he ignored me. After a while, I became angry with him and gave him the cold shoulder, too."

Beth picked up her spoon and stirred her almost empty cup, searching for words before continuing.

"Then one day my Dad received word that he was to transfer to Florida, a permanent change of residence. His company would move us and we were to leave right away. I was excited at first and didn't give a thought to notify my friends that we were leaving, which included Ben too. At that age we don't think anything is truly permanent. It was only after we arrived in Miami that I realized I had not told Ben I was leaving. I cried for a while, but with the excitement of meeting new friends, Ben's memory started to fade. We heal fast when we are young."

"Did Dad ever find out where you had moved?" Julie asked, trying to break the spell. "Did you contact any of your friends in Michigan later?"

"Yes, I sent letters to my close friends back home and kept up some communication with them for a while. I never knew then if Ben ever tried to find me. Soon I met this guy in my sophomore year and I thought I was in love. We dated, things got pretty serious and I soon found myself pregnant. We married and before long my daughter was born."

"Oh, you have a daughter; what is her name?"

"Karen. As things turned out, she was the most wonderful part of my marriage. She is the light of my life."

Julie smiled. "Were there other children?"

"No. For whatever reason, Jerry~~~oh, I'm sorry~~~my husband, became a very jealous and mentally abusive person. He accused me of all sorts of things for no apparent reason. I felt so belittled and worthless. I was made to feel inadequate as a woman, a wife, a human being. I had lost all self esteem."

It was apparent to Julie that Beth was having a hard time relating this to her and feared if she pushed her too hard, she might end their conversation and leave. Julie did not want that; she had to know what this woman was to her father, what happened and when. Instead, she sat quietly and waited for Beth to regain her composure.

"I'm sorry Julie," Beth offered, her voice a bit shaky. "I don't know why I'm telling you this."

"Maybe you've wanted to talk to someone about it and I just happen to be the one you feel comfortable with. I hope so. I'm just so interested in what sort of relationship you might have had with my dad." Julie smiled as she went on. "Dad could always spring a surprise on me when I would least expect it. He could make me laugh at the craziest things. Yet, there was always a side of him that he kept locked up. Never too obvious, but I could tell there was something that was very private to him."

Julie paused to see if Beth would go on, but she sat motionless as if she was deep in thought. She then decided to push on, only very gently.

"Did you patch things up with Jerry?" she asked. "Did he ever hit you?"

"Oh no, there was never anything physical. Just the mental, almost constant, it never changed. After fifteen years of marriage, we divorced. I shut so many doors around me as a protective shield, determined to never become involved with a man again." She paused for a moment to collect her thoughts and then continued.

"I returned to school and poured myself into classes, working hard to prepare for Med School. Karen had become the beautiful person I am so proud of today. She provided the lift I needed to pursue my goal of becoming a pediatrician."

Julie felt that Beth was feeling more at ease with her, so she decided to go for it. "Where does Dad come into this?" she asked with a chuckle.

Beth echoed the chuckle with one of her own. "Well, I guess I went over my past life so many times trying to make sense of what all had happened. My parents and sister were very loving and supportive of me in everything I ever did when I was growing up. No one had ever belittled me like Jerry had and it made me wonder why. Looking back at the only other experience I had with boys, was with Ben. Those memories were so good! Sweet and loving, even at that young age. He made me feel important and worthwhile. Even when he was hurt, he never said a cross word to me~~~ just never said anything at all." Again she paused, but this time a faint smile crossed her lips.

"I began to think about those times more and more and how Ben had been so different. But, we were so young! I found myself wondering what ever happened to him and what he would be doing."

"You never tried to find Dad?" Julie asked as if she might have.

"No, I don't think I ever gave it a thought. But there were many times he would pop up in my memory and I could never quite figure out why."

"How did you come to choose pediatrics as a profession?"

"Oh, that was easy! Not so easy *getting there,* but easy to decide that is what I wanted to do. In my freshman year in high school, we were required to take a nine week health course. Part of that was reading about certain medical vocations and in particular about children with learning disabilities. At the time that seemed very interesting to me, but sometimes things happen in life causing a change in your direction somewhat."

"Did you date any during that time?" Julie asked.

"No, not until after I was through with residency and set up a practice. I became quite active in civic affairs and I enjoyed a good reputation that afforded me plenty of opportunities to meet many men~~~not all eligible," she said with a wink.

"There was one man several years ago who was very interested in a long-term relationship. While I was comfortable with a close friendship, I was never able to become truly involved. Those fears were always in the back of my mind~~~fear of failure, fear of rejection. I was afraid of being completely open, relaxed and honest with anyone~~~man or woman. I had resigned myself to being alone the rest of my life. Those doors, walls or that shell I put up around me those years ago were still there and would not go away. I once considered therapy but rejected it, as I didn't want to go over the past again."

Julie pursed her lips trying to digest all of what Beth had just told her. Surely a single, attractive, professional woman could have virtually any man she wanted. "You must have been awfully lonely. Did you stay in touch with Karen?"

"Yes, as much as I could, but she married and has a life of her own. I never wanted to be a burden to her. After a few years of practice, I decided it was time for a little vacation~~~time to get way for a while. It had been a long time since I had been in Michigan where I was born and had spent so many happy times. So, I decided to take a trip back here a number of years ago."

"Did you try to look up any old friends? Ohhh, did you see Dad?"

"Well, yes and no. I did try to locate some of my old friends, but was not successful. I did not see your dad, nor try to contact him." Beth paused as if in deep thought before going on, "But something very strange happened while I was here. I went to the place where we lived and found it pretty much as I remembered. I looked at the porch where I experienced that first kiss and suddenly found myself crying. I couldn't stay there; I felt so alone and lonely, like something was missing."

She paused, looked away and reached in her purse for a tissue and wiped her eyes. She could not hold back the tears now, but controlled them immediately.

"I'm sorry. I guess that's where your dad comes into all of this. I realized what was missing was Ben. I could not stop thinking about him. I wandered around town, but everything I saw seemed to remind me of him. I kept seeing this cute young boy with eyes that sparkled and smiled at me, not realizing he was no longer a boy but a grown man, probably with a family of his own. I found a phone book and my heart almost stopped when I saw his name and number. But I couldn't call him. I was afraid that he would not remember me and I would be embarrassed."

Beth paused, looked intently into Julie's eyes trying to read what she was thinking. "You must think I'm terrible." she whispered almost inaudibly.

"No, nothing like that; I'm just trying to let all this soak in~~~trying to grasp how you must have felt." Julie paused, and then added," So you didn't call?" she asked as if she found this little bit of information hardest of all to believe.

"No, I didn't, but from that moment on the memory of Ben kept popping up in my mind and each time that happened it warmed my heart. It seemed to sort of open up a little crack in that protective shield I had wrapped around myself for so many years. For the first time in a long time, I felt loneliness." Beth seemed to drift off into another world for a moment, staring past Julie before returning her gaze to her with a bewildered look on her face said, "And we were just kids."

Julie studied her face and thought she detected pain and sorrow in her eyes, as if a part of her had died. But as suddenly as that look presented itself, it was replaced with a warm, inviting smile as Beth continued with a vibrant, energetic tone in her voice, "Now you must tell me something about your life. Tell me about the relationship you had with your dad. What was your life like when you were growing up?"

Julie was sure that Beth was interested in those years and probably wanted to know more about what life was like for her father, rather than her. But for some reason, she felt compelled to tell her what life was like living with her dad during those early years. Besides, she did have a good relationship with her father and loved him very much, so why not?

"Oh gosh, I think the first recollection I had with dad was when I fell down the porch steps and busted my head open. I think I was three or four. I saw the bright red blood and thought I was surely going to die. Dad heard me scream and was the first to get to me." A smile crossed

Julie's face as she looked past Beth, remembering that special time. "He was so cool! He took me into his arms and showed no sign of alarm. His gentle voice soothed me; told me I was okay and that everything would be all right. He hadn't yet looked at my head, even though the blood was getting all over him. Head wounds bleed a lot and he knew that. He just seemed to know that the best thing to do right at that moment was to keep me calm, and he did. Mom brought him a cold washcloth; he held it against my head and made me think that the bleeding had stopped. Of course it had not."

"Did the wound require stitches?" Beth asked, obviously interested in what Julie was relating.

"Yes, it required two. I didn't even know we were going to the hospital until we were there. I started to cry again, but Dad said that he wanted to show the doctor what a big girl I was. I remember he told the doctor that I had bumped my head and he wanted the doctor to put that stuff on it to make it feel better, like what he had put on his head once. I remembered thinking that Dad must have fallen down the steps, too. And soon it did feel better."

Beth smiled, "You trusted him, didn't you? He was your guardian angel."

"Oh, yes! Dad always made it easy to talk to him~~~about anything. He always insisted that dinnertime was family time and that was the time to share whatever was on our minds. Funny~~~there were only the three of us, but Dad made it sound like we all had something to talk about. I was an only child, did you know that?"

"Yes. Ben related that to me in an early email."

"Did he tell you why?"

"No. I never felt that was any of my business, so I never asked."

Julie leaned back in her chair, took a deep breath and decided it would be all right if she told Beth about this part of her life. "Dad traveled a lot then and I think they had planned on having another child, but had put it off for later, thinking Dad would not have to travel so much. But, Mom was in an automobile accident and it very nearly killed her, leaving her paralyzed from just above the waist, involving both legs. Her spleen and uterus were severely damaged and both had to be removed. Many super infections racked her body, one right after another."

Julie paused and bit her lower lip before adding, "Even after the initial crisis was passed, there were months of rehab that turned into years of all sorts of complications. The sleeping arrangements were not working, as neither of them could sleep due to the constant tossing and turning in bed. Dad had to get up early in the mornings for work, so naturally he was not getting the rest he needed~~~besides he now had to work as well as tend to Mom's needs. Fortunately, I was old enough then to help out some. I remember one time I got up in the night to use the bathroom and I heard Dad crying in the living room. When I went there to see what was wrong, he feigned sleep." Julie looked down at the table shaking her head from side to side. Beth reached across the table and touched her hand as she said, "Oh honey, he was lonely and hurt. His life was put on hold too."

"Yes, I guess so. Of course I didn't know about those things then and Dad never talked about it. In fact, after Mom's accident, he seemed to withdraw into himself. I noticed that a few years later, as I grew older; he became more secretive and sort of moody and I blamed it all on Mom's condition." Julie paused and was thoughtful for a moment, then continued."But wait a minute~~~that was pretty clever. Get me talking about my life and there are still so many questions unanswered about yours!" Julie said with a laugh and a smile. "I still don't know what happened with you and Dad. Certainly you must have made some sort of contact that went beyond emails."

"Oh Julie, I feel strange telling you some of this. After all, Ben was your dad."

"Well of course he was, but he was human. I knew him as a warm and sensitive man. He had a keen sense of humor, liked to make people laugh and was very outgoing. He seldom held things back, except for something that I knew was underneath the surface, but I never could get a handle on what it was that he kept locked up inside. Sometimes he would drift off somewhere sort of like in a trance~~~millions of miles away. Funny! His facial expressions would change, from a sort of blank stare, to a sort of evil smile." Julie then laughed and added, "Like he was having an erotic dream."

Beth laughed and felt a little flushed. Julie was quick to notice the blush and said, "You know something about that, don't you?" Julie smiled a sort of knowing smile and added, "Do you know what he might have been thinking about during those times?" Julie now had a pleading look on her face, telling Beth that she genuinely wanted to know the answers to her questions. "Beth, please don't feel that I would be offended by anything you tell me. If Dad had some skeletons~~~and I'm sure he did, it doesn't matter. Gosh, if there was something that gave him pleasure in his life, then I'm happy he found it, because he deserved whatever pleasure he could find."

Beth sat quietly for what seemed like hours to Julie. How could she tell this beautiful young woman, who clearly worshiped her father, that she too loved him? How could she explain the events that happened to her and to her father, in ways that Julie could understand; how their lives had reached across time and rekindled an ember that started a flame? How could she ever understand? How could she tell her without hurting her?

"Julie, I can't expect you to understand any of this. Some things happened as if in a dream, a dream I never wanted to end." A tear ran down Beth's check as she stared past Julie.

"Beth, were you in love with my dad? She asked almost already knowing the answer, yet wanting to know more.

Beth hesitated before answering. "Our emails became more and more personal. Ben told me things about his past and how he often times thought of me, wondering if I was happy. He talked about that first kiss and how he never forgot about it. He told me about how his life had changed course so many times and how his most precious memories were your birth and that one kiss we shared." Beth paused and tilted her head to the side as if deciding what to say next. "Soon I found myself telling him very personal events in my life and the sad ending to my marriage with Jerry. I couldn't believe I was telling him these things. I had never told Lynn about any of this and she was my very best friend, as well as my sister. Ben listened and never offered any criticism, only his gentle understanding. I think he must have felt my tension as I was telling him these things, so he broke the spell by saying he couldn't remember the sound of my voice. I told him I could not remember his voice either, but it had been so many years and I was sure our voices would not sound the same anymore. He then asked if I had a cell phone and of course I did. He very carefully~~~and by the way, he was very skillful at this sort of thing~~~asked me if I would have any objections if he was to call me." Julie noticed the smile that crossed Beth's face with this disclosure.

"And did he call you?" Julie asked, feeling the excitement Beth must have felt at the time.

"Yes, he did. I was so nervous when the phone rang. He told me when he would call and I was so afraid he wouldn't like my voice or that I would say something wrong. But it was not like that at all. Almost instantly he had me laughing and feeling that I had known him all those years. It was fun! His laugh was contagious. My nervousness soon vanished; I found I was totally relaxed and enjoying our conversation. But there was so much to talk about and so little time. Even after all the hours we had spent with emails, it was like we had to go over all of it again. It was so personal."

Beth sat back in her chair and let out a sigh as if there was a weight lifted off of her shoulders. She noticed the smile on Julie's face and it told her that what she had said agreed with her, so she continued.

"Julie, after that phone call, something was very different~~~I felt warm inside. I could still hear his laughter and the way he could mix laughter with words. We agreed to trade phone numbers to use in a case of an Internet failure, so we could keep in touch. But, I wanted to hear his voice again and soon called him. He answered with 'Emergency on this end, too' and we were both laughing again. We soon found that the phones were rapidly taking over what the Internet once provided."

"You never answered me. Were you in love with my dad?" Julie asked with a knowing smile on her face.

"Ben kept saying things to me that made me feel very loved and appreciated. I could tell he had strong feelings for me, but never came right out and said anything like what you're suggesting. He just sort of 'danced around it'. I don't think I even thought about my own feelings right then. I was just trying so hard to understand what Ben was trying to say to me. I just~~~~" she stopped and let her words hang in the air, clearly not going to finish her sentence.

Julie knew it was time to change the subject, as clearly this was still too emotional for Beth and maybe not the right place to pursue this line of questioning. She suddenly had this idea.

"Beth, this place is getting crowded. Why don't we go to my place? It's private and a lot more comfortable."

Beth was still dabbing her eyes as she said, "Oh, I couldn't do that! I would be intruding."

"Nonsense, you would be my invited guest. Besides, it gets lonely there at times, as I live alone since Mike and I divorced eighteen months ago. I still have not been ready to get in the dating scene yet. I'm not really in much of a hurry!" Julie said with an air of disgust.

"That's very nice of you, Julie, but I really have to get back. My plane leaves at 4:45, and I should be there early to get through security."

"We can fix that problem. I know this guy who works for United and he's been wanting to date me. He can get your flight delayed for a tomorrow departure. There will be no problem. And the bed sheets in the spare bedroom are fresh. We have lots to talk about, so I will not take no for an answer!" Julie's voice carried with it a certain degree of authority.

Beth laughed. "You sound like your dad when you talk like that. He was never bossy, but always liked to sound like he was in charge. It always elicited laughter from both of us. His eyes would sparkle when he laughed, much like yours just did."

"Well, that's where Dad and I differ~~~I mean it!" she said with a wink. "So let's get out of here and let me take care of the rest."

They rose to leave and Beth picked up the tab before Julie could get it. "Oh Beth, let me get that. It will make me feel like I'm earning the information I'm going to get from you," Julie said, laughing out loud.

Beth smiled and handed the bill to Julie. "I don't know about that or about any more information you might extract from me. But whatever that might be, it will be free. It just feels so awkward as I was not prepared to meet you. My work sometimes puts me in precarious positions and I find it difficult to tell parents some things that they do not want to hear. I hope this is not the case now."

"No, no! I want to hear everything you can tell me about Dad. I know he looked happy before he~~~before he left us. He looked peaceful, like he had found peace." Now it was Julie that was tearing up. "Come on! Let's go!"

Beth dutifully followed Julie but wondered if this was a wise thing to do. What all could she tell Julie? She felt an instant affection towards her, but this was her father she was talking about. She had not even been able to think about all the memories she had shared with Ben, and certainly was not sure if she could talk about them. How close is Julie to her mother? Surely she would not want Ben's widow to know about her. Why was she doing this? Why did she let Julie talk her into this? She did not have the answers but felt this amazing warmth being with this young woman; this wonderful feeling of closeness to Ben.

CHAPTER III
Revelations

Soon they arrived in front of Julie's home, a small dwelling in a pleasant neighborhood. "This is nice," Beth said as she got out of her car, "and quiet."

"Yes, it's mostly older people living around here~~~no kids and they keep pretty much to themselves. Come on in and welcome to my humble abode," Julie invited as she opened the door.

Beth noticed that the decor screamed female, with nary a masculine article to be found. Reading Beth's mind, Julie quipped, "Yes, I've cleared everything out of here that resembled manhood," Julie chuckled. "I do not want to look at them for a while or anything that closely relates to them."

Beth could not contain her laughter."Oh, you will in time. I walled myself in so tightly, I gave up any thought of what it would be like to be held by a man or make love again."

Julie picked up on that instantly. "Are you saying something happened~~~with my dad, that changed your mind? What was it? When did it happen?"

"Not so fast!" Beth replied very quickly. "I didn't say that. I just meant your perspectives can change in time. We can learn to feel again, to live again~~~and yes, to love again! It will happen in time, Julie. You are young and very beautiful with so much to give to the right man."

Julie was hanging on her every word and realized that even though she had not said so, she knew Beth had somehow, somewhere been her dad's lover. Yet, there was something else, something different and something beyond just being a lover. She had to know. She had to know more. How did this happen and what happened.

"Well, take off your jacket and make yourself comfortable. Would you drink some coffee if I put some on?"

"Yes, that would be nice. I think I caught a chill driving to the cemetery. The years in Florida spoiled me with warm weather. I can't get used to Michigan's cool fall temperatures. Even Columbus isn't this chilly so early."

Even as she said those words, Beth knew it wasn't the weather that caused her chill. She suspected that Julie also knew.

While Julie was busy getting the coffee started, Beth used the time to look around Julie's living room. She found a family photo framed in an 8x10 sitting on top of an entertainment center. Clearly, it was Julie and she assumed the man was Mike. There were no children.

"Is that Mike in the photo?" Beth asked as she returned to the kitchen.

"Yes," Julie said, and then asked, "How do you take your coffee?"

"Just black and steaming!" Beth said with a chuckle. "You have no children?"

"No." Julie paused before continuing. "I lost one shortly after we were married. It was a messy miscarriage, late in the pregnancy. I lost a lot of blood and had to be hospitalized. I was told that another pregnancy could kill me, so I had my tubes tied. I hated that, as I wanted a child so much."

Julie took a sip of her coffee and looked away to hide the sadness in her eyes. Beth could feel the pain she must have felt during that time. "I hope it doesn't sound like I'm letting my professionalism run away with me, but did you ever considered adopting? There are so many babies out there that need loving homes." Then as quickly as Beth offered that advice, she relented. "I'm sorry. That is really none of my business! I had no right."

"No need to apologize. I considered it, but Mike wouldn't hear of it. He wasn't too fond of the idea of being a father and I think he was happy I lost the baby. It was a boy and I thought he would have liked to have a son, but I guess I was wrong."

"How did Ben and your mother take the loss? Weren't they looking forward to their first grandchild?"

"Oh yes! Dad was ecstatic when he learned I was pregnant. Before long, my belly was bigger than his!" Julie said with a laugh. "While he never let his disappointment show, I know he was hurt. He was so full of support for me, telling me I could try again. I never told him that I couldn't. I didn't want to disappoint him anymore."

Julie realized that this conversation was going in the wrong direction. Instead of learning about Beth and the relationship with her dad, Beth was playing doctor, extracting information about the relationship she had with her father. She knew that this had to change and change quickly as she exclaimed, "Oh, wait a minute! You did it again! You escaped my inquisitive mind! I'm supposed to be asking the questions." Julie said with a slight smile.

"Oh Julie," Beth said with a chuckle, "I think I've told you all I can." We spent many times chatting on the Internet and on the phone. We got to know each other fairly well that way."

"Are you trying to tell me that you have never met my dad?" Julie asked with some semblance of authority and annoyance in her voice.

"That would have been impossible. The distance between us was too great." Beth said, averting Julie's eyes.

"No, that would not be a problem. Dad traveled a lot. You knew he was a consultant, didn't you?" Julie asked pointedly.

"Yes, I knew that. We had talked about his work."

"Uhuh, and I'm sure he could have worked in a special stop during one of those visits. If Dad was nothing else, he was very efficient and knew how to make the most of his visits," Julie said with a sparkle in her eye.

"No, he would never do that. He never combined business with personal interests."

"So you are saying that you have never seen my dad since 1956?"

"Julie, I think that is what I have said."

"Then how did you know I have Dad's sparkle in my eyes. When did you see that sparkle~~~when he was fourteen? I don't think it would have been there yet."

Beth looked away from Julie and was silent for what seemed an eternity. Yes, how did she know? How did she let Julie trip her up? She, the doctor that asks the questions and is always filling in what the patient doesn't say; then she slips and lets Julie catch her in a major mental lapse. She felt tears forming again as she pondered how she was going to answer Julie's charge.

Finally, Beth again faced Julie and looked into her eyes.

"Julie, you must understand that Ben and I talked at great length over several months, both over the Internet, then over the phone virtually every day. We instantly were drawn to each other and wanted to learn so much about what each of us had experienced through the years~~~where our lives had taken us. We agreed from the start to be very honest with each other or~~~why even bother." Beth paused, but Julie did not speak for fear she would let Beth drift off subject again.

"From the very start," Beth continued, "we felt this intense closeness, almost like we had never been apart or as if we had been together in another lifetime. I know that sounds silly and we even talked about how we both had the same impression since our first email. Ben began to tell me about his early life at home. He was rebellious as a teenager. He wondered many times what had happened to me and was angry that he couldn't find where I had gone. He became very impulsive, becoming involved in some things he later regretted. I could hear the pain in his voice as he was relating stories he had never shared with anyone before."

Julie was fast losing her patience with Beth. "What does that have to do with my question? I'm sure Dad had some problems when he was young. He had told me about some of that. Did the two of you meet~~~or not?"

Beth sensed the frustration that Julie was feeling and she feared the frustration would soon turn to anger if she tried denying her any further. She did not want to anger her, but still found it hard to admit to Julie that her father had committed adultery.

"Ben~~~from the very start, told me how much of an impact I had on his life and how he could not stop wondering about me. That I was very special~~~that he had tried to find someone who would fill the void he felt. Instead of fading, his desire became even more acute. He kept saying words to me that made me feel very loved and appreciated. I could tell he had strong feelings for me, but never came right out and said anything like what you're suggesting. He just sort of danced around it."

Julie looked away as if she was losing interest in this story. Beth knew that she was going to have to get it out or she would ruin what little chance she had of establishing a friendship with her.

"Finally one night while I was reading Ben's email, I decided it was time to meet this situation head on. I told Ben I was going to use the L word. I slowly and hesitantly typed, 'Ben, I love you. There is no doubt, as I think right from the start, I was sure'. I stared at what I had just typed and had a hard time touching the send key, as I was worried that I might have misread what Ben had been trying to say~~~I was afraid he might not respond~~~ever."

"You thought you were in love with Dad?"

"No Julie, I knew it! There was no doubt. I could hear in the tone of his voice, the way he said certain phrases, the feelings he projected to me. I think we were in love all those years ago, before we even knew what it was. Julie, I realize this is hard for you to believe, or even begin to understand, but it is true. I remember how painful it was when I saw the hurt in his eyes that night in the basement. There was nothing I could do about it; I felt so helpless and Ben told me the same thing."

Beth then looked Julie straight in the eyes and said, "Yes, I was in love with your dad. I have never loved anyone quite like I loved your dad. I still do!"

Julie was almost shocked at how direct Beth finally became, but she composed herself and asked, "How~~~did Dad respond? I assume he did."

"Oh yes," Beth chuckled, "he was so excited! I have never deleted that email. Now that our feelings were finally out in the open, we couldn't say the words enough. The tone of our conversations changed, becoming so tender and caring. Virtually every day we talked on the phone, loving in a very special way, with words, tender loving words. I doubt that couples who are together physically seldom say these words to each other. We knew eventually we would have to find a way to meet, to feel that magic again."

"And you did!" Julie quipped as a statement instead of a question.

"Yes, and it was magical! It was all I ever wanted or needed. For the first time, I felt I had found the one true love of my life, my soul mate"

Julie gazed across the room, her head filling with more questions than answers. "But when did you do this? How and where did you meet?" Julie asked incredulously.

"It happened a few years ago. We decided to meet half way, so we both flew into Indianapolis. Because we deplaned at different gates, it was hard to find each other, so we used our cell phones to describe where we were. Ben told me he was heading toward the baggage claim area and described a sign on the wall he had just past. I finally saw him, and told him so. He said that wasn't fair as he could not see me. I described to him where I was in the crowd of people, against the wall to his right. He then spotted me and I could see the frown on his face break into a broad smile~~~the most wonderful smile I had ever seen! I watched him walk toward me, his eyes sparkling brighter with each step."

Beth paused and looked past Julie with a faraway look on her face. Her eyes filled with tears, but they did not leave her eyes. Julie knew she was reliving that moment in her mind.

"Without stopping, he walked right into my arms. We held each other for what seemed like an eternity and felt the years drift away. The only words he spoke were 'I love you', whispered in my ear. I never wanted the moment to end."

Beth looked at Julie and waited for her response. "I can't believe this! Didn't either of you feel any guilt? Did you ever think that what you were doing was wrong?" Julie searched Beth's face, her eyes, trying to read what Beth was feeling.

"No, for the first time in my life, everything felt right. I felt this is where I was always meant to be. I felt that this is where Ben was meant to be. We belonged in each other's arms. There was no guilt. We knew the life we both had been living all those years was wrong. That is what we felt guilty about."

Julie sat quietly letting what Beth had just told her sink in. Her mind was racing, not wanting to accept the notion that the years she spent with her dad were all wrong, that the love she felt in his arms was wrong? That the times they spent together he would have rather been with her, this~~~woman? No, she could not accept that. She knew her dad loved her and that there was nothing wrong with the love she felt for him.

"You are wrong! You are just wrong! I know my dad. I know he was happy with me~~~with us~~~with his life." Julie's voice was breaking up as she continued. "How can you say that? I know he loved me. I know he loved mom. You are just wrong!"

Julie was now sobbing uncontrollably and Beth knew that soon her hurt would turn to anger.

"No Julie, I'm not saying Ben didn't love you or your mother. Oh dear God, that's not what I meant! He did love you both! That's why he could never leave. He loved you so very much. When he spoke of you, and it was often, his eyes would shine and he would smile that smile of his. There was no doubt how much he loved and cared for you. His love for your mother was one of deep devotion and commitment. It was very clear from the beginning he would never leave or abandon the two of you. I understood and I respected his feelings. I knew from the beginning that he would give me all he could, but there were things he could not give and I accepted that. He was always very honest with me."

Beth paused and wondered if Julie was hearing anything she was saying.

"Julie, you said it seemed like your dad was very secretive about something~~~ that he would sometimes drift away. Do you remember saying that?"

"Yes", she said quietly.

"Was it always that way or just most recently?"

"Oh, I don't remember. When I was younger I wouldn't have noticed those things. I just seemed to think he was getting older and was reflecting on his life." Julie mused.

"Julie, he told me most of his life was spent without the deep passion he had always dreamed he would have. He was looking for something that seemed to evade him. He met Helen and at first everything seemed good. He was happy, especially after you were born. But soon something changed and he was restless again, feeling that drive to search for whatever it was he felt was missing." Julie was now looking at Beth and seemed to be hanging onto every word she was saying.

"Did you know if your dad was ever unfaithful to your mother?"

Julie was silent a long time before answering. "I suspected that he was, but I never wanted to believe it was true. I heard them talking once and Mom was very upset. I was pretty young then," she stopped abruptly, and then added quickly, "did Dad tell you that he had?"

"Yes. It was a deep hurt he carried inside for many years. It hurt him deeply when he told me, like he was finally getting it off his chest, but never trusted anyone enough to say how much it bothered him."

Julie lowered her head and stared at the floor not wanting Beth to see her eyes and asked, her voice barely audible, "What did he tell you?" wanting to know what Beth would tell her, yet not sure if she was ready.

They were both quiet for what seemed an eternity before Beth finally continued.

"Oh Julie, it was after we had moved on to cell phones and he called me on his way home from work. He said I wouldn't like him much after he opened up about his past, but if we are going to be honest, I may as well hear it all now, as opposed to later. I told him what had happened to each of us in all those past years was just life happening and that those events are long gone and past now. I added I already knew how I felt about him and nothing he could tell me would change my mind."

Julie was torn, wanting to know what her father had told Beth, yet not wanting to hear anything that would destroy the respect she always had for him. "Was it bad?" she asked, feeling her face twist in recoil. "Were you shocked?"

"No, I wasn't shocked. I could feel how much he was hurting from the baggage he had been carrying. I think it was he who didn't like himself very much, not me. He had been carrying this around for a long time and he wanted to get it out and start over."

"What baggage? What baggage was he carrying? You must tell me, Beth~~~please!"

"Oh honey, if I told you, I would feel like I'm betraying his confidence."

"Did it have something to do with another woman?" Julie asked. "I thought Dad had slipped once. He didn't say so in so many words, but it was a feeling I had. Is that it?"

"Yes, but you must understand how it happened. In a way, it was sort of what Jerry was so sure would happen to me if I was working around other men. I've seen that sort of thing and I knew it happened, but I think it is hard for a man to ignore when a woman makes it pretty clear that she wants him~~~that way. Ben had never been with any other women before Helen. It was something he wondered about and when it became clear to him that this woman was offering him that opportunity, he~~~slipped, as you say. Your father was human and the excitement he felt at the time had nothing to do with love. What he felt was as old as the ages."

Beth again looked away from Julie before she went on. "Julie, what I'm going to tell you now is not easy for me. I can only hope you will understand the pain your father felt. I can tell you this~~~I never had a problem understanding him and I knew how he felt about himself at that time. He destroyed his own self-esteem and was heading down a path of self-destruction. I wonder if you might have noticed a change in him after he finally came to grips with his past."

Beth again paused, as if to make a final decision as to go on or just let it stop right here.

They sat quietly for what seemed like hours, Beth nearly hearing her heart beating hard inside her chest. She could only guess what Julie was thinking~~~what she might be feeling Then without warning, Julie reached for Beth's hands, squeezing them tightly. "It's okay. I know my dad was happy before he died. I also know he was not always happy in earlier years. I had no idea what might have changed him, but I think I'm beginning to understand. I think Dad would want you to tell me all that you can."

"Oh yes, he was happy. He also wondered if you noticed the difference in his demeanor." Beth paused only slightly, then went on, knowing now she was going to get it all out and let things fall where they may.

"Ben entered into his marriage wanting to be the perfect husband~~~ the perfect father. He had this belief he would always just share his life with Helen and his family. When he failed by having an affair, he was very hard on himself. He felt he was dirty and that there was no way he could atone for that. He then sort of went on a binge, a sort of self-abuse and began hanging around bowling alleys during women's league bowling, finding it a good place to meet and yes, pick up willing women. The numbers were not important, as each one just drove him further into self-loathing. It got so bad he never even bothered to make up excuses to go out~~~he just went~~~with no explanations when he would return home. He jeopardized everything, his marriage, his home, your custody and even his health."

Beth paused, looked down at the floor shaking her head from side to side. "He was crazy, sort of insane. It went on and on like this until he met this woman, one that was not the type who would engage in a casual one night fling. Ben knew this, but was attracted to her very much. She was a widow who had lost her husband about a year earlier, over Guam during the war. She was a nice person and Ben lied telling her he was single, never been married as he had never met anyone that he would want to marry~~~until now. He used every ploy he could think of to seduce her. As if by surprise, he found he still had a conscience when this woman told him she thought she was falling in love with him. This scared him so much he found he could no longer perform sexually with her. His guilt gave him away and when the woman questioned him about what was wrong, it all came out~~~all the ugly truth. The lady was hurt and her pain quickly turned to anger. Ben was also hurt, as he had developed some very strong feelings for her as well."

Beth again paused to gauge Julie's apparent feelings. Finding her still intent on what she had been telling her, she continued.

"They never saw each other again. Ben tried to shake off the guilt, but as soon as he was with someone, he found he didn't want to stay. He felt ill and wanted to leave instantly. It was then that he started asking himself why he was doing this, but there was no answer. He then crawled into a sort of shell and began eating himself up inside. There were no more women, no more sex, and that is how it was for over 15 years~~~until he found me."

Beth waited for a response from Julie, but there was none. She was staring at the table top, so Beth could not tell what she was thinking.

"Julie, Ben was a good man. You knew the man he was. You loved that man and your love was returned in great measure. Please don't let what I have told you change any of that. What he went through during that time was not Ben. That is why he was ill. He carried the guilt of his behavior for a very long time, causing him much pain. His actions had caused irreparable damage to his marriage; even though it was over, he could not leave. He would not walk away from the commitment he made to Helen and to you, knowing he would not be able to live with himself if he abandoned the two of you. Many times he told me he was glad he stayed, feeling he didn't deserve any real happiness and he would just have to make the best of a bad situation. I think he did pretty well."

Julie looked up and wiped tears from her eyes. "I think~~~ he did too," she said through her sobs." I wish I would have known. I wish I could have told him~~~it was all right," as the tears started rolling down her cheeks again and her sobs became much heavier.

Beth went around the table and embraced her, holding her head close to her chest, her tears wetting Beth's blouse. "I know you would, dear. I know you would. He loved you so much~~~he was so proud of you! You were the apple of his eye."

Beth held Julie until her sobs subsided. As she straightened up she felt the stiffness in her back.

"Ben told me that he had always thought he would be the perfect husband and father. It devastated him when he realized that he had failed his responsibility. He wasn't ready to admit he was human. He was angry, finding it impossible to forgive himself, all the while being haunted by this desire to find that which he felt he was missing so desperately."

"But~~~he was~~~a good father!" Julie sobbed through tears that were starting again.

"Yes, my dear, I know he was!" Beth said as she took Julie in her arms again, shaking with sobs of her own.

Beth's mind was swimming through so many thoughts as she held this young woman in her arms, wishing she could tell her something~~~anything that would turn her tears to laughter, like Ben always seemed to do. She remembered Ben telling her how Julie would come to him with tears in her eyes, knowing her daddy would make everything well again. But he failed to tell Beth what it was he did or said to Julie that would bring the smile back to her face. If only Ben could somehow help her now.

"Julie, I'm sorry that this has happened and yet I'm glad it has. I'm sorry it has caused you pain, but in time you will come to understand your dad, and realize he was a real live human being, with wants and needs much like your own. You'll know the frustrations he felt living in two separate worlds, one with you and your mother and one that gave him the fulfillment we all need. He needed and loved both of his worlds. His love for me never diminished his love for you and Helen, it actually complimented it. Did you notice your dad seemed happier during the last few years?"

Julie seemed thoughtful before answering, "I noticed he seemed less sullen, but I thought it was because he was feeling better physically. He suffered from arthritis for years~~~" Julie paused and then went on, "I noticed he would sometimes sit alone in the living room just staring at the ceiling like he was ready to take a nap. He looked peaceful and relaxed. Now~~~I'm wondering if he was thinking about you during those times."

"Does it bother you thinking that he might have? Can you understand why he would?"

There was a long silence between them and Beth feared that she was losing Julie. She wanted so much to have a good relationship with her. She shared something very special with Julie, such a deep and abiding love for the same man, albeit in very different ways.

"Julie, there are some who believe that extramarital affairs are selfish and self-centered. There are affairs that are shallow and strictly based on the physical instead of something deeper and lasting; those are selfish and immature. I knew your dad would do anything to prevent that sort of a relationship with anyone. He suffered too much from the scars of that sort of thing in his past. That is not what Ben was searching for. He wanted to love with passion again and be loved in return the same way before his life was over. To love and be loved without reservation, without pressure to try to be something that he wasn't; to just be who he was and be able to let that be visible to someone he could trust, someone who would never betray that trust. He found that in me and it was the very same with me. We both wanted the same things, a true and loyal friend; a soul mate~~~to want to give up that part of ourselves completely, not fearing the hurt and pain that would come from rejection~~~complete and total abandonment. Do you understand what I'm telling you, Julie?"

"Yes, I think so. I loved that way once and it hurt so badly when I found that love like that was not felt for me. I never let myself go like that again. It hurts too much."

"Yes, it is a defense mechanism that we build up around ourselves. We deny ourselves the most intimate and loving experiences in life by allowing fear to take over. Some never experience the ultimate of sharing two people can have with compete trust. There is an old saying that states 'it is better to have loved and lost, than never to have loved at all'. Yes, it hurts to lose that kind of love when we are so vulnerable, but some search for that feeling, that passion again and that was what Ben was searching for. It was what he had found with me all those years ago and lost it when he lost track of me. We were just too young. We are not supposed to fall in love at that young age; it happened, but we never realized what it was. We recognized it almost instantly when we met on Facebook. It was like we had never parted~~~that those years had never passed us by."

Beth looked away and became quiet as if carried away in thought. Julie thought she could feel Beth's innermost feelings as she looked at her. She suddenly had an overwhelming urge to take her hand in hers and as she did, she felt she was touching someone who had been very close, very precious to her father. She pulled Beth into her arms and cried silent tears, feeling some sort of relief that she did not yet understand.

"Our coffee is ready. You drink it black, right?" Julie asked as she got up to pour the coffee and wipe the tears from her face.

"Yes~~~and hot! The cold air chills me to the bone these days. You will find that as you get older."

"I think I already have," Julie replied. "Since the divorce, the nights are cold and I find myself sleeping in a fetal position. It's not that I miss Mike~~~I just miss a warm body next to me during these chilly nights. I'm not ready to go out looking for another one, though."

"Was Mike abusive?" Beth asked, not sure if she wanted to hear Julie's answer.

"No. I think Dad would have killed him if he had been. He just liked other women too much, if you know what I mean. I got tired of sharing my husband with someone else."

Beth could sense what Julie was saying without actually saying the words directly to her. It was clear to her that Julie was intimating that Beth was sharing her father with her mother and that bothered Beth. She knew that Julie had to know more about the relationships that existed with herself and Ben, and with Ben and her mother. It was important that she understood why her father behaved the way he did.

"Julie, it wasn't like that with your father. He wasn't sharing anything. He gave to your mother the companionship and support she so desperately needed. He spent most every hour of every day with her, something I would have given almost anything to have had. He cared for her and protected her. What he didn't give her had nothing to do with me. That part of their lives had ceased long before fate brought him back to me. He gave to me what he had not given to anyone for a long, long time. He gave me the passion and love he had felt all those years before~~~ that time and opportunity didn't permit. The time we had together, while very precious, was also very scant. Nevertheless, our love was very intense. We loved, we laughed and we cried together. Our words to each other would chase the loneliness away. His voice soothed me, made me feel very warm and comfortable, as if I was lying next to him with my head on his shoulder."

Beth paused and sipped her coffee, which was still hot. She gauged Julie's face and noticed that she seemed very intent on what Beth was telling her.

"Was this on the phone?" Julie asked as if it was hard to understand.

"Oh yes, it was. Most of our time was either on the phone or on the Internet. We only had a few short days together and those days provided us with memories that sustained us."

"I don't understand. When did Dad call you? Where was he when he called? How did that work?"

"Ben would call me from work or sometimes I would call him. While our time was brief, it was often. We both had jobs that would permit the time and freedom to call. There were times that it didn't work because of what either of us was doing, but not too often."

Julie sat back against the back of her chair, her eyes wide open, "Oh! That must be why Dad didn't want to retire! Why~~~that fox! We kept pushing him to retire, but he kept saying he wasn't ready. Years before, it was like he couldn't wait until he could retire." She paused as if she was searching for the words to implore Beth.

"Please Beth~~~please tell me what Dad was like when you were with him~~~not the~~~you know~~~personal things, but the things you did," she paused again, then continued, "I guess I do want to know what he was like~~~ when he was like~~~that way. It's like I'm seeing him for the first time and I feel like I ~~~didn't really know him at all."

"No, Julie, you did know your father the way he was; as a warm and very loving man. What I have told you should not have changed your perception of him at all." Now it was Beth's turn to search for the right words; the right way to approach the sensitive nature of what Julie wanted to hear.

"Maybe if I take you back to those early days when we were teenagers, you might learn what he was like then to appreciate what he was like when alone with his most private moments. Are you sure you want to hear this?"

"Yes. Oh yes! There were many times I wondered what he was like when he was younger. He always had this sparkle in his eyes when he was thinking about something frisky. We all knew he was going to say something a little off color and no matter how much we prepared for it, he always caught us off guard. So yes, I want to hear everything."

"Okay then. Let me warm up this coffee, and we'll get started."

"Oh, I'll get it. Go ahead and start." Julie said as she got up to retrieve the coffee pot.

"Well, I think it was very near the end of the 1956 school year, the latter part of May. We were in the park for our school picnic~~~~~~

CHAPTER IV
Early Awakenings

~~~~~Late May 1956

Ben suddenly turned to Beth and said, with a sense of urgency and hope in his voice, "I know a place close by we can go to be alone."

"Where? Do you mean now?" she asked.

"Yes, take my hand. Hurry before anyone sees us leave.

Taking his hand she found it hard to keep up with him. On the other side of the hill was a thick timber, so thick finding one's way in and out could be very difficult. As they neared the edge of the timber, Beth tugged Ben's hand and stopped.

"Do you want to go in there?" she asked. "It's dark and kind of scary. I've heard there are bears in there."

"No, there isn't. I've been in here before and it's okay. I know a neat place; it's not very far and no one will see us."

"All right, but just don't let go of my hand."

"I won't. Come on~~~let's go."

Slowly and carefully they entered the timber and soon came upon a small clearing. Sun filtered through the thick trees and added some warmth to the thick grass that grew there. As Ben surveyed the clearing he noticed a group of daisies, almost as if they were glowing in the rays of the sun. Bending down, he picked the largest one handing it to Beth, and then touching her face, he tilted her head to his lips giving her a light, tender kiss. She put her arms around his neck and returned his kiss, still holding the daisy in her hand.

"I love your kisses," he said breathlessly. "They make me dizzy."

Beth laughed as she pulled him down to the grass which was soft and warmed by the sun. Neatly she placed the daisy next to her, framed by the lush green grass.

"Now you can get as dizzy as you like and you won't have to worry about falling down," she replied with a little giggle.

He then put his arms behind her shoulders and gently laid her back in the grass. Resting on his left shoulder, he positioned his body partly over hers and kissed her more firmly. Her lips parted slightly and his tongue touched hers, which had never happened before when they kissed. Beth felt the contact and pressed her tongue against his. Ben's head was spinning as he pushed his tongue deeper into her mouth. Now they were exploring each other's mouths, their tongues doing a dance as old as time immemorial. Suddenly, he became aware of pressure in his groin, finding it uncomfortable lying on the ground in this position. He shifted his body to one hip, then the other, until finally moving his body slightly away from her to relieve the pressure.

"What's wrong? Is someone coming?"

"No nothing is wrong and no one is coming. I just feel funny."

"I do too~~~and I'm so hot! Feel my face."

Ben touched her forehead, then her cheek and found they were flushed and felt hot to the touch. As he touched her face, Beth reached out and touched his cheek and noticed he felt hot as well.

"Gosh, you're hot too!" she said, surprised at the sound of her own voice. "I had my tongue in your mouth~~~I think that is a French kiss."

"Yeah I think so. Mine was in yours, too. Wow! That really made me dizzy! Want to do that again?" he asked.

"Yes, let's do it again." she said excitedly.

Ben leaned forward, cupped her face in his hands and gently brought his lips down to hers. Their mouths opened slightly at first, then wider. Beth's tongue entered Ben's mouth first and he received it by gently sucking it in further, running his tongue along the side of hers. His head was spinning wildly as he felt her shaking in his arms. He released the suction and she withdrew her tongue, with his tongue following hers back into her mouth. Beth then applied the same suction, flirting with Ben's tongue as he had done to hers. Finally, he removed his tongue and finished the kiss in a more conventional way, with a series of light tender kisses, leaving him breathless as he pulled away. Beth's body was trembling uncontrollably; her face appeared much differently than he had ever seen it before.

Her eyes were glazed and her voice shook as she said, "Ben~~~I think I bit your tongue~~~did I? Ohh, I didn't mean to~~~I'm so sorry! I love you, Ben!"

He was shaking too, not fully understanding what was happening to them. "No, you didn't bite me, but I just about didn't get my tongue back out in time"

He clearly wanted to do more~~~something~~~but what and how. "I love you too Beth. I think~~~I think I want to make love to you but," he paused almost too embarrassed to continue, before finally adding, "I don't~~~know how."

Beth touched his cheek, smiled and replied, "Ohh, I think we have to take our clothes off, but I'm scared. I think we better go back."

"Yeah I think you're right. I've heard some older guys say some things, but I don't know if it is right or how to do that. Yes~~~we better go back."

As Ben got up and reached back to help Beth up, she was looking right at his crotch and asked, "Oh Ben! Did I do that to you; does it hurt?"

"On no~~~it's nothing," he stammered, "It just does that sometimes." His face was bright red as he added as an afterthought, "Yes, it was you~~and what we did. But it doesn't hurt, it just feels kinda crowded and tight~~~ I'm~~~ I'm sorry."

"No, no, don't be sorry. I'm glad that happens to you with me. I hope I can always do that to you."

Still feeling awkward and embarrassed, he looked away and uttered, "Let's go Beth. We better get back."

"Wait Ben, I have to get my flower."

Bending over to retrieve her daisy, Ben found he could not take his eyes away from her. Even though Beth was only one year older than Ben, she had already developed the shape of a ripening, young woman. Her hips flared outward as she bent over, tapering smoothly to her thighs. He could not understand the strange new stirrings he was feeling as he watched her move. Swallowing hard, he took her by the left hand, her right hand tightly clasping the daisy. His stride was much shorter and slower as they left the clearing.

Near the edge of the timber, Ben stopped, turned toward her, looked deep into her eyes and said, "I love you Beth. I really do~~~I think."

Beth laughed and said, "You think? I love you, too~~~I think."

He bent slightly to place one last light kiss on her lips before walking out of the timber making their way back over the hill.

~~~~~*Return to present day*

Julie laughed as she said, "My dad red-faced, embarrassed? I would have thought it never happened to him. He was always so free and open with everything he said. The only time I remember seeing his face red was when he would laugh real hard or be really angry. I would have loved to have seen him embarrassed."

"Yes, he was so embarrassed that I had seen his erection. We were so young and inexperienced, but I did know about that sort of thing. We just did not have any idea what to do about it, or how. In retrospect, it probably was a good thing that we didn't."

"Did you ever get any closer back then?' Julie asked.

"Yes, one other time. We almost went too far, shortly before I started high school. I think I was a little more knowledgeable at that time than Ben. I had a pretty good idea of what we were supposed to do, but not exactly how. I think I was ready to figure it out, though."

"Do you mind sharing it with me?" Julie asked hoping that she would not refuse her.

"Of course I don't; it was all so innocent and so good! Those times were so exciting~~~times I wish I could relive, but of course we can't."

"Well go ahead and start, while I get something out of the fridge for dinner," Julie said as she got up to head toward the refrigerator.

"We had taken a walk back to the old school, kind of like for the last time sort of thing. As we came back to my house, we went into the garage and sat in one of my father's cars. I wanted to kiss him again, like that day in the park. As we turned to look at each other~~~~~~~~~~"

~~~~~*Early August Evening 1956*

Ben had just sat down behind the steering wheel, when Beth almost flung her body next to him. Surprised at her aggressiveness, he nevertheless recovered and placed his arm up and around her shoulders. He started to say something, but Beth pressed her mouth tight against his, her right hand touching the side of his face. Her kiss was firm and demanding, prodding him with her tongue to open his mouth. As he did, she darted her tongue into his mouth and he quickly sucked it gently. Ben felt his temperature rising and a stirring in his groin, his mind swirling with crazy thoughts. He was shaking and starting to perspire, finding it difficult to breathe. Finally, the kiss ended, and Beth kissed his neck.

"Wow!" Ben said, almost out of breath. "You've never kissed me like that before. Did I bite your lips?"

"No. You were all right." She was silent for a moment, as if she left her thoughts hanging, letting him know that she was going to add something. "Do you remember that day in the timber~~~in that little clearing?"

"Yes, how could I ever forget that?"

"Remember how you felt, what it did to you?" she asked, knowing that he certainly remembered.

"Yes, I remember." Ben felt his face flushing with the thought of that event and how she had seen what had happened to him.

"Has that happened now? I can't see~~~ it's too dark in here," she asked excitedly, secretly hoping that it had

"Uhhh, yes, I think so." Obviously flustered, he asked, "Why?"

"Can I~~can I feel it~~~just touch it?" Beth asked almost afraid he would think she was terrible for asking.

Ben felt his throat tightening as he tried to swallow. He suddenly felt that familiar dizziness sweep over him again.

"You mean you want me to~~to take it ~~~out?" he said, his voice quivering with the shaking of his body.

"No, I just want to~~~just touch it this way." she said as she reached down and gently placed the palm of her hand against the firmness of him.

Ben sucked in his breath sharply, as if he had been stuck with a thousand needles.

"Oh! You didn't wait for my answer, but I guess it's okay. Could I touch your uhh~~~boo~~breast?"

"Yes." she said as she placed her hand against his face again and kissed him.

He slowly brought up his left hand and cupped her right breast, feeling at first the firmness of her bra and then feeling the softness of her breast as he gently squeezed it. What was at first a stirring in his groin, was now a pounding, as he could feel his heart beating there. He returned the firmness of her kiss, not letting go of her breast as her hand dropped back to his groin. Soon their breathing was like the sound of a hurricane and the car windows were fogged as if it was winter. They were both wet with perspiration, exhausted and wanting more, but not knowing exactly what it was that they wanted. What was a pounding in his groin was now becoming an ache. He could no longer continue this without pain. He released her, and sat back against the back rest of his seat.

"Beth, I feel like I want to take off my clothes. I'm so hot and I can't breathe. I think I might have strained something, because it~~~it hurts."

"Oh, I know; it is so hot in here. What did you hurt?"

"You know~~~here," as he took her hand and placed it back where she had so feverishly touched earlier, "a little lower~~~and kinda in my belly."

"What happened to it, did I do something wrong? What can I do?"

"I don't know. I've never felt this before. I don't think there is anything you can do. Maybe I can fix it later. We better get out of here and get some air."

"Okay~~~I hope you will be all right. I hope I didn't hurt you. I love you, Ben."

"I know~~I think. I love you, too."

~~~~~Return to present day

"We got out of the car and he walked me to the house. I know my face was flushed, as it still felt hot. I had this feeling that Mom would look at me and know that we did something~~~different. If she did, she didn't say anything."

"Did Dad ever tell you what it was that caused his pain?" Julie asked with a knowing smile on her face.

Beth chuckled and said, "No, he never did and I never asked. I remember I asked him if he was all right the next day and he just said 'Oh yeah, I'm fine.' We never went that far again. It wasn't long after that, my family moved to Florida."

"Was the party shortly after that time?" Julie asked.

"Yes it was, just a matter of weeks. Ben and I never saw each other
~~~~~

much between those times. I remember he looked different during that time, but I never knew why."

"Did you have any ~~~I mean dates~~or see anyone else like that before you left?" Julie asked, not quite knowing how to ask Beth without prying.

"No, it was only Ben. I knew it was something very special at the time, but never really realized just how much until sometime later, much later, after I was in Florida. More things happened, but they were different."

Julie noticed Beth had that distant look on her face again and was suddenly perplexed by what she had just said. "After we eat, will you tell me about your life in Florida?"

"Sure, if you like. I enjoy talking to you, Julie. You are a good listener~~~so much like your dad."

"Thank you. I understand why Dad liked you, but I'm sure glad it didn't work out for you," Julie said with a sly smile on her face.

"Why would you say that?" Beth asked incredulously.

"Simple! I wouldn't be here if it had!"

They both laughed heartily as they got up to fix their dinner. Julie moved around the table, placed her arms around Beth and embraced her with a gentle hug, as tears formed in Beth's eyes.

Their dinner was simple and quick. Some warmed up meat loaf, sweet corn, instant potatoes, bread, butter and iced tea. Beth picked at her food and appeared deep in thought. Julie broke the silence and asked her what she was thinking; "I think you left me. You seem to be far away in your thoughts."

"Oh, just bringing up all this makes me go back over those years." Beth paused before going on. "It was tough at first, getting pregnant so soon and unexpectedly. When Karen came, I was so wrapped up in her that I didn't have time to think about anything else. It was fun watching her grow, teaching her new things. I don't think I ever thought about Ben during those years. Oh, there were times when Jerry and I were quarrelling, I would lie in bed and think about those times in the woods and in the car. It would make me tremble until I would have to block them out so I could go to sleep. I was pleased that it didn't happen often."

"Did you keep in touch with anyone from here, some old friends?" Julie asked.

"Well, Lynn did more of that than I did. She kept me informed somewhat. If it had not been for Lynn keeping in touch on Facebook with some of her old classmates, Ben and I would never have connected."

"Yes, I remember you mentioned that. What did you think when she told you about Ben?" Julie asked, now wanting to know more about that connection.

"Ohhh, my pulse increased. I couldn't believe it. I was excited and I felt like if I didn't reply right away, he would be gone. I was very nervous, and didn't know quite what to write. Ben had mentioned in the message to Lynn that I had been his first kiss. Of course, I was single when Lynn received this message from Ben, and I had no interest in starting a relationship with anyone at my age. Yet, I was keenly interested in Ben and what he was doing, where his life had taken him~~~if he was happy. I just knew I needed to talk to him."

"Did you write back to him right away?"

"No! I mean yes, I did, but Lynn doesn't get on her computer every day and by the time she received Ben's message, I received it a couple of days later. I was afraid I was already too late and that he might have given up on Lynn being the person he was seeking out. I was almost in a panic!" she said with a chuckle.

"But obviously, he didn't." Julie said. "What did you say to him~~~what did you write?"

"Oh I think I said `Yes, I am the same Beth that you kissed for your first time and yes I do remember you. No one ever forgets their first kiss'. I went on with a lot of questions, you know, like where are you, what are you doing, are you married, do you have children. I wanted to ask him a lot of questions not only because I wanted to know the answers, but hoping it would entice him to reply."

"Did he answer all your questions~~~right away?"

"Yes he did and then some! He told me that he had thought about me many times, wondered if I was happy, or even alive. He said he was almost afraid to send a message to Lynn for fear of what she might tell him, but he felt he had to know. I could feel something in his writing that told me more than his words. It was strange. There was this pull, a magical thing that was happening. We were communicating in a way without words~~~more like feeling. I cannot explain it, Julie. It was almost like we had never parted. He did not feel like a stranger to me, even though I had not seen or spoken to him in over 50 years; we were just kids! Instantly, I knew I wanted to exchange email addresses with him so we could talk freely and more privately. When I suggested it to him, he agreed right away and said he was about to ask me the very same thing."

Julie was silent, almost mesmerized by what Beth was telling her. Beth was right, she could not explain it. Could this really have happened? Could two young kids hold this attraction inside all these years only to ignite it again with just an email message? While there was doubt in Julie's mind about how that could happen, one thing was very clear in Julie's mind; there was no doubt this woman loved her father very much, but did her dad feel that love for Beth? Is that what brought peace to him before he died? She was now almost obsessed with the desire to learn more about Beth, wanting to understand more of not only the relationship she had with her dad, but also about the one she had with her husband. She wanted to know everything about this woman and what it was that drew her father to her after so many years. She hoped Beth would not be offended if she probed deeper into her past.

"Beth, would you feel comfortable sharing some details of your life with Jerry and Karen? If you're not, that's all right. I understand that you might want to leave the past in the past and not rehash it."

Beth looked away as if in thought. She wanted Julie to fully understand the profound effect Ben had on her life and did not like the thought of dredging up the past, but yet she wanted to form a lasting bond with Julie, especially now that she had met her and felt the chemistry of her father in her.

Finally, she faced Julie and replied, her voice much quieter, yet resolved. "Julie, I hope if I tell you some more about my marriage you might understand why I'm here to visit your father's grave and why I will continue to return every year as long as my health allows me to travel."

Julie was silent, waiting for Beth to continue, merely nodding in agreement, not wanting to interrupt her thoughts.

"The first years of my marriage were," she paused, "what I thought, good at the time. Everything was new and exciting and Karen was on her way. I was thrilled when Karen arrived~~~she was so beautiful~~~so soft and perfect. I thrilled at how tiny and perfect her little fingers and toes were." She again paused and a slight smile crossed her lips as she recalled those early memories.

"I didn't enter the work force until Karen started first grade, for a couple of reasons. She was my only child and I wanted to give her the best start in life by teaching her all I could before she started school and being with her all day. Also, Jerry did not want me to work. We really needed the extra money a job could provide and I didn't want to stay at home all day with nothing to do. Eventually, I found a part-time job at an insurance company as a receptionist, being able to leave work in time for Karen when she arrived home from school. Karen had always had a difficult time with reading and her first grade teacher told me she thought Karen was dyslexic. She recommended a private company which tutored children with this problem. Of course it was expensive, but the money I earned as a receptionist would cover that expense for the rest of the school year." Beth paused again, biting her lower lip before going on.

"Jerry was furious that I went out on my own, finding a job that would allow me to be home with Karen and pay for the special tutoring. He did not want me 'out in the public', especially working around other men. This led to all kinds of accusations and arguments, almost daily. He was positive I was flirting and going out with some of the men where I worked. None of his accusations were true! I was seeing a side of him I had not seen before, a side I truly disliked. I offered to go to counseling with him, but he refused. After many years of demeaning words about me and to me, I moved out of the house to an apartment with Karen and filed for divorce. Jerry was livid and started harassing me at work, at my apartment and on the phone which prompted me to obtain a restraining order against him with no end date, so it still stands today. I closed myself inside many barriers for both physical and mental protections. My self-esteem was shattered. I wanted no part of any man for over five years, not even as much as a date. During this time, I would have thoughts about my childhood in Michigan and of course thoughts of Ben and the fun we had together would creep into my mind. I never forgot his smile, his tender kisses, and the innocence we shared. I found myself wondering why life could not be like that now, so simple and safe. I could not have realized it at that time, but there was a little ember smoldering in my heart for him."

"Did you tell Dad about all of this?" Julie asked, now feeling much empathy for Beth.

"Oh yes, at the very beginning, when I suggested that we be very honest with each other. Ben was so agreeable with this, that he started telling me about where his life had taken him and that drew me to him with such a feeling of trust; I felt I could tell him anything. I don't know if I could have opened up to him if he had not done that first."

Julie was by now listening intently to what Beth was saying. She felt a surge of emotion well up inside her as she reached for Beth's hands, squeezing them tightly. As a woman, Julie understood full well what Beth had been through. "So when did you go back to school?" she asked in a lighter tone, to break the somberness a bit.

Smiling slightly, Beth continued, "I knew that soon Karen would be going away to college and my life would be quite empty with her living away from home. That's when I decided to devote the rest of my working life to pediatrics. It was hard going back to school at that age, but I was determined. Being with children helped fill some of the voids in my life. I loved every one of them, being unafraid to be open with my young patients. Being around other men was always somewhat uncomfortable."

"So you started back to school when Karen left for college"?

"No, not right away. I waited until I was sure Karen was settled in and comfortable. I must have vacillated several times about going back, as the thought scared me some, but I finally made the move."

"How did Karen feel about it?"

"She was elated. She always supported me in most everything I did. I felt we were more like sisters, at times. I could not be more proud of her."

"Could you tell me about how you and Dad~~~what you did~~~I mean, what was it like when you met. It's like, you know, we don't think our parents have sex~~~like we can't imagine it. I don't mean to be nosey. I just cannot imagine my dad being a lover~~~a~~~a sexual person."

Beth could not contain her laughter. "Ohhhh Julie! Your dad was very sensual. Yes, I understand what you mean. We just don't think they ever `do it'. But we don't die sexually when the kids leave the nest. In many ways, I think we just begin to fully discover the true joys of our sexuality. It was your dad who told me that casual sex is cold, meaningless and even brutal. That it is empty of anything of value, that it is love we seek, not sex. When the two come together, a beautiful, warm bond forms and that is what is truly beautiful. Age has nothing to do with it at all. Yes, it is true our bodies don't move like they once did and we aren't as agile or inventive as we are in our 20s. But we have something that is even better."

"What is that?" Julie asked, her interest now piqued to the limit.

"If I can take you back to that fall day in early November~~~~about 5 years ago, maybe you will discover for yourself what it is. It started in the airport in Indianapolis when he came into my arms. The first thing we had to do was pick up our luggage and get a car. I had already made reservations at a nice hotel and with Hertz to rent a car. As we went to the Hertz counter, the gentleman there looked at me and said~~~~~~~~~~~~~~~"

~~~~~Late October 2005

"Hello Elizabeth~~~is this your father?" nodding toward Ben. Ben was not to be out gunned by this brash young man and quickly zoomed in on the fact that the man was quite bald.

"I'd say judging by our common hair style, or lack thereof, we are about the same age," Ben quipped. Not able to contain her laughter, Beth's outburst readily told the man that he had lost that exchange and shared her laugh, albeit with a slightly red face. Ben felt his chest swell with pride, but contained his exuberance. Beth completed signing the papers and the man directed them to their car.

"It is a red Toyota with Texas plates and is parked in the number one slot~~~just for you." Beth accepted the keys, turned and walked away from the counter as Ben looked at her smiling and quietly whispered, "He likes you too and was flirting with you; thinks I'm your dad. See, I told you what a striking figure you are! And you say I'm biased. Ha! You are still a very beautiful, enticing woman." He fell back a step or two behind her as they went through the door of the terminal to search for their car. He delighted watching her walk in front of him, watching how she placed her foot so accurately in front of the other, the slight sway of her hips, the grace she exhibited as she walked was more like floating motion; her movement was so fluid. He could not remember her walk all those years ago, realizing her gait was probably a lot different, as she was so young. As he followed her now he felt a strong urge to continue watching her from behind~~~and yet he wanted to walk beside her and take her hand, proud to be next to her.

Beth felt his eyes on her as she walked. She was thinking about the dream he had related to her a month or so before. In his dream she was walking away from him in a sort of "huff" as if she was angry with him, swinging her hips in an exaggerated way as if in a form of defiance. She hoped she wasn't walking that way now, as she only wanted to welcome him with her walk.

Ben picked up his stride and moved up next to her, taking her hand in his, "I love to watch you walk," he said, "you carry yourself in a very professional way. You make me feel very humble, yet very proud."

"You mean I don't walk like in your dream?" she laughed.

"No not at all; you kinda take my breath away. Do you have any idea how striking you are?"

"Oh sweetheart you are so biased, but I'm glad you think so."

"No, bias has nothing to do with it. Fact ma'am, just fact," he replied as they arrived at their car.

Beth opened the door with her key and assumed the driver's seat. Ben went around to the passenger side and was glad he would now have a chance to watch her as she drove. He was impressed how she was able to take charge as if she was used to doing that. This was not only a very beautiful and professional woman, but also a very independent and self confident woman. Ben was quietly hoping that he would not disappoint her. She took note of the controls, adjusted the seats and mirrors, started the engine and put the car in gear. As she turned her head to back out of the parking space, she glanced at Ben and smiled warmly at him, a smile that told him she was very happy to be here with him, in this car, at this moment. He returned her smile, winked and reached across the car and lightly touched her knee. "I love you", he said almost so quietly she barely heard him. She smiled and continued to back up until she had cleared the parking space. She then placed the transmission in drive before she looked back to Ben and said, "I love you too."

"Do you know how to get to the hotel?" Ben asked.

"Yes I think so. I Googled a map and studied it before I left. It's not far from here."

He settled back in his seat, sighed, folded his arms across his chest and said, "You know, this is pretty nice. I can just sit here and let you take care of everything and admire you. Just like back in study hall, when I used to stare at you all the time. You still look as exciting as you did then. I could look at you all day."

"Stop that!" You'll make me have an accident." she laughed.

"Oh, well I guess it's out of the question if I was to move over closer to you then?"

"You just stay right where you are and keep your seat belt fastened! We'll be at the hotel soon and then I don't want any distance between us."

"I can't wait to kiss you again. I didn't want to do that at the airport. I want it to be very slow and deliberate, like the very first time. I want to feel that magic again. I've looked for it all my life before I realized it could only be found with you. It was not easy to keep from kissing you right away," he said while looking out the side window, as if he was remembering that time~~~again.

"I know, I felt the same thing. I thought you were going to but I remembered how you had said you wanted it to be very private and slow. But I thought I was going to kiss you, too." she laughed.

They were quiet for a while as Beth maneuvered the car expertly through the busy traffic of Indianapolis. Ben watched her intently and soon felt very comfortable with her driving, which was not usual for him. He was seldom comfortable in an automobile with anyone else unless he was behind the steering wheel. However, he noticed how she kept her eyes moving and both hands on the wheel at a 4 and 8 o'clock hold as opposed to the more conventional 2 and 10. She explained this to him in a way that he had never thought about before.

"I'm not very tall and I sit pretty low in the seat. If I was to have a collision with something and the air bag would go off, it might break my arms or dislocate my shoulders."

Ben was not only admiring this woman whom he already was deeply in love with; he was learning things about her now that made him very proud of not only her face and body, but of her mind as well. He knew from their correspondence that she was very bright, but now he was seeing her display that intelligence. Shifting his body forward, he gazed out the windshield as they continued on their way. His mind was racing, going over all the years and finding it hard to believe that he was with her, right beside her, in this car. He felt a cold chill course down his spine as he wondered, "Will I be okay~~~after all these years of abstinence~~~can I perform? Will everything work? What if it doesn't? How will I be able to handle that?~~~Damn! After all these years why am I worrying about this now?" he thought. "I have to put this out of my mind~~~or it might not"

"We're here. I'll go check in and you can get the bags, if you would." Beth offered.

As she exited the car, she turned to smile at Ben as he opened the back door to remove the two bags. She walked ahead of him and again he felt his mouth go dry as he watched her walk. He wanted this woman; he wanted to make love to her in a way that he had so many times in his mind, in his fantasies. Now she was here with him. They were going to be together, finally, in each other's arms for three days and nights. Why were his hands so cold and wet? Why was he already shaking? He did not approach the counter as Beth registered; instead wondered how she registered~~~but didn't ask. They entered the elevator and he considered putting the bags down to take her into his arms, but thought better of it. He could wait just a few minutes more. They were silent in the elevator, both engrossed in their thoughts. What was she thinking? What was he thinking?

Before they were aware, the elevator stopped and the door opened. Ben put his hand against the door frame as it finished opening, to keep it from closing on her as she slowly stepped out of the elevator. He watched her walk to her left toward the door of their room and felt a thrill shoot across his chest, knowing it would not be much longer before he will taste her lips again. Beth had already inserted the card key in the lock before he could leave the elevator, finding that his knees were weak and not propelling him behind her. She opened the door of the room, turned to see him still standing in the open elevator.

"Honey, are you coming with me, or are you thinking about servicing the elevator? I need servicing more than the elevator," she said with a giggle. The humor in her voice broke his trance; he smiled and hurried across the hall to the open door and toward two arms that were anxiously waiting for him. Entering the room, he slowly put the bags on the floor without taking his eyes from her, and then reached behind to lock the door. Standing in front of him now with a warm smile on her face, her lips quivering slightly, reminded him of the way she looked at him some 50 years ago. Stepping toward her, he looked down to her upturned face and into her eyes, his heart pounding as he reached out with his left hand and lightly touched her face. His voice was weak, shaking and not recognizable to him as he said, "No baby, I don't want to service the elevator. I just~~~I just want you."

Beth tilted her face against his hand, as he brought his other hand up to her face and gently cupped her face between his shaking hands. He didn't wonder now if his hands were cold or not; he was lost in this moment. Lowering his face to hers, their lips finally touched, so lightly and he felt the electricity flow into his body again, as it had all those years before. His mind swirled for a moment, but he quickly recovered. This time the kiss was a bit more knowledgeable, as their lips moved against each other, in a slow tender movement. As the kiss ended he pulled back slightly and looked at her face. She looked different, her eyes slightly closed; a look he had seen only once before, building in him a new sense of confidence. He brought his lips back to hers again, only this time the kiss was a more urgent one. His hands went around to the back of her head; her hands went up around his shoulders, her fingers on the back of his neck. Their lips were pressed hard against each other, moving feverishly as if looking for some special spot that could somehow quell the fire that was burning inside them, knowing that the kiss could not, would not dampen this tremendous urge that was building, that had been building for so many years. Moving his hands down to her waist, then to her bottom, he pulled her tight against the pressure he felt in his groin.

As the kiss ended, Beth pulled back a little and said, "Do you remember what you told me that time in the car~~~in Dad's garage?"

Ben was still holding her tight, kissing her neck as he whispered in her ear. "What thing do you mean?"

"About how you felt like you wanted to take off your clothes."

"Yeah, I remember." he chuckled.

"Well, I want to take off your clothes. I want you to undress me too," she said as she looked directly into his eyes.

"I ain't nothin' to look at Baby and I was thinking about pulling the curtains shut and have you close your eyes."

Laughing she said, "Well I'm not a bathing beauty anymore either, but I don't want you to think about that sort of thing. Of course, we are no longer teenagers and our bodies are different, but that doesn't matter. I just want to feel you next to me, with nothing~~~nothing between us anymore, not miles, not time, not even clothes."

"I'd like to freshen up some first. I haven't showered since early this morning and that little jet was crowded," he said, starting to shake again, feeling the fears and doubts starting to creep in again.

Sensing his fears, she replied, "Me too, but I just want to slowly take off your clothes. I want you to undress me and then we can shower."

"Okay~~~but you can shower first, then I will. We can shower together later~~~deal?"

Beth laughed. "Okay, deal! Now hold still while I take off your shirt."

He was wearing a blue sweatshirt with a white T-shirt underneath. She placed her hands to either side of his waist, lifting the bottom of his sweatshirt up to his arms, where he had to help her by raising his arms as she wiggled it up over his head.

In a shallow attempt to lessen the tension he was feeling he chuckled, "Don't mess up my hair darling," as if there was any hair to mess up. Being prematurely bald since high school, all that remained was the band of hair around the sides of his head. He was a tall man, over 6 feet, while Beth was much shorter by over a half-foot. As she reached up to lift the shirt over his head, her face came close to his and with his hands still above his head, he lightly kissed her lips. She froze for an instant, returning his kiss and then said, "If we don't get this thing off, either one of two things is going to happen. Our arms will tire from lack of blood or we will crumble to the floor right here and never make it to the shower."

Visualizing the scene that would present, he countered, "If we crumble to the floor, as you say, at our age we may never get back up. We better concentrate on getting this shirt off of my arms."

Beth could not contain her laughter as he dropped his arms and she slid the shirt the rest of the way off. She quickly grasped the tail of his T-shirt and lifted it up over his head. Dropping it to the floor, she quickly ran her hands across his chest, enjoying the feel of his hair combing through her fingers, much of which was gray. Ben felt his nipples harden as her fingers teased them before kissing one, then the other. While teasing him with her mouth and lips, her hands went to his belt which she quickly unfastened, opened the clasp at the top of his jeans and lowered the zipper. Stepping back, she tugged at the waist pulling them down over his hips, down his legs and letting them fall to the floor.

Anxiously, she reached for the waist band of his jockeys, but he stopped her saying, "I think it's my turn now." He reached for the bottom of her sweater, slowly pulled it up revealing her lace trimmed black bra. Black lingerie had always turned Ben on and she being blond and fair-skinned, the contrast of the black against her skin took his breath away.

He pulled her to him, pressing her breasts firmly against his chest and whispered in her ear, "You are so beautiful. I love you so much." As he spoke his hands went to the clasps of her bra. He had not done this for such a long time and was surprised at how deftly he unfastened the hooks, feeling the two sides quickly come apart. He felt her shoulders shrug forward against him, allowing the straps to slide off of her shoulders. Moving back a bit, he slipped the straps the rest of the way down her arms and the bra fell away from her breasts. Ben sucked in his breath in a gasp. Her breasts were small, but sat high on her chest, not looking like a woman of 60 plus years. They were proud, with light pink circles around pert nipples. He stepped back and brought his hands up to cup them, marveling at the soft, yet firmness of them. As he started to bend forward to kiss them, she chuckled and said, "These jeans are getting hot; can you get me out of them?"

Ben began to work on the belt of her jeans when Beth noticed that Ben's jockeys appeared a little different. She reached out and touched him there and he jumped from her touch. He now worked even faster at her jeans until he had them down to the floor and she stepped out of them. Her black panties matched her bra; they were low cut, but not scant. They fit her hips well and had that little bit of loose material in the crotch that Ben always found very sexy. He did not recognize his voice as he said, "Your~~~turn in the~~~shower."

Beth smiled as she bent over to pick up her clothes. He had to look away, fearful that he would not let her get to the shower. She straightened and glanced at him, smiling before entering the bathroom and soon Ben heard water running in the shower. He was still standing where she had left him, still shaking with desire~~~feelings he had not felt in so many years. He slowly picked up his clothes, neatly folded them and placed them over a chair. He walked into the bedroom and sat on the edge of the bed; his mind filling with doubts again. What if? While he was worrying about this, he noticed the erection he had just a few moments ago, had faded, adding even more fear. Because his mind was fixated on his insecurities, he failed to notice that the shower had ended and Beth appeared in front of him in a blue loose fitting sleep shirt that reached to her knees. She had touched up her hair and was absolutely a vision that would turn any man's head. She smiled as she said, "Your turn."

Rising from the bed, he took her into his arms. He liked the feel of her night shirt and dropped his hands to the small of her back, just above the swell of her buttocks. The love he felt for this woman could not be denied, wanting so much to be able to make love to her like when he was much younger, but was so afraid he would disappoint her. This beautiful woman deserved, no, commanded special attention. Beth felt his apprehension. "Go take your shower. I'll be right here waiting for you. I'll wait forever if I have to, but don't make me wait too long. I want you, my love."

Feeling somewhat elated hearing those words, he turned to enter the bathroom not feeling his feet touch the floor. Pulling off his shorts, he stepped into the shower still having those haunting fears when a cold spray of water hit him on his chest. He jumped as the sudden cold took his breath away. "Oh great," he thought, "Just what I needed~~~a cold shower!" He struggled with the shower until he managed to get it at least warm and wondered if Beth had taken a cold shower.

Finally stepping out of the shower he dried off, put on a pair of lounge shorts, pulled on a T-shirt and moved back out to the bedroom. Beth was on the bed, her head and shoulders propped up against the head board. She smiled as she held out her arms welcoming him to her bed. He went to her and melted into her arms. Lying beside her, he pulled her to him as he kissed her lightly at first, then kissing her nose, her forehead, and her closed eyelids, then down to her neck. He loved the softness of her skin, the sweet scent of her freshness. She was fresh and young again in Ben's mind, holding that sweet little girl whom he fell in love with all those years before. The vision of her in that little clearing in the timber so many years ago and the memory of their kisses came rushing back to him; how they first touched each other in the car and the pain he felt in his groin. It was all surreal to him. How the clothes disappeared, he did not know, he was only aware of her soft body first next to him and then as he was kneeling over and above her. He felt thousands of thrills and spasms, as he felt her touch. His mouth showered kisses on her, finding it hard to be everywhere at once. Somehow he was now on his back and she was kissing him, touching him in the same way he had touched her. Their movements were slow and deliberate, giving away the toll the years had taken. He heard the sounds that she was making, deep in her throat and quiet. He felt her tugging at him, trying to bring him up onto her, wanting him inside her. But he was unable to continue, as his worst fears and doubts were realized. He had been concerned that possibly after all this time nothing would work, as he had heard that if one didn't use it they would lose it. Anger and frustration were quickly overtaking him. What would he say? What *could* he say?

He didn't have to say anything; Beth said it all for him. "Sweetheart it is okay~~~I understand. I know you are nervous~~~I felt it earlier. You are here in my arms, so I am not worried. This is what I want more than anything. I can touch you, kiss you and hold you next to me. The rest will come, you'll see. Just relax and hold me close~~~don't worry about anything. You thrill me in ways you don't even know, so just hold me. Know that I love you and that I will always love you."

Ben felt tears welling up in his eyes. He had never felt such love for anyone in his life and wanted to love her in every possible way. She was giving herself to him without any demands, just patience, love and understanding. This woman knew and understood him better than he knew himself, as if she had lived with him somehow all those years.

"I love you Beth, I love you so much. I want to give you the very best of me."

"I know you do and you do give me the best of you~~~even now you do. I have never doubted that. The other things will come as you relax and get comfortable. You have absolutely nothing to worry about. What you've done already, has given me much joy. We will get over this hump~~~I promise you!"

Ben rolled back over on his back. Beth smiled as she put her head on his left shoulder and placed her left leg across his belly. She ran her hands through the hair on his chest as he ran his right hand up and down the length of her thigh. His left hand curled up against her back and stroked her side and the curve of her hip. It was comforting and warm. He could feel her breath on his chest, tickling him as it moved through the hair. Beth glanced up to his face and smiled, then kissed his left nipple. Ben thought to himself, "How in the hell could it not work now?"

As she lay there feeling the warmth of his body tight against her own, feeling his chest rise and fall with his breathing, hearing his heart beating close to her ear, she smiled as her mind sorted through the various thoughts and feelings of the day. She remembered her feelings while jetting toward their rendezvous, as each mile passed quickly behind, her pulse quickened, knowing she was on a heading toward the arms of the most meaningful person ever in her life. The daily sound of his voice had brought to her more joy and happiness than she ever imagined. Thousands of words shared over the phone and emails have brought with them an understanding of each other. But the warmth of his arms around her is what she had longed for over the past months.

She knew now that a spark was born over 50 years ago that did not die and was now a flame of want and need. She felt it was like she was on her way to a first date~~~like the first time they kissed~~~only now with years of adult experiences between them to enrich each moment they would share. She thought she would be nervous about seeing him face to face the first time after all those years, but the feeling soon disappeared as she found herself so excited to see him and touch him. How could she be nervous when he walked right into her arms, holding her tightly as if he never again wanted to let her go~~~ whispering 'I love you'? She could close her eyes now and see the look in his eyes after closing the door in the hotel, lowering his face to kiss her. It was like the first time all over again, tender and sweet, but then becoming more passionate, full of want and desire, touching in ways they could not touch during the past six months.

Now, lying in bed next to the man she should have been spending the past 50 years with, spending only the past few hours making love to him, feeling the gentleness in his touch, drawing her to him, making her want to never leave his arms~~~~ she could feel the completeness of his love. She could see in his eyes, the strain of so many emotions that had overwhelmed him. He at last had the love of his life in his arms, but was emotionally unable to let himself go. Yet for Beth it was so easy, so comfortable, as if she had been with him before~~~like they knew each other in another lifetime and were simply saying 'Hello' again.

"Baby I'm sorry, I was afraid something like this would happen. It's been so long. I want you so much, but I'm afraid I'll disappoint you."

"Oh sweetheart, how could you ever disappoint me? Even if nothing else happens other than just holding me close like this, I feel more love than I have ever felt in my life. I can feel and sense the love you have for me. You make me feel warm and safe in your arms. I know you will never hurt or disappoint me."

"But there is so much more I want to give you. I want to give you now those things I wanted when we were younger, but couldn't. It's~~~just been too long."

"No it hasn't, Ben! Neither of us are teenagers anymore. I'm older too and it's been years since I've had any form of intimacy. I was afraid that you wouldn't find me attractive any more. I'm old and wrinkled, but I am filled with all the love for you that I had when we were young. When I saw the look in your eyes as you undressed me, I knew then that I didn't have to worry. I realized then that the years didn't matter. We are still the same two kids that fell in love before we knew what love was all about. It is you I want~~~all that you can give me, in any and every way possible. I need you more than just the physical pleasure you can give me. I need your touch, your gentleness and your understanding. I need you because of the way you make me feel about myself~~~like I'm worth something~~~to someone~~~~to myself. I know you love me~~~and this is the first time I have ever believed that so completely."

"Oh my God baby, you are not old and wrinkled! I don't see you that way at all. You are as beautiful today as you have ever been, maybe even more. You are every bit a woman now, no longer a girl, but a warm and loving woman who needs a man; I want so much to be that man. I need you in exactly the same way you have just told me~~~the ways you make me feel about me. You give me a reason to go on as life now has meaning again. I don't want to think about living the rest of my life like I have the past half century~~~without you."

While Ben was telling her this, Beth's hand had moved down to his groin and the same soft strokes she had been making on Ben's chest were now arousing stirrings much lower.

"Remember the first time this happened?" Beth asked with a chuckle.

"I will never forget. I was so embarrassed."

"Oh it shouldn't have embarrassed you. It made me feel good when I saw that because I knew what we had done together had caused that to happen. I felt proud that I could have that effect on you. I thought about that many times after that and it excited me."

"You should have told me," Ben laughed.

"Oh yeah, right, that would have probably gotten us in all kinds of trouble," she chuckled.

"Well look what it's gotten us now~~~a different kind of trouble."

"Nothing we can't handle, nothing I can't handle~~~this time," she said with authority.

Ben rolled over toward her and moved his hands to her in much the same way she was touching him. He kissed her firmly as her tongue slipped between his lips. Their hips were moving in unison, as their passion rose again. He moved his body to prepare to enter her, feeling a surge of passion he had never experienced before. His arms were weak and shaking as he supported his weight off her upper body, seeing the flushed look of passion on her face. Funny, he thought, 'Why did that look appear to be one of pain, when it was pure joy?' He slowly entered her hearing her moan as she wrapped her ankles over his legs. Ripples coursed through his body, feeling them run up and down his spine. He dropped his head to her neck, kissing her ear and whispering something that made no sense, or that she could comprehend. Their bodies first moved at random, but then moved as one. Beth arched her body upward and raised her hips up hard against him, making sounds deep in her throat that he did not recognize. But there was still a barrier that Ben could not get over. He could get so close, but the climax eluded him. He collapsed against her and was close to tears. Why was it like this; what was wrong with him?

Beth softly kissed his cheek and whispered in his ear, "It is okay my love; it will happen. I promise you it will happen~~~we will get you over this hump. Just don't think you failed me, because you have not! I love you sweetheart~~~I love you so much"

As darkness started to fall, Ben suddenly felt exhausted and soon drifted off to sleep. Beth could tell by the different sound of his breathing that he was sleeping. She did not want to wake him, as she knew his exhaustion was brought on by the emotional upheaval he was going through. Instead, she spooned up against his back, pressing her breasts tight against him, placing her hand across his side to his chest. Soon her breathing matched his and she joined him in peaceful sleep.

Ben stirred at the first sign of dawn and found Beth asleep against his back; apparently he had not moved in his sleep. When was the last time he had slept this soundly? He slowly eased his body away from her and out of the bed as he made his way to the bathroom. His bladder was full so he sat down on the seat to avoid waking her with the sound of falling water. It didn't work, as Beth sensed he was gone. She found her nightgown and quickly pulled it over her head as she got up off the bed.

"Are you getting in the shower Sweetheart?" she asked.

"No, I'm on the can. I'll be done in a minute. I didn't mean to wake you."

"It's all right; I was ready to get up. I don't want to waste any time while we are together."

Ben grabbed a towel to wrap around him and asked "Do you want to go find that cemetery today? It's supposed to be a nice day."

"Yes I would like that. Do you mind if we go?"

"Not at all; I enjoy doing everything with you. I want to see you with the sun on your face and the wind in your hair. We will still have time to come back here."

"Okay we will do that first and then we will come back here."

Ben took her hands in both of his and pulled her into his arms, giving her a morning kiss. When they pulled back, his towel fell to the floor.

"Sounds like we better get ready to go. Do you want the shower first, or do you want to share it with me?"

"Beth looked at his naked body, smiled and then said, "Now how am I supposed to answer that except one way with you standing in front of me like that?"

Looking down to the floor he saw his towel in a heap and replied, "Well then let me help you get that thing over your head, then you get in there first and adjust that damn shower. It nearly froze the~~~you know what off me when I tried to adjust it yesterday."

She laughed as he was lifting her nightgown up over her head. He bent and kissed her breasts as they came into view. "Honey you'll have to excuse me first~~~I have to pee."

"Oh of course, I'm sorry. Just yell when you get that shower warm and I'll wash your~~~back, or anything else you might need help with."

He walked back into the bedroom and caught his reflection in the mirror. "Oh what a disgusting sight!" he thought as he was parading around naked. "I've got to get rid of some of this gut."

"The shower is ready. I need some help with my back." she called. With that announcement Ben forgot about the mirror and his gut. It was time to shake a leg, or wash a back, or anything else that might need washed. He might have a few places he needs help with, too.

CHAPTER V
Indianapolis

~~~~~*Return to present day*

Julie asked, "Did you leave then for the cemetery~~~I mean, leave then or~~~?"

Beth laughed and said, "Yes, we dressed, gathered up our jackets and my camera, then we went down for breakfast. It was only a Continental breakfast but a very good one. My grandparents had a farm just outside of Indy and I wanted to drive there to see it. I wasn't sure if any part of it was still standing and Ben agreed to go along to help me find it. My parents used to go there in the summer to visit them when I was very young. I loved to play with all the dogs and cats that lived in and around the barns.

"And did you find it?" Julie asked.

"Yes, but most of it was gone; just a few broken down barns were all that were left. I think Ben saw the hurt in my eyes, as he touched my hand and said 'Let's go.' So we left and set out for the cemetery. It didn't take long and soon~~~~~~"

~~~~~*Early November 2005*

"Here it is~~~ this is the road; we are close now," Beth said as she started a turn to the right.

"Have you been here before?" Ben asked. "I didn't think you knew how to find it."

"No, I never have but I looked it up on the net and downloaded the directions. How did you know where it was?"

Ben laughed, "By reading the directions you sent to me. You did good!"

Beth glanced at him with a sly smile on her face and said, "You had me thinking you knew exactly how to get here and you didn't know any better than I."

"Sure I did! Besides, I had you as my pilot; how could I go wrong? Even if we got lost~~~so what? I couldn't think of anyone I would rather get lost with." He then shifted his body toward the front, leaned back against the seat and started singing 'Let the World Go Away' until Beth could not stand the noise anymore.

"Hey Pavarotti, we're here. Grab your jacket; the concert is over."

"Does that mean you don't like my singing?"

"I didn't know you were singing," she said with a twinkle in her eyes.

Laughing, he leaned over and kissed her. "I love you! I know you really can't wait to hear the second verse."

After grabbing her camera, she exited the car while Ben was still putting on his jacket. It was a beautiful sunny day, but there was just a hint in the air of what was soon to come.

A worn and neglected sign at the entrance to the cemetery read Established 1865. Weeds grew abundantly around an old stone church that looked like it may have been used years earlier for services before interring the dead. The graves were laid out on the side of a sloping hill, most of which were hard to distinguish, as the indentations in the earth were long ago eroded. The headstones were worn from years of the elements.

"What are we looking for?' Ben asked.

"Headstones with Morgan inscribed on them. I think there are three, maybe four. "If you look over there, I'll look here. Call out if you find anything and I'll do the same." Ben walked over in the direction she pointed out for him but instead of looking at the ground for headstones, he continued to look at her. "My God," he thought, "She is beautiful even at this distance!" His gait as he walked was more like the stumbling of a robot, aimlessly wondering; his attention was so focused on her he failed to see a broken headstone, tripped over it and almost had to run to regain his balance. Immediately, he sheepishly glanced at her to see if she had seen him trip, breathed a sigh of relief, satisfied she had not.

"Over here; I found them!" Beth cried out.

"Of course she did," he thought. "It couldn't have been me that found them 'cause I wasn't even looking for them."

Beth not only found the graves, she also found a small group of daisies growing between the cracks of a headstone lying on the ground that was broken into three pieces. She was staring at the daisies as Ben approached her.

"Are these the ones you were looking for?" he asked.

"Yes and look Ben~~~look at these daisies. It is almost like they are trying to tell of a broken heart. Do you remember when you gave me a daisy from those in the woods back in the park when we were kids?"

"Yeah, I remember; I thought it was strange that they were the only flowers growing back there. Not many flowers could compete with you. The daisies and you were the only flowers around, just like now," he observed as he looked around the cemetery.

"Yes, they looked so lonely all by themselves, just like these." As she spoke she bent down, picked one and handed it to him. "This time this one is for you."

"For me~~~what will I do with a flower?"

"Let me show you." She took the flower and held it by the stem in her left hand. "When my sister and I were young, we used to pick them and pluck the petals off one at a time and say, 'he loves me, he loves me not' like this." Ben watched her gently pluck the petals off the daisy until there was only one petal left. "And the last petal would answer the question. If the last petal left is up for he loves me, then you love me."

"Uhoh! What are you going to do now?" he asked, as the last petal up was for 'he loves me not'.

"Oh we would just get another daisy, as the first one was a bad one," she laughed. "Besides, I already know that you love me."

"You're right, I do. But here, you need a daisy to hold next to your heart as a reminder of that first time in the woods and how innocent and sweet that time was. Always remember that I do indeed love you~~~very much," as he handed her a fresh daisy.

"Thank you. I'll always see your face in a daisy and be reminded of your love every time I hold one. Here, hold it for me while I take some pictures of these headstones."

After she had taken pictures of all her ancestor's graves, she pointed the camera toward Ben and said, "Give me your best smile. I want to take this back with me." Ben smiled and she instantly snapped the picture, and then quickly reviewed it. She smiled with the results and clasped the camera to her chest.

"Oh Ben, it is so nice here. The sun feels so good and we are so alone. Hold me."

He didn't need to be asked again. He took her into his arms and held her tight against him; her face against his felt cool from the chilly air. He then pulled back a bit and kissed her full on the mouth, a long deep kiss, his tongue tracing the curve of her lips. She parted her lips allowing his tongue to explore a little deeper, as she sucked it gently. Their lips parted and her eyes gave away the passion she was feeling as she said, "Let's go back to the hotel; I have plans for you."

"You do; are we going to play cards or something like that?" he asked as they started back to the car.

"Ummmm yeah, something like that. But we won't need any cards and you won't have to ask any questions," she said with a wink.

"You might have to teach me this game," he paused, "is it hard?"

"I hope so; I'm going to try my best to make it hard for you!"

"Sounds like a challenging game to me."

"Oh you'll like it and it will get much easier as you get into it," she said as she opened her door.

Ben was smiling as he climbed into the car, pulled his belt up tight with one hand, while still holding the daisy in his other. Beth leaned across the console, winked at him, touched his hand with the daisy and gave him a light kiss.

~~~~~RETURN TO PRESENT DAY

"Did you go back to the hotel after you left the cemetery?" Julie asked.

"No. We wanted to find a nice place for lunch. We looked around for a while, just driving enjoying the sights until we found a quaint little Italian restaurant. Ben and I both like Italian food so we decided to have lunch there. It was comfortable and the scent of garlic and oregano really whetted our appetite. We found a cozy table for two near the rear away from the crowd where we could talk and touch across the table. I ordered Chicken Cacciatore and Ben ordered Beef Ravioli. After the waitress left with our order, we sat holding hands across the table and chatted about our lives when we were teenagers, not about our current situation."
~~~~~

"Did you or Ben wonder how Mom was doing back home?" Julie asked.

Beth sensed more than a simple question in Julie's inquiry. "No~~~not right away, but I'm sure he must have thought about her during that time. He became quiet once and had a faraway look in his eyes; they looked sad and hurt. At the time I didn't know if he was thinking of yesterday, of earlier times or perhaps his home~~~I was afraid to ask. I felt I knew him pretty well by then but there were still times I could look into his eyes and not read him. His eyes were usually very descriptive but not this time. I could feel something across the table that was bothering him, but I just did not know what it was."

"Yes, I know what you mean. Sometimes you could look into Dad's eyes and tell what he was going to say before he said it. There was a twinkle in them especially when he was going to say something funny."

Beth chuckled and said, "Ben still had a lot of little boy in him; he loved to play and tease. He loved to say and do things that would get a rise out of people and then he would laugh. He did that to me all the time. He was ornery."

Julie smiled knowing exactly what Beth meant. "What did you do after lunch?"

"Well, I couldn't eat all of my lunch as I'm not used to eating that much for lunch, so I asked for a container to take the leftovers with us. As we got up to leave, Ben asked if there was anything else I wanted to do before we go back to the hotel. I told him that I just wanted to go back~~~~~"

~~~~~Early November 2005

"Just take me to bed right now or lose me forever!"

"He laughed and said, "You've been watching too many movies. I would not have thought you were a Top Gun fan."

"Ohhh the movie wasn't so hot~~~I just liked Tom Cruise," Beth chuckled.

"Are you trying to make me jealous?" Ben asked with a twinkle in his eye.

"Did I?"

"Nope."

"I didn't?"

"Of course not."

"Why not?"

"Too many miles from here to Hollywood and I'm right here. Besides, I know you don't like Tom Cruise."

"How do you know that?"

"Because you love me; I'm sure of that"

"I'm glad you are. I love you because you are real, not a fake make-believe person. I like what you are, you are right here and you are mine!"

"Yes I am all yours, now and forever!"

As the waitress returned with Beth's take home container, Ben picked up the check, paid the tab and they left. As she drove back to the hotel, he watched her intently trying to imagine what this plan she had for him was all about. She had already surprised him with how comfortable she was with her sexuality. Could there be something that she had not shown him up to now? Whatever it might be, he resolved to just relax and enjoy every moment with her. He marveled at the way she navigated through the busy city traffic, safely making their way back to the hotel. Her aggressiveness was sufficient to find a safe place in the roadway, yet cautious enough as to not take the right of way, yet accept it when given. He was able to sit back and relax while she was driving; surely he could relax with her when she wanted to make love with him.

"You aren't tired, are you?" Beth asked as she glanced over to him.

"No, just calm and contented like a happy bull," he chuckled. "I'm trying to figure out what you have planned when we get back."

Chuckling she replied, "Oh just be patient~~~~I promise I won't hurt you."

"Hurt me? Hey don't forget I'm an old man!"

"You are not old, you're just experienced! I promise I won't make you stand on your head or anything like that."

"Well that's a relief! I don't think I could do that anymore," he laughed.

"You don't have long to wait; we're almost there," as she turned into the parking area.

Pulling into a parking space, she placed the Toyota in park before Ben jumped out of the car and ran around to her door. He opened it, then bowed placing his arm with the daisy in his hand across his waist and said, "May I escort you to your chamber, my Queen?"

With a look of total bewilderment, she exclaimed, "My goodness, have we gained royalty? Of course you may, my Prince. Please lead the way~~~but I better turn off the engine, first."

Hand in hand they walked together to the lobby of the hotel. As they entered the elevator and the door closed behind them, he suddenly took her into his arms and kissed her long and deeply. He could feel her breath increase against his face as she exhaled through her nose. Her tongue darted between his lips as if she would not be denied entrance. "Yes," he thought, "she is ready. Oh I just hope I am!"

The kiss ended as the door opened to their floor. Before they moved to leave the elevator, he again took her hand and squeezed it without saying anything. There were no words for what he was thinking.

Quietly, they walked the short distance to the room. She looked at him, flashing a devilish smile and a twinkle in her eye as she inserted her card key into the slot. Ben opened the door and held it for her as she barely entered before turning to wait for him to follow. He entered and reached behind to close and lock the door as she reached up to him and started to unbutton his shirt. He watched her without a word, her fingers working deftly on the buttons, her face displaying that same devilish smile as she looked up at him, still holding the daisy in his hand, wondering where she was going with this. As the shirt came off she lifted the bottom of his T-shirt and quickly pulled it up over his head and it too joined the pile she was starting at his feet. His upper body now devoid of any clothing, she lowered her head to kiss his chest, flicking her tongue across his nipples, lingering at each of them while her hands went to his belt buckle. He was amazed at how she worked the buckle without watching what she was doing, all the while sending little charges through his body with her mouth on his chest. The buckle opened, followed quickly with the button and zipper of his jeans. She stopped the therapy on his chest as she kneeled to pull his jeans to the floor, taking first one leg out and off, then the other. Still kneeling at his feet, she reached up to the waist band of his shorts and slowly slid them over his hips, down his legs to his feet. She kissed his belly as she rose up to put her arms around him and said, her voice sounding very sultry, "Take my clothes off Ben~~~please undress me."

Ben's pulse was racing as he dropped the daisy to the floor. He reached for the bottom of her sweater and quickly raised it up over her head, taking care to not mess her hair. He liked the way the wind had tossed it, adding to this feeling of abandonment she was projecting. He added it to the pile that Beth had started, as he reached behind her and released the hooks on her bra. He brought his hands back over her shoulders, picking up the shoulder straps, taking them forward with his hands down the length of her arms. The bra fell away and joined the pile. He cupped her breasts in both hands and held them as he lowered his face to them, kissing first one, then the other. Taking his cue from Beth, he kept his mouth busy while he went to the top of her jeans, opening the buckle first, then the button and the zipper. He knelt to the floor, pulling her jeans over her hips, down her legs and to the floor. He reached up to the low cut top of her panties, pulling them down off her hips, but before they reached the floor, he put his arms around her hips and pulled her body close against his face.

"I love you baby! I love you so much!" he said more to her lower belly than to her face.

Her voice was shaking as she softly said, "Ben, let's get in the shower. I want to bathe you. I want to run my soapy hands all over every inch of your body."

"Well, 'tell ya what. If you help me get up off of this floor, I'll be more than happy to oblige you." Ben said laughing.

Beth laughed and extended her hand, "Grab on sweetheart. If I can't get you up, I'll just join you there."

"Ohhhh, you'll get me up all right," Ben said with a wink.

"Oh yes, that's a given. It appears we're half way there."

As he slowly got up from the floor, he became acutely aware of what she had just said. "Good," he thought, "things are looking up!" He followed her to the bathroom, watching her bottom sort of wink at him as she walked in front of him.

Taking her hand as she stepped into the shower he said, "I'll wait for you to adjust that shower; it doesn't like me very much. What do you want me to do with your daisy?"

"Ohhh, where is it, did we forget it?"

"No, I dropped it on the floor by the door."

"Oh good; just put it with some water in one of those glasses on the lavatory and set it over there out of the way. I have the water just right now, so get in here and join me."

He went back to where the daisy was on the floor, picked it up and straightened the petals a bit and placed it in a glass of tepid water. As he turned to get into the shower, he noticed the daisy rotated in the glass as if it was following him. He was still thinking it strange as he stepped into the shower, the water feeling warm and invigorating on his back. Beth turned him around to face her, allowing the water to cascade down his face and chest. She reached for the soap, put a generous amount on her hands and then positioned her body to block the spray from the shower with her back. Starting at his bald head she gently washed it with her hands, not using a washcloth, as she wanted this to be a very sensuous time for both of them. She smiled at him as she added more soap, adjusted her attention to his face and neck, down to his chest. After lathering his back, she wrapped her arms around his body placing her hands on his chest, pulling his back against her breasts. He threw his head backward and smiled as she worked the soap around his back with her breasts. Adding a little more soap, she again reached around him, only this time down lower. As she stroked him gently with her soapy hands, she found him firm and ready. Ben found it difficult to swallow, as he felt his pulse pounding in his groin. If she continues this, things were going to happen that he was not ready for and he was certain she was not as well. Beth sensed this, filled her hands with soap again and finished by washing his legs and feet. He had never felt anything quite as sensuous as having her kneel before him washing his feet, her face so close to him.

"Okay, now it's your turn." as she rose up and handed the soap to Ben.

He moved around and behind her to take advantage of the water to rinse the soap from his body and to block the water from her. Started with her shoulders, he worked the soap around them with a massaging motion, moving down the length of her arms and sides, gently teasing her under her arms. Retrieving more soap, he reached around to her chest, bumping her bottom with the hardness of him. Sliding his soapy hands over her breasts, the nipples firmed against his palms.

"Ummm, that feels so good," she murmured. "Feels like you have an extra hand.

"Sorry it isn't a foot," he laughed.

"What would I do with that?"

"Ohhhh, I'd bet you could find something."

Ben turned her around, added more soap to his hands, pulled her close against him and ran both hands up and down her back. He moved his hands down to her buttocks massaging and kneading them slowly until he reached the upper back of her thighs. He poured some of the liquid soap over her belly, catching some of it in his hands, some running down between her thighs. Placing one hand on the flare of her hip, he moved his other hand to where the soap had run, extending it between her thighs to her backside, moving it up and back and forth against her body. He could feel her opening against his hand as a soft sigh arose from her throat. Moving his hand from her hip down and over to her bottom, the same motion continued from back to front. She moaned and moved back away from him, signaling that it was getting hard to stand on rubbery legs. Feeling her tremble, his hands moved down her thighs, on to her lower legs and feet, kneeling in front of her with her hands on his shoulders to steady her. Before rising he kissed her tummy, tasting the soap and not minding it at all. He helped her turn to rinse and noticed the flush look on her face; the devilish look and twinkle had turned to passion. Ben stepped out of the shower first, grabbed a towel and held it open for her to step into as she slowly stepped out of the shower and into his arms. She placed her arms over his shoulders as he briskly rubbed his hands all over her body through the towel. Beth looked down and began laughing.

"What are you laughing at?"

She could not contain her laughter. "You are moving so fast, you have 'motion in the back field'. It's swinging back and forth. It's so cute."

Ben laughed, "Cute? I just think it's flirting with you."

As her laughter finally subsided, she grabbed the other towel and began drying him. Her method was different; she held the towel open with both hands while she slowly moved it over his body, until she reached down between his legs and took him in both her hands, gently rolling her hands back and forth. Satisfied that he was dry, she walked out of the bathroom. He followed her until they reached the bed, when she turned to him, positioned his back to the side of the bed, sat him down and then pushed him backward onto his back. She stood up straight, took the towel off her body, looked down at him with a look on her face that Ben had not previously seen and said, "I'm going to do things to you that will exceed your wildest dreams!"

Ben swallowed hard and meekly said, "Be kind."

She smiled and said, "Ohhh honey, I will be more than kind; just lay still and enjoy. Close your eyes and~~~just be aware of all your senses."

He closed his eyes and felt the bed move as she climbed astride him. She lowered her face to his and kissed the top of his head, raising her body upward to allow her breasts to touch his face as she stretched above him. He started to reach for them with his mouth like a child searching for its teat, but she pulled away, clearly teasing him. Moving to his forehead, she kissed his eyelids, then his cheek down to his ear, circling it with her tongue, closing the circles in tighter until she arrived at the opening, then flicking it lightly with the tip of her tongue. He felt goose bumps rising all over his body, the hair on his legs standing straight out. She moved down to his neck, kissing and flicking her tongue toward his throat, kissing it before moving down to his chest, not touching him with anything except her mouth and tongue. Her hands supported her weight just above his body, pressing into the bed on either side of him, her knees to the side of his legs. Adjusting her body lower over his, she kissed his right nipple, slowly sliding her tongue over the tip of it, then moving around the edges in concentric circles before placing her lips around it, gently sucking it into her mouth.

Ben sucked in his breath as sharp jolts shot down toward his groin. While holding his nipple in her mouth, Beth rolled her tongue across the tip, wrinkling the areola like a dried prune. Satisfied that she could get no more out of this one, she moved to the left, finding it already swollen in anticipation, in conjunction with the goose bumps that had erupted all over his body. She again dragged her tongue over the top of his nipple, before taking it into her mouth. This time she sucked firmly on it, hearing him moan and feeling his hips move in response to the electric-like shocks conducting to his crotch. Releasing his captive rudiment by giving it a parting kiss, she moved down to his navel, circling it with her tongue, and darting into it, before leaving to move lower yet. His body tensed as he surmised where she was heading and his pulse quickened. With each kiss, he felt his insides begin to shake, feeling both excitement and apprehension. The feeling was so intense, as the only thing touching him was her mouth and tongue; almost like a butterfly, flicking its wings across his body. Each tender touch feeling more like every touch he had ever felt before~~~all rolled into this one light touch~~~until she arrived at her destination.

Her face moved upward away from him and all he felt was her breath on him lightly and yet feeling as strong as a hurricane. His mind instantly went back to that day in the clearing at the park, over half a century ago, alone with this girl that he wanted so much, but didn't know how to love her. Now, she was about to show him a way to love he never would have dreamed of at that young age. His closed eyes burned as tears began forming, feeling very uncomfortable with what she was about to do. He wanted to make love to her in a way that would bring them both the ultimate in not only sexual pleasure, but a binding of the heart and the soul.

She did not speak when she noticed the tears running down the side of his face, as she sensed his feelings. Ever since their very first days when using email to communicate, they both seemed to have an uncanny ability to read, or perhaps feel, each other's mind. And now, seeing the tears, she sensed his feeling of despair. With a parting kiss, she positioned her lower body over his and slowly slid down on top of him, her breasts falling near his face. He opened his eyes and gently cupped her breasts with his hands; their hips moving in synchronized rhythm.

Beth tossed her head backward and ground her hips hard against him as she felt the spasms starting to rise deep inside her. She collapsed her upper body down against his chest and made noises that Ben did not understand as she was overcome by the waves that rippled through her body. But she did not stop; she continued to move with him, wanting so much to give him pleasure. Still again, he felt it slipping away; holding him back~~~something he did not understand. He ran his hands down her back, kissed her neck and cheek, feeling the convulsions inside her gradually slow and stop, her final spasms gripping at his now flaccid member.

"I love sweetheart~~~I love you," Beth murmured as her breath was returning to her.

Ben rapidly rolled his head from side to side, both in frustration and futility. "I'm so sorry honey~~~I don't know why~~~what~~~it's not you baby~~~it's just me. I love you so much~~~I just don't understand~~~just don't know why. I want you so much, but~~~"

Beth did not immediately move or reply, as she loved lying on top of him, feeling the rise and fall of his chest as he breathed; her mouth close to his ear, he could feel her breath tickle and send little chills through his body. Finally, she elevated her upper body above him, supporting herself with her hands on either side of his head. She smiled down at him as he opened his eyes, reading the sadness and disappointment he was feeling. She leaned forward and lightly kissed his lips. He reached up and cupped her face like he did the very first time he kissed her, his finger tips near the lobes of her ears. It sent thrills down her spine as his touch was always so gentle and soft, like he was touching some fine delicate work of art, savoring the richness of its texture, the beauty that the years have added to its value, fearful of hurting or damaging this one of a kind, this love of his life. Beth knew that she would have to convince him that she was not fragile, that she wanted to give him all of herself completely, without any reservation. That every kiss, every touch comes from her heart, that it was he who opened her up, wanting so much to give him everything she has to give.

She rolled off him onto her side, leaning on her left elbow and asked, "Are you thirsty; can I get you something to drink?"

"No, not right now. What do we have here to drink besides water?"

"Nothing in the room, but there is a vending machine in the lobby that has all sorts of drinks. I could put on some clothes in a jiffy and run down to get something."

"No way, you ain't goin' nowhere! Why would I want you to get dressed? What's that the kids are saying these days about candy?"

She laughed and replied, "Do you mean 'eye candy'?"

"Yeah, that's it, eye candy. You make these old eyes feel good. I love to watch you walk from behind." Ben paused and chuckled deep down in his throat. "It looks like you are flirting with me with your butt~~~winking as if to say 'follow me'."

"Well, that's what I want you to do, but I never thought that my rear had any flirting ability. You are just so biased!"

"I like your cute little butt."

"How did you twist this around to my butt by asking you if you were thirsty?" Beth laughed. "And besides, it isn't so little."

"Oh that's easy; when you are laying on top of me bare butt naked, how can I think of anything else?" he chuckled. "And why is it that women always think their butt is so big?"

"I don't know; maybe because our hips are wider due to the differences in our pelvic bone. Men have been referring to us as 'broads' for so long, I guess we think of ourselves as having a big rear. And we do carry our weight in our hips and thighs, as opposed to guys carrying it around their waist."

"Well, I don't think you are a 'broad' and I like your butt just the way it is~~~soft and enticing."

"Okay," she smiled, "but I do have to get up; I have to pee. I'll try not to flirt with you so much. On the other hand~~~watch this."

She slowly and seductively got up off the bed, took a step or two and then walked very deliberately away from him, slowly swinging her hips from side to side in a very suggestive way, looking back over her shoulder at him as if to say, 'Come and get it' "

He rose up on his elbow and watched her as a broad smile spread across his face. "Yeah, that's it~~~that come-hither look."

She stopped, turned around and faced him shaking her shoulders from side to side, her breasts jiggling slightly, her hands on her hips and her legs slightly apart. Smiling, she said in a low sexy voice, "For you sweetheart~~~just for you."

Swallowing hard, he looked at her standing in front of him, totally comfortable with her nakedness. The years had been kind to her; small pert breasts pointed outward from high on her chest, the waist flaring gracefully to wide hips curving gently to soft thighs. Her lower legs were firmed from miles of walking, tapering smoothly to her ankles. The small five foot-two inch frame was topped with a head of stark blond that the years had turned to a mix of silver and gold, framing a face that held a smile that warmed his heart and eyes that shined with love as she looked at him.

"You better go pee before I drag you back here," he uttered, his voice cracking as he spoke.

"You can drag me back anytime, but I'll be right back. Don't go away." she winked.

Ben sat up, turned and stared out the window. It had been so many years since he had been sexually active, thinking those days were gone forever and had accepted that fate. His mind now turned to thoughts of the ED drugs on the market and wondered if he needed those. "Maybe that is what is wrong," he thought. "Have I neglected that part of my life so long that I have lost the ability to make love to a woman? Is it true that if it isn't used, it is lost? How important is this going to be in this relationship?" That question was answered in his mind as soon as it entered. He knew it was going to be very important, especially to him. "No," he thought, "I haven't lost it. I look at her and I'm filled with all this desire. I want her and yet~~~I'm afraid~~~but what the hell am I afraid of?"

"What are you thinking about?" Beth said as she tied the belt around the waist of a pink robe she had put on as she left the bathroom and sat down beside him on the bed.

"Oh, I don't know~~~lots of things."

"Want to talk about them?"

"I don't know where to start. I don't even know how to start."

"Well, why don't we start with how you make me feel?" Ben's heart sank as he thought how his inability to perform might make her feel inadequate, and that made him feel even worse.

"Do you know how wonderful I feel when I'm with you? You must know how complete I feel when I'm in your arms."

"I~~I know~~and I feel like that with you too. It's just~~~I don't know."

"Ben, be honest with me now~~~do you feel guilty being here with me?"

"No~~~this is the first time it's ever felt right. Oh honey, there have been many times I made love to you in my mind. I'd close my eyes while I would be with someone else, but it was you I was with. I would feel guilty about that later, but not at the time. In my mind I still saw you as that 14 year old girl who was with me on the porch, in the woods, in your dad's car."

He paused and stared out the window. Beth reached up and placed her hand at the back of his head and slowly combed her fingers through the hair. She said nothing, allowing Ben to verbalize his thoughts.

Slowly, he continued in choppy bits and pieces as though he was searching for words. "After a time, I put it out of my mind completely~~~thinking I would never find you. Those times in the woods~~~in the car~~~I wanted you so much, but I was afraid~~~I didn't know what to do and afraid we would get caught." He paused and looked at her with eyes full of tears before going on. "Now I want you in the same way and I know what to do~~~but I'm still afraid."

"But what are you afraid of~~~there is no one here but you and me? I can tell you that you do know what to do and you do it quite well. Are you afraid of me?"

"No of course not~~~I'm not afraid of you~~~it's more like I'm afraid of me."

"What do you mean, Ben? I don't understand; you are so kind and gentle. I love your touch and I know there is nothing you would ever do to hurt me. What is it about you that scares~~~you?"

"No, I'm not afraid I will hurt you. I would die before I would ever think of hurting you~~~*I'm just afraid there isn't going to be enough of me,*" he said with a tone of finality as if he had finally gotten it out and off his chest.

"What? What could you possibly mean? Not enough of you? My God Ben! Look at me! Look in my eyes," a hint of anger in her voice.

As she spoke, tears started falling from her eyes. "Ben~~~you have given me more in just these few short months than I have ever felt in all those years before. I am alive with feelings I have never experienced before. I have never let myself go like I do with you. You have opened me up and I've found things within me I never knew I possessed; a whole new way of loving~~~of giving myself up to you~~~all of me. I want to belong to you because I feel I have always belonged to you. You fill me with so much of you. You are my first thought in the morning when I wake and the last thought before I go to sleep. God only knows how many times I think of you between those times. How could you possibly think there is not enough of you?"

Ben brushed away her tears with his thumbs, cupping her face in his hands and looked at her for what seemed countless minutes, their eyes locked to each other, searching each other's souls, before he spoke.

His voice sounded tired as he said, "Sometimes I feel like I hurt you without even knowing it. Honey, everything you have just said is exactly how I feel. It is how I've felt for so many years, almost hauntingly. Now that we have found each other, it still seems like it is all a dream and it is going to disappear. I *know* it is not a dream, but I still fear it might disappear."

"But why do you think it might? You know I love you and you love me. Ben, that is forever for me and I know it is for you. How could it not be after loving me all those years? I am not going anywhere~~~ever! You're stuck with me buddy!" she said with a smile.

"I know, I know. I know all of that. But what if I can't give you everything that you need?"

"And what is it you think I need that you can't give?" she asked with a tone of authority in her voice.

He smiled at the sound of her voice. He loved it when she sounded off like that. She had some fire inside her and he could see it when she brought that out. There were times when she would not be denied. Ben knew that and loved that about her.

"Well, beings you asked in such a stern way, I guess I better tell you," he said as if the mood was much lighter now, as there was a bit of humor added.

"I'm waiting dear," she said with that tone again.

Ben looked past her to the wall behind, staring at it as if to gather up his courage. Finally he sucked in his breath and spilled it out in one long flowing sentence."Honey, I'm afraid that I might not be able to give you all the physical things that you need. I'm an old man~~~I ain't a teenager anymore."

"Phew~~~is that all? Ohhh for God's sake, Ben! And you think I am? I am not fourteen anymore! Sex~~~you're worried about sex? Oh Ben~~~we aren't about sex! We are far beyond that~~~sex is just an extra. We have talked about this before; you said it yourself~~~sex without love is shallow and empty. Ben, we love each other, deeply and completely. Sex will happen and it will be only a small part of what we need. All I need is what we have~~~together and you give me that. Don't you see you have already given me everything I need? I just want to give you the same~~~and I will dammit! You'll see!"

"But when we were younger~~~"

"Dammit, we are not that young couple any more, we never will be!" she said with firmness in her voice that cut Ben off before he could finish. "But we are still the same people~~~the same souls that touched and fell in love with each other. That love did not fade. If anything, it has become much stronger over those years as we found the things that were not important in each of our lives and now realize what is truly important." Her voice then softened as she said, "Ben, I know we won't have the stamina we could have had back then, but we have something much more than that now. We have years of experience~~~years that have taught us much about life and now we have learned how to really love and be loved. The mechanics aren't important. Only what we feel in our hearts is important. *I love you Ben! With all my heart and everything that is in me and that will never change!* You have nothing to be afraid of."

The emphasis in her voice told him it would prove fruitless to disagree with her. Taking her into his arms, he held her tight against him, not wanting her to see the tears that were flowing from his eyes as he said, his voice quivering, "I love you my sweet Beth. I will never let you go!"

"No need to worry sweetheart, I'm not going anywhere~~~unless you want to get dressed and we could go out and find a little pub where we could have a sandwich and a drink and maybe dance. I've never asked you~~~do you dance?" Beth asked.

"I've been known to step on a few toes, but I've not danced in years," he said as he sniffed through his nose.

"I haven't either and I was never very good, but I'd like to sway with you in my arms. Do you think we could find a place with a jukebox?" she asked excitedly.

"You really want to do this, don't you?"

"Yes I do. Come on~~~~ let's go," as she took his hand tugging to get him up off the bed. "Maybe someone in the lobby will know where there is a place to eat, drink and dance."

"You just want to get your toes stepped on, don't you?" Ben quipped as he rose to get up off the bed, with a look of resignation on his face.

"Well, if you step on them, you'll kiss them for me when we get back, won't you?" she asked with a wink.

"Ohhh, you have a foot fetish? I've never been there before."

"Nooo, I didn't say that!" Beth said with a laugh. "I just figured if you step on my toes, it will be okay if you kiss my injured piggies."

"What if I trip you and you fall on your rear; what then?"

She smiled that devilish smile of hers as she replied, "I shouldn't have to tell you what to do in that case. But you won't let me fall, will you?"

"No. If you start to go, we'll both end up on the floor. But hey! No fast stuff. I don't move that fast any more, okay?"

"Yes, that's a deal!" she chuckled. "I don't either. Now let's get dressed and ready to go."

Chapter VI
Footwork After The Dance

Beth made her way to the bathroom as Ben walked over to retrieve his clothes from the couch. As he sat down to pull on his socks, he wondered where they might find a place with a jukebox. Did any place have them anymore? He remembered one back in Michigan in a bar he used to frequent a few years ago, an old one that held some classic country tunes that had been well played. As he thought about it, he remembered that the bar had been demolished under those Urban Renewal programs that dictated anything still standing around seventy or more years had to be removed to make room for new and better things. Figuring someday those folks will look at him and get the same idea; he made a mental note to keep his powder dry.

"Your turn for the bathroom," Beth announced as she stood there in a pair of jeans and a red turtleneck sweater. Ben was amazed at how quickly she could be ready to go and how young and sexy she looked in a sweater and pair of jeans. She had a look of excitement on her face, almost bubbling with life. She wanted to have fun and he knew he was going to be proud being seen with her.

"Wow! You look nice~~~and very patriotic with your white sneakers to match your red sweater and blue jeans," he remarked with a wink.

"Oh, I never thought about that. Do you want me to change?"

"Of course not~~~you look terrific and there is sure nothing wrong with patriotism~~~at least not yet," as he stood up with only his socks on and moved toward the bathroom.

Beth could not keep from laughing at the sight. "Are~~~your feet~~~cold?" she asked laughing.

Looking at his feet he realized how stupid he looked with only a pair of socks on his feet and began laughing as well. "No not really," as he turned toward Beth to hug her, but she stopped him in his tracks.

"Don't you dare start something now. You know if you touch me now looking like that, we won't get out of here, so behave yourself and put some clothes on!"

She had that familiar tone of authority in her voice that he was becoming accustomed to and knew she had read his mind again. Even though she was creating visions in his mind standing there so enticing and vibrant, he knew he would have to wait. He shrugged his shoulders, picked up his clothes and went into the bathroom pouting like a little boy that just had his toys taken away, knowing this would have the right effect on her, as she loved the little boy that still resided inside him. His nearly seventy years had taught him that most women loved the little boy that sometimes live on in men.

Ben emerged from the bathroom fully clothed, still slightly pouting. Beth smiled as she walked over to him and said, "Now you can give me a hug," as she took him in her arms.

"Chicken! Why didn't you do that before?"

"You know why. We would have been over there now moaning and groaning," she replied pointing to the bed.

"What's wrong with that?"

"Nothing~~~as long as we save it for later. I just want to dance with you now."

Smiling broadly he bowed, offered his arm to her and asked, "Would you like to go dining and dancing with me? I would be honored with your presence."

Why, yes sir! I would like that very much," she replied as she looped her wrist in the bend of his arm.

Ben smiled broadly at her; already swelling with pride as they left the room and made their way to the elevator. She was still holding his arm as they entered the lobby and approached the young lady attending the registration desk. Ben winked at her and asked if she knew of a place that might have a jukebox and a place to dance. She thought for a moment before answering, "No, not a jukebox~~~but I know a neat little bar that has a local singer with one of those machines that plays like background music. He sings with it and is quite good; it's a real cozy place."

"You mean a Karaoke?" Ben asked.

"No, just some sort of rhythm thingy that he can adjust and simulate drums or other stuff that he might want; it's better than Karaoke. He also plays recorded music when he takes his breaks."

"Can you tell us how to get there from here?" Beth asked.

"Oh yes, it is not too far from here. My fiancé and I go there quite often on Fridays after I get off work. I think he wants to go there tonight. It's called The Haven."

"Does he play every night?" Ben asked.

"Every night except Sunday; I think he's very religious," she laughed.

"I would imagine business wouldn't be so hot on Sunday night," Ben added.

"Don't know; never been there on Sunday. I can give you directions, if you like."

Beth quickly replied, "Ohh that would be super, dear. Thank you!"

After getting directions, Ben took Beth's hand and headed to the parking lot and their car. "She handed the keys to him saying, "You drive this time."

"Ohh is that the reason you asked for directions?"

"Well, I know how men hate to ask for directions and besides, I want to grade your driving."

"How fast do you want to go?"

"You don't move fast anymore, remember?"

"Yeah, I do remember," he replied as he unlocked the car, opening the door for Beth. "Are you always this much of a gentleman?" she asked.

"No, so you better enjoy it while it lasts," he said with a chuckle.

After driving for only a few minutes, Ben pulled into the parking lot of The Haven. There were a lot of cars and very few empty spaces.

"It looks crowded; do you want to stay?" he asked.

"Yes it's okay, as long as you are there any place is fine."

He parked and again went around opening the door for Beth. She ducked her head as she got out of the car, then surprised him as she reached up and gave him a quick kiss on his cheek and said, "Thank you, my Prince."

Ben blushed and stammered, "You're welcome, Your Grace." Taking her hand in his, they entered the bar. The young lady at the hotel was correct; the man was playing and singing some country tune and he was very good. There were a few couples on the dance floor; the lighting was soft and low. There were still some empty tables and he guided Beth over toward them.

"Do you have a preference?' he asked.

"Let's take this one~~~it's a little farther away from the dance floor. I might want to steal a kiss or two from you without making it a public display."

Ben slid the chair out from under the table and held it for her as she seated herself. He sat next to her facing the dance floor and was about to say something when the waitress approached their table to take an order for drinks.

"Do you serve food?" Ben asked.

"We have sandwiches," she replied, "until 11:00 o'clock."

"Great! I'm kinda hungry. Would you like a sandwich, baby?"

"Yes, I think I'd like to have a grilled cheese on rye."

"One grilled cheese on rye and could I have a Reuben?" he asked the waitress.

"I don't think I know what that is," she replied.

"It's corned beef and sauerkraut on rye," he said.

"I'll have to ask them in back and let you know," she said. "Can I get you something to drink?"

"Yes, I'll have a double CR on the rocks," Ben replied. "What would you like, honey?"

"I think I'd like a small glass of a nice, sweet white wine. Any brand is fine and a glass of water." Beth replied.

"Fine, I'll be back with your drinks and let you know about that~~~Rue~bun?."

Ben chuckled as she left. "I hope she knows what a CR is."

"What is it?" Beth asked.

"Oh, it's like lemonade. When she brings it, I'll give you a sip. You may like one for yourself."

As they were waiting for their drinks, their attention turned to the man that was entertaining. He was singing 'Behind Closed Doors', an old Charlie Rich tune. Ben turned to Beth and said, "That song reminds me of you."

"Of me~~~how is that?"

"You are a striking, professional woman that appears so prim and proper. One would never guess the fire behind those glasses and clothes. But when you get behind closed doors and shed those clothes, you are a very sexy, sensuous woman! And you make me glad I'm a man!"

"Only because of you I am that way. I feel that we have always been together, never really apart, with love that has always been present~~~tucked away somewhere deep inside. I've never been so wanton like this~~~feeling like I've missed so much all those long years. You just bring so many emotions out of me I never knew were hidden inside."

She paused for an instant and Ben knew she was still thinking of something more when she continued, "I remember feeling like this when we were together back in the 50's. I didn't understand it then, but~~~sweetheart I do now. But only with you~~~it was always you."

"Excuse me," the waitress announced as she returned with their drinks. "We do make Reuben sandwiches and I will bring it right out in a jiffy." She then placed the drinks on the table, turned and quickly returned to the kitchen. Ben winked at Beth as they realized the young woman was very new at her job. "I'm ashamed I made the crack about the CR." But before he could say anything else, the waitress returned carrying the grilled cheese and Ben's Reuben.

"Wow! You not only make them here, you already have one for me. That was quick!" he retorted

"Thank you. The lady in the kitchen knows what they are~~~she also likes them."

Ben paid the tab after he sipped his CR, satisfied that she or the barkeep knew what that was. He then offered it to Beth for a sip. As it came close to her lips, she smiled at him and said, "Lemonade my ass! That's whiskey!"

He laughed heartily and out loud. There is a certain look in her eyes when she says things like this, and so atypical of her, yet so cute. "But very good whiskey", he countered after composing himself.

"I just don't like hard liquor; a little bit of wine goes a long way with me. We eat and then you are going to dance with me buster," she winked, as he grinned and wondered if that was a threat or a promise. He knew she was not going to be denied this night.

The Reuben was very good and Ben surmised the lady in the kitchen did indeed like them as well. There was just the right amount of sauerkraut giving it a snappy taste, but not too sour.

"Your cheese sandwich looks good; so does that little piece of cheese that is clinging to your lower lip," he chuckled.

Beth touched her lip and found that indeed a small string of cheese was sticking to her lip. She smiled as she used her index finger to slowly push it up and into her mouth, lingering long enough to suck any remaining piece of it off her finger. Ben was taking another sip of his drink, and nearly missed his mouth as he watched her seductive display.

"Yes, it is very good~~~would you like a sample?" she replied with a devilish smile on her face.

"Uhh, no~~~not now~~~uhh I have my Reuben to take care of at the moment. Besides, I'm waiting for this fast song to end so I can abuse you on the dance floor."

"Abuse me? Ohh honey, you will probably have to hold me up after drinking this wine."

"The pleasure will be all mine and I think this fast one is about over. Are you ready for this?"

Before she could answer, the song ended, but instead of the singer launching into another number, he announced it was time 'to pause for the cause'. Ben looked at Beth and said, "Ahh, I was saved by the 'cause'.

But as soon as he said that, the man put on some recorded music with Garth Brooks singing 'The Dance'. "Oh no you're not," she said as she took his hand, nearly pulling him out of his chair, leading him to the dance floor, "this is a good one."

As she turned to him, she moved smoothly into his arms and they moved together farther out to the center of the floor. While he had not danced in years, he managed to avoid her toes. Soon his hands were both behind her, one around her waist, the other clasping his other wrist. It allowed Beth some freedom to move, yet holding her close. She put her head against his chest and felt his body move against hers in sync to the music. She loved this and wondered why she had never danced very much before?

As Garth ended, Kenny Rogers was next with 'Lady' and their movements never stopped. Ben pressed his head against Beth's, her hair soft, gently brushing his face. He kissed her forehead as the music came to an end, followed by a Jerry Lee Lewis number that was way too fast. He looked at her and smiled, "Time for another sip of CR." She laughed as they left the dance floor and returned to their table. When they sat down, she took his hand between both of hers, looked into his eyes and said, "I love dancing with you. Can we stay a while and dance some more?"

"Yes, as long as you like, my love. I love dancing with you, too; maybe we can turn the radio on in our room, take off all our clothes and dance in our room," he said as if it was a question.

"I think it would end up being a horizontal Mambo." she laughed.

"Who knows~~~it might be fun," he winked.

~~~~RETURN TO PRESENT DAY

"Oh Julie, I'm starting to feel the effects of a long emotional day and I think we should call it a day. I don't get a second wind like I used to."

"I'm sorry; I didn't mean to keep you going so long. I'm flabbergasted over what you are telling me! Can we continue in the morning?"

"Are you sure you want to hear more of this, Julie? I feel rather awkward talking about your father like this."

"Yes, I want to know it all. I want to know what it was that gave Dad the peace he seemed to have before he died. Mom thought he was just happy to be dying to get away from her, but I never believed that. I always felt he was devoted to her and was worried about what was going to happen to her after he was gone. He talked to me about that toward the end."

"He did?" Beth asked, very interested now with what Julie could tell her about Ben that she did not already know. "What did he say?"

"Well, he said he wanted me to look after her after he was gone, as she would need some help taking care of herself. Actually, it's more than just *some,* now that I know just how much of a job it is. I spend a lot of my time with her, which is another reason I have not had much of a social life."

"I know it was hard for Ben and it was hurtful wanting him, knowing I could never spend the time with him that I wanted," Beth responded softly. "Had he left Helen, he would have never forgiven himself and I wouldn't have had the caring man that I always knew and wanted. We
~~~~

just had to take what we could manage and make the most of it. I would not have wanted to lose that precious time."

Julie stared at the floor digesting what Beth had told her, wondering how she should feel about all she had learned about her father and how she would feel about this woman in the morning. Finally looking up to Beth, she noticed her eyes looked tired. "Well, I better let you get some sleep. I have a bath off my room, so the one in the hall is all yours. Help yourself to the towels and the shower. Breakfast at 0700."

Beth laughed and quipped, "You sound like your dad again with that military time. I'll be up before seven and I'll help you with breakfast."

"Okay, sounds good. Thank you Beth~~~for~~~sharing with me. It means a lot to me."

Beth took Julie into her arms, her voice choked up as she said, "It is so~~~strange my dear. I feel close to Ben talking to you about him. I'm so happy we have met and I see now why Ben was so proud of you."

"I'm happy we have met, too. We still have so much to talk about, but for now, we both better get some rest~~~busy day tomorrow."

"Yes. Good night, Julie."

"Good night."

Julie retired to her room; her mind busily going over the events Beth had related to her. She was learning things about her dad she had never imagined; never thinking of him as a sexual being and certainly not as a lover. She refused to conjure up the vision of her father that way, preferring to remember the gentle times he held her on his lap and conveyed all his love to her in a paternal way~~~not a sexual way~~~to this~~~woman. No, she concluded her father was not a sexual being, before drifting off to sleep.

Her alarm clock went off at 5:30 AM. She picked up her phone and called her manager's voice mail to report that she would not be in for work today, as she was not feeling well. She hoped Beth was not awake to hear her make that call. After taking a quick shower, she pulled on a pair of sweatpants and a matching sweatshirt before entering the kitchen, finding Beth already dressed and brewing a pot of coffee.

"Good morning. I hope you don't mind I found the coffee and put on a pot. Did I wake you?"

"No, not at all~~~I'm delighted that you did. I didn't hear you out here as my alarm blasted me out of bed like it does every morning," Julie moaned. "I hate that thing!"

Beth laughed and said, "That sound gets worse as you get older; try some nice soothing music~~~works for me."

"Do you eat eggs? I thought I'd scramble some with some ham and hash browns," Julie asked.

"Yes, that sounds fine~~~is there something I can do to help?"

Julie went to the cupboard, fetched a loaf of wheat bread and handed it to Beth. "If you like, you can toast some bread. There is a toaster oven over there on top of the microwave," as she pointed to the oven. "It's the only other available electrical outlet not already used in the kitchen."

Beth took the bread and busied herself with the toaster while Julie began cracking eggs. Soon the kitchen was filled with the scent of fresh coffee and toast. Julie had two skillets going, one with the eggs and cubed pieces of pre-cooked ham, the other browning the hash browns. Beth suddenly felt hungry as her nostrils filled with the delicious aroma of the food being prepared, sending messages of delight to her brain. As the toaster bell sounded, she removed the toast and spread some butter on four pieces and set them on the table.

"Beth, would you grab a couple of plates and silver from right above the toaster and the drawer right below? The eggs are just about done."

The table was set, the food brought to the table and they sat down to eat. They were both silent as they enjoyed the hot coffee with ham and eggs. As Beth finished her breakfast, she pushed back from the table and said, "That really hit the spot, Julie; it was all very good. Let me wash up these dishes."

"Oh no, the dishwasher will take care of them. It only takes a moment to load. While I do that, you can tell me more about what happened at the bar. Did you close the place?"

Beth laughed hard and replied, "Ohh, no! It didn't take long to wear us out at our age. No, we stayed until the singer took another break, then left."

"Did you continue with the radio back in your room?"

Beth again laughed and replied, "No, I think Ben had enough dancing for one evening. When we returned to our room, he flopped on the bed~~~~~~

~~~~~Return to November 2005

"Oh my legs are tired," Ben said as he rolled over on to his back. I sure couldn't agree with that song about dancing all night."

Beth kicked off her shoes and slithered up on the bed beside him. "Oh, you held up very well. Thank you for taking me dancing; I really had a good time."

"I did too. It's been a long time since I've done that. Never had much fun before, but it was fun with you."

"Do you feel like a shower? I could sure use some help washing my back," she asked.

"Umm, that sounds great. My back could use some attention, too. Sounds like we might do this together?"

"You learn fast, darling; beat you in there!" Beth said as she jumped up off the bed.

"No contest; I need you in there first to adjust that cold-blooded shower."

She quickly began shedding clothes as she made her way to the shower, stepped in and adjusted the shower to just the right temperature. Turning toward the shower door to call out for Ben, she was startled to find him already in the bathroom watching her while she was adjusting the shower. Seeing him grinning there, she retorted, "Voyeur!" Did you get your eyes full?"

He had to hold onto the railing around the shower to keep from falling, as he was laughing so hard. "How could I not be a voyeur when you are in the shower? Besides, I was right behind you as your behind became more and more visible as you went ahead of me. I'd have to be a eunuch to not look at you."

"I think that's the first time I ever had someone peek at me in the shower," she chuckled.

"Well, I'm betting it won't be the last. Did you like the feeling?" he asked as he applied some soap to her back.

"Yes, only because it is you. I'm pleased that you enjoy looking at me."

"I've never been able to take my eyes off you. You are so beautiful to me~~~always have been."

"Silly man, you forgot to take your glasses off and they are steaming up," she laughed. "No wonder you think I'm beautiful~~~you can't see me!"

Ben suddenly realized that he had indeed forgotten to remove his glasses before stepping into the shower. Thinking quickly, he responded, "No sweetheart, they steamed up *after* I saw you!"

She gave him a gentle jab with her elbow and said, "Yeah right, now turn around and let me wash your back."

He turned and let his head tilt backward, closed his eyes and reveled in her touch as her hands gently massaged the lather into his back in small tight circles. Satisfied that his back was clean, she kissed the top of his head, stepped out of the shower to allow the water to rinse his back and quickly wrapped a robe around her small frame to dry and keep warm. She stepped into her slippers and made her way to the bed, sliding between the sheets, removing her robe as she did. Ben was just finishing with a towel, as he looked for a pair of loose fitting shorts to put on before leaving the bathroom. Entering the bedroom he looked at her under the covers and said, "Are you cold?"

"Not anymore~~~I'm all dry now. Come in and join me."

Instead, he pulled back the sheets and sucked in his breath. He swallowed hard before sitting on the bed next to her. He ran his hand gently and lightly along her body, loving the feel of her soft skin under his finger tips. As his hand reached her feet, he felt a sudden impulse and turned his body around to more squarely face her feet, lifting the one closest to him. He held it in his right hand and ran his fingers slowly under the arch of her foot. Her toes curled as he did this, telling him that her feet were very touchy. Then he wriggled his fingers faster, back and forth on the bottom of her foot, making her squirm and giggle. A devilish smile spread across his face as he learned that she was ticklish, inspiring a thought to try something very different. Her feet were fresh from her shower, so he lowered his head to her foot, first kissing the top of it, then lifting it higher and tickling the bottom of her arch with the tip of his tongue.

"What are you doing?" she squealed as she squirmed around making it hard for Ben to hold on to her foot. "You didn't step on my feet!"

"I know, but I was trying to. You kept moving them out of the way."

"But why did you want to step on them?' she asked bewildered.

"So I would have an excuse to do this," he said as he took her big toe into his mouth and sucked it gently while moving his tongue up and down the length of it.

"Eww, Ben! What are you doing?"

"Worshiping the feet you walk on," he said, as he moved the tip of his tongue between the big toe and the one adjacent to it. "I like it! My God, I like it," he said.

Before she could respond, he had already moved over to the other foot.

He held firmly to her foot as she squirmed and giggled, her toes curling against his mouth. He was delighted he was having this effect on her, but also knew he must not take it to the point of torture. Moving his tongue to her arch and gently stroking it like a cat pruning itself, she purred deep in her throat and settled back against the bed, languishing in these new sensations. He slowly took one, then the another toe into his mouth, massaging them with his tongue and soft sucking motions.

She sat up to watch as he ministered to her feet. "That is so intense! Where did you learn that?"

"Right here, right now." he replied.

"Do you mean you have never done this before?"

"Yes. I mean no, I've never done this before. I've never had any desire to do it before. Do you like it?"

"Yes, but not too much between my toes. That drives me crazy. Do I get to do that to you?"

"No".

"Why not; what's good for the goose is good for the gander."

"I'm too ticklish; I can't stand to have my feet tickled."

"Ohh, wait 'til I get hold of them," she threatened.

"How are you going to do that while I have you by your feet?"

"Ben if I have to, I'll wait until you go to sleep and I'll get them then."

Not being able to contain his laughter, he said, "Look at us! Senior citizens playing footsy games like a couple of adolescents. Why did it take us so long to find this much happiness?"

"I don't know Ben; I'm just so glad that we have. I never thought I could have this much fun and be so happy. I feel like a teenager again, like we were just put on hold for a while."

"If we would have been put on hold much longer, there wouldn't be anything left. I hope my battery doesn't run down when I sleep," Ben quipped.

"Battery~~~do you have~~~uhhh~~~something I don't know about? I don't like toys."

"No," Ben laughed, "nothing like that. Just a figure of speech, darling~~~meaning I hope I have the energy to keep up with you."

"Don't forget sweetheart, I'm no teenybopper either. Now just relax, lay back and get your feet up here."

"Ohh, no you don't. My feet aren't cute like yours. They're big clods, not dainty, pretty painted, kissable pinkies like yours."

"Listen here Benny boy, if you don't let me work on your feet, I'm going to get on top of you and tickle your arm pits until you can't stand it. Then I'll get your feet when you are too weak to stop me."

"What makes you think I'm ticklish under my arms? Besides, I think I'd like you on top of me, so carry on."

Beth's eyes narrowed and a devilish smile crossed her face hearing him say that. Rising up on her hands and knees, she slithered like a cat toward him with a look in her eyes that made him attempt to slide away from her. He was too slow, as she approached him with a kiss full on his mouth that brought his defenses down like the walls of Jericho. He sank down on his back, taking Beth down on top of him. As promised, her hands went to both of his arm pits and started a light wriggle at first, then picking up the tempo while keeping her lips tight against his. Without warning, she removed her hands from under his arms and aborted the kiss, quickly sliding down his body to his feet, grabbing one in both hands pulling it to her mouth. Swiftly, she kissed the underside of his arch, making him jump and try to pull his foot back, but she had a firm grip on it. She laughed and ran the tip of her tongue across the bottom of his arch, making him laugh almost hysterically. Sensing he was not kidding about having ticklish feet, she slowed the movement of her tongue to a more caressing motion, again cat-like.

He groaned, feeling the tension start to subside as she moved her mouth slowly up the underside of his foot, moving toward his big toe. Dragging her tongue upwards toward the tip, she gently sucked it into her mouth as her tongue welcomed it with a massaging motion up and down the length of it. Beth was surprised at how pleasant this was and wondered why she had never thought of this before. However, no matter how amused Beth was by this new experience, it could not match the sensations that Ben was feeling.

"Ohh wow!" he gasped as her tongue moved over to the area between his big toe and the one adjacent to it. "Eww, that tickles!"

Beth grinned as she moved over to the smaller toe, taking it into her mouth, and then adding the middle one with it. She was gaining confidence in this new found method of titillating him and noticed that he had settled down and was enjoying this new found pleasure. He offered no resistance when she moved to the other foot and repeated the treatment on it as well.

"Now I suppose you want me to kiss you after you sucked my toes?" Ben asked.

As she moved up to his face, she murmured, "Why not? What's good for the goose is good for the gander," she chuckled.

He cupped her face in his hands and kissed her long and deep. Ending the kiss, he looked at her and smiled, "I don't think you would want to do this in the summer after I just finish mowing the lawn."

"I don't think I would want to kiss you anywhere when you are that sweaty," she laughed. "I can wait until after your shower, then we'll see what all I will do."

"Umm, sounds like a promise to me," he winked.

"Just wait and I'll give you a sample later," her voice low and sultry, as she rose to get up off the bed.

Leaning back, he hooked his fingers behind his head and mused, "I can hardly wait; I love everything you do. I never dreamed I could be so happy. I keep wondering what our relationship would have been like if we would have found each other much earlier. Do you think we would have made a go of things if you would have stayed in Michigan instead of moving to Florida?"

"I don't know," she replied, "we were so young. I think we would have probably gotten into trouble. We would have eventually learned what to do with all those impulses."

"Yeah, your dad would have killed me!"

"No, he wouldn't have. Dad didn't have a mean bone in his body. He would have been disappointed just like he was when I did get pregnant. I think he would have liked you," she added as she stretched, swinging her feet off the bed before rising to go to the bathroom.

It had been a long day and they were both tired. Ben switched on the TV to check the weather forecast when Beth called out from the bathroom, "What do you want to do tomorrow?"

"I don't think I want to go anywhere. It is going to be our last day together and I want to spend it right here with you. Maybe we can call up room service and have breakfast in bed. What do you think?"

She came out of the bathroom in her blue nightgown, walked over to him taking his hands in hers and tugged at him. "I think that is a wonderful idea! Now get in there and get some clothes on. You look cold sitting there."

"Oh, I get it, tired of me already~~~got to get dressed, huh?"

Laughing she said, "No such luck buddy, I'm not done with you yet. That will never happen!"

He stood up from the bed and she rose up on her toes and gave him a full bodied kiss, letting her hands drop down behind to cup his butt pulling him tight against her.

"See what I mean? I want a lot more of you, but I want to curl up next to you and rest with your arms around me now. You look tired too, so hurry up in there and get back in bed with me."

"Yes ma'am~~~anything you say ma'am. I'm on my way, sweetheart~~~on my way."

"Don't you dare salute me, buster!"

He laughed as he moved around her on his way to the bathroom. As he arrived at the bathroom door, he looked back to see if she was watching him. She was. He smiled as he entered the bathroom; enjoying the fun he has teasing her.

After brushing his teeth and putting on a pair of sleep shorts, he hurried back into the bedroom.

"What are you doing in those?" Beth asked pointing at his shorts.

"You told me to get some clothes on; I am just trying to please you," he replied with a laugh.

"You won't be cold when you get in here with me, so take those silly things off."

"What about you and that blue nightgown you have on?"

Tossing the covers back she replied, "What nightgown? Now get in here and keep me warm."

He smiled and quickly complied, shedding the shorts and climbed in beside her. He felt the warmth of her body coiling around him as he moved tightly against her. Placing her head on his shoulder and draping her leg across his belly, she gently stroked his chest with her hand. She loved this position and Ben knew that she would soon be asleep.

"Good night my love~~~sleep well, "he said with a kiss on her cheek.

"I will sweetheart~~~~you too," as she returned his kiss.

CHAPTER VII
Past Experiences

Beth was first to awake, as she was the lighter sleeper of the two. Years of staying at hospitals with a critical child who was fighting for its life, conditioned her to be alert at a moment's notice; still finding it hard to fall into a very deep sleep. She could function with very little sleep, grabbing short power naps whenever they availed themselves. She was amazed at how fast sleep would come to her after making love to Ben; how relaxed and calm her body would become while spooning against him. Now as she lay there listening to him breathe, feeling his chest rise and fall, she felt a chill course through her body at the thought this would be their last day together. Tomorrow they would have to part and go back to their dismal lives~~~no longer free to reach out and touch the other. Gently she rolled away, leaning back over him to plant a light kiss upon his forehead before rising off the bed. Slipping back into her nightgown, she made her way to the bathroom to freshen up before picking up the house phone to order breakfast. She ordered orange juice, coffee, scrambled eggs, toast, a fruit plate and some donuts, as she knew Ben had a weak spot for donuts. She went back to the bed, crawled up over him and began lightly kissing his head, face and neck, until he stirred and opened his eyes.

"Are you still awake; can't you sleep?" Ben's voice was deep and weak as if he was still not fully awake.

"No honey, it is morning~~~time for breakfast." Beth laughed.

"Already? I better order something for us."

"I already have sweetheart; scrambled eggs. Are you hungry?"

Rolling over to his back, he stretched and yawned, "Umm, sounds good. Did you order some black coffee and OJ?"

"Yes, dear~~~I know what you like," she said with a deep throated chuckle.

"Yeah, I know you do. I'm pretty easy, ain't I?"

"No, I just know you very well, like I've known you all my life. You better get up before our breakfast gets here or you might get caught with your pants down," she said with a wink.

"Aren't you coming back to bed? I wanted to serve you breakfast in bed."

"Yes. I'll get back in after the food gets here. You can get the door, if you get your pants on."

"Okay, but first I have to pee like an exhausted race horse," he said as he reached for his shorts. "What time is it?"

"0730, just like always. I'm always up by this time."

"Wow, using military time now? I'm rubbing off on you."

She pulled herself away from him and got up off of the bed, "Yes I guess you are, but you can rub all you want. Better get up honey."

Ben weaved his way to the bathroom, emptied his bladder, washed his face and brushed his teeth. He looked at his reflection, noticed he needed a shave and knew that Beth's sensitive skin would soon be irritated if he didn't knock off those whiskers, making a mental note to do that after they finish breakfast. As he was leaving the bathroom, a knock on the door prompted him to look through the little security lens and saw their breakfast had arrived. Beth quickly slipped on her robe, as he opened the door and the bellboy entered the room with the cart carrying their breakfast. Ben signed the tab, as Beth handed him a couple of dollars for the tip. The bellboy thanked them, turned and left. Ben smiled and said, "Thank you darlin'; I forgot about the tip."

"I saw you standing there with just your shorts on, so I knew you didn't have your wallet with you. I had you covered; besides, I got the money from your wallet," she laughed.

"I might have to take that out in trade later."

"Better wait until you see what you signed for first."

Ben lifted the cover on the cart and his eyes lit up when he spotted the donuts. "Ohh, you are after my heart. You didn't say anything about the donuts."

"I already have your heart; I'm after the rest of you now. But you don't get to eat all of them; I have to look out for your good health. Besides, I'm going to sin a little, too."

~~~~*Return to present day*

Julie smiled as she said, "Yes, Dad struggled to keep his weight under control, but he did like donuts. Did he eat them all?"

"Oh no, I wouldn't let him eat all of them. We devoured the eggs and fruit first and then I decided to tease him with the donuts. He loved to tease and be teased~~~did you know that?"

Julie laughed as she replied, "Yes, I know how Dad liked to tease. He knew just how far he could go and always seemed to set himself up for revenge. But I noticed that when the laughter stopped, he would sink back into that sort of daydreaming he would do and I knew then that he wanted to be left alone."

Beth pursed her lips in thought before replying, "I never noticed that; his eyes would light up when the teasing started. I'd pick up a donut to offer him a bite of it and as he leaned forward to take a bite of it, I'd look away as if I didn't see him going for it, then let my hand slip down a bit so the donut touched him on his chin. When he tried for it again, I would raise it up and it would poke him on the tip of his nose. Finally, I'd let him capture it, but he looked so funny straining to grab it in his mouth, almost like a baby searching for a breast."

"Oh gosh, I can almost see him doing that! What was his reaction?"

"He was real cool, like he didn't notice until he picked up a donut to offer me a bite. I think I knew he was going to do something with it and I was right. He put it up against my face and sort of smeared the frosting all around my mouth and chin, with that devilish grin on his face."

"What did you do next?" Julie asked on the edge of her seat.

"I stuck out my tongue slowly and as seductively as I could, licked my lips and as much of my chin that I could reach. I looked at him while I did that with a look in my eyes that I had given him before, knowing what effect that would have on him. When I took the donut out of his hand I noticed the frosting on his fingers and thumb. I took his thumb into my mouth and began sucking the sugar off. Seeing the look on his face, I could not hold back my laughter. I was still laughing when he came at me for another bite. He was like that, always looking for fun in everything
~~~~

we did. He loved to laugh~~~to play. I never did much of that before and I discovered I loved playing with him. He would not allow long faces and would try most anything to get a laugh or at least a smile. Already, I found in just three days, how much fun it was being with him."

Julie looked away in quiet thought before replying, "I remember when I was very small, Dad would tease me and laugh, always seeming to know when I didn't want to play that game anymore. He would then pick me up laughing and hug me. His laughter was infectious and soon I was laughing too. Yes, you are right Beth~~~he would not allow long faces."

Tears started to form in Julie's eyes as she remembered those days with her father~~~now gone, along with her youth. Collecting herself, she turned to face Beth and asked, "How did you spend the rest of your last day together with Dad?"

"Oh Julie, it was a mixture of pure happiness and sadness all combined in one beautiful, heart wrenching day. After we finished playing with the donuts, we~~~~~~~~

~~~~Return to 2005

Beth was still working on the last of Ben's fingers and thumb when he was overcome with a strong desire to kiss the remaining frosting off of Beth's face. He removed his thumb from her mouth, placed his hand along the side of her face and gently kissed her mouth, her chin and her cheeks, slowly running his tongue over the areas to taste the last of the sugar. He felt his heart beating faster as he did this, feeling so much love for this woman, wondering how many ways he could express his love for her.

Her hands went up to encircle his neck pulling him down against her as she slid back down on the length of the couch. He followed her without ending the kiss until they were both half way off of the couch. She chuckled, saying "We should get more comfortable or our backs are going to give us fits if we stay here like this very long."

"Yes, you are right," he said as he brought himself up to a sitting position. "Come sit next to me and tell me all your dreams."

Beth scooted over to him and placed her head against his shoulder, her left arm across his lap.

"Ben, tell me what you did after we moved to Florida. I want to know your thoughts and who you were with after we left."

Staring at the ceiling, he thought about her request, wondering what and how much she was expecting. "Oh baby, you're really going to tax my memory. I don't remember half of those names."

"The names aren't important. I just want to know what you felt and how your life unfolded after you entered high school," she replied as she looked up to his face and noticed it suddenly looked sad; the ever-present smile in his eyes faded before he spoke again.

"I remember that first summer was bad~~~you were never home. The thought never entered my mind that you might have already moved; in fact I don't remember when it was I first learned that you were gone. I recall I felt anger thinking you were avoiding me for some reason. I think during my first year of high school I figured I would see you in the halls, but of course I never did. I went to the Dean's office and asked him if you were there. He told me I'd have to check with the girl's Dean, as he had all he could handle keeping track of the boys." He paused shaking his head from side to side. "That's how it always went~~~a hassle trying to find you."

"Did you go to Mrs. Gordon's office to ask her?"

"No, I would have felt silly going in there. Maybe I should have. I never knew where you went until I found you on Facebook. I just knew you weren't in Midland anymore. I remember going around like I was lost for a while before the realization hit me that you were gone."

"What did you do after you gave up? Did you find another girl friend?"

Ben looked straight into her eyes, "You know, I don't think I ever gave up~~~not ever. I just ran out of ideas. I knew even if I found where you went, there wasn't anything I could do about it at that time. I thought after I finished high school I would have the freedom and resources to find you, knowing if I ever did, I was going to chew you out for not writing me to let me know where you were. But it didn't get any easier, as I didn't have much freedom while in the military. I did look in telephone directories everywhere I was stationed, searching for your last name. Even found some that I called, but they were fruitless~~~some not very cooperative."

Beth chuckled sensing how frustrated he must have been. Ben smiled, adding, "I'm sure glad your last name wasn't Jones or Smith or I would still be making calls!"

Again she laughed, but pressed on, "You didn't tell me about any other girl friends."

"What makes you think I'm going to?" he laughed. "Besides, you never told me who your girl friends were, else I might have been able to find you though them."

"Ohh, honey, that's not fair. I want to know everything about you, especially those young innocent years. I know about the later ones, but I want to know how you learned about girls. That's the time I remember about you and what I loved about you even way back then. We were so close! Please tell me~~~Ben~~~please."

"Oh sweetheart, you don't have to beg me; I'll tell you what I can remember." As an afterthought, he winked and added, "I'll try not to brag too much."

"Okay," she said excitedly, "I'm waiting."

He grinned, noticing that his last remark had no effect on her. She was obviously anxious to hear about those times. He starred at the ceiling letting his mind wander back across the years, trying to settle on a place to begin.

"Okay, I think I'll start with this one. I met this girl in the movie theater once during my freshman year. I don't remember her name, but she was pretty forward, sitting behind me with another girl. I was with a buddy of mine and I kept feeling something in my hair," he paused before adding, "and yes, I still had some then. I soon learned it was popcorn as some of it fell into my lap. I turned around and saw this girl holding a bag of popcorn sitting there smiling at me. I said 'Hi' and 'thank you for the popcorn'. She continued to put popcorn on my head, so I got up, went around to the end of the aisle, then down the aisle where she was sitting and sat down beside her. I reached into her popcorn bag and took out a handful and told her I'd rather eat it this way."

"Ohh, what did she do?"

"She was with another girl that moved several seats away from us when I sat next to her. As I reached into her bag for another handful of her popcorn, she put her hand over my hand and told me her name. I told her mine and before long we sank down lower in the seats and started making out. After the movie was over, her girl friend split and I walked her home. When we arrived at her house, she led me into her garage and proceeded to suck my lungs out. I had those familiar feelings again and decided it was time I learned what to do about it."

Beth laughed again and said, "It seems like we girls love to get you in garages, doesn't it?"

"Yeah, I was beginning to think I wasn't worthy of better accommodations, that I must have produced an aura of low-life or something like that."

"So did she seduce you in the garage?"

"Oh no, it was nothing like that. I eventually excused myself and left. My next stop was to the library to check out some books."

Beth smiled and asked in a teasing way, "What kind of books were you looking for?"

"I was looking for any book that had the letter S in the beginning of the title, an X at the end of the first word and an E in the middle. I found one titled 'The Illustrated Encyclopedia of Sex'. I checked that one out and took it home hidden under my jacket. Upon reading it, I was totally blown away at all the things I did not know. Hell, I didn't even know how I was put together or how my stuff worked. Of course, I knew what things looked like on the outside, as I'd seen girls, but never knew what was inside those folds and little buns. I was losing sleep at nights, as I would read that book with a Boy Scout flashlight under the covers in bed. I could not put it down until I had read every word several times, trying to memorize everything."

"Did that bolster your confidence after you read that book? Did you feel you knew what to do the next time the opportunity presented itself?"

"Well, I felt it was about time I learned some of this stuff~~~but no, I didn't feel any confidence yet because I didn't know how much of what I read was true in all cases. I did know I was ready to experiment and felt I knew where to touch~~~just didn't know how yet. I made up my mind that the next girl I was with, I was going to try things out and see what happens. I just hoped I didn't get slapped, but knew I was never going to leave with my head hanging down and feeling ashamed from being so ignorant again."

"And you did, didn't you? How did it go?"

Ben could not contain his laughter. He let out a huge roar as he hugged her and said, "My love, you are not only a voyeur, you like to hear details too, don't you?"

She chuckled and grinned that flirting grin she loves to flash at him at times and replied, "It's part of my profession, remember? Doctors have to know details, so tell the Doc all about it."

"And exactly how many kids have told you stories like this?" he asked with a smile.

"None, but one big one is about to now," she said with a wink and a kiss full on his mouth. "I love you, so please continue."

"Pretty sure of yourself, aren't you? What exactly is it you want to know?"

"I want to know how you approached the big moment, where you were, if it was a success and what you thought it would be or if it was a flop. Purely in the interest of medical science of course," she chuckled.

"Oh, but of course it is," Ben smiled. "Never let it be said that I obstructed the advancement of medical science. Next I suppose you'll want me to donate my body for scientific research."

"No, I'll take care of that all by myself. Any research done on this body will be done by me and me only," she said with authority and a wink. "And I'll start right here," as she squeezed his right thigh.

"Too bad you weren't the very first. I have a feeling you would also have been the last."

"You can bet on that, as there would have been no way you were going to get away from me! But enough stalling, who was she and how did it go?"

"Aww, I don't remember her name and I guess it was okay."

Beth was silent and stared at him before finally speaking. "Ben, just who are you trying to fool? No one forgets the name of the first one. You're teasing again!"

He winked at her and said, "If no one forgets the first, then you must remember yours too."

"And you know too, I've already told you that Jerry was the first, so come on buddy, you're holding out on me."

Yes, he knew that was true and he had no reason to doubt her."All right, it was Helen and you must have known that. But it didn't happen the first time I tried as I developed cold feet after I started and backed off. It didn't take long before I wished I hadn't."

"Why did you stop and why did you regret it?"

"Well, I could feel her tense up when I touched her breast. I was kissing her when I did that and I was afraid she was going to pull away from me when the kiss ended, but she didn't. I thought I lucked out that time, so I didn't try it again. Later, when it was time to go, she asked me why I stopped. Hell, I didn't know what to say, so I just shrugged like I didn't know what she was talking about."

"Where were you when this happened?"

"We were in the front seat of my car. I came up with a different strategy the next time we went out."

Beth noticed he was getting a bit cockier now as he was starting to relate this information and she liked that. She smiled at him as she asked, "What was this new strategy?"

"Well, we went to our favorite parking spot and I mentioned that we should get in the back seat where it is more comfortable. I told her my legs get cramped in the front seat. She agreed as she started crawling over the back of the front seat. As I watched her do this, I became very excited watching her move her legs and butt to get over that seat. She had on short shorts and they fit her like a glove. She had a button down blouse that was not inside the shorts, but loose over the top of the shorts. After she went over, I followed and found that two of her buttons had opened from moving over the seats and the cup of her bra was exposed. I then did a stupid thing."

"Well~~~come on; what did you do?"

"I put my hand over the cup and said 'I think you broke some buttons off your blouse, but it looks better this way anyhow', or something like that. She just smiled, said nothing and made no attempt to move my hand or to button her blouse. So I moved my head closer to hers and finished unbuttoning the rest of her buttons until her blouse was fully opened. My hands were shaking and that bothered me because I wanted to be cool. But when I put my hand back over her breast and squeezed it, she put her hand up to the back of my neck and pulled my lips down to hers. That's it."

"What do you mean that's it? Don't tell me you stopped again~~~I don't want to hear that nonsense," she said in such a way that he knew he wasn't going to get off this easy. But what all did she want to hear, certainly not all the details~~~did she?

"Well, I ran my hand up and down her thigh and it felt so much smoother than my own. When I did that she moved her leg closer to me and made it easier to touch the inside of it. I moved it slowly up her thigh until I could feel the heat of her body against the back of my hand." Ben paused and asked Beth, "Do I have to tell you every little detail?"

"No, I don't want to hear what you did with her. I assume you took her clothes off."

"No, we somehow managed to get her out of those tight shorts and her panties, but nothing else. We were both nervous and she was afraid someone might see us. She didn't do anything to help me get my jeans and shorts down. I touched her and she was wet. It was easy to find the places that the books illustrated and I soon found that certain areas had to be touched very softly and easy. It was a great learning time and it was enthralling to learn all of this. It was having a tremendous effect on her and on me, too. Soon our breathing was out of control. I tried to lie down on top of her to do it, but my legs were too long to get positioned right. So, I sat upright on the seat, pulled her up on my lap facing me and that is how we did it. It didn't take very long, but it left me thinking something was missing. Helen was ready for more, telling me how good that felt, making me wonder if she had done this before. There was no blood and it didn't feel like there was anything impeding my entrance. I felt empty and wanted to get my pants back on right away. It was only after it was over I remembered that I had not used a condom and was worried that she might get pregnant." He paused as if he was thinking about what else he was to say.

"You asked if it was successful and I guess I don't know. I think she enjoyed it and I felt it was a learning experience, but it left me wondering what was so special about losing one's virginity. I didn't feel any different. Now, that's it~~~no more."

"Ben, most first time experiences are not that successful. I don't know why you felt something was missing. What were you expecting?"

"I think I was waiting for the thrill I felt when I kissed you the very first time, the feeling that made me dizzy, like I was floating. I didn't feel that way~~~I kept thinking it was going to happen but it didn't. I felt I was cheated. Maybe that's why I'm afraid to let go again~~~afraid it won't happen and the disappointment will come crashing in again."

"No honey, you won't be disappointed again. There is love now and lots of it. Love that has been waiting for decades to be fulfilled and it will happen~~~I promise you that!"

He hugged her, nuzzling her cheek followed by a light kiss.

"Ouch, you stuck me!" Beth yelped.

"Stuck you~~~what do you mean?"

"Your beard honey, you haven't shaved since we've been here," she said as she rubbed the three day growth of stubble on his chin. "You need to shave."

"I hate to shave baby and besides, you haven't given me any time for that," he said with an ornery chuckle.

"You didn't seem very interested in taking time out to shave lately," she countered. "But neither did I. But hey, I have an idea! Why don't I shave you?"

"What~~~you must be kidding me! How do you propose to do that?"

"Well, get your stuff and follow me. I'll show you what I can do with a scalpel."

"Oh, oh, oh, hey, wait a minute. You never told me you were a surgeon and my razor is not a scalpel! I think I better do the shaving!"

Beth doubled over from laughter at the look of fear on his face. "No sweetheart, I am not a surgeon and I will not hurt you. I promise I will be as gentle as you. Now come along with me my love. Momma's going to shave her baby!"

Chapter VIII
The Greatest Gift

Reluctantly he followed her into the bathroom and handed his razor and shaving cream to her. A look of concern crossed on his face as she asked, "Do you soak your beard first with warm water?"

Wondering if she had ever attempted anything like this before, he replied,"I like it hot, not warm. These gray ones are tough and hot water softens them making them easier to cut off," he said as he adjusted the water temperature and began soaking his beard.

"Yes, I think it must have been one of those that stuck me. It felt like a needle."

"I'm sorry; I didn't mean to hurt you. There, that should be enough. Now we're ready for the cream."

Beth extracted some shaving cream from the can onto her fingers. Reaching up as high as she could, she found she could not spread the cream evenly on his face.

"You're too tall; maybe you should put the cream on your face, or you could bend down for me."

"How are you going to shave me that way? I have a better idea; why don't you sit on the vanity? That should give you the boost you need," Ben offered.

"Oh yes, that should do quite well," she said as she backed up against the vanity top. Lifting her right foot up off the floor, she placed her right buttock on the edge of the vanity and scooted the rest of her small frame up onto the vanity. "Now come closer so I can reach your face."

"I can't honey, your knees are in the way. You have to spread them apart so I can move up against the vanity top."

"Oh heck, I can't; my nightgown is in the way."

"Well, I guess you're going to have to take it off then. Want me to help?"

"No, I'll have to get back down first~~~I'm sitting on it. Besides, you sound too anxious." Beth laughed as she jumped down off the vanity.

Ben reached down for the hem of her nightgown and raised it up over her head, admiring the expanding view of her body. He felt a knot swell in his throat as he watched her maneuver back up on the vanity top again. "This ain't gonna work," he thought to himself.

"This must look silly, me sitting on the vanity naked shaving you in your shorts," Beth mused.

"Well maybe this will make you feel better," he said as he quickly dropped his shorts to the floor. "They were starting to feel constricting anyhow."

"Now remember, I am shaving you, so you better not make my hand slip!"

"Well, my face is dry now. I'll have to wet it down again. Lean over a bit so I can wet the washcloth."

As he leaned forward against her, their reflection in the mirror took his breath away. The view of her back, with her arm around his neck balancing him as he leaned around her, excited him. It was a different view, one he found very erotic. Suddenly it became harder to swallow, and he knew she was not going to get down off that vanity for quite a while.

"Okay sweetheart, it's ready for you," he said as he put the washcloth down, knowing that his beard was not the only thing ready for her.

Beth placed more shaving cream on her hand and spread it over his face. Her hands felt magical to him, soft and caressing, gliding smoothly across his face, yet making scraping noises as she worked the lather into his beard.

"Hand me your razor honey; I'm ready to get these nasty things off you."

His hand was shaking as he picked up the razor from behind her, giving it to her with the admonition, "Remember, this is not a scalpel!"

"You know I will," she laughed. "Now just relax and let me get at those tough gray ones."

She took the razor in her hand making the classic shaving mistake, sliding the razor down his face with a slow long stroke, the way TV commercials brag about their product, causing Ben to feel the whiskers pull instead of a crisp, clean cut.

"Baby, let me show you how to shave my face. Everyone's face is different. My beard grows downward, so it is best to shave uphill against the grain, instead of downhill with the grain. Also make the strokes short and fast. You won't cut me with this razor~~~unless you want to," he winked.

"Okay, but you have to get closer to me, because I certainly don't want to cut you!"

"I'm as close as I can get~~~I'm already against the edge of the vanity; you have to scoot closer to me."

As she started scooting out toward the vanity's edge, she suddenly stopped and said with a wink, "Oh, I think I'm too close now."

"No, you're just right." His hands reached around her gripping her bottom, pulling her tight against him. "You feel exactly right, now."

"Oh Ben, let me shave you first. I don't want to get scratched up by this porcupine that lives on your face."

"Okay, just hold the bottom of my face with this hand like this," placing her hand in the right position, "and then pull the razor up against the whiskers like this," taking her through the procedure.

She then repeated what she had just learned, first with one stroke and then another until she became comfortable with her efforts. Soon all that remained was trimming around his nose and sideburns which Ben quickly dispatched.

"There, all done~~~smooth as a baby's butt," he said.

"Oh honey, I hate to burst your bubble, but I've felt a lot more baby butts than you have and your face does not compare to any I've felt. But I'll take it just like it is nevertheless," she said as she moved forward to come down from the vanity top.

Ben caught her in his arms as she came down, supporting her with both hands under her bottom. "There can't be very many baby butts much smoother or softer than this one," he said as he squeezed it tenderly.

"You are so biased! Now put me down before you hurt your back. I have plans for you and those plans require a good pain free back."

"I love the way you think! I hope your plans are the same as my plans," he said as he lowered her to the floor. Before she could turn to walk into the bedroom, he cupped her face in his hands, kissing her again like the very first kiss, soft, tender and light. His heart jumped every time he kissed her like this and Beth sensed it. She pulled him down hard against her lips in a way she wished she had done so many years ago~~~never letting him go. But she knew it wasn't Ben that left, it was she, and there was nothing either one of them could have done to prevent it.

Those thoughts raced through her mind as she resolved to never let another day, another moment pass without letting him know that she would never leave again.

Taking his hand, she led him from the bathroom to the bedroom where she turned and sat down on the edge of the bed facing him, still holding his hand.

"Sweetheart, I want you to remember and think about the day you took me to that little clearing in the woods when we were kids. Think about what you wanted to do but didn't know how. Remember I said I thought we had to take off our clothes?"

"Yes, of course I remember that day. I've thought about it many times over the years. We were afraid someone would see us."

"Well my love, there is no one here but you and me and we already have our clothes off, so just do what you wanted to do that day under the sun on that soft green grass. I promise I won't bite you, but I will nibble a little here and there. Don't think about anything else except just you and me, right here, naked and alone."

Ben looked down at her and felt his heart tempo increase. She looked like that little girl again, sitting there looking up to him holding his hand, her eyes imploring him. Yet, here she was all grown up and wise in the ways of touching, feeling, kissing and yes, loving. She knew what she wanted and he not only knew what that was, he also knew she would not be denied. As he pondered those thoughts, his fears of inadequacy began to return again. He suddenly felt old as she pulled him down on the bed with her.

She smiled as he sat next to her, still holding his hand. "Remember how you took my hand leading me in and out of the woods? I still need to hold your hand Ben. I need to feel you there next to me. I feel safe and secure when I hold your hand, your arms around me. They are still the same hands with the same needs." He looked down to her hand in his, brought it to his mouth and softly kissed it. "Yes, it is the same hand;

one I wanted to touch so many times," as a tear coursed down his cheek onto the back of her hand.

"Oh honey, don't cry. There is no time for tears anymore. Just love me my sweet, sweet darling, just love me!" She reached over to his face with her other hand pulling his face to hers, kissing first his lips, then his eyelids as she gently lowered him onto his back. Positioning her upper body above his chest, she continued to shower his face with tiny little kisses, again arriving at his lips with a long deep kiss, imparting all the feeling and emotion she felt for him at this moment.

Ben felt alive and his senses multiplied, as he felt her move slowly down his chest, leaving a trail of kisses as she moved even lower. His mind went to the times he was a child at the carnival, riding the rides and thrilling with each one. He remembered his first airplane ride and the first time he took the controls and felt the exhilaration of flying alone for the first time. He remembered the fast roller coaster ride along the Boardwalk in New Jersey and the time he stretched out on the grass as a child on a warm summer day as a butterfly landed on his chest and he thrilled at the slight touch of its tiny feet; the thrill of touching a newborn baby's fingers and marvel at the perfection of the tiny finger nails. His mind reviewed every thrill, every moment that held special meaning to him, especially the first time he kissed this woman. Suddenly none could compare to the feeling she was imparting to him now.

Grasping the bed sheets in both hands he clenched his fists and cried out a moan that was a mixture of pain and joy combined as the great dam broke. His breathing was short and fast as it felt he would surely die from the incredible rush convulsing over his entire body. Spasms continued to shake him to his very core, gradually subsiding into an increased sense of extreme sensitivity, as he returned to the present time with her still kissing and loving him in this special way. He reached for her and brought her to his face kissing her like he had never kissed her before.

It was some time before either spoke when finally he whispered to her, "There are no words to express how I love you. There has never been anyone touch me like you. It's as if you have a special key to my heart. Honey, it's been so long; I never thought I would ever experience that feeling again. Oh baby, I love you so much!"

"I have never wanted to feel anything like this before; never able to let myself go. I love you so and feel as if I cannot get enough of you. You make passion well up inside me I have never felt before. I want always to feel this with you; to always love you like this~~~and I hope someday we will." As she spoke, she looked at him, found his eyes closed and looked so peaceful.

"Are you going to take a nap?" she asked.

He opened one eye, smiled at her and said, "It would be very easy to right now. I'm more relaxed now than I've been since we arrived here; you drew all the knots out of me. Come lay your head right here," patting his left shoulder.

She positioned her body over and next to him placing her head on his shoulder and her left leg over his belly. "Oh I love this," she said as she ran her fingers through the hair on his chest. "It's the best way to cuddle."

He reached down and ran his hand up and down the length of her thigh as he asked, "What would you like to do the rest of today? "

"I want to stay right here with you. We can have dinner brought up or we could go out for dinner. What do you want to do?"

"We can go out for lunch tomorrow before we have to leave," he said. I don't want to share your vision with anyone else today. You are all mine!"

"Now it is I who likes the way you think! We could plan what we want to do the next time we meet," Beth suggested.

"Oh, when are we going to do that and where are we going to meet?" Ben asked, surprised.

"Ohh Ben, have you ever been to Mackinac Island? It is so beautiful and romantic. I would love to go there with you."

"No, I've never been there. What would we do on an island?" he asked with a sly smile on his face.

"We could take a carriage ride that tours the island, or ride a bicycle and move around at our own pace. We could stay overnight in one of the historic inns. We could visit the Grand Hotel or we could~~~"

"Whoa! Hold on a minute," Ben interrupted. "You're flooding me with information. I think I get the message; you really want to go there. I take it you have been there before?"

"Yes, Lynn and I went there some time ago. It is a really special place and I know you would like it."

"When do you want to go?"

"I'm not sure, but I think in late summer would be nice~~~maybe in September?"

"Were you thinking about next year, or the year after next?"

"Would next year be okay with you?"

"Well, I'd have to check my busy schedule. I'm usually booked up a year or two in advance," he teased.

"No, I'll have none of that~~~I have priority. You are not supposed to keep the doctor waiting."

"Oh yes, I remember. Sorta like the military~~~hurry up and wait."

"But I offer much better fringe benefits than Uncle Sam," she winked.

"Yeah baby, you can sure say that again!"

~~~~RETURN TO PRESENT DAY

Beth was quiet now and was starring off into space as Julie broke the silence, "Did you go out for dinner or stay in?"

She turned to her as if she had just been awakened, smiled and replied, "We stayed in and had dinner brought up to our room. The rest of the day was quiet as we talked some, went back over some old memories together and made some plans for our next meeting. We turned on the TV and ordered a romantic movie, but I don't recall the title. Neither of us had ever seen it before and I doubt we saw much of it then as we were holding each other, already quietly thinking about tomorrow."

"Did you have trouble getting to sleep later?"

"I think I could tell by the sound of Ben's breathing that he was asleep, and his body would suddenly jerk every once in a while. I knew I didn't want to sleep; I just wanted to lie there touching and feeling his chest rise and fall as he breathed, knowing that very soon I would not be able to do that again. I suppose I must have dozed off eventually, as morning came way too soon." She paused and Julie decided to let her gather her thoughts, as she could sense that what she was remembering now was painful for her. Finally she continued; her voice lower in volume as she went on.

"Ben stirred first and went into the bathroom. I stared at the ceiling and kept praying that it was Saturday~~~not Sunday, but I knew it was not. When he came back to the bed, he leaned down and kissed me
~~~~

lightly on the forehead without a word, then turned and sat down on the edge of the bed next to me. I sat up and leaned against him as I felt my eyes filling with tears. I did not want to cry now~~~I knew there would be more than enough time for that later."

"He turned his head and the look on his face was one of sadness and loss. It was one of the few times he seemed to be at a loss for words. He twisted his body around to face me, placed his left arm behind me and leaned against me letting my body sink back down on the bed. He placed his other arm around me and pulled me against him so tightly I could hardly breathe. He kissed me long and hard, harder than he ever had before. I felt his body shaking before I realized that he was sobbing. I pulled back to look at him and he said 'I don't want to let you go'. I thought that I had to break this depressing moment, so I said 'Honey, you have to let me go for a minute now because I have to pee'. He suddenly laughed and let me go."

"Ohh, that's funny," Julie said. You were saved by the call of nature!"

"Yes, it seemed our bladders were always getting in the way of some of our most intimate moments. You will understand as you get older. It was a source of laughter for us, so I was grateful for the interruption. I didn't want our last day to be filled with nothing but sadness. I knew there was going to be a lot of that for both of us as we journeyed back to our respective homes."

"After I finished with my~~~business, I adjusted the shower and announced the shower is ready and waiting for another body. Before I finished the sentence he was there already out of his shorts and stepped in the shower. He took the soap, worked up a thick lather on my back in a soft sort of massage; I closed my eyes and it seemed as though my back was the only part of my body that had feeling, as it felt so good. We didn't talk much as we bathed each other; just relished each touch knowing it would be a long time before we could do this again. What was even worse was the thought of something happening that would prevent us from *ever* doing this again, or even seeing each other after this day. I forced those thoughts out of my mind as I could not deal with them then."

Beth was silent before continuing, "We finished the shower, dried, dressed and decided to go out for breakfast. Without a word, we packed our luggage so that we would not have to do that later when it was closer to our departure time. I finished first, looked at him and smiled. He took my hand and we left for breakfast. We found a nice little place close by that offered light breakfast fare and it was very cozy. Ben ordered eggs, bacon and toast and I ordered a fruit plate and coffee. I couldn't resist pointing out to him that he should have ordered fruit instead of bacon and eggs. He frowned and ignored me, like we were an old married couple."

She paused again and mused, "It was like that a lot of times, like we had been together forever. We were not strangers at all; so comfortable with each other, not afraid to say what was on our mind. It is just so hard to explain, Julie. It was almost like all those years had passed, but we were never really separated. We felt so secure with each other, but yet hated being apart so much. The awareness of our situation was becoming unbearable, probably because we were not getting any younger. I did not want to live without him anymore. He had told me he was beginning to feel very selfish~~~that it was time for~~~us. Even as we expressed those feelings we knew our circumstance would not change. Neither of us were the type that could walk away from commitments. We both knew we would lose some respect for each other if we did. I could never ask Ben to do that and he knew that as well. He always said 'We were doomed'." She then looked at Julie with a questioning look on her face as if to ask, "We were, weren't we?"

Julie reached for Beth's hand and gently squeezed it. "No, you were not doomed. Beth, the two of you found something in a short time that so many couples never find in an entire lifetime. While some may question the morality of it all, it was based on love that spanned a half century. In a much truer sense, it was your sense of morality and decency that sacrificed your own selfish desires, so as to honor previous commitments. It would have been wrong to abandon those commitments. We cannot help how and who we fall in love with, or control how powerful that emotion is felt. We can decide what we do with it, how we handle it and ultimately how we allow it to affect other lives around us. When I sort through what you have told me so far, I think you were far from doomed. You managed to find a path to real happiness without hurting anyone else. I don't see anything wrong with that."

They were both quiet until Julie asked, "So how was breakfast?"

Beth's voice was weak and shaky as she whispered, "What you just said was very sweet, my dear. You made me feel really good inside to hear you say that." She straightened in her chair, cleared her voice and then continued.

"Breakfast was quiet but very good. We took our time making small talk about what we would do upon returning home; that we would continue planning our next rendezvous via the Internet and our phones. Knowing that we would still be in daily contact with each other lessened the angst of departing. We topped off our coffee several times and soon it was time to head back to the hotel, pickup our bags and get to the airport. Ben placed a tip on the table, took the check to the cashier and we departed. As we were making our way back to the car, Ben handed the keys to me without a word. He was very quiet on the way back to the hotel; he just sat there starring out the side window. I had no idea what he must have been thinking, but I instinctively knew not to interrupt his thoughts. As I pulled into the parking lot and turned off the ignition, he unfastened his seatbelt, shifted his body toward me, then gently touched my face lifting my chin and looked right into my eyes. The look in his eyes was so deep~~~as if I could see all the way inside him~~~to his soul. He didn't say a word and yet I could read what he was thinking~~~what he was feeling."

Julie was shaken with what Beth had just told her. She had seen that very same look in her dad's eyes when her mother was close to death after the accident. She knew the look was one of despair and utter helplessness. "What did you feel he was thinking?"Julie asked.

"It was like he was being torn up, as if he wanted to do something to end his pain, but he felt helpless to do anything. He then turned around, opened his door and got out of the car. He came around to open the door for me and we walked together inside the hotel. When we entered our room, he took me into his arms and held me close to him for what seemed like an eternity. He had not spoken since leaving the restaurant until then as he whispered in my ear that he didn't want this moment to end. But~~~it did~~~they always do," Beth said sadly.

"We broke away from each other, gathered up our luggage and moved to the door to leave. He leaned over to me and kissed me that light tender kiss that he loved so much before opening the door. We then left the room~~~~~~"

~~~~Return to 2005

While waiting for the elevator to arrive at their floor, he looked at her and said, "You know, I will be living just for our trip to that island you mentioned."

"Mackinac~~~yes, I know. We can continue to plan our time there after we get back home during our talks. It will give us both something to anticipate."

The elevator arrived and delivered them to the lobby. After checking out, they made their way to the car, with Ben taking the keys this time. After loading the bags in the trunk, he entered and found Beth already buckled in, smiling at him as he searched for the buckle of his seatbelt.

"Your departure is before mine, so I'll just walk with you to your gate and sit with you until you have to board," he said as he started moving the car. "Then the walls will close in on me."

"No sweetheart, they will not. We will still be together and we must not think of leaving. We are just going back to our other world, the one where we found each other. We will be all right; we will have our time. Please don't be so sad~~~I want to see you laughing when I look back at you."

Ben drove through the airport traffic as if no one else was around. He was used to this after all the years of traveling in and around airports. He learned it was a mixture of the right amount of aggressiveness and anticipation; figuring the other guy is going to screw up and being ready for it. He maneuvered the vehicle as if on an auto-pilot, making his way to the "Car Rental Return" lane and soon pulled the car into an empty space close to the terminal.

"We have arrived," he said as he killed the engine and turned to her.

Beth exhaled a sigh of relief as she replied, "Yes, but I had my doubts a time or two!"

Ben let out a roar of laughter that triggered Beth's laugh, the one that he loved to hear so much. It is a little girl's giggle that comes from down deep and makes her eyes light up and sparkle as they fill with tears of laughter. He knew this is what she wanted to see, to feel before they parted.

"I was beginning to think you were trying to extend our time together~~~in the hospital," she laughed.

"Well, that's a thought, but they would have put us in separate rooms," he said with a wink, "not a good idea." He leaned across to give her a kiss on the forehead, unbuckled her seatbelt and then reached across her to unlatch her door. He then straightened and opened his door as he said, "We better go," and then exited the car.

After opening the trunk, he removed their bags, handed Beth's to her, and took her arm in his right hand. They slowly entered the terminal as if it was a funeral home, neither of them saying a word as they walked, both engrossed in their private thoughts.

Beth finally spoke as she said, "Ben, I want to check this bag as it is too hard to get in and out of the overhead. I can carry the other one on with me."

"No problem; sometimes there isn't enough room for everything in the overhead anyhow. Seems like some assholes think they own all that space. I've actually thought about throwing the stuff that is in the overhead above my seat on the floor and put my stuff up there~~~but I never have. Just another thing I admire about you."

After processing Beth's bag, she walked through the metal detector without a problem. Ben had forgotten to take off his belt buckle, a big unsightly thing that always triggers the bell. He passed the shakedown after removing his buckle. They then picked up their carryon luggage and moved in the direction of Beth's gate.

"I noticed my gate is not far from yours. I won't have to hurry after you leave. The weather looks good for flying. I like those little two engine jump jets."

Beth realized that Ben was rambling on about nothing, as he was not ready yet to accept the inevitable; knowing he was searching for something funny to say that would elicit a laugh from her. As they took their seats at her gate, she leaned over to him and placed her head on his shoulder as Ben put his arm around and behind her neck.

He felt his eyes begin to burn, so he closed them just as he heard the announcement for Beth's flight to begin loading. He did not want to let her see him hurting. She did not move until the second announcement came, then slowly moved her head, looked up to him finding his eyes closed, so she kissed his eyelids and detected the saltiness of the tears that were held behind them.

"I have to go honey and you have to go too. I'll call you as soon as I'm on the ground." She then stood up, picked up her carryon bag and started to move toward the boarding area. Ben hurriedly jumped up, walked toward her, cupped her face between his hands and gently kissed her.

"I'm sorry honey; you must think I'm a cry baby. It's just so hard to watch you walk away."

Smiling up at him she replied, "I love you my darling! Thank you for a wonderful time~~~I'll talk to you in a few hours." She then turned and walked away before her voice betrayed her. Ben found his voice was gone and felt a piece of him slowly dying as he watched her disappear through the doorway. He peered at the shiny jet through the terminal window as if he was somehow blessing it, trying to insure a safe voyage with the most precious cargo in his life aboard. Finally, the silver bird backed away from the terminal and made its way toward the runway. He watched until it was no longer visible to him before turning to slowly navigate his way to his gate.

Ben's small jet lifted up off the ground swiftly and soon climbed to altitude. He peered out the window watching the landscape change, rapidly putting more and more distance between them. His hand clenched the cell phone in his pocket wishing he could turn it on to call her; talk to her while in flight, but knew regulations forbade using them while in the air. He knew it would be some time before he would know she was safely on the ground and at home.

He loved to fly, but in later years there was a feeling of intimidation connected with it, not knowing with whom he was flying. Apprehension was especially keen now with Beth flying home alone and he in the air so many miles apart unable to help her if anything went wrong. As he pondered these thoughts, he realized there would be very little he could do if anything did indeed go wrong, but at least they would be together. He would not relax until he knew she was safely on the ground and home again.

His mind drifted back to the past three days and of the range of emotions he felt when he first saw her in the terminal. It was like seeing her again in the spring~~~fresh and new~~~for the first time. He closed his eyes and could almost feel the softness and texture of her skin when he touched her lightly, marveling at the touch of a face he thought he would never see again. He remembered how it felt to take her into his arms after so many years and how everything in this world became meaningless except her~~~and the moment. The way she gave herself to him that made him feel both significant and magnificent~~~feeling good about himself; yes, he knew that is the magic about her that he loves so much. It is the way she makes him feel about himself~~~that he is still worth something~~~that there is still value to his life. He opened his eyes and smiled, realizing that his need for her is immense and unrelenting.

Meanwhile, Beth's flight was moving along uneventfully. She too was going over in her mind the events of the past three days, capturing and engraving certain visions in her memory. She rested her head on the headrest of her seat, closed her eyes and could see him as he approached her in the terminal. It was the first time she had seen him walk in well over 50 years, and really could not remember how he walked when he was so young. Now she smiled as she saw him in her mind, a sort of swagger, a confidant stride but not as long as she would have thought for his height. He was smiling as he became closer, looking straight at her and into her arms without breaking stride. "Funny," she thought. "I had never seen this man before in my life, and yet I welcomed him into my arms as if I had known him all my life." Yes, she knew she had known the boy, but never the man. And yet she knew him better than anyone else in her life. From their first Facebook words, she had found herself completely at ease chatting and laughing with him, but sensing his loneliness and pain.

She knew his touch, his gentle kisses from all those years before and had learned so much about him from their correspondence over the Internet, as well as the conversations with their cell phones. She now knew that this was the same boy with whom she had shared some very sweet, innocent memories and how time had not permitted them the opportunity to let love blossom into full bloom. Now their love had blossomed, much like the daisy she was carrying back with her, to place between some wax paper and press along with the one Ben had given her from the park clearing so many years before.

The jet bounced a little as the wheels touched the ground and brought Beth out of her reverie. She was back in Columbus and would soon be home. She decided she would wait to call Ben until she was home, which would allow enough time for his plane to be on the ground.

Ben felt the jet bank sharply to port and knew he was in the MBS landing pattern. The rush of the lowered flaps and the clanking sound of the gear extending told Ben he would soon be home. He was tired and emotionally exhausted.

He had just unlocked his car when his cell phone rang; answering it he said, "I miss you already! Did we really get together?"

Beth laughed, "How soon you forget. Yes my love, we now know the thrill of what has been denied us all these years. We now know each other's touch and I still feel the warmth of your embrace, which will keep me warm until we spend time together on Mackinac Island. You have given me some very sweet memories. Are you home yet?"

"No, I was just getting into my car~~~are you?"

"Yes, I've been here about 20 minutes, long enough to get out of these travel clothes and get into something more comfortable. I think I will take a long bath and go to bed."

"Ohh, I wish I could wash your back."

"Yes, I'll bet you would," Beth chuckled. "This bathtub isn't as big as the one in the hotel," she laughed.

"Yeah, I didn't think I could sneak that one in past you. I'm glad you're home safely. I'll call you in the morning. Sleep well, my love."

"I will sweetheart. I love you."

"I love you, too! 'Nite."

"'Nite."

CHAPTER IX
Visiting Midland

~~~~*Return to present day*

Beth was looking past Julie as if she was caught up in the memory of those precious days they spent together as she spoke, "That was the first time we met after all those years. In many ways it was exactly as I would have thought it would be and yet more than I ever dreamed it could be. I was amazed at how comfortable I felt with him and how natural it all seemed. He walked toward me as a stranger, but he did not feel strange when I was in his arms. For three days, five decades disappeared and there was only now."

Julie sat motionless, spellbound by what Beth had just told her; this was about her father who had spent three days with a woman who was not her mother. She did not know quite how to feel about this, thinking how her dad always took care of her mother and seemed happy to do so, yet he was obviously in love with this woman. "How could he do that?" she wondered. He was a good father, seemed solid and had never given her any reason to think he was having an affair with anyone. Yet she knew he had moments when he seemed distant, far away somewhere in his private thoughts and Julie knew not to disturb him when he was like that, as he always returned in his own time. Some things were now adding up; making a bit of sense to Julie.

They were both silent for what seemed like hours before Julie replied, "Dad must have been under a lot of stress during this time; his heart was not strong."

"Yes, I know he was under some stress and we struggled with that. I was concerned about him because he put so much stress upon himself. It became my mission to get him to relax and not worry about being
~~~~

nearly seventy years old. That weighed heavily on his mind and it soon became clear it was going to take some doing to get those silly thoughts out of his head."

"You must have felt some stress too. Did you worry that Dad would not like you when he saw you?"

"Of course, there was some apprehension he would expect to see a young, sexy looking vixen~~~which I never was even when I was younger," Beth laughed. "But we had exchanged pictures over the Internet so we both knew what to expect. I was mostly concerned with what he would feel when he kissed me. He was so enthralled with the memory of our first kiss and had longed to feel the rush he experienced so long ago; I just cannot explain it. Yet when he was in my arms, I felt so good about everything and was sure this meeting was going to go well~~~especially when his first words were 'I love you' ".

"Did you feel any shyness getting undressed in front of him?"

"I thought I would~~~I didn't think I could bear to have him look at me naked, but when it came to that, I didn't have any reservations at all. Ben felt the same way at first, but it just seemed natural when it came to that time. Love is blind, Julie. Everything is beautiful when you are so deeply in love. The lines, wrinkles and stretch marks are merely a part of our history and the milestones of our lives while we were apart. I loved every wrinkle he had and I think I kissed everyone of them."

Julie stood up, cleared off the breakfast dishes and placed them in the dishwasher. "How would you like to take a ride around town and visit some of the old places?" she asked Beth.

"Oh I would love that! I noticed as I drove in from the airport three years ago how much everything had changed, but I didn't get to look around much as it was pretty painful at the time."

"Yes, it has changed quite a bit since you left. We have a new high school now, but still use the building you and Ben attended. The city has grown a lot since you left fifty years ago, however like a lot of communities around the country, the economy has really slowed."

"I remember a new high school was being built while I was still there. Is that the one you are talking about?"

"No, the newest one is Dow High. It was built around 1968 I think. The one you are thinking about must be the current Midland High School. Didn't you attend the new one?" Julie asked.

"No, we left before it was finished. I completed my freshman year at the old high school. So Ben must have attended the new one, correct?"

"Yes he did. Dad went out for football, but didn't make the team. They had a good team in 1957 and won the State Championship. He always said it was a good thing he didn't make the team or they probably would have lost," Julie said with a chuckle. "Grab your jacket and we'll go for a ride."

As Beth gathered up her jacket and purse, Julie asked, "Do you remember the name of the park where your class held their school picnic?"

"No, I don't~~~it's been so many years ago and there are so many parks. I just remember the hills, the wooded area, some softball diamonds, picnic tables, concession stand and that it was very nice," Beth replied.

"Yes, I know there are so many and it's hard to tell which one it might have been. We will go past a few of them during our ride."

As Julie started the car and moved out into traffic she glanced over to Beth and began, "After Mike and I married we moved out west to Wyoming as Mike loved to hunt. I hated it out there~~~it was so cold and desolate! We lived there quite a few years until I started insisting we have a child to keep me company while he was out chasing prairie dogs all over Wyoming. I finally became pregnant, but lost the child. We were so far away from civilization that by the time we got to a doctor, it was too late. That seemed to be the impetus to get him to move back here, but so much had changed while we were gone. I'm still learning my way around, but I'll do my best to show you our city."

"I know you will, and I really appreciate that. I'm so sorry you lost your baby." She was curious as to how Julie had lost the baby but did not feel like she should pry. She felt that maybe in time Julie would talk about it as she became more comfortable with her.

Julie drove through traffic expertly, turning onto Rodd Street, proceeding northeast past Central Park toward E. Nelson Street.

"This is one of our older parks where a lot of band concerts used to be held in the summer months. It has been the center of some controversy over the years lately. I don't get too involved with that sort of thing, so I can't tell you what it was all about, except it involved some demolition of sorts. I'm not your best tour guide," she laughed.

"You're doing well and I enjoy seeing some of the old sites, even though they are very vague."

Julie turned east onto E. Nelson Street continuing to Eastlawn Drive. Soon she approached Midland High School, "This is where Dad went to high school and is the one that was being built while you were still here, 'The Home of The Chemics'. It soon became overcrowded and the need for another high school soon became evident."

Julie then moved on east to Swede Avenue turning north on Swede, then left onto E. Sugnet Road. As she passed the Northeast Middle School she looked over to Beth and asked, "Does this look familiar to you?"

"Yes, I thought the neighborhood was starting to get familiar. Is this my old school?"

"Yes, I think so. It used to be the old high school; does it look different?" Julie asked.

"It looks so much smaller. Funny how everything seems smaller as we age~~~except our hips," she chuckled.

"Or our thighs!" added Julie with a laugh.

Julie moved the car further westward toward N. Saginaw Road, on past the Medical Center until they reached the newer H. H. Dow High School.

"This is the newest high school and is pretty elite. It is more of a campus setting as you can see."

"Yes, it is very nice and so much bigger than the older one. Incidentally, I meant to mention earlier when we drove past Elgin Street~~~isn't that the street where Ben was living before he died? Your place on Elizabeth is very close to Elgin Street."

"Yes, it took a while to find a place close to Dad. I wanted to be close to help him with Mom. I'm sorry, I should have taken you past the house~~~I will on our way back."

"Thank you; that would be nice. Could we go by my old place and where Ben lived when we were kids?"

"I know where Dad lived, but you will have to tell me where you lived. I think I can find it as my job gets me around town more now," Julie replied.

"I'm sorry Julie; I meant to ask you what you do for a living. I am wondering how you can make yourself available for me. I sure hope I'm not inconveniencing you or causing you any trouble where you work."

"No you are not inconveniencing me at all! I work for Century 21 and show real estate. I say I show it~~~hopefully I can sell it," Julie said with a chuckle. "Where did you live?"

"I lived on Lingle Lane, not too far from where Ben lived. He used to walk to my place to see me." Beth replied.

"Yes, I know the street. It will be easy to run past both places," Julie retorted as she turned the car around and headed back eastward to Eastman Avenue. Turning south, she proceeded past the Midland Country Club. "This is where the more affluent play. Dad never belonged there. He spent his time drinking at home," she laughed.

"I knew Ben drank from time to time. I remember talking to him on the phone a couple of times when he had had a few. He was so funny when he had been drinking," Beth said with a smile. "But he didn't drink much when we were together~~~just a few times."

"Mom said he used to drink quite a bit when he was younger, but he really slowed down as he got older. I remember a few times when he got his nose wet, and yes, he was funny. He loved to have a good time." Turning left onto Helen Street, then left onto Holyrood Street, Julie slowed and said, "Tell me if you recognize Dad's house and I will stop."

Beth studied the homes but did not recognize Ben's house. "I~~~don't see it. I think it was right here, but it doesn't look familiar to me."

Julie smiled as she replied, "There's been a lot of remodeling in this neighborhood. You are right; it is the one you picked out. Looks a lot different, doesn't it?"

"Yes, it surely does, but I can almost see Ben walking down this street."

Julie continued on to Noeske Street, turning right onto Noeske, then a left onto Balfour Street and a very quick jog across W. Nelson Street to Lingle Lane. As she slowly drove around the arc, she said, "Let me know when we are there and I will stop again."

"There it is and it still looks so nice. I really loved that house! It was on that back porch~~~," letting the sentence hang as she smiled to herself remembering that special kiss so many years ago.

Julie was enjoying this, watching Beth reminisce, soaking in all the scenes taking her back in time. In some strange way she felt her dad's presence in the car with them.

"I will never forget this place. It is engrained in my memory," Beth said so quietly, Julie barely heard her. "Thank you Julie for taking me past these places. I cannot tell you what it means to me."

"You don't even have to try; I can see it in your face. Are you ready to head back?"

"Yes. Ohh, this was so nice of you. Thank you so much!"

Julie drove the short drive back to Noeske Street, then down to Elgin Street. "This is where Dad was living when he died and where Mom is living now. Did you want to meet her?" Julie asked without thinking.

"Oh no Julie, I would not know what to say and I would never want to hurt her. I did see her the day of the funeral, but it is best she never know about me. While I loved your father, I never wanted to hurt your mother. I never wanted to hurt anyone. I think Ben and I were the only ones who felt any pain from our love~~~and I guess that is how it was supposed to be. It is enough that I have met you and have come to understand your father's great love and admiration of you. I trust it will always remain that way."

"It will. I know Dad would never want anyone to suffer from things that are already done and past. I want him to rest in peace and I believe he is. Having met you Beth, I can understand my dad's love for you. He was a pretty good judge of character. Your secret will forever stay with me and I hope we always remain friends."

"Yes, I do too. In fact, I've been thinking about retiring and moving back here soon. When I'm ready, could I have you search out a nice place for me?"

"I would truly love too! Just let me know when you are considering it and I'll put out the feelers. But hey, you ain't goin' nowhere yet~~~let's go back for some lunch and you can tell me some more about the times you spent with Dad."

"Okay, but why not let me take you out for lunch? I would like to do that," Beth said.

"Oh Beth, you don't have to do that. I have plenty at home and I love to cook, Julie replied.

"Nonsense! I love to cook too, but I want to express my appreciation for~~~well, for everything! Do you like Italian food?"

"I love food! I know a good place and it's not too far from here," Julie said as she wheeled the car around to head back toward the business district. "This place used to have a very good lunch buffet~~~I hope they still do."

"Ben loved pizza; I don't think he could ever eat enough pizza or cheese. We found a very good pizzeria while we were in Indianapolis."

"Oh, I know he did. I think that is just one of the things he consumed way too much of that contributed to his heart attack. He knew it was not good for him to eat so much of it, but he just could not stop. He always responded by saying, 'If I can't have what I enjoy in life, I might as well be dead anyhow,'" Julie mocked.

Beth laughed and added, "I can hear him saying that. He told me there was a time he denied himself a lot of things he really enjoyed until one day he decided what good is living when one lives in denial. So, he resolved that he was going to pacify his desires and push the envelope. There was no changing his mind when it was made up."

"Yep~~~you knew my dad!"

"He really sort of felt me out before he made up his mind and took my opinions into consideration. I found he would bend and blend my wishes into his. I really respected that, as I was so used to getting things my way. I learned to bend a little too. We really complimented each other so well. We just did not have enough time together," Beth lamented.

"Did you ever see Dad angry?"

"Angry no~~~hurt, yes. There were a couple of times he could have become angry, but he didn't. He used to say we don't have time for any of that nonsense and he was so right. Your dad was not afraid to show his emotions. I could always tell what he was feeling. He accused me of reading his mind," she laughed. "And I guess I could."

"Well, here we are. Let me see if I can find a parking space and hopefully you will enjoy some of the best pasta you have ever tasted."

Julie soon parked and they entered the restaurant. The scent of Italian spices filled their nostrils and excited their senses, whetting their appetites. Julie led the way to a neat little table away from the serving line where they could talk. Before long a waitress appeared and asked, "Would you like the buffet or would you like to order from the menu?"

"I think we would like to look at the menu," Beth replied.

As she looked over the menu, she found so many entrées that appealed to her, but remembered that it was lunch time, not dinner. She finally made up her mind and laid the menu aside. As she looked over to Julie she found she too had apparently decided what she would have.

"Are you ready to order," the waitress asked. Beth nodded to Julie and smiled, "Go ahead dear."

"I think I will have whatever you are having." she replied.

"Okay, I think I will have a bowl of hot minestrone soup with a small house salad and some garlic bread. And a glass of water with no ice, please," Beth ordered.

"I will have the same except I would like a glass of iced tea," Julie added.

"Thank you," the waitress retorted, "I'll bring your drinks right away."

Beth breathed in deeply, exhaled and sighed, "Oh, it smells so good in here. They make their own bread, don't they?"

"Yes and the soup is their own recipe too. Their house salad is also great."

Julie took a small sip of her tea, leaned back from the table and asked, "Did you and Dad make it to Mackinac Island like you had planned?"

"Oh yes, and it was absolutely wonderful. I have never had such a more exciting or memorable time in my life. Everything was so perfect, except how quickly it was over. Ben was so happy and full of excitement. His eyes sparkled at everything we saw, as there is so much to see and experience there. Have you ever been there?"

"No, strange as it might seem, I have never been there. We never seemed to go on vacations when Dad was younger. I guess I know why now, but that is no excuse as Mike and I could have gone there after we were married. He just seemed to want to go hunting all the time."

Beth glanced up toward the ceiling as she said, "One place I remember visiting before we left Michigan was Crystal Lake. It is such a beautiful place and I fell in love with the area when I was so young. I had wanted to go there with Ben, but we~~~ran out of time."

"Where is that located?"Julie asked just as their food arrived.

"Oh everything looks so good and smells so good!" Beth exclaimed as the minestrone was placed in front of her. "Oh~~~Crystal Lake is on the Lake Michigan side of the state and is northwest of here. It is very near

Frankfort, a little southwest of Traverse City. My dad used to go there when he was a child and loved to take us there when we were small."

"I guess I don't get around much as I have never been there either. We did go to Traverse City once and I liked it a lot. The beaches were beautiful and it was one place Mike liked too, which was unusual, as we seldom agreed on much. I think he liked all the bathing beauties, if you know what I mean."

"Yes, I know what you mean. I don't think they ever stop looking. I think I would worry about one if they did." Beth chuckled.

"Yes, I suppose so, but Mike would get upset if he saw me looking at some hot guy in a Speedo. I never did like that double standard. I guess men expect us to ignore that sort of thing."

"Some do, but things are changing today. As we women have become more liberated, a lot of men have also become liberated and are accepting us as equal human beings. It has taken a while, but it is not hard to find the ones that have. I see the way the younger doctors relate to me at the hospitals as compared to some of the older ones. Some actually pay attention to what I'm telling them. I guess they know this ole broad has been around a while and been around the block a time or two. "

Julie could not contain her laughter as Beth related this to her and nearly forced some minestrone up her nose.

"Oh I'm sorry dear; I didn't mean to make you nearly choke on your soup."

"That's okay, Julie laughed, "I wasn't expecting you to refer to yourself as an 'ole broad'. That was so funny! You are not an ole broad; you are a very elegant lady."

"Oh thank you Julie, you are so sweet. I just think that some of the younger ones think of me that way~~~you know, still hanging around and don't retire. But I love my work and the children, finding it just too hard to walk away from it all. I've reduced my hours, but I still keep my hat in the ring, so to speak. How is your salad?"

"Excellent. I have had it before so I knew it would be very good. Do you like it?"

"Yes I do, very much so. You were right about the quality of the food. The minestrone is absolutely delicious."

They finished their lunch quietly, and then left the restaurant. As Julie pulled out of the parking lot and into traffic, she glanced over toward

Beth and asked, "Will you tell me about the trip you and Dad made to Mackinac Island?"

"It's a longer story, but if you want to hear about it, I will be happy to tell you. It was such a beautiful trip; the happiest few days of my life. Everything was perfect," Beth continued on their way back to Julie's house, "It is such a picturesque place and so romantic. They made a movie there you know; 'Somewhere in Time'. Do you know the movie?"

"No, I don't think I do; who were the actors?"

"Jane Seymour and~~~Superman~~~I can't think of his name right now."

"Christopher Reeves?" Julie asked.

"Yes, yes that's it. Oh what a hunk he was!"

Julie laughed again, finding that she really enjoys this woman, her keen sense of humor and wit, and how she expresses herself in such warm and funny ways. "Yes he was; I was saddened when he had that terrible accident."

"Yes it was a terrible tragedy and loss. If you get a chance see that movie, I think you will enjoy it very much. It will give you an insight of what Ben and I enjoyed while on that island."

"Did you meet out there~~~I mean on the island?"

"Oh no, I flew from Columbus to Detroit~~~~~"

Chapter X
Mackinac Island

~~~~Late September 2006

As her plane left Columbus early in the morning, her excitement rose knowing that soon she would be in Ben's waiting arms. After long months of planning this meeting over the phone and through emails it would soon come to fruition. She knew their love had grown stronger over the long, lonely months of want~~~remembering those special moments in Indianapolis. She remembered the time her sister Lynn and she had visited the island, how they both had admired an historic house which had been converted into a majestic hotel, and knew this was a place she and Ben would be comfortable and relaxed.

Her pulse quickened after changing planes in Detroit for her final leg to Midland. Thinking about Ben's kisses, she found she was becoming less patient, harder to wait any longer for the soft, tender kiss he loved to give her first, much like the very first kiss many years ago. The small jet finally touched down at MBS and her steps quickened as she was walked into the terminal toward the baggage claim area. As she came down the escalator, she immediately spotted Ben in his usual blue jeans, sweatshirt and light blue windbreaker. Never slowing or diverting her eyes from his, she walked directly into his embrace, instantly saying, "I love you! I've missed you so much!" Ben held her close, tightly against his body, repeating the same words over and over with her for what seemed like a long, long time.

Finally, ending their embrace, he stepped back a short distance from her, still holding her shoulders in each hand and said, "Hi. Where have I seen you before?"

Beth smiled broadly with a twinkle in her eyes as she replied, "How soon you forget. I think we shared a bed once, a long time ago."

"Oh yes~~~too long ago. I remember now; your feet were cold, but your lips were very warm. Have your feet warmed up any?"

"Well, come with me my dear; you can see for yourself," she remarked, taking his hand in hers leading him to retrieve her bags.

Ben's smile was as big as Texas as they found her luggage and made their way to the car he had rented. After placing her bag next to his in the trunk, he opened the door for her to enter, then walked around the car, ducked inside his door, fastened his seatbelt only to unfasten it again, leaned across the seat, gently cupped her face between his hands, then slowly and tenderly kissed her lips long and very lightly. He loved this kiss as he felt the same old electricity course down and around his body from the light contact made with Beth's mouth on his, making goose bumps pop up all over his body, the way it did so many years before. Firmer, more demanding kisses would come later, as they both knew, but this was their special kiss. It left Beth weak and breathless, wanting more.

"I have missed that so much," he whispered in her ear. "It is the magic I have searched for all my life."

"I have too, along with your touch, your hands, your eyes~~~just everything about you! We are going to have a wonderful time; I have everything planned. I am going to keep you very busy, Benny boy," she said with a wink and a hint of excitement in her voice.

"Uhoh, I better get this car moving then," he said with a smile. "We're on our way to U.S 10," he quipped as he shifted back in his seat, buckled up and put the car in motion.

They were soon out of the heavy traffic and moving north on U.S. 10 when Ben reached across the seat and took Beth's hand in his. "I cannot tell you how many times I have wanted to reach out across a table, a bed, a room and touch you. Now I can and I don't want to let go."

"I have had the very same thoughts. I sometimes think we communicate mentally even when miles apart, much like when we say the same thing at the same time."

"Yeah, I know, it's like you can read my mind and that can be dangerous for me sometimes," he laughed.

"No, never dangerous; just might give you away though. Ohh, look at the cherry trees, Ben! And the apple and plum orchards! Can we stop and get some apples and some jelly and butter? I have an idea what we can do with some blueberry jam."

He smiled saying, "Mercy, how can I say no," as he slowed to exit the highway.

The weather was a perfect sunny 75 degree day with a light, gentle breeze. The scent of the fresh apples, apple butter and jelly was more than they could withstand. They made their purchases and each began eating a fresh apple as Ben pulled back onto the highway.

"Onward to Mackinaw City and the ferry trip," Ben announced. "Is this apple going to hold you or are you getting hungry?"

"It is delicious and is filling a void, so yes I can wait until we get to the ferry. I'd like to wait until we get out to the island before we eat. Can you hold out that long?"

"Yes, if that is what you want to do; I'll eat another apple if I have to," he laughed.

"Ben, I can't believe we are actually on our way and we are going to be together for 3 whole days and 4 nights! Sweetheart, pinch me to see if I'm dreaming all of this," she sighed.

"How 'bout if I just squeeze your hand instead? Any pinching that I do will be done later when I can get a good hold on the right spot!" he said with a wink and a smile.

"Ben have you noticed sometimes when we touch it feels like an electric current passing back and forth to each other, or do I just have such a heightened tactile sensitivity when you touch me?"

"No it is not just you; I feel it too. It was that electricity racing through my body all those years ago and still does, especially when I kiss you. That is why I like that soft, light kiss~~~it is like sparks jumping between us. I guess our batteries are still charged pretty well for a couple of old fossils, huh?" Ben joked.

"We are not old fossils! Fossils are hard and petrified! We are still soft and pliable~~~warm and alive," Beth proclaimed with a tone of authority in her voice that Ben loved to hear. He knew how to trip her levers and get a rise out of her and it delighted him to see her set her chin out and tighten her lips. It instilled a strong desire in him to kiss her right then, but driving made it impossible. Instead he laughed and said, "I love you my sweet! You will never be old. I just love to tease you and watch your eyes light up." To lighten the tone, he added, "Tell me something about this ferry we are headed for."

"I know you love to tease me and I guess I earn it because I love to tease you, too. Maybe someday I'll get used to some of the things you get me with, but you always seem to find something else."

"Well, it's my way of getting back at all the doctors that took my money and cut me all the time," he winked.

Her voice dropped a few decibels and took on a sultry tone as she murmured deep in her throat, "But sweetheart, I don't do any cutting. I soothe and perform therapy when it's needed. I just stroke and make everything better."

"Oh baby, I'll say you do~~~but enough of that; I'm trying to drive! Now tell me about that ferry."

"Well, it has been a family owned business for many years and is the most known service to and from the island. Their fall schedule leaves Mackinaw City every hour on the half until 6:30 pm. But I hope we can get there as early as possible as there are so many things to see on the way over. The route the ferry takes is across the strait that separates Lake Michigan and Lake Huron."

"I've never been on any of the Great Lakes other than just the shore line of Lake Michigan. Are they very much like the ocean?" Ben asked.

"I don't know~~~I've never been out very far in the ocean; we only played along the Atlantic coast when we lived in Florida. The beaches were nice, but my fair complexion made my skin very susceptible to burning. I really limited my time in the sun."

"How long will it take to get across the strait to get to the island? Will you be in the sun too long?"

"It doesn't take very long~~~about a half an hour. If you like, we can sit in the enclosed area of the ferry. I've learned to avoid too much exposure to the sun over the years."

"No, if the sun doesn't bother you, we can sit outside so we can feel the wind and spray of the water in our face," Ben replied.

She smiled her approval as they entered Mackinaw City and Ben spotted a sign advertising the ferry. He decided to follow the directions on the sign and before long he entered the parking area.

"We have arrived," he said to Beth as he took her hand in his and squeezed it gently. "Let me get this thing parked and we'll venture up there to see about getting tickets, what do you say?"

"Sounds like a plan to me. Anything you say, Captain."

"Whoa honey, we'll let some other fella be the captain. I'll just be another passenger holding onto your hand and enjoying the ride," he laughed.

After finding a parking spot, he turned in, killed the ignition and went to the trunk to retrieve their luggage. Beth grabbed what she could carry and together they made their way to the ticket office. After purchasing their tickets, they boarded the ferry which was due to leave on the half hour.

"Whew, we just barely made it before we would have had to wait another hour," Beth sighed. "I can hardly wait to see your face when you see the island. Oh Ben, you are going to love this!"

Ben could not only feel the excitement in her, he could see it in her eyes as well. They were emitting sparks like fire and he knew that yes indeed, he was going to love it on this island.

"Baby, I hope I can keep up with you when we get there," he winked. "Don't forget, I'm an~~" Beth cut him off before he could finish. "You are not, and I don't want to hear that again! You will feel like a boy again~~~you'll see."

Ben was getting very familiar with the tone in Beth's voice and knew when to change the topic, as he knew he had worn this one pretty thin. As he looked out over the water, he knew this woman, this girl he fell in love with so long ago, was the best thing that had ever happened to him and was grateful she was right beside him. He knew he needed her as a great stabilizing force in his life. She knew him like no other and he could not explain the thrill he felt when he teased her, knowing that she loved every minute and was always ready to give it all back to him. But, feel like a boy again~~~that brought a smile to his face. As these thoughts were going through his mind, the ferry lurched forward as it started its departure from Mackinaw City.

"We're on our way, Sweetheart," Beth said as she grasped Ben's arm and leaned against him. Ben could feel her trembling as she pulled him tight against her. "Did you go to the bathroom before we left the dock?" he asked.

"No, why do you ask?"

"Just wanted to know how safe I was sitting this close to you the way you are shaking," he laughed.

The elbow in his ribs told him she either didn't like that crack or he was going to get a crack back later. His laughter triggered a laugh from her, which is what he wanted to hear as he loved her laughter.

"Not to worry my love; my bladder is under complete control. I'm just so excited about going to the island with you."

"Me too honey, I know how you've been looking forward to this time. Heyyy, this is starting to feel like we're on the ocean. We might be soaked before we get there."

"No, it's not that bad. I think it feels pretty good, don't you?" she said as she laid her head against his shoulder.

"Yes, a bit chilly, but refreshing. I'll bet it's pretty crisp out there on those sailboats."

The island soon appeared on the horizon and the ferry quickly closed the distance, making a smooth, gentle docking. Ben regained his land legs, stepped off the ferry and helped Beth up and onto the dock.

"Don't worry about our suitcases Ben; they will be transferred to our hotel. We have the rest of the afternoon to look around and take a short walk to our hotel."

Ben was immediately impressed by the beauty of the island, the gulls that hung around the docks and the magnificent building sitting high up on a hill overlooking the bay area. "Is that our hotel up there?" he asked pointing up the hill.

Beth laughed and replied, "No Dear, not that one. That is the Grand Hotel and I didn't think we could afford that one. Ours is up the street a few blocks from here. Hold my hand and I'll take you there."

Taking her hand, they slowly walked the three blocks along Main Street to the hotel. It was painted white, 3 and 4 stories, with a reddish brown roof, pink awnings and a veranda spanning the front. It looked out over the marina and Haldimand Bay. The lawn in front was plush with green grass that impressed Ben this late in the year. It was beautiful with many flower beds containing both colorful perennials and annuals.

"This is where I'm going to take you and have my way with you, Sweetheart. I felt we could be very comfortable here. The room I reserved is one of the king bedrooms on the 3rd floor with triple windows overlooking the bay. There are two restaurants and a buffet breakfast, so we won't have to leave the hotel to eat unless we want to go elsewhere."

"Well if we couldn't afford that one up on that hill, how much is this one setting us back?" he asked.

"Oh, you don't want to know, at least not now. Come on honey, wait until you see our room," she said as she took his hand and led him up the walkway.

Ben admired the surroundings as they entered the hotel. He noticed the charm of the Victorian era and the beauty of the adornments. After checking in at the desk and receiving their keys, they made their way to the elevator. The door opened on the 3rd floor as Beth led the way to the room, inserted the key and opened the door. Ben sucked in his breath as he scanned the room~~~it was truly breathtaking. The room was bright with sunlight pouring in from the three windows facing the bay. The king-sized bed was covered with a bedspread in a floral pattern of greens, yellows and pinks. The valances at the top of the windows were in a matching fabric. Typical for a Victorian-style hotel, the wallpaper was in a floral stripe with many of the same colors as the bedspread. On the other side of the room there was a pale green, queen-sized pull out sofa bed and matching overstuffed chair. A television, refrigerator and coffee pot added other amenities to the room.

"Quite a shack," Ben winked. "When do we start washing dishes?"

Beth laughed and said, "Silly! Let's freshen up a bit and take a look at the grounds. I have to straighten up my hair a bit as the wind on the bay messed it all up."

"Me too," Ben said as he licked his hand and ran it over his bald top, "I'm ready to go!"

She laughed again adding, "It won't take me very long," as she came over to him looking up to his face. Ben knew the time had come again for their special kiss as he cupped her face between his hands and slowly lowered his head toward her until their lips met very lightly. It was always like the world just stopped spinning when he kissed her like this~~~all the spinning was inside his head. When the kiss ended his eyes were glazed and his knees were weak, once again. It was like the first time for him.

"Are you sure you want to go out?" he asked, his voice low and suggestive.

"Yes, we have plenty of time now. Let's enjoy the sun while it's still up. I'll be right back," as she turned to enter the bathroom.

Ben walked over to the windows and peered out over the bay. The sun had started on its downward path toward the west, reflecting its rays off of the water making the surface appear to be laced with flashing diamonds. The seasonal southward travel of the sun was making the sunlight slant across the room toward the sofa, casting shadows off the window panes upon the vertical stripes of the wallpaper, creating images that seemed to move as Ben stared at them.

He then walked around the room trying out the firmness of the bed, the chair and opened the refrigerator door, disappointed as it was not stocked with beer.

"Fancy place has everything in it except a cold beer," he thought to himself. "But I'll take care of that later."

"I'm all ready to go now," Beth said as she emerged from the bathroom. Ben was amazed at how in so short a time she could work such miracles. She could look windblown one minute and a few minutes later she was ready to go to the prom. With very little makeup, she was truly a prize, of what he was well aware. He smiled as he walked across the room, took her into his arms and whispered in her ear, "You are the most beautiful thing on this island."

"Nonsense! How do you know? You haven't even seen everything on this island yet. Besides, you are still going to have to wait until later for your reward," she chuckled. "Now let's go before I change my mind."

Ben grabbed the key, opened the door, departed their room and entered the elevator. He was just about to plant one on her lips when the door opened to the lobby.

"These things are usually slow as molasses until you want to horse around a little," he mumbled as they exited the elevator.

Beth could only smile and chuckle a little as they walked hand in hand across the lobby. She was still smiling as they exited the hotel and began a slow stroll around the grounds. They were thoroughly enjoying the ability to touch each other after so many long months apart. As they rounded the corner of the hotel they spotted a gazebo area where weddings were performed. Surrounding this area were flower beds bursting with vibrant perennials. As Ben's attention was drawn to the gazebo, Beth cried out, "Look Ben! The gardeners must have known we were coming and grew these just for us," as she pulled him over to a bed of daisies.

"Well, I'll be," he remarked as he leaned over and picked one, handing it to her with a kiss on her cheek and added, "You can press this one and add it to your collection in your old high school yearbook. I hope I don't get extricated from the island for picking this," he laughed.

"Oh I don't think so; there are so many of them. We can take it to our room and then venture down to the Bar & Grill for a bite to eat. You are hungry, aren't you?" she asked.

"Heck, I'm always ready to eat. Lead the way baby!"

After returning to their room and placing the daisy in a glass of water, they navigated their way to the Bar & Grill, located inside the hotel. Soups, sandwiches and salads were offered and after viewing the menu, Ben decided on a Black Angus burger with cheese, fries and a glass of Burgundy wine. Beth selected a chicken Caesar salad and her typical glass of water. Ben had to admit, she was a cheap date as she did not enjoy alcohol. She seemed to find laughter and fun from the flame burning within her.

As their drinks came, Ben sipped his wine and smiled his agreement. He put his glass down and smiled across the table at Beth as she said, "Do you mind if I taste your wine? I thought you would opt for a beer."

"No~~~of course not. Maybe I'll have a beer later. Would you rather have a glass of a sweet Rhine or Zinfandel?" he asked.

"No, I just want to check yours to see if it meets my strict standards," she said as she raised the glass to her lips. She took a tiny sip, held it in her mouth for a few seconds before swallowing. A sort of frown creased her forehead before taking another small sip. "It is bitter; how can you drink this?"

Ben smiled his widest smile then laughed, "No darling, it is not bitter; it is just a bit dry. Burgundy is a dinner wine and should be dry to the palate. It has a nice finish and goes well with red meats. I think you would prefer a sweeter wine, perhaps a white or a blush?"

"No, I'll just stick with my water. I think the last time I drank any wine was with you in Indianapolis~~~do you remember?"

"Yes, how could I forget? We danced and I didn't step on your toes."

"No you didn't, but do you remember what you did after we went back to our hotel? She asked.

"Uhh~~~no~~~I don't think so. Did we watch some TV?" he teased.

Beth laughed and quipped back, "You do too remember!" She then leaned over the table toward him and whispered, "You kissed my big toe."

"Ohh, I did not! You must have been dreaming!" Ben could not continue with a straight face as he started laughing as he studied the look on Beth's face, "No, I didn't just kiss your toe~~~I sucked it! And yes, I remember every moment~~~I loved it~~~and so did you! Do you want to go dancing again?" he asked with that devilish sound in his voice and a wink.

Beth laughed and her eyes twinkled as she replied, "Oh honey~~~not so loud; someone might hear you! We could skip the dancing and pretend that you stepped on my toes," she whispered.

Before Ben could reply, the waitress returned with their dinner. As she was placing it on the table, he looked across at Beth, into her eyes with a warm and relaxed smile on his face. She was aware of his eyes and could see how relaxed he was in his manner, and the physician in her told her how important that was, as she knew and understood the daily stress and pressures that weighed on him. As they talked, she could see the love and affection in his eyes. They both knew how much they needed this time to themselves; time to enjoy each other's company, to laugh and have fun.

With dinner consumed, Ben finished his wine, leaned across the table and looked at Beth with a gleam in his eyes as he said, "We need to get outa these clothes, crawl into bed and do a little~~~uhh, snuggling. It's been way too long a time between snuggles."

Smiling, she replied, "My thoughts exactly, Sweetheart," as she reached across the table to touch his hand. Ben grasped her hand and brought it to his mouth, looked directly into her eyes and gently kissed the back of it and said, "I love you more than you will ever know."

They left the restaurant and returned to their room. After Ben closed and locked the door behind them, he turned and took her into his arms pulling her tightly against his body, her head against his shoulder. He knew how much she loved this feeling; the same feeling she had felt all those many years before and again last fall in Indianapolis. He was enjoying the feel of her closeness when she pulled back a bit and reached for the bottom of his sweatshirt, pulling it up over his arms and head, tossing it aside, then following it with his T-shirt. She then pulled him back to her, showering kisses on his chest whispering against him, "I'm going to freshen up~~~want to wash my back in the shower?"

Ben's face broke into that wide grin and instantly came back in his usual evil way, "Not only your back, but also some other very special parts too~~~including your *feet.*" He walked away from her to sit on the sofa to remove his shoes, making a deep, throaty chuckle that told Beth he was getting all sorts of fertile images.

She smiled as she made her way into the bathroom, undressing as she went, then adjusted the shower for the right temperature and stepped in. She was enjoying the feel of the water cascading down her back when Ben stepped in and again took her into his arms. There was something very special with their bodies pressed together feeling the water flow around them fusing them together as one. She closed her eyes as he washed her back, gently, almost reverently moving the cloth over her body followed by his hands on her most tender places. He then knelt down making sure she had a good hold on the rail, lifting first one foot and washing it, then the other, kissing her as he raised himself back up. Beth was shaking as she took the cloth from his hand, added more soap and performed the same feat on him. Ben felt the same stirrings he felt with her as a young boy and again with her in Indianapolis. His mouth was the only place that was dry by the time Beth finished with him, as he was visibly shaking when he stepped out of the shower. They didn't speak as they dried each other, both of their hands shaking but not from the cold; rather from the heat that was building inside them.

Beth draped a plush terry robe over Ben shoulders while he was brushing his teeth and then draped the other one on herself, pulling the front closed. Ben rinsed his mouth and walked back into the bedroom while Beth brushed her teeth and touched up her hair. Ben pulled back the bed, dropped his robe and crawled in under the covers, finding the mattress comfortable and very relaxing. Beth then entered the bedroom and stood next to the bed looking down at him lying there so peacefully. He reached over to her and untied her robe, letting it fall slowly to the floor. As he did this, she wondered if anyone else had ever seen this part of him, the sensuous, sensitive, tender, wanting and needing side of him, convinced he did not allow many to see him this way, fearful they would find him very vulnerable.

"I have missed you terribly," he said as she climbed in beside him and their bodies seemed to melt together. Their hands seemed to never stop caressing and touching all over, everywhere as if they knew not where they wanted to go. Showering kisses upon kisses, hungry like they had been starved from one another forever. They didn't speak, as all the words had already been spoken so many times over the long months apart. There was no need for all the verbal 'I love you' whispers as it was now being pronounced in Braille and in no uncertain way. Ben felt no fear, no feeling of inadequacy, not this time. He was relaxed and they were like one with each other, like the time in the timber when they were so young. It only took 50 years, but they had finally found each other and all the years simply vanished and passed into history. The time was now and this love, this great love they had for each other was finally realized in all its fullness.

As their breathing gradually subsided, they were both quietly crying, tears of relief, of joy finally found, of a bonding that would last the rest of their time. As Beth lay beside him with her head on his left shoulder and her left leg across his belly, she felt the tears run from her cheeks onto his chest as she realized this man, this most important person in her life, was finally relaxed and at peace with himself. She smiled as she drifted off to sleep, feeling Ben's slow and steady breathing, knowing that he was already asleep.

CHAPTER XI
New Friends

The sun had not yet peaked over the horizon when Beth opened her eyes. The room was illuminated with the first glimmer of light from early dawn and she noticed she had not moved during the night. Ben had turned his head slightly toward her, but was clearly still asleep. She gently kissed his chest, then looked at his eyes which were still closed and offered no indication that he had awaken. She nuzzled his left nipple with the tip of her nose, but there was still no response from him. Now determined to wake this sleepy head, an idea flashed across her mind. Very gently pulling the sheet off him, she slowly slid down the length of his body, facing his feet as she positioned her upper body over his lower legs. Her face broke into a wicked smile as she stared at his left big toe sticking up in the air as if to say 'I dare you'. Holding his ankle with both her hands, she cautiously approached his toe with her lips, first kissing the tip of it, then the first big joint, then down to the top part of his foot. She ran the tip of her tongue up the back side of his big toe, to the top and then carefully took it into her mouth. She felt his foot flinch as she did this, but still he did not wake up until she moved her tongue to the area between his big toe and the one adjacent. His toes curled and his eyes popped opened wide, a bewildered look on his face, as he looked down to Beth and exclaimed, "What the devil are you doing?"

Beth laughed as she replied, "Worshipping the feet you walk on~~~remember," as she took his toe back into her mouth and ran her tongue up and down the length of it, producing a massage that was causing Ben to laugh and squirm over the bed. His legs were captivated by her body, finding himself totally at her mercy.

"Ohhhh baby~~~stop~~~that tickles~~~you're driving me crazy!"

"Okay, I'll try this one then," she said as she moved to his right foot. Showing him no mercy, she administered the same treatment to his right big toe as she had the left one. Realizing he could not escape, he tried to relax and ignore the sensations she was causing; to control the reflex that was making him jump and squirm. Propping a pillow under his head to watch her movements, he found her slow and deliberate motion very sensuous, both visually and tangibly. He felt the nervous tension drift from him, relaxed his head and let it sink back into the pillow as a smile creased his face.

"Ohhh, did you decide you like this?" she asked with a tease in her voice and a smile.

"Yes, it is like when you sucked the frosting off of my thumb in Indianapolis. I've never felt anything quite like that. Now get up here and cut that out!"

"Okay, but you haven't seen the last of this," she chuckled. "Are you ready to get up now, or would you like to snuggle a while?"

"I think I'd just like to lay here a while with you, snuggle and dream. Maybe we can just watch the sunrise."

She slowly snaked her way back up the length of his body, stopping only to plant short, quick kisses along the way, until arriving at his chest. Placing her head on his shoulder, her left leg across his belly, she gently stroked his chest and kissed his chin. Ben was silent, feeling her breath filter through the hair on his chest, tickling him until he smiled and spoke.

"Aww honey, remember when we were kids~~~before I had any hair on my chest?"

"Yes. What made you think about that?"

"Oh, I don't know. I guess I was wondering what would have happened if we would have had a moment like this in the woods~~~me with no shirt on~~~you with no~~~

"No, no, that would not have happened then! I would have been far too shy and scared to take any clothes off in the woods!"

"You didn't let me finish; what makes you think I was thinking about you with no clothes on?"

"I just know you, my dear. You don't like clothes remember? I'll bet you were a little streaker when you were a child, squealing, running around the house naked after getting out of the bath tub. Yes, I think I know you very well!"

Ben chuckled knowing she was right, as they continued reminiscing, going over the years when they were apart; living separate lives. Beth told of some funny things that happened while in med school; Ben talked about some of his travels.

Soon the room became flooded with sunlight. Beth slowly disengaged her body from him and climbed out of bed.

"I'm up first, so I get the bathroom first," she said with a wink. "You can put on a pot of coffee."

Ben smiled and stretched before rolling out of bed, his feet swinging in one swift motion to the floor, a practice he perfected over many years on the road. He learned that his back was much better throughout the course of the day if he did this before rising. He picked up his robe, threw it over his shoulders, cinched up the tie and made his way to the kitchenette to start the coffee, then walked back over to the window to survey the morning. The gulls were busy seeking out tidbits for their breakfast, but there was not much else going on yet at this early hour. The lake seemed very calm giving the impression of a lazy day. He turned on the TV to check the news and weather as Beth came out of the bathroom.

"You're up next, "she announced, "Is the coffee ready?"

"I haven't checked yet, but it might be." He quickly turned and entered the bathroom, feeling as if his bladder was about to burst.

"I was beginning to think I was going to have to open the window," he announced.

Beth laughed and replied, "I would have liked to have seen that," but as an afterthought, she quickly added, "No, I would not want to see that! Don't you dare even think about doing that," she teased, as she poured herself a cup of coffee. "Hurry up darling; we can go down and try out the breakfast buffet."

Eventually, Ben emerged and found Beth all dressed and with every hair in place. "Sorry it took me so long~~~I had trouble with my hair. Looks like I'm going to have a bad hair day," he quipped.

Beth laughed, "I know it must be difficult keeping track of all 20 of them. You look fine, so let's go."

As he picked up the room key, he couldn't help thinking how quickly this woman could be ready to go most any place in record time. This observation was very unusual and a very pleasant surprise. He was also impressed by how eager she was to do so many things. She was not the type to sit around much; she liked to stay on the move. This thought suddenly made him feel older than this woman.

"Maybe I had better have spinach for breakfast", he mumbled to himself. Beth evidently had not heard his mumbling before taking his hand as they made their way to breakfast.

"You had better fill up on breakfast because it might be a long time before I let you have lunch."

Ben smiled thinking this wasn't exactly what he had in mind, but remarked, "Before you *let* me have lunch? Is that some sort of a threat?" he laughed.

"No, it's just that we have a full schedule this morning and it will be some time before we will be able to have lunch."

Walking through the buffet line, he was already having questions about how he could cram enough into his stomach now to hold him over until lunch time.

"I wish I was a cow," he mumbled to himself, but Beth heard him this time.

"What did you say about a cow?" she asked.

"I said I wish I was a cow," he repeated. "Cows have more than one stomach."

Beth smiled and gave him a teasing poke in his ribs with her elbow, "Oh sweetheart, if you had more than one, they would all be hungry at the same time."

He knew she was right; she knew him too well. He piled on some scrambled eggs, hash browns, ham and toast, a side of hot cakes, orange juice and cantaloupe. Beth settled on orange juice, scrambled eggs and mixed fruit. After they had both picked up a cup of hot coffee, Ben led the way to a table that was close to a window where they could watch the pedestrian traffic pick up in intensity as the island became more alive with activity.

"I love this time of day," Beth mused as she sipped her coffee. "Everything is starting to hum like a beehive."

"Yes and it looks like it's going to be a beautiful day. No clouds in sight and the sun is sparkling across the bay. But the best part of the morning is looking across this table at you. You get more beautiful with each passing day; you~~~you seem to glow."

Beth reached across the table and took his free hand in hers, as her other hand was delivering a load of scrambled eggs up to his mouth. He glanced over the fork and winked at her, knowing he had struck a tender spot in her heart. Beth could not speak; she merely smiled and shook her head from side to side. She was astounded at the way he could so casually say the sweetest things as though they were facts and beyond dispute. She suddenly felt an urge to hug him, but it would have to wait until later. She finally regained her voice as she carefully fed him another mouthful of eggs and said with a mischievous grin, "You are so full of bull shit!"

Ben nearly choked on his eggs, not expecting this from her. She never ceased to surprise him in the most amusing ways. He loved this about her~~~quick, ornery at times, fun loving and teasing.

Her eyes were still sparkling, proud of herself as they finished their breakfast and made their way outside into the crisp early morning air. Beth took Ben's hand and looked up to his face and asked, "Honey, are you warm enough?" She had dressed in layers that included a hat, but Ben was in his customary jeans, sweatshirt and light jacket. He did not have a hat, as he had an aversion to anything on his head after so many years of not having anything up there~~~including hair.

"Yes I'm warm enough, but I'm thinking I should have brought a hat. My bare dome might take a beating from that sun later on."

"Well, we are going right past some shops and we'll just pick up a hat for you," she said with authority.

Ben felt he was developing a mild case of lateral whiplash as they walked past the various businesses on both sides of Main Street. Flowers could be seen everywhere, in hanging baskets, window boxes, flower beds and large planters. Every old-fashioned street light had two large wire baskets hanging from it, lined with brown cocoa matting and filled with red geraniums, asparagus ferns, vinca vines and trailing purple and yellow flowers. Northern Michigan's cool nights allowed these flowers to thrive until frost. Along the way they passed another hotel, a pancake house and a mercantile shop, where Beth guided Ben inside to find a hat.

"See if you can find a hat while I pick up a couple bottles of water," Beth quipped.

"What do we need water for~~~are we about to leave civilization?"

"No, but we will have a long ride and besides, none of us drink enough water, "Beth replied.

"Yes Doc, you get the water and I'll find a hat," Ben chuckled as he made his way to the rear of the store. He didn't find a multitude of hats, but there were quite a few that had various images of the island over the bill. Finally having decided on one that depicted The Grand Hotel, he proceeded to find Beth. As he approached her, she smiled and said, "Oh, I like your hat."

"There was not a whole lot to choose from," he replied. "There were just various scenes of the island. I liked this one as it reminds me of that movie Superman was in."

"Well they are just promoting the island and the hat will serve as a souvenir for you later on. Let's get over to the Tourism/Information office and pick up a brochure with information about places to see and also check on the times the carriage tours begin."

"See that bicycle rental place over there?" she asked Ben. "Maybe we can rent one of those that are made for two and we can ride it around on our own, later."

"Ben chuckled and replied, "I've never rode one of those before, but if you feel brave, I'm game." As soon as he said that, he wished he had not.

They entered the Tourism office and Beth started a conversation with a lady who was more than ready to answer Beth's questions. Ben was looking through the many brochures and discovered there were many points of interest on this rather small island. Beth had a brochure the lady had given her and together they walked out and sat down on one of the benches outside the office.

"Ben, let's decide which one of these carriage rides we want to take. There is this one the lady told me about that really sounds great and it leaves pretty soon," as she pointed to one that was a three hour tour which included a visit to Fort Mackinac, Wings of Mackinac butterfly conservatory and then on to see Arch Rock.

"Sounds good to me, especially that trip to the old fort," he said. "Are we ready to go?"

"Yes, we better hurry; they are starting to line up."

Ben surveyed the carriage that was pulled by two horses. There were five bench type seats painted bright red and yellow that would seat four across. The undercarriage was red and it rolled along on rubber tire wheels. The roof of the carriage was white with a white fringe, much like a surrey fringe, hanging from the edges. He soon learned that the driver was also the guide and was able to answer any questions anyone might have along the trip.

"Let's try to get the seat right behind the driver," he whispered to Beth. "I'll wear out the driver with questions."

As they boarded the carriage, a younger couple was the first to occupy the front bench, but left room for Ben and Beth to sit beside them. As Ben settled into his seat and became comfortable, he took Beth's hand, kissed the back of it and squeezed it tightly and said, "I never want to leave this place."

Hearing him say this and feeling her hand in his, her thoughts went back to that day in the wooded area of the park when they were teenagers. Now finally, this was their time and she also never wanted it to end.

Pulling away from the curb, the driver made an immediate left turn and headed for Market Street which parallels Main Street. As he made the turn onto Market Street, the Mackinac Post Office appeared on their right; a post office like none either of them had ever seen. It looked like a small cottage home, white with blue shutters, perfectly landscaped with window boxes that were alive with flowers, a picket fence surrounded the yard and a bicycle rack was at the front. The next building was a museum, which was not a stop on this tour.

"Ben, maybe we can come back here later on our bicycle and visit this museum." Ben was busy surveying the sights as he mumbled, "Sounds like a plan to me."

As the carriage neared the end of Market Street, the driver made a right turn and started up the incline on Cadotte Street. Ben caught a whiff of a foul scent, looking first toward the young couple to his right and noticed the young lady wiggle her nose as if she too had caught the scent. He then leaned over to Beth and pronounced, "The horse or the driver has a gas problem, and I ain't talking about gasoline."

Beth also had detected the scent and leaned closer to Ben as she whispered, "I think it is the horse. When they pull hard they sometimes vent."

Ben laughed and replied, "Vent? Is that what they called it in med school? I always called it~~~"

"Yes I know what you called it," she cut him off, "and by the looks of that young man to our right, that is what he calls it too," she chuckled, nodding toward the young man who was also visibly laughing.

Then to change the subject she added, "Look to your left Ben," as the huge Grand Hotel came into view. "That is the hotel you mentioned where Superman was filmed and is illustrated on your hat. But it wasn't Superman, it was 'Somewhere in Time'. Did you see that movie?"

"Yeah, but it was a long time ago. I didn't mean it was a Superman movie~~~I just meant that the guy that played Superman was in it. What was his name?"

The young lady sitting next to Beth overheard Ben's question, smiled toward him and replied, "That was Christopher Reeves. He starred in that movie with Jane Seymour."

"Oh Yeah, I remember now, thank you. By the way, my name is Ben and this is my dear friend Elizabeth."

"I'm happy to meet you both. My name is Shannon and this is my husband John. We are on our honeymoon."

"Ohh, how sweet," Beth exclaimed as she took Shannon's hand in hers as Ben nodded across to John and extended his congratulations. "Do you live near here?"

"No, we are from Illinois~~~near Peoria. We only have a week before we both have to be back to work. Are you from around here?" Shannon replied.

"Yes originally, we both grew up in Midland, south of here. I now live in Ohio, but Ben still lives in Midland."

"Are you engaged~~~oh, I'm sorry~~~I'm being rude!" Shannon quickly added, her face turning slightly red. "I saw Ben kiss your hand so I thought~~~"

"Ohh, think nothing of it," Beth laughed. "No, we just go back a long time and ~~~well~~~we are just enjoying this time together. At our age one doesn't think much about marriage anymore; we're more concerned about surviving," Beth said with a hearty laugh and a wink. "You two, on the other hand, have your whole life before you. Don't waste a moment! Enjoy every day you have together and never stop being lovers."

Shannon smiled, leaned back against the back of the bench and thought about what Beth had just said. Beth was also thinking about what she had just told Shannon, realizing the import of what she had just revealed to her, as they approached the Little Stone Congregational Church, a much photographed stone structure built around the early 1900's. The driver halted the carriage in front of another museum that housed various antique carriages, restrooms, and snack and gift shops. But what instantly attracted the ladies' attention was next door at the Wings of Mackinac butterfly conservatory. Their guide told everyone they could spend as much time at this location as they wished, and they would later board another carriage with seating for 35 persons, pulled by three horses.

Hearing that, Ben looked at Beth and said, "I ain't so keen about sitting in the front seat anymore; might have fresher air in the rear~~~err, I mean in the back."

John overheard Ben's remarks, laughed and said, "I was thinking the same thing; mind if we sit with you?"

"Not at all~~~be glad to have you," Ben replied.

"Not so fast you two, we want to go in here and see the butterflies before getting on that carriage," Beth quipped.

"Oh we didn't mean right now~~~by all means we want to see them too, right John?"

"Yes, that's right~~~of course," echoed John.

Beth winked at Shannon and the two of them smiled as they entered the conservatory. While the guys thought they slipped past that one, the girls knew better. They observed a room that explained the life cycle of a butterfly and behind a glass window there were many chrysalises hanging from branches. If you were lucky you might see a butterfly emerging from one. Then on to narrow paths leading through beds of flowers surrounded by hundreds of colorful butterflies, flitting all around and sometimes landing on visitors. As they were making their way past the beds, a beautiful Monarch landed on Shannon's rather well endowed breast, its wings opening and closing as if to invite John to remove it. As if she knew what he was thinking, she commanded in no uncertain terms, "Don't you even think about it!"

Ben could not contain his laughter. "My gosh John, I think they are all alike! They can read our minds!"

Beth chuckled and replied, "We learn that at an early age, don't we Shannon?"

"Yes," she replied as she placed the back of her hand in front of the butterfly to allow it to move to her hand, "It is our only defense. Now John, you can see if it will go to your hand," as she extended her hand over to John.

"Naw, it won't be the same now; won't be spontaneous," he quipped.

"That's right," added Ben. "It has lost the urge."

"The butterfly or John?" asked Beth with a wink. As she said this she looked at Ben and began laughing. Ben had removed his hat upon entering the conservatory and a butterfly had taken up housekeeping on the top of Ben's bald dome.

"Look Shannon, that butterfly must think it has escaped to the desert!" Beth said with a hearty laugh.

As Shannon spotted the butterfly, she too erupted in glee at how the butterfly looked as if it was 'King of the Mountain'. John seeing it too, could not contain his laughter. Ben knew instinctively what they must be laughing at and said, "He knows a quality landing strip when he spots one," and joined their laughter. "But he won't find any nectar up there; it's been barren for a long time!"

As they made their way through the remainder of the conservatory, they exited and decided to find a seat on the larger carriage. They were in time to lay claim to the rear seat and made themselves comfortable. Ben and John had engaged in some chatter about jobs and retirement, seemingly oblivious to the two ladies. Shannon turned to Beth and asked, "Can I ask you a personal question?"

"I guess so; what is on your mind, dear?"

"Were you and Ben ever married?"

"Yes we were, but not to each other. We fell in love when we were so very young, too young actually and circumstances beyond our control separated us. Broken hearts heal very fast when hearts are young and before long I had found new friends and a new love. Ben went on with his life as well, making a home and family of his own."

"Are you a widow?"

Beth hesitated before answering as she had already decided it would be the last question. "No, I've been divorced for a number of years. I never remarried or ever considered that possibility, as I went back to school and received a medical degree in pediatrics. I think that answers your questions."

Shannon sensed by her tone that it was the last question. It was obvious that she had no intentions of answering any questions concerning Ben. Shannon understood and respected Beth's privacy. She felt a keen sense of admiration for this woman and she also detected a bit of sadness in her voice. "I'm glad the two of you found each other again; you seem so right together."

"Thank you, Shannon," she paused, then added, "We are right for each other~~~very right."

The carriage now loaded, began its journey up the hill to Arch Rock. It is a very short stop, but a very picturesque area. The arch frames a view of Lake Huron some 146 feet above the shoreline and is surrounded by thick woods. Ben and Beth left the carriage to use the restrooms, as Shannon and John ventured closer to the arch to gain a better view of the lake.

"John, what is your opinion of Ben?"

"I like him, I guess. He's funny and easy to get to know. Why do you ask?"

"Do you detect a sense of sadness in him?"

"No, I don't think so. He seems very happy with Beth. Is something wrong? Did Beth say something to you that indicated there was some trouble?"

"No, not really, but she is very protective of Ben somehow. I really like her; I just wondered how you felt about him."

"I think he's okay. She's kinda cute, too."

"Watch it, buster!" she chuckled.

They re-boarded the carriage and resumed the trip down toward the Avenue of Flags at the entrance to Fort Mackinac. As they arrived at the entrance to the fort, Shannon and John opted to view the old fort and departed the carriage. Ben was feeling his stomach starting to growl and expressed his desire to head downtown to find an eatery to pacify his noisy stomach. Beth agreed, so they bade farewell to the young couple, not knowing if their paths would cross again before leaving the island. After boarding another carriage, they were on their way down the hill toward town to have lunch. There were numerous restaurants on Main

Street and Ben's belly was not allowing him much time to make up his mind. He noticed a rather huge American flag flying over the doorway of a tavern at the corner of Astor and Main and said, "That's it; that's the one. Any place that flies 'Ole Glory' is where I wish to eat."

Beth laughed and replied, "What if they serve dog food?"

"Well, I'll remember that and bring my dog back the next time I come here."

"Does that mean we will be coming back here?"

"I would like to," Ben paused and went on, "Who knows? I'd like to buy one of those cottages on the West Bluff and stay here."

"Oh yes, I know you would like that, along with thousands of others as well. That is out of the question. But~~~could we come back here again?"

"Honey, this is only our second day and we still have another to go. I don't even want to think about leaving~~~at least not now."

"I know we do and I'm sorry I seem to be pushing you. It's just that it is so romantic here and I~~~~

"I know baby~~~I know," Ben cut her off, "but let's go inside here and have some fun. Time's a wastin'! Should I give a rebel yell as we enter?"

Beth sensed he was feeling the time passing too quickly and did not want to think about leaving~~~at least not now. She knew he was right~~~now is the time for fun, not lamenting what may or may not be in the future.

Gathering her best smile, she replied, "Don't you dare! If you do I will act like I don't know you," she laughed.

The interior of the pub was decorated in red, white and blue, very pub-like making Ben say, "I'm liking it more all the time!"

They chose a table toward the back of the dining room and settled in to check the menu which offered appetizers, soups, salads and sandwiches. Beth selected a Chicken Salad Wrap with Michigan cherries on tomato basil flatbread served with fruit while Ben ordered the Stacked Reuben with corned beef, fresh sauerkraut, Swiss cheese on rye served with kettle chips. To wash it all down he ordered a schooner of draft Michelob. Beth had her customary glass of water.

"Is your Reuben good?" Beth asked.

"Umm yes, very good and so is the beer. How 'bout your Chicken wrap?"

"Yes, it is very delicious. You should eat more chicken and less beef. It is better for your heart."

"Oh Doc, I know I should, but I love beef. Besides a couple of beers a day will keep the doctor away."

"Oh really? You will have to explain that to me," she laughed.

"Well, most of them; there are a few exceptions~~~but only the ones I want, mind you," he was quick to add.

Beth looked at him with a stare that was meant to be a glare, but she could not keep the smile from forming across her face. Ben was already laughing before she said, "You had better make that singular, buster!" Ben reached across the table and took her hand in his, squeezed it and looked into her eyes. Beth knew without a word being spoken what he was saying with his eyes, as they were so descriptive and spoke much louder than his voice. He didn't have to say a word~~~she knew. He loved to tease with his words, but loved her deeply with his eyes. Finally, Beth smiled and mouthed the words that he was saying to her with his eyes, "I love you, too! Are we ready to leave?"

"Yes, I'll take care of the bill and meet you outside."

As Ben made his way to the cashier, Beth walked outside and caught the scent of freshly made fudge. "Oh what a nice dessert a piece of fudge would make," she thought. After Ben joined her on the street, she tugged his hand, "Let's go over to the fudge shop and get some fudge."

"Are you sure that's on my diet, Doc?"

"It's on your prescription, along with some exercises later to work it off! Come on, let's go."

After crossing the street the scent became even stronger and Ben felt his mouth watering for a taste of some rich fudge. "Ben, it is so rich and the pieces are so large, let's just get one piece and share it? What kind would you like?"

"Oh heck, whatever kind is on the prescription is fine with me. I like it all; it's chocolate ain't it?"

Beth picked out a piece of chocolate pecan and they began nibbling it on their way back toward their hotel. They stopped to sit on the benches that were along the boardwalk to watch the sailboats and catamarans in the bay.

"When I was 11 or 12, my father taught me to sail a small sailboat when we vacationed at Crystal Lake and I still enjoy watching them glide effortlessly through the water. Would you like to sail on one of those catamarans before we leave?"

"You never told me that before. Yes, I think I'd like that. Will you be the skipper?"

Beth laughed, "No, it's been too many years ago; you will be much safer if one of those young men do the sailing."

"Some of those make some pretty quick turns," he remarked. "They won't tip over, will they?"

"No, not very likely as it would take a lot of effort and rough water to do that, I believe. You aren't having second thoughts, are you?" she chuckled.

"No, not as long as you are on board; I know you would save me if we tipped over," he laughed, "I don't swim very well, so my life is in your hands"

"Not to worry my love. If you go down, I will go down with you."

"Well, that's not very encouraging! No Honey, I want you to keep us both *up!* I'm not ready to blow bubbles or push up daisies. Speaking of daisies, did you remember to water your daisy this morning?"

"Ohhh, I forgot all about that. Well, let's go up and take a nap before dinner and I'll check on it when we get up there. I hope it isn't wilting already."

"No problem sweetheart; I can steal another one for you if it is dying already."

"It's not really stealing~~~they grow fairly wild with little attention and are pretty hearty. Besides, they will not be missed. I have loved daisies ever since you gave me the first one in the woods when we were in school together. They remind me of you and how happy I was during those days."

"That's so ironic; every time I would see a daisy, I too remembered that day in the park with you. I think it was the way the sun was shining on it~~~like it lit up when you walked into the clearing. It seems they are always around us when we are together. And yes, they are very hearty, and thrive without much attention~~~so very much like our love. It has thrived through all these years without any attention, touching or caring.

Yet it comes to life as though it had never died~~~only slept through a very long winter."

Ben squeezed her hand and winked at her, "Gee, speaking of sleep, I'm starting to get tired~~~what about you?" he said with a yawn.

"Is that a hint you want something?" she asked with a smile.

"Yes it is; a nap," he quipped.

Beth leaned toward him placing her head against his shoulder while still holding his hand as she replied, "I'm tired too and I'm ready to curl up next to you for a little nap."

"Okay, sounds like a plan," Ben said as he stood up taking both of Beth's hands to help her up. A low flying gull swept down just above Ben's head, causing him to duck. "I think that bird likes my hat; I think he was trying to steal it."

Beth laughed, "Just make sure you keep it on or he might recognize that quality landing strip you have up there and decide to land"

"Yeah, or maybe start a bomb run!" Ben added.

They entered their hotel room and Beth immediately entered the bathroom, as Ben crossed the room to the bed. He sat down to remove his shoes and socks, then his jeans and sweatshirt. He then lay back across the bed in his T-shirt and jockey shorts. He loved getting out of clothes, as they always made him feel restrained. If *streaking* would have been thought of when he was a teenager, he always felt he would enjoy trying that in one of the various malls around Saginaw, as long as he could depend on his friends to pick him up after his run. He smiled as he thought about this, knowing that his buddies would delight in abandoning him there, naked as a jaybird.

Beth entered the bedroom, having shed her jeans and blouse; seeing Ben smiling piqued her curiosity, "What is so funny," she asked, "Are you plotting something evil?"

Ben laughed and replied, "No, just remembering something from long ago. You wouldn't understand."

"Now don't do that; don't make me wonder what you were thinking!"

"Oh it was just some ornery stuff a bunch of us guys used to do when we could still run. I always thought I'd try streaking if it had been thought of back then. By the way, is your daisy all right?"

"Yes, my daisy survived my negligence quite well. It's is still beautiful. Oh yes, I can just see you streaking; your dislike for clothes would make you a natural. There is no doubt you *were* one of those little kids that used to streak bare-assed naked through the house, soaking wet after getting out of the bath tub," she winked as she crawled up on the bed next to him.

"Actually, I never really stopped enjoying running through the house that way, but I had to control the impulse in later years. Would you like to see if I still have it in me?"

Beth laughed and replied, "No, you don't have to show me~~~I believe you. Let's get your head up near the head of the bed so you will be more comfortable." Ben moved over to his side of the bed, lying flat on his back, allowing Beth more space. She moved against him placing her head on his left shoulder, her left leg across his belly and stroking his chest with her left hand. She loved this position as it was so relaxing and warm. Ben's left arm was under her neck enabling him to stroke her back and left side down to the flare of her hip, his right hand resting on her left thigh.

Ben could barely hear her as she whispered, "Sweetheart, I want you to know I have never been this happy before in my entire life. Everything I have always wanted in a relationship, I have found with you. I keep thinking so much that I wish we could have had all those lost years together. We would have ran, played ball, raised kids, went fishing and boating, laughed, cried~~~just so many things together~~~all those years~~~"

She didn't finish the sentence and Ben knew without looking that she was quietly crying.

"Baby, those years are gone and behind us and we can't ever bring them back. But there is no need to weep over that which we cannot do anything about. Our time is now and we must make the best of every moment we have together. What we have now and what we had all those years before, is more than most ever find. Yes, I know all the things we could have enjoyed if we had not lost those years. But you know, we may even have drifted apart back then. We don't really know; Julie and Karen would never have been, so just be glad for now, grab on and hold on tight. Our love is enduring and the moment is now."

He listened for a response, then noticed Beth's breathing was slow and regular; she was asleep. Ben smiled, kissed her forehead, closed his eyes and joined her in a much needed nap.

CHAPTER XII
Ominous Signs

Beth was first to wake from their nap, finding that they had not moved. Ben was still sleeping with his mouth slightly open, looking very peaceful and emitting a slight snore when he inhaled. Beth watched him, feeling his chest rise and fall with his every breath. She wondered what her life would have been like waking up next to him like this. She could not imagine being this happy every day; surely something would happen that would spoil the perfection of moments like this. As soon as the question entered her mind, she knew the answer~~~they would have had to go to work. She smiled as she realized even work, especially work, would have only added to her happiness. She would have had everything she ever wanted, the work that she loved and was devoted to, plus the love of her life. What more could she possibly want?

As if by magic that question was answered as Ben stirred, opened his eyes and caught her gazing at him. "Did I die? Are you an angel?"

"No my dear, you did not die and I am not an angel," she paused, "just your lover who loves you very much. Do you feel rested?"

Ben placed his right arm over his head and extended his left one straight out under Beth's neck, stretching and yawning as he replied, "Ohewwahh~~~yes~~~much better." Sighing and relaxing his body he added, "How about you~~~did you sleep well or did you just stare at me while I slept," he asked with a chuckle, quickly adding, "Did I snore?"

Beth smiled and replied, "I just woke up a little bit ago but didn't want to disturb you. You looked very peaceful and yes, you snored so loudly I thought the windows were going to crack."

"Really? I didn't think I ever snored. I stayed awake one night and never heard a sound. You're kidding me, right?"

"Just exaggerated a little bit; your snoring is very slight," she teased, "but why do you sleep with one eye open?"

Ben laughed knowing that it was hard to get one over on her. Her mind was quick and her wit was sharp keeping him on his toes and he loved this about her. "Well, because I can't bear to lose sight of you even for a moment."

Beth was moved by that response as she propped herself up, looked into his eyes and replied, "I guess you know that kind of talk is going to reap you rewards later," she said with a seductive look on her face.

"I'm counting on that and I have plans for you too. How would you like to have a nice slow back rub starting at your neck and shoulders that extends and includes a foot rub after dinner?"

"Ohhh, that sounds like heaven. Remember, what's good for the goose is good for the gander. I also have a surprise for you later."

"Uhoh, what do you have on your mind?"

"You'll just have to wait and see or it won't be a surprise," she said as she slowly got up off the bed and made her way to the bathroom. "What do you feel like for dinner tonight?"

"You know me; I'm always ready for pizza. What would you like?"

"Pizza sounds fine. There is a pizzeria on the east end of Main Street. We can get it by the slice or get a whole pizza."

"Well, we may as well get the whole thing as slices don't cut it for me, no pun intended," Ben laughed thinking he just nailed a good one.

Beth had to give him that one, as it was a natural. "You may want to reconsider, as I think I might want a veggie pizza. How do you feel about that?"

"That fine, besides I need to eat more veggies and less red meat, right Doc? As long as it has lots of cheese, I'm good to go."

"That's right~~~and I'm not your doctor. If you keep calling me Doc, I'm going to have to send you a bill."

"Uhoh," he said as he got up off the bed and walked over to the bathroom door, "I don't think I could afford you, so I better behave. Are you decent in there?"

"Yes, I'm just freshening up some. Do you need the bathroom?"

"No, I just need you; I need a hug."

Beth came to the door and as she opened it Ben took her into his arms and whispered the words in her ear that she never tires of hearing,

"I love you baby! I just love and need you." As he pulled back a bit, he framed her face between his hands and lightly kissed her lips, a long gentle searching kiss, always leaving them both breathless. Her hands went to his wrists returning his kiss as her lips opened slightly allowing his tongue to trace the curve of the inside of her lips, moving across her upper front teeth and gums. He loved her mouth, the softness of her lips, the way she searched his lips as he moved his gently over hers.

As the kiss ended, Beth looked into his eyes, her face slightly flushed and said in a low and sultry voice, "We better stop this and get ready to go or we won't make it for dinner."

"Umhuh, you're right. Just one kiss from you cranks my engine over; makes me weak in the knees, bringing back memories of that very first kiss. Ain't nothin' else in the world quite like your kiss," he said as he released her, moving around her to enter the bathroom, "but if you will excuse me for a moment, I have to pee."

Beth laughed, "What a mood breaker that is! Do you need some help?"

"No, not now; I'm afraid if you were to *help* me we won't get out of here at all."

"Okay, I'll finish up out here; you can have the bathroom, then we can leave."

Beth moved to the mirror on the bedroom wall, smiling as she faced her reflection, reflecting on the many things in her life that had changed since they found each other. Never before could she be so free with her innermost thoughts with a man, amazed at how openly she could say the most seductive things to him, totally fearless of what he might think of her. Finding also this newfound freedom seems to have brought them even closer together, fostering a degree of trust she had never felt with anyone else. She noticed her smile had widened further with the realization she had never felt more a woman, more in want of this man who had opened her in ways she had never thought possible. She was still smiling when Ben finished in the bathroom.

He dressed in his usual jeans and sweat shirt, put on his sneakers and was ready to go. Beth also dressed in jeans and a light blue turtle neck sweater that accented her long neck and the graceful lines of her face, framing it as if she was royalty. She slipped on her sneakers, made one last look in the mirror to check her hair, then turned taking Ben's hand and simply said, "I'm ready, my man; let's go."

They departed the hotel making their way down Main Street as the sun was starting to set behind them. Ben felt something strange in his chest and wanted to stop for an instant to get his breath, but did not want to alarm Beth. Instead, he stopped her and said, "Let's check the sunset; it feels good on my back." They turned and looked towards the sun, seeing nothing unusual about it at the time, as it was still a bit early and still too high in the sky for the brilliant color and hues that would appear over the water a little bit later.

"Oh you're too anxious darling; the sun isn't low enough yet," she remarked. Ben agreed as he was silently assessing his chest and his breathing. Thinking that whatever it was had passed, he shrugged, took her hand and continued on toward the pizzeria. Off in the distance somewhere they could hear the sound of music and the laughter of younger voices making Ben wince at the reminder that he was not young anymore~~~and wondered why he had thought of that now.

Ben held the door for Beth as she entered the pizzeria and the scent of the spices in the sauce filled their nostrils. "Umm, something smells mighty good," he mused, as Beth spotted a table and guided him toward it. "How is this one?" she asked.

"Oh, this is fine," he replied as he glanced at the menu and noticed that they did not serve alcohol. "Uhoh~~~pizza without beer; I'm not used to that."

"Well, you aren't used to veggie pizza either, so you shouldn't miss the beer. Maybe you would like some chilled vegetable juice or just water." Hearing that, Ben frowned but had no comment as the waitress arrived to take their order.

Beth took the initiative and said, "I think we would like a medium size veggie pizza on a thin crust. I would like a glass of water without ice."

The waitress agreed and asked if she would like a salad to go along with it. "Yes, that would be nice~~~with your house dressing."

"And you, sir?" the waitress asked. Ben gave her a blank stare as she reiterated, "What would you like to drink?"

"Oh, I'm sorry. I would like a double V-8 straight up on the rocks with a water chaser."

"Pardon me," the waitress asked. Beth laughed and replied, "He just wants a glass of chilled vegetable juice and a glass of water.

The waitress chuckled as she said, "Very good. I'll be right back with your drinks."

Beth reached across the table and took Ben's hands in hers. "You really would like to have a beer, wouldn't you dear?"

"Naw, not really; I was just teasing her. She is so young; I figured that would go over her head."

"If you want, we can find a little pub after we leave here and you could get a beer."

"No really, I don't need another beer. I had one for lunch and that is plenty. I think after we leave here, I'd like to take a walk down by the docks, then around the hotel grounds. How does that sound to you?"

"That sounds marvelous, but honey, you didn't bring your hat, and the gulls might~~~"

Before she could finish her sentence, Ben started laughing. "Yeah, they might make a carrier landing."

Ben, still holding her hands across the table looked deeply into her eyes, totally oblivious to his surroundings, his mind drifting back over the years of loneliness and longing for this woman, remembering the agreement they had made for complete honesty and how it had resulted in the huge changes in his life. Now, looking into her eyes he could see her soul, knowing they were always meant to be together, neither complete without the other. There was no doubt in his mind that this was so.

The waitress returned with their drinks, waking Ben from his reverie. "Your pizza will be right out shortly," she announced. Ben sipped his vegetable juice, finding it lacking of something, and then deciding it was Vodka.

"How is your water?" he asked with a grin on his face.

"Very wet; how is your double V-8?"

"Very dry; like something is missing."

"Well, it must be the pizza, but I see it coming now."

The waitress delivered the pizza along with some fancy napkins. The aroma of the vegetable pizza filled Ben's nostrils and made his mouth water. Something about the scent of pizza triggered something in his brain that made him ravenously hungry, even when he was not.

As the waitress left, Ben waited until Beth picked up a piece, carefully placing a bite of it into her mouth. That was Ben's signal that it was okay to dig in. He picked up the next piece, took a huge bite of it, finding it pleasantly very good.

"Umm, I never knew veggie pizza could be so tasty. This is very good; maybe we should have gotten a large one."

"Honey, if you are still hungry, we could order another slice or two."

"No, I've had plenty. I just have to wash it all down with this cocktail."

Beth had finished eating and was quietly watching Ben sip his V-8 juice, listening to the Italian music playing softly. "I like this place; maybe we can come here again before we leave," she whispered across the table to Ben.

"Yes we can, if you like. Are you ready to leave?"

"Yes."

Ben left a tip and made his way to the cashier as Beth moved to the door. She looked outside, saw the sunset was now complete and the moon was taking over the night sky, shining off the smooth water of the bay. It was a cool, yet warm evening at the same time. There was hardly any breeze but it would soon be time for a jacket. She knew they would not be out walking very long.

He joined her at the door, taking her hand as they began the walk back toward the hotel, passing the docks as they continued on. The gulls were quiet, showing no interest in Ben. "They must be all grounded tonight; maybe they have a big bombing mission scheduled for the morning?" he laughed.

They moved on to the hotel grounds and walked slowly around to the rear of the building. There were so many flowers, and the sounds of night creatures were already starting their evening serenade.

"Oh I love the sound of night time, Ben!"

"I do too! I always feel everything is good when the frogs, tree frogs and crickets are making racket. It is when everything suddenly gets quiet that really gets my attention. This is music to sleep by."

"Ben~~~hold me," Beth said as she turned toward him. He took her into his arms and felt the warmth of her body against his, but also felt her trembling a bit.

"Oh baby, you're getting cold. We better get inside before you catch a chill." Beth felt there was more than just the night air that caused her to tremble, but she did not know what it was.

"Not before you kiss me," she said as she reached up to him and touched her lips to his. He returned her kiss, tasting the garlic and spices that they had both enjoyed just a short while before. "You have a much different taste tonight," he remarked.

Beth laughed and replied, "I was just thinking the same thing about you. Let's get inside and brush our teeth. I think I have some broccoli stuck between my teeth."

As soon as the door to their room opened, Beth jumped inside quickly. "I get the bathroom first; why don't you see what's on the television."

Ben accepted her dash and readily complied with her wishes. Besides, for some reason he felt tired as he picked up the remote and turned on the TV. What could possibly be on that they would want to watch? He surfed the channels, but found nothing of interest except for a hockey game from Canada. He decided to keep that channel as he was sure Beth would have no interest in watching that and would want to turn it off. He was curious about what she had planned for this evening. He also felt in an ornery mood, but wanted to spend a quiet evening just having fun with her, teasing and laughing.

Beth soon emerged from the bathroom and announced that it was all his now. "Did you find anything on the TV that is worth watching?"

"Oh yes I did; a Canadian hockey game. Do you like hockey?"

"No I don't; I don't understand anything about the game. It seems like they just skate around, start fights and the crowd love it when that happens. Why don't the officials try to stop the fighting?"

"Maybe because they fear the crowd would attack them if they did; ya think?"

"Well, go brush your teeth and I'll see if I can find something better."

"So much for the hockey plan," he thought to himself as he got up off the bed and made his way to the bathroom. As he stood in front of the toilet to urinate his thoughts returned to the walk down Main Street earlier. Why did he suddenly feel out of breath? But the thoughts vanished as quickly as they appeared when he flushed the toilet. He found his toothbrush and began the chore of trying to get rid of the garlic scent from his mouth, finally discovering that it was emanating from his pores as much as from his mouth. Oh well, it seems she wants to watch TV anyhow, so why worry about such a small thing. Besides, she probably will not know what is permeating from him or from her.

He switched off the light in the bathroom and walked toward the bed where he found the TV was still on, but the sound was muted. "Are we going to watch silent movies tonight?"

Beth laughed and replied, "No, I thought we would turn off all the lights except for the light the TV is making. I think it is very sensual."

Ben smiled and hurriedly flipped off the table lamp before climbing onto the bed beside her. As the scenes changed on the TV, so did the light patterns that fell across her body. She had put on a thin see through light blue nightgown that hit her just above the knees. The changing light was just enough to tease, causing Ben to think he was seeing things that perhaps he wasn't. She looked very seductive and he found he was moving toward her as she said, "Just lay back and relax. I want to take off your T-shirt so you will be more comfortable."

"Won't it be easier if I sit up to take it off?"

"Maybe, but I want to do it this way," she said as she began tugging on the bottom of the shirt, right above the band of his jockey shorts. Ben found that he was rolling his body back and forth to ease the shirt up over his belly and chest until she had it up around his neck. She then leaned against his chest and licked his right nipple. First thinking she was going to do a number on his chest, he was surprised when she instantly moved to under his right arm, first kissing his arm pit and then slowly licking across it like a cat licking milk.

Always being extremely sensitive in this area, he immediately started wiggling, trying to get away from the onslaught. But Beth was holding both of his arms above his head and was holding him down with her body. She teased his armpit, licking, sucking and kissing it, moving her face back and forth tickling him, making him laugh and beg for mercy. Without hesitating, she moved over to the left side, stopping just for a brief moment to kiss his left nipple before going for his left arm pit. By now, Ben was beside himself, squirming and laughing out loud.

"Be quiet! Someone will hear you!"

"My God, I hope so", he laughed. "Maybe someone will come in and save me!"

All the squirming and wrestling caused Beth's night gown to rise up around her waist. As she got up off the bed to remove it the rest of the way, Ben reached out and goosed her. She jumped in surprise and yelped.

"Be quiet," he quipped, "someone might hear you!"

Beth laughed as she crawled back into bed, straddling Ben's legs with her own as she tugged at the waistband of his shorts, pulling them down over his hips.

"There, now we are even and you look much more comfortable. I like lying next to you with nothing between us."

Ben placed his arm under her neck as she placed her head on his shoulder and her left leg across his belly. "Baby, if we were a hundred years old do you think we would still be doing this?"

"I will never tire of doing this with you. I just hope we make it to be a hundred and then we will see what we can still do. But honey, you will have to stop that goose thing you just did; I might fall on my face," she laughed.

"I couldn't resist; the target was there and besides, you had that one coming. What's that you say about the goose and the gander?"

"Oh you loved that and you know it!"

"And you loved that goose, too! I could tell from the sound of that yelp you made," he laughed. Beth looked in his eyes with a look that told him that yes, she had. She loved the fun and play they had found with each other.

Ben stared at the changing light patterns on the ceiling, then turned his head toward her and asked, "What do you have planned for tomorrow?"

"We can have breakfast here again, if you like. Then later I thought we would take a carriage ride up to the Grand Hotel for a tour and then enjoy the buffet lunch they serve. After that, I think you would like to take the carriage ride to The Bluffs. And for dinner~~~"

"Okay," he laughed, "It looks like all I have to do is be ready on time~~~and I can do that."

"Good," she said as she tilted her head up to kiss his cheek, "you will enjoy tomorrow."

"I enjoy every minute I spend with you," he replied as he lowered his head to lightly kiss her lips. It never changes, he thought; the kiss always brings back the sweet memory of so many years ago. He knew he would never get enough of this woman! He knew that life was too short for that possibility. What he didn't know, was how short it was to be.

Off somewhere in the bay, the sound of a bell could be heard peeling intermittently, varying in intensity as the sound waves rode on a slight breeze blowing softly against the docks below. As Ben listened to it, he realized what a lonesome sound it made and likened it to some creature that lives in the water, searching for its mate. Or even a lost sailor who went down with his ship during one of the many wars that may have been fought around this island. He suddenly felt alone as he tightened the pressure of his arm under Beth's neck and pulled her closer to him.

"Are you awake?"

There was no sound from her except for the gentle sound of her breath moving across his chest; she was asleep. The TV was still on and there was enough light to see her face. She looked so peaceful and serene. They were both nude and soon she would be chilled. He moved his body slowly, trying to avoid waking her as he reached for the remote control for the TV and to grab hold of the bed sheet near his feet. Somehow he succeeded without waking her, although she moved slightly, moving her hand across his chest to make sure he was still there.

He then pulled the sheet up over her and turned off the TV. Moonlight flooded the room, casting a sort of blue hue to the white sheet. Ben now wondered why he didn't wake her, as the room took on such a suggestive appearance. Smiling when he thought of how she would react, he bent his head down to plant a kiss on her forehead. No, he would let her sleep; there would be more time for loving later. He turned his head back toward the window and listened one last time to the lonely bell before falling off to sleep. He did not feel alone anymore.

Chapter XIII
Shopping and the Grand Hotel

Moonlight gave way to the first shades of early morning sunlight, changing the hue of the room from a subtle blue to a dull shade of yellow and pink. Beth had already awakened and had just finished putting on a pot of coffee. Satisfied with her efforts, she padded back to the bed and peered down at the sleepy head that looked so warm and peaceful. She gently pulled back the sheet exposing Ben's chest and belly. A devilish smile spread across her lips as she leaned down and gently kissed his right chest, dragging her tongue across his nipple. Slightly raising her head to see if her teasing had had any affect and finding there was none, she moved over to his other side planting gentle kisses as she moved over to his left and most sensitive nipple. A light touch with her tongue and again she gauged the effect; there was none. Something had to be done soon as this bending was killing her back. She took his nipple into her mouth and sucked it gently, then a little firmer. Still nothing! She nibbled it with her teeth and felt him move. She glanced up at him with one eye and caught him smiling.

"You've been awake all along, haven't you?" she asked as she teasingly bit his nipple.

"And good morning to you too," he replied. "How far were you going to go?"

"I was about ready to fetch a glass of cold water," she chuckled.

"Aww you wouldn't do that, would you?"

"Oh yes I would, but I'd warm you back up in the shower."

"Is that an invitation?"

"Would you like some coffee first? I have a fresh pot made."

"Yes, that would be nice. What did you do with my shorts?"

"I just tossed them somewhere; I'll find them." After looking on the floor and under the bed, she suddenly burst out laughing.

"Look where they landed," as she pointed to the wall.

On the wall to the right of the bed is a painting of a sail boat. His shorts were hooked on the top of the painting, appearing to be on the top of the sail mast.

"You couldn't do that again if you tried," he laughed. "Can you reach them?

"Yes, I'll get them," she said, still laughing.

Beth reached up to retrieve his shorts. He admired the way her breasts jutted forward as she reached above her head, her nipples straining her thin nightgown. "I should have awakened her last night," he thought.

He swung his legs out over the bed and pulled on his shorts as Beth handed him a cup of coffee. Sitting down beside him on the edge of the bed, she went over the tentative plans for the day. "Are you hungry, my love?"

"I'm always hungry, especially for you," he replied reaching behind her head gently pulling her face toward him and kissing her cheek.

"You have to wait until later for that. Meanwhile, I'll go start the shower. You can join me and after you get my back squeaky clean we can go down for breakfast."

"Uhh, yeah, something like that! My *back* needs some work, too," he chuckled.

Smiling, she replied, "Okay, I'll get the water started, but why did you think you needed your shorts just to have coffee with me."

Ben stared off into space with a bewildered look on his face. "Yeah, why did I need my shorts?" he thought. He was still shrugging his shoulders as Beth disappeared into the bathroom.

Hearing the water running in the shower, he finished his coffee, returned the cup to the kitchenette and walked into the bathroom. Through the shower door he could see her standing facing the shower head letting the water cascade down the front of her body. Even through the frosted glass of the door, she looked inviting.

"Are you ready for some company?"

"Yes, the water feels wonderful. Did you bring everything with you."

Ben thought for a moment before dropping his shorts to the floor. He wondered what her reaction would be if he would have entered with them still on. Opening the door, the distortion of the glass pane disappeared and he was treated to a vision that caused his heart rate to increase. She was a small woman~~~5'2", no more than 110 pounds, with a distinct flare to her hips from a very trim waist. Small breasts sat high on her chest, proud with pointy pink nipples. Her thighs were tapered nicely to calves that slimmed sharply to petite ankles; her legs exhibited signs of being very athletic, strong and well defined. In her youth her hair had been starkly blond, now hosting traces of gray mixed well among the blond, appearing like a mixture of silver and gold, kept short and neat. She was still a very beautiful woman, carrying her age in a way that defied her years; the sight of her immediately arousing desire in him.

After swallowing hard, he asked, his voice quivering slightly, "Room for one more in here?"

"Yes there is. Did you bring everything with you?" she repeated.

Realizing she had caught him off guard the first time she had asked him, he quickly gathered his wits and replied, "Yeah, even in the expanded version!"

"Oh that's good! It will be easy to clean that way."

He could not contain his laughter. She was so open with him, unafraid to say anything and he loved that immensely. Her sense of humor so closely matched his; in so many ways they were so much alike~~~truly soul mates, if there is such a thing.

"Well, beings it is so easy, I'll just let you have the honors," he laughed.

"First things first, Sweetheart, there is a back side facing you that is in need of your tender touch."

With that, Ben reached around her to take the washcloth in his hands, shivering as he pressed his body against her back, applied some liquid soap to the cloth and began to move it around her back. After liberally soaping her back, he put the cloth aside; using his hands he kneaded and massaged her back with the slippery soap, slowly making his way up to the back of her neck. Beth threw her head back and moaned, "Ohh Ben~~~that feels like heaven."

After applying more soap to the cloth, he shifted his attention lower, to her waist and bottom. He applied the same methods he had used on her back, with an added motion or two that included the top of her thighs. As she turned to face him, the look in her eyes said she was ready for the flip side. He found he didn't need or want the cloth anymore. There was only one way to do this and it involved gentle touches with lots of loving care, without the coarseness of the cloth. The soap added an exotic element, a slick gliding sensation that was soon leaving them both breathless. Her voice was shaking as she moaned, "Ohh honey, my legs are getting weak! We better tend to you before something happens in here."

Reaching behind her, he turned off the shower. Beth picked up the cloth and filled it with soap, spreading it all over Ben's chest, his belly, groin and his legs. Putting the cloth aside she used her hands the same way Ben had with her, administering loving touches and strokes across his chest and belly. Kneeling slightly, she ran her hands up and down his legs, ending at his groin, softly stroking him there until she could sense it was time to quit. Turning around, she turned the shower back on and laughingly, squirted him in the face with the multiple streams of water flowing from the shower head, rinsing him from head to foot. Ben took her shoulders and moved her around under the warm stream, rinsing all the soap from her body. With her back to him, he bent and kissed her back, and the top of her butt. Turning back to him she took him in her hand and caressed him gently and said, "You are squeaky clean now and this is a promise of things to come later," she said as she turned off the shower, opened the shower door and stepped out onto the towel.

"Uhh, what am I supposed to do with this?" he asked with a chuckle.

Beth laughed and replied, "Well, we got it cleaned while all the wrinkles were out of it, so it should be easy to dry off. So get dressed so we can get something to eat. I'm hungry!"

Ben could only smile and shake his head as he stepped out of the shower to grab a towel. He wondered what he loved the most about her; her face and body, or her quick mind. He concluded it was the total package, as he began dressing.

They soon made their way down to the breakfast buffet. For whatever reason, Ben felt he would have a healthier breakfast today, concentrating on fruit and melons. Beth noticed the change, but said nothing for fear he might go back to eating the fattening things. She knew he needed to lose some weight and this was a good start. Beth picked up an extra glass of orange juice as she noticed Ben failed to add one on his tray. Knowing how he loved orange juice, she smiled as she thought how much men needed women to look out for their best interests. She loved doing things for him, wishing she could do more and especially more often.

"You're welcome," Beth smiled at him as they returned to their table and she seated herself.

Ben looked across at her with a bewildered look on his face as he muttered, "For what?"

"For your orange juice; you forgot to get your juice."

"Ohh, yeah I guess I did," he stammered. "Thank you darling; how can I repay you?"

"I've got it all figured out. You can take me shopping after breakfast. We will have some time before we have to leave for our ride to the Grand Hotel and there are so many shops I'd like to visit."

He smiled as the realization she is not unlike other women, struck him that she is in fact very much like all women~~~they love to shop! "Uhh, can I take the juice back?"

Beth laughed, "No sweetheart, it doesn't work that way. You know you will enjoy shopping, too."

"Is that a promise? Do they sell guns out here?"

"I don't know. Maybe we will find out."

After finishing breakfast, they embarked on a journey that Ben felt was going to be a bore. He reluctantly went along, trying to appear interested in her interests as they went in one fudge shop after another. However, they soon entered a neat toy shop and Ben had finally found his niche. This shop not only sells toys, but also allows one to play with them before purchasing them. Ben spotted some yo-yo's and because he had become quite astute with them when he was younger, his eyes lit up. Like riding a bicycle, once learned it comes back rather quickly with very little practice. He found one that looked very well constructed and adapted to doing tricks. It was called the *Fireball* and was made by Yomega. Ben thought that sounded like a good Japanese name and they were experts when it came to yo-yo's.

He picked one up and attached the string to his middle finger of his right hand and flipped it down over the back of his hand for a few test runs to get the feel of this simple, yet amusing toy. The first flip was straight down and resulted in a quick return to his hand. Good! His coordination was still very good as he made a clean catch. His next flip was out somewhat away from his body, causing the yo-yo to 'sleep'. Ben noticed it had good bearings and spun for a very long time before he gave it a tug to bring it back up to his hand. His smile was broad as he decided it was time to see if he still remembered some of the old tricks the Japanese guys taught him back in the 50s. His first was what was called 'Around The world' He flipped it out straight away from his body, causing the yo-yo to rise up over his head, around behind him, back to the front of him and with a slight little twitch of his hand, it returned back to his hand.

Ben grinned as he knew this yo-yo stored up a lot of energy and that it would easily make two trips around the world and still have energy to spare. He then flipped it down sharply and let it sleep, lowering it to touch the floor and 'walked the doggie' toward Beth's feet. She jumped back laughing and before long Ben was drawing a crowd. Returning it to his hand again, he put it to 'sleep', very carefully gathering up the string forming a sort of loop in front of him with the yo-yo still spinning. He gently caused the body to swing back and forth through the loop thus 'Rocking the Baby'. The kids were delighted and begged Ben to teach them how to do that trick. Beth meanwhile tried to pull him away from the crowd. He finished his routine by 'Shooting the Moon', a series of underhand flips out in front of him, back and forth without stopping, rolling his wrist in such a way to continue the motion, slowly moving the arc of the movement upward toward the ceiling. The excellent yo-yo obeyed his every command.

Beth finally succeeded in getting him drawn away and outside the store.

"Where did you learn to do all of that?" she asked.

"When I was in grade school, there was a group of Japanese gentlemen that used to come around selling yo-yo's to us on the school grounds, selling them by demonstrating all the neat things one could do with them. They were terrific! They could work two of them, one in each hand somehow twisting them together in the air, but still separating them and returning them to their hands still spinning. There were so many tricks, only a few of which I learned to do. I never could do anything with my left hand. I used to own a Duncan Yo-yo which was kinda top of the line in those days, but the one I just played with in there would run circles around that old Duncan."

"Well, we didn't find any guns, but there are still a few shops left to go."

"You go ahead. I think I'll sit here and watch traffic go by while you check out the rest of them."

"What's wrong? Did the yo-yo wear you out~~~or are you going back there to play some more?" she laughed.

"No," he chuckled, "my feet are tired~~~that's all."

"Okay. I won't be long," she said as she started off down the street.

After she disappeared from view, Ben got up and went back to a store they had visited earlier. He had spotted a Lover's Knot bracelet made of sterling silver and decided he wanted to buy that for Beth as a surprise later on.

After making his purchase, he stuck it under his sweat shirt hoping Beth would not notice the bulge around the other more natural bulge that resided there and returned to his bench. He returned back not any too soon, as Beth returned and announced that she had seen enough. "We can go see about getting our tickets for the carriage ride to the Grand Hotel now. We are a little early, but we can sit there and rest a while. My feet are tired now."

Ben chuckled, "I never knew women ever got tired shopping."

She reached down to him and took his hand in hers, drawing him to his feet and said, "There was a time I could shop 'till I dropped, but not so much anymore. Come my love, let's go get our tickets."

He smiled as he rose to his feet and together they walked back toward the Carriage Tour Ticket Office. When they arrived, Ben stood back and let Beth take over to negotiate a deal for a private ride that would take them to the Grand Hotel, pick them up after they toured the hotel and enjoyed the buffet lunch served there, then taking them for a tour of the Bluff Cottages, returning them back to the downtown area. Ben was in awe of her negotiating skills as she tried desperately to get the best price possible for a two hour tour. He found himself moving away from her as his ears were burning indicating that he was embarrassed by her maneuvers. He was surprised at the way she handled herself as if she was used to this sort of thing.

Finally she walked back to him with two tickets in her hand and replied, "We will depart in about 15 minutes. Are you excited?"

"Excited? I think my ears are still red! Where did you learn to dicker like that?"

"Oh that comes with dealing with Pharmaceutical salespersons and insurance companies. I've not only had to look out for my own interests, but also those of my patients," she replied. "I didn't embarrass you, did I?"

"I sort of felt like we were Bonnie and Clyde trying to rob the bank," he chuckled. "How did you make out; did you get a good deal?"

"You don't want to know! It was an exercise in futility, but I did get the schedule that we wanted."

"You know, you're a dynamo wrapped in a small package! I learn something new about you every day!"

"Just stick with me sweetheart; we've just begun!"

Soon a carriage arrived and they climbed aboard. The driver smiled and welcomed them and stated, "We're going to the West Bluffs, right?"

Beth replied in a stern voice, "We are going to the Grand Hotel first. *Then* you are taking us to the West Bluffs!"

The driver chuckled and retorted sharply, "Yes Ma'am! We're off to the Grand Hotel".

As the carriage topped the hill, the hotel appeared much larger and more majestic. The wide porch seemed to be endless and Ben found he was again in awe. "Wow! It is much larger than it looks from below. It is so huge and majestic. No wonder it is called the Grand Hotel."

"Don't you remember it from the movie, darling?"

"I guess I was just caught up in the story and missed the scenery. This is really beautiful."

The driver, hearing their conversation turned around and remarked, "I've worked here going on 25 years and I never tire of coming up here. The whole area is so beautiful; just wait until you go inside."

He pulled the carriage up in front of the hotel and brought it to a halt. "Watch your step getting down, Ma'am. Take your time and enjoy. I might not be the one that returns to pick you up for your ride to the Bluffs; if not, you folks have a nice day."

"Thank you," Beth replied, "you just make sure you are the one," she said with a wink. The man smiled and replied, "Yes Ma'am," as he then snapped the reins and departed.

Ben took her hand, turned her toward him and said, "You amaze me; in no time flat, you charmed his socks off," he said with a smile.

"Why are you so surprised? Did you forget what I did to you?"

Ben laughed, "No; how could I ever forget that?"

"Come on, dear; let's go visit the Grand Hotel."

A few steps up the red carpeted stairs put them on the huge front porch. Ben turned around to take in the view of the bay, Lake Huron, the Mackinac Bridge and beyond to Lake Michigan. The steep yet beautifully manicured hills that rolled from one flower garden to the next were inspiring. "Wow, the view from here takes my breath away," he remarked. As he was admiring the view beyond, Beth wondered out loud, "How many bulbs, annuals and perennials had to be tended to each season with such massive flowering areas."

"Huh? Oh, I have no idea," Ben replied.

"I know you don't," she chuckled. Yes it is so beautiful~~~come on, let's go inside."

Ben was beside himself as he entered the huge lobby. My God, he thought; this place reeks of money! "Baby, I don't think I belong here. Someone is going to ask me for my credit card and after they see that, they'll toss me out on my butt."

Beth laughed and added, "Nonsense darling. Remember we aren't staying here; we're just visiting."

Ben gazed down the long lobby at all the various shops and remarked more to himself than to Beth, "You don't even have to go downtown to shop. I wonder how much a beer cost in here."

"What did you say, dear?"

"Oh nothing really; I was wondering where a guy could get a beer in here, but I doubt they sell beer here~~~probably just champagne."

"Oh sweetheart, are you uncomfortable here?"

Ben grinned, "No, I'm just a little out of my league." He then threw out his chest, put a scowl on his face and tried to look important.

"Stop that," Beth retorted with a laugh, "you look fine just the way you are. But I must admit, you look somewhat like a politician with that look."

Ben quickly removed the scowl and lowered his chest. He then took Beth's hand in his; smiled down at her upturned face and replied, "Don't need that! I look pretty important enough just holding onto the hand of the most beautiful woman in the joint! Come with me my princess, we have places to explore!"

They moved down the long lobby viewing the many shops, the tea room and salon as well as a long seating area decorated with lots of foliage. At the east end the walls were covered with historical artifacts covering the past years of the Grand Hotel. They wandered aimlessly through the hotel through the various rooms including a spa, a children's playroom, children's game room, the Terrace Room that was equipped for dining and dancing nightly to a small orchestra and the Geranium Bar Room. Finally working their way back to the front of the lobby, Ben announced, "My feet need a rest. Let's go out and sit on the porch for a while before going down to the gardens."

They found a bench for two and sat down to enjoy the soft early fall breeze that wafted across the porch. Around the entire perimeter of the porch were long white wooden planters bursting with vivid red geraniums. "This place is heavenly, Ben. I wonder what it would be like in the winter."

"Ohh, very cold I would imagine. It gets cold enough in Midland and this island is out in the lake. There is no way I would want to live out here during the winter months. I would think it would be very imposing."

"Yes, I know it would be cold, but can you imagine the snow on these hills and icicles hanging from the railings around this porch?"

"Yes I can and it makes me cold to think about it. A picture would suffice nicely."

Beth laughed and pulled him closer to her saying, "I would keep you very warm," she winked.

"Yeah, and I know where you would park your feet~~~against my back," he laughed.

"Speaking of feet, are yours ready to walk the gardens?"

"I reckon so; the grass will be much softer than those hard floors inside."

They rose and started to make their way down the steps when a handsome black gentleman approached Beth and offered to help her down the steps. "May I give you a hand down the steps, Ma'am?"

"Why yes, thank you! That is very nice of you," she replied.

Ben stood back smiling and watched as they made their way down the steps in front of him. As they reached the bottom, Beth thanked the gentleman then turned to take Ben's hand.

Ben could not contain his remark as he smiled and said, "See what I mean; they all want to take your hand."

"Ohh, that's silly! You're not jealous, are you?'

"No, of course not; I'm just very proud to be with you!"

Beth squeezed his hand when he told her this, sensing he did not fully understand the impact his words sometimes had on her, as he said them so casually like they were just a known fact. But it made her feel so good when he said them and she wanted him to know that.

They began slowly strolling between several flower beds on either side of the wide and winding path they were walking. Beth glanced up to Ben and asked, "Wouldn't it be nice to be married here amongst all of these flowers?"

"Oh, I don't know; seems the guy wouldn't be hooked any firmer here than if a judge hooked 'em in a court house. Just cost a lot more, I guess."

"Hey, you know it would be nice! Besides, look at the money that could be saved by not having to buy any flowers."

"Well, you might not have to buy any, but you sure would be *renting* all of these," Ben teased.

"You're too funny, today!"

"Someone sure spends a lot of time trimming up these bushes forming them into these animal shapes. And do you see what I see? Look over there to your right," he said as he pointed to a flower bed of huge daisies. "I bet I'd go to jail if I pulled one of those."

"Ohh those are so big and beautiful. No, we would not be able to hide that one. The stem is over a half inch in diameter. We shouldn't even be thinking about that," Beth said with a larcenous chuckle.

"I'd have to get some criminal tools~~~like a scissors to cut through that stem," Ben joked. He then bent over to smell of them, but found they were very faint. "One would think they would have a lot of aroma as big as they are, but they don't seem to have much."

"Their beauty is subtle; more like a smiling face of a shy girl," Beth mused.

"Yeah, that's perfect~~~you've nailed it perfectly. The first daisy we found in that clearing in the timber when we were kids. It was a reflection of your face, pure white with a shy, shining smile radiating sunshine from inside. I've never realized that it was like looking into your face until now."

"So~~~you're saying that I look like a daisy~~~like a flower?"

"No no, I'm saying the daisy reminds me of your beauty, so subtle, shy, warm and yet so inviting~~~pure, clean, sweet and fragile, yet durable and enduring. Aw, I can't explain it!"

"No, on the contrary, I think you just did. You aren't aware of the nice things you say, are you, Ben?"

Laughing out loud he replied, "Of course I am! There's a method to my madness. I'm stroking the strings of your heart, knowing it will pay back big dividends later!"

He then took her into his arms and gave her a long, big hug, followed by one of those light tender kisses. Beth was so full of love and happiness at that moment she could not help but wonder how life could get any sweeter~~~or how long it could last. They continued to wander through the gardens and around the swimming pool until Ben decided his stomach would take no more denial. "What time does that buffet start? According to my belly it must be very soon."

"It starts at noon dear and by the time we get back inside, it will be time. Has all this walking worked up an appetite?"

"Yes it has; aren't you hungry?"

"Not really. I could admire these flowers all day long! There are so many and they are so beautiful."

"Let's go eat before you have me picking them," Ben chuckled.

Chapter XIV
Random Thoughts

Upon entering the hotel, they were ushered to the buffet line where they were offered an array of garden salads, fresh vegetables, various dressings, fruit, hot pasta, soups, cheese platters, meats and desserts. Ben knew it was going to be difficult deciding what to choose, but finally after filling their plates, they selected a table and sat down to enjoy the many delights.

"Everything is so delicious and there is so much," Beth remarked. "We are going to be ahead of time for our carriage to return to take us to the Bluff Cottages, but I know what we can do while we are waiting."

"I'm almost afraid to ask," Ben groaned.

Beth put down her fork and smiled across at him. "I know you spotted that Wine Bar we passed earlier and I think I saw you lick your lips. We could go back there and sample some of the wines. Now that wasn't such a bad idea, was it?"

"I didn't think you saw the Wine Bar. I wasn't going to suggest it, but beings you have~~~"

"I know," she cut him off with a laugh; "it was the farthest thing from your mind."

After finishing their lunch, they found their way back to the Parlor Room and the eight foot entrance to the Audubon Wine Bar. To Ben's delight, wine was not the only spirit served, as the best single malt scotches and fine Kentucky bourbons were also available.

"No wonder I was licking my lips," Ben said as he eyed the bottle of Makers Mark. Beth went along with him as they bellied up to the bar.

"What'll you have, sir?" was the question Ben had not heard for quite some time.

"Oh, I'll have a double Maker on the rocks and whatever my lady prefers."

"Could I just have a glass of water please? I'm not much of a drinker," Beth added.

"You sure can Ma'am~~~whatever you like; ice with the water?"

"No thank you; no ice."

After the bartender returned with their drinks, Ben picked up the glass holding the dark amber liquor and held it in front of him as he said to Beth, "I may never be able to toast you in a more conventional way, so I'll drink not only to your health, but also long life and every happiness. To the most wonderful person I have ever known. You so richly deserve the very best of life. I hope you are always as happy as you are this very moment." With that said he put the glass to his lips and took a small sip.

Beth smiled and lifted her glass of water in front of her and said to him, "I raise my glass of low octane water and offer a toast to the person who has brought me to the happiest time of my life, by teaching me how to love without reservation~~~and that he does not drink too much of that whisky," she paused, then continued with a wink, "because I have plans for you later."

Ben laughed heartily and the barkeep hearing her toast burst out laughing as well and added, "Not to worry ma'am! I'll shut him off after this one!"

Ben smiled at her, "There's no way I would want to do anything to ruin those plans. A drink like this really relaxes me and makes me mellow. I might even start talking to the horse when the carriage driver returns," he chuckled.

"You're joking, I hope."

Turning to face her head on, he took both her hands in his, looked into her eyes and said in the most serious voice he could muster, "Yes, of course I am." He paused as he searched her eyes, first one, then the other before adding, "However, if I hear the horse talking to me~~~we're both in trouble." He winked and laughed when he saw the expression on her face change from one of seriousness to a wide smile, her laughter joining his.

"You are so full of it! I never know what you are going to say next~~~and I love that!"

"I know you do. I just love to hear you laugh. Your laughter makes me feel really good inside."

"Oh, look at the time; we better get out to the porch or we'll miss our ride." Ben finished his bourbon, left a tip nodding to the barkeep, "She talked me out of having another."

"Good choice," he laughed, "what she has planned for you sound better than anything I have here! You folks have a good day."

Walking out on the front porch with some time to spare, Beth took his hand and led the way to a seat, settling in to await the arrival of their carriage. She looked at him, smiled broadly and asked, "Do you think there is anybody else our age that behaves like we do?"

"Oh yes; I remember this old couple once when I was a kid that used to almost sit on each other's lap when they would watch black and white TV~~~holding hands munching on Planter's peanuts. I think they had been married at least 50 years back then."

"I mean people our age~~~not old people."

Ben looked at her with raised eyebrows before speaking. "Honey, if they had been married 50 years and were married when they were 20, they would be close to our age."

Beth shrugged and replied, "But, I don't feel old with you." Then in a stern voice she added, "We are not old and I don't think that couple you are talking about thought they were old either. They were just still very much in love with each other." She paused and then continued, "Love keeps people young; we will never be old."

Realizing he was not going to win points with her over this subject, he quickly added, "No, I don't think we will ever be old either, but I can't help wonder how much time we have left."

"That's why we have to take advantage of every moment we have together," she relied. "Is that our carriage coming up the hill?'

As it drew closer, Ben could see the driver and recognized him as being the one who brought them here. "Yep, I think that is ours, even though he has some passengers on board."

"Well, let's go down then, but don't you dare say anything to that horse."

Ben laughed out loud knowing that she had already read his mind. "Ohh, you spoiled it! How did you know that is what I was going to do?"

"I'm getting wise to you," she laughed. "I can't always know what you are going to say or do, but I figured you were going to say something to that horse."

"What am I supposed to do if that horse starts talking to me from his back side again?"

"If that happens, just ignore it," she laughed.

"Remember you said that," he quipped with a wink.

The carriage pulled up next to them and the driver brought it to a halt. "I picked up a couple of hitch-hikers on the way; hope you don't mind."

"No, not at all," Beth replied as she took Ben's hand to help her board the carriage.

After they were seated, the driver looped the reins with a little snap, and the horse continued onward.

"Folks, we're on our way to the West Bluff area. In 1895 this island became the state of Michigan's first state park. The Mackinac Island State Park Commission leased some of the lots on the bluffs for the construction of some summer cottages. These Victorian cottages were built by wealthy Midwestern families. As you will see, they are multi-storied with architectural designs that include wraparound porches, gables and stained glass windows, thus the term 'cottages' are a bit of understatement. You will find my description is also an understatement."

As they drew closer to their destination, the driver continued, "There are 16 cottages on the West Bluff and were built between 1886 and 1891 and include a variety of styles such as Queen Ann, Classical Revival, Shingle Style and Carpenter Gothic. They are all built with Michigan White Pine. While they are privately owned, the Park Commission lease requires that the architecture must remain unchanged and must comply with The Secretary of Interior Standards for Historic Preservation."

As the cottages came into view, Beth inhaled sharply. "Oh my gosh! They are fabulous! Does anyone live in them?"

"The owners can do with them as they wish as long as they don't change anything. They could stay over the winter months I suppose, but it is not a very comfortable place during the winter," the driver responded. "I don't stay here, that's for sure."

Beth leaned against the back of the carriage seat and was quiet for a while, her thoughts wondering far away from this island. Instead of the winter scene the driver had just instilled into her mind, she closed her eyes and a vision of daisies in a warm clearing with rays of sunshine filtering through the trees, overwhelmed her thoughts.

She saw a young boy and girl getting up off of the grass, the girl clutching a daisy in her hand. She reached out to grasp the boy's hand but the distance between them grew wider the more she stretched and reached. The boy was quickly leaving her behind until he disappeared from view. The girl suddenly became frightened and felt lost and alone. She turned to her right, then her left, but could not find her way. Collapsing on the ground, she began sobbing uncontrollably. Where did he go and why did he leave her like this?

"Are you all right honey? Ben asked as he took her hand in his. "You're very quiet all at once and you're trembling."

Beth opened her eyes, looked up to his face and replied, "Oh, I'm fine. I was just thinking about something, that's all."

"What were you thinking about that would make your eyes water so? Are you sure you feel okay?"

"Yes, I feel fine; I was just thinking how happy I am being here with you."

The carriage turned and started making its way back toward the downtown area. The clack-clack of the horse hooves was melodic and soothing to Beth, as she wondered what the thoughts meant that rushed through her head just moments before. She surveyed the beauty surrounding them as they made their way back to the carriage depot. They disembarked, thanked the driver and then slowly walked toward the various shops.

"Where would you like to go for dinner this evening," Beth asked.

"I don't have a preference but after eating so much during lunch, I'm really not very hungry. What do you think?"

"I think if you are not very hungry, I should check to see if you are not feeling well," she laughed, "but you did pig out during lunch. Maybe we could check out a little soup and salad shop I saw earlier yesterday. They have some light entrées and we should be able to find something that isn't too filling."

"That sounds fine, but I would like to go back to the room for a short while to rest my feet. I think I might have a blister on my heel."

"Oh, yes; let's go back and I'll have a look at it," Beth replied.

She had noticed he was walking with a slight limp and was hoping she could get him off of his feet before the blister broke open. She smiled a devilish smile at the thought she was going to have an opportunity to perform a medical service on him. "This is going to be fun," she thought.

After entering their room, Beth announced, "Take your shoes off and sit on the chair over here; the doctor is in the house. Now let me have a look at that heel."

Ben did as she instructed, and moved to the chair. Beth supported his foot with a hand under his calf. "Ohh, looks like we are going to have to perform some surgery on this," she mused quietly to herself.

"What? It's~~~only a blister! I've had them many times. It will go away on its own."

"But honey, this is a big one! I think I'm going to have to lance it."

"Ohhhh, nooo you ain't!" Give me back my sock!"

Beth laughed and replied, "Oh sweetheart, I'm just teasing you. I'll wash it off and open it to release the water. Then apply some antibiotic and dress it with a Band-Aid. That's better than having it burst while you are walking. You won't feel a thing. Haven't you done that before?"

"I don't remember. This is the first blister I've had in years. I must have had a wrinkle in my sock or something."

It was clear to Beth that he did not want to talk about the blister. Instead, she cleaned it, opened it and applied the antibiotic and a Band-Aid.

"Do you always carry a first aid kit in your purse?" Ben laughed.

"Yes, I do. You know what they say about an ounce of prevention."

Ben put on a clean pair of socks and a different pair of shoes.

"How does it feel? Do you think you can walk okay without irritating it any further?" Beth asked.

He walked across the room, turned and walked back to her. He took her hands in his, helped her off the chair, took her into his arms and kissed her full on the mouth. As an afterthought, he ended the kiss with a single tiny peck, smiled at her and said, "Doc, that will have to hold you until you send me a bill."

Recovering from the surprise, she laughed and replied, "Are you sure you can afford me?"

"No I'm not, but I hope my credit is good with you. I'm willing to work it off in any way you see fit."

"Ohhh, I think I have a number of ways you can do that. And yes, your credit is very good with me."

"Good! Now that all the finances are settled and I can walk again without pain, my appetite has returned. Let's go eat!"

Beth smiled as she took his hand and headed for the door. "That sounds more like the guy I love so much. Just give me a second to freshen up my face."

Before Ben could think about sitting down, she was ready. He could only shake his head in disbelief as he had never known a woman that was so efficient. He opened the door and they were off to dinner. Ben was happy to find the soup and salad shop Beth had discovered earlier was only a couple of blocks from their hotel, very near the docks.

After they entered and were seated, Ben found there were a multitude of soups, fresh greens and salad toppings offered. He was pointing this out to Beth as the waitress approached to take their order. Beth already knew what she wanted, deciding to build herself a Mediterranean-type salad with mixed greens, feta cheese, black olives, tomatoes and cucumbers. Her soup choice was cream of broccoli and her drink was water without ice, as usual.

Ben listened intently and rather than come up with something differently, he decided to go with what Beth was going to have except he was not going to have cucumbers~~~or water. He opted for a big vanilla milkshake. Beth raised her eyebrows, but said nothing.

"I thought I'd better exercise a little restraint," Ben quipped, "I had them hold the cucumbers and chocolate."

Beth shook her head from side to side, struggling to contain her laughter. She knew he should not have the milkshake, but could not find it in herself to criticize him. She was aware he knew he shouldn't, but he was having fun and she did not want to spoil his mood.

They ate quietly, both glancing at the other and smiling. Ben had noticed before how dainty she was when she was eating, slowly and making each bite look tastier than it really was. He could tell she enjoyed eating, but did not overeat. Even though he was eating the same thing, he knew his was not as good.

When they arrived back to their room, it was already dark, and moonlight filtered into the windows. Ben flipped on the lights and went into the bathroom. Beth crossed over to the TV and turned it on to check the weather and local news. She heard water running in the shower and moving back to the bathroom, she spoke through the door, "Are you getting into the shower?"

"Yes, would you care to join me?"

"I think I had better~~~so the temperature is adjusted properly," she laughed.

"Yeah that's right and my back needs some attention, too."

Beth quickly undressed and joined him in the shower. It was so strange how she so enjoyed showering with him especially since she had always preferred this to be a very private thing. Just one of many things she was finding so different in her life since they had found each other.

"Ben, did you shower with Helen when you were younger?"

"Oh yeah, I guess we did a few times~~~but not often. Our first apartment didn't have a shower; just a bath tub. Then Julie came along and there was never time for that sort of thing. I think showering was a time for solitude and a time to reflect on the day, so we seldom did it together."

He added some soap to the wash cloth and began washing her back before continuing, "We started drifting apart shortly after that and not only didn't shower together, didn't do much of anything else either. That was my fault. We argued a lot~~~had plenty of that. But what about you~~~did you shower together with Jerry?"

"No, I never liked showering with anyone. I always felt it was something very private, like using the toilet. I enjoyed the private time," she responded.

"What about now; would you prefer to shower alone?"

"No! I want to spend every possible moment with you and I enjoy the touch of your hands on my body. I actually look forward to this time with you."

"I do too~~~besides I can't reach my back to wash it, so I need the help. And we both know how inept I am at adjusting the water temperature."

"So, are those the only reasons you want me in the shower with you?" she asked with a chuckle.

"Uhhh no, not exactly. Those are just a couple of extras. There are a few other areas besides my back that you seem to wash better than I do. You get me much cleaner and I love washing your~~~back."

"I hope we always enjoy this~~~and this," she said as she washed him in one of those aforementioned areas.

"You can put me in the ground when I stop enjoying that," he said, his voice shaking. "But I think we will maintain privacy while sitting on the throne."

"Yes! Exactly!"

"Did you ever see or use an outhouse when you were younger? The old wooden kind that was so prevalent in the country?" he asked.

"Yes, I hated those spider infested places. I remember one that had a wasp nest in the upper corner near the door. I couldn't get out of there quick enough."

"I always wondered why they had two holes. Did anyone ever share that moment? Or was it just for emergencies?" he asked with a bewildered look on his face.

Beth was flabbergasted and could not contain her laughter. "Only you could come up with something like that. I never gave it a thought, but maybe there was his and hers as she didn't want to sit where he might have splattered. You know how guys are."

Ben winced at that statement, but knew it was true. "I remember seeing one that had a seat attached for that purpose. Must have been the first time a guy heard the command to lower the seat when he was done."

"I'll take your word for it, honey. This has been a very enlightening shower, but I think I'm ready to get out and move on to other more educational endeavors."

Ben was still smiling as she stepped out of the shower. He followed her, took the towel and rubbed her back and legs down to her feet. He then reached over to the counter and picked up some body lotion and applied a liberal amount on his hands, applying it on her thighs and lower legs. He sat on the stool as she raised each leg to him, one at a time as he worked the lotion in and around her legs.

"When we get in bed, I'll do this to your back, too," he said.

Beth then wrapped her terrycloth robe around her body, stepped into her slippers and moved into the bedroom area. Ben finished drying his feet and examined the blister on his heel. It looked good, but he knew she would want to put a new dressing on it after he joined her. As soon as he approached her sitting on the bed, he noticed her first aid kit in her hand and instructed him to sit next to her on the side of the bed and place his foot up on her lap. Ben had only wrapped a towel around his waist and he suddenly became exposed when he lifted his foot to her lap.

"What a position I'm in now," he laughed. "I must look pretty silly like this."

"I think you look pretty enticing and sexy," she replied. "I wish I had a picture of this. You look like something from the Roman empire days."

Ben laughed, "You mean like a Gladiator? Or more like a Christian after the lions got hold of him?"

"No, I was thinking of the lavish times in Rome when guys sat around in those short loin cloths flashing the ladies every once in a while," she giggled.

"Well. I think I'm more than flashing you~~~I'm overexposed!"

"I know you are and I love it! So do you!"

After Beth applied another coating of some medicated cream, she put another Band-Aid over Ben's blister, then stood up and removed her robe before lying down on the bed. "Now we're even," she smiled.

Ben retrieved the body lotion, leaned back on his elbow and gently moved her over onto her stomach. He removed the towel from around his waist and straddled her body, applied the lotion onto his hands and then to her back. Starting at her neck, he began a slow and methodical massage, moving down her spine, kneading and applying pressure on both sides of her back, moving down to her buttocks. He then gently massaged first one, then the other, squeezing and kneading them until he heard her moan. Looking at the side of her face, he saw that her eyes were closed and that she was totally relaxed. He lifted his body off of her, bent down to plant a departing kiss on her rump and then lay down beside her. Beth rolled over onto her side and faced him, kissing his lips before reaching down to the foot of the bed and pulled a sheet up over them. Lying back beside him again, she looked into his eyes and asked, "Ben, what is going to become of us? What happens when we have to leave here?"

Ben was quiet a long time before he answered. "I don't know, baby~~~I just don't know. We'll just have to wait and see."

"But~~~will we see each other again? We have no plans."

"How can we plan when we both have other obligations? Honey, fate somehow brought us together for whatever reason. I have to trust fate has something in store for us beyond here and now. Maybe we can get away again later." As he said this, he knew that the likelihood of that happening was very remote.

"Time is not on our side sweetheart. If I would retire and move to Midland could we~~~"

"And you become my mistress? What would you do when I couldn't see you? How would you keep busy? You would miss your work with the children!" Ben's face was red as he cut her off with such veracity, as the thought of keeping her as a mistress was not the vision he had of her. He paused to allow his pulse to slow before adding in a more gentle tone, "I don't know honey~~~I just don't know."

But Beth would not let it drop there, touching his face as she replied, "Maybe I could find some work in Midland; maybe help in the pediatric ward at the hospital."

Ben's mind was tired. He had been worrying about the same things, but had not brought them up as he didn't want to think about them yet. "I'm tired my love. Just stay close to me so we can snuggle."

Beth put her head on his shoulder and her left leg across his belly. She ran her hand across his chest combing the hair between her fingers. Soon she could tell from his breathing that he was asleep. Tears ran from her eyes as the realization swept over her that this may be the last time she would know this joy. Her eyes were still wet when she closed them and found sleep.

Chapter XV
Sailing

The pale blue glow of moonlight that had splashed over the couple while they slept, gave way to the yellow and orange of the first sign of dawn. Beth again was the first to awaken, as she opened her eyes feeling both elation of another day with Ben, yet sadness that today was the last full day they would spend together on this romantic island. She was lying on her back and Ben had rolled over onto his right side. His breathing was very shallow and regular, telling the doctor in her that he was still asleep. Her right arm was next to his back feeling both the warmth of his body and the expansion of his chest as he breathed. She rolled over to her right side pressing her body up against his back, placing her arm across his waist, letting her hand lightly rub his lower belly. She was hoping to wake him this way; lightly kissing the back of his neck.

His sleep was more of a light doze, so he soon became aware of her actions. He smiled as he thought he would feign sleep to see what else she would do to arouse him. But what he was not aware of was the fact that Beth was much attuned to the sound and feel of his breathing and sensed that he was awake. She remembered he had done this before, so this time she was going to get the best of him.

She rolled back over onto her back and made sounds as though she had gone back to sleep. Ben, now thinking that he had blown an opportunity, waited a few seconds to be sure she was sleeping, then carefully rolled over to his left side. With Beth lying on her back, he had ample access to the complete playground. With his right index finger tip, he very lightly touched her throat, slowly moving it down the center of her chest, to her navel, but stopping short of going any further. He made very light, little circles around her navel while he watched her face for any sign of reaction. There was none.

He then moved his finger tip back to her face and lightly traced the curve of her lips. He thought he detected a slight movement of her eyelids. Rising up on his left elbow, he leaned over her and gently brought his lips down to hers giving her a light, gentle kiss. Beth's arms encircled his shoulders bringing his body down across her chest, returning his kiss.

"You're awake," he mused. "I thought you were awake earlier."

Beth chuckled and replied, "I know you did. You were playing possum with me again. It was my turn to play with you," she said with a wink.

"I love playing with you. I wish we could wake up every day like this. Did you sleep well?"

"Yes I did. I was awake early and watched the sunrise. It was beautiful."

"You didn't get out of bed, did you?"

"No, I just watched the colors in the room change. It was a nice feeling lying here close to you; it was so peaceful."

Ben rolled back onto his side and ran his hand down the length of her body, feeling the softness of her skin and the fullness of her breasts. She rolled over to her right side pressing her body against his, and putting her left leg across his thighs.

"Will we always be limber enough to do this," she asked.

Ben laughed heartily, "I just hope we have the opportunity." Then his laughter erupted again, "I also hope we never mistake the Ben-Gay for the K-Y!"

"Oh my~~~oh my goodness! We will have to make sure one is kept in the bathroom and the other next to the bed!" she laughed.

"All this laughter is making me hungry. What's on the program for today?"

"Are you satisfied with the breakfast buffet we have here at the hotel?" she asked.

"Oh yes, that is fine; there is plenty of good stuff to eat there."

"I thought for lunch we could go to that little bistro we saw near the ferry boat docks. There were some people sitting at the outside tables and that looked so very inviting. But for this morning, we could go shopping if your heel feels up to it. Let me have a look."

Ben, still naked as a jaybird, sat up on the bed and raised his foot up to her. Beth laughed and said, "It is amazing how comfortable we are with each other. I thought we would have to do everything in complete darkness and look at you now."

"Well, I figure you're a doctor and you're used to this sort of thing; you see it all of the time, right?"

Beth laughed and replied, "Well, not exactly like this. The ones I see are just a little bit smaller."

"Oh, just a little bit, huh?"

"Yes, just a little bit," she winked. "Now hold still and let me take a peek at that heel. I've already had a peek at the rest of you and I approve."

Ben smiled and felt his chest swell with the pure joy of her. He truly loved this woman and enjoyed the fun they shared with each other. When he felt these feelings, it brought tears to his eyes. He knew there was nothing he would not do for her except the thing he wanted the most; and that was not possible.

"It looks good; I think we can put another dressing on it and be careful how we walk and limiting the amount. I will be easy on you today," she promised. "Maybe best you bypass the shower this morning so you can keep it dry."

"Yes, you are probably right. You go ahead and I'll shave while you shower, then we can get down for some badly needed nourishment. If you want, I can reach in and do your back."

"Yeah, I bet you would. But you would not just do my back and you know it. You would be in there too, so put that thought on hold for later."

Ben chuckled as he got up off the bed and turned on the TV to check the news and weather. He knew she was right and it was best she showered alone this morning, aware she would be in and out of the shower before he finished shaving.

Beth picked up her robe and headed for the bathroom. The news as usual was gloomy, but the weather forecast was great; they were going to have another beautiful day on the island. As expected, Beth was already out of the shower and dressing before Ben had taken care of the prickly devils on his face. He put things in high gear and found Beth waiting for him to depart for breakfast.

"For someone who was so hungry, it sure takes you a while to get ready for breakfast," she quipped with a wink. He merely smiled a sheepish grin and announced he had decided he would eat a little healthier this morning.

Taking his hand they left the room and made their way to the cafeteria. She was impressed as she watched him select more fruit and less fat, taking just one small serving of scrambled eggs without the bacon or sausage. He had his usual glass of OJ and coffee. Beth finished her usual breakfast of fruit and cereal with a banana. Ben watched her work on the banana and marveled at the entertainment she was inadvertently providing for him. There were just some things that would never be quite the same after spending time with her and this was just one of those things. How could he ever eat a banana again without this vision engrained in his mind? He wondered if she knew what she was doing to him.

Finally finishing the banana, Beth looked at Ben as he was sipping his coffee. "Are you ready to go shopping? There are just a few shops I wanted to check out. You may not want to go inside of them, but you can sit outside on one of the benches and wait for me. Then we will get some more of that famous fudge."

"Oh that's fine; I'm ready to go. I don't mind waiting while you shop. I would never deny you one of woman's most treasured desires," he winked.

"Oh, you are too kind, sir," she laughed. "Shall we go, then?"

Leaving the hotel the early morning air felt crisp and clean. "Do we need a sweater," Ben asked. "It's supposed to be pretty warm again today."

"No, I don't think so, she replied as she looked up to the top of his head. "Do you think you need your hat?" she asked with a chuckle.

"I might when I walk past those gulls. I still think they look at me as a practice landing strip."

Beth soon approached the first shop that she wanted to browse. "There is a bench right over there with a beautiful view of the bay. You can relax and wait for me there~~~and I promise I won't be too long sweetheart."

"Oh honey, don't hurry. Take your time and enjoy. I will be fine out here; the sun feels wonderful."

Ben walked across the street to the bench as Beth entered the shop. He now felt he had some time to think about what Beth had asked him before they fell asleep the night before. The more he thought about that question, the more the answer evaded him. The solution was more than what he wanted~~~much more than that. Selfishness had brought such disarray into his life, living long ago with the gnawing, aching pain of self-loathing brought about by the infidelities of his past. It was not until he found Beth that he came to grips with why he had failed so miserably in his marriage. He knew he could not live without Beth~~~not anymore~~~but he also knew he could not abandon the woman he had committed to all those years before~~~not when she was totally dependent on him for her every need. If he did, he could never forgive himself as the beauty he now shared with Beth would be forever marred and damaged.

No matter how much he thought about it, the answer would not come to him. There was no simple answer; no magic 'fix all' presented itself that would address all the concerns and problems that confronted them. Fate brought them together again in a way that was both beautiful and cruel. What the future held for them, he did not know. Fate would have to supply the answer, as he knew that he could not. He did not want to lose her~~~not ever again~~~but he knew he would never truly have her~~~or would he? He was shaking his head as she walked up and sat down beside him.

"Hi Shannon~~~what a surprise; where's John?"

"Oh, we separated," she laughed.

"Already? This place is supposed to bond a couple together, not separate them," Ben replied.

"Oh, just for a while. I was doing some shopping and John went to get the tickets for some Catamaran sailing this afternoon. Where is Beth?"

"She went shopping too. I think we are going sailing later today, as well. She had mentioned that earlier, so I guess she still wants to go. She used to sail when she was a child, but it's been a long time ago. Her father taught her and she loved to do that."

"Look who I ran into," Beth announced as she and John approached the two of them.

"Yes, I see that, and I found John's other half," Ben winked. Shannon just told me they are going sailing later today; weren't we thinking about doing that, too?"

"Yes we were and when I ran into John he told me about their plans to go sailing as he was getting their tickets. I hope you don't mind darling, but I went ahead and purchased two for us as well. We are all scheduled to go at 2:00pm this afternoon."

"Oh, that's great~~~really great! John, can you swim in case I go over board?" Ben chuckled.

"Yeah, I got you covered. I was a state champion swimmer in high school and competed in college. Actually I was a diver, but all that means is I will get to you right away," he laughed.

"Do you kids have any plans for lunch?" Beth asked.

"No, not yet," Shannon replied.

"We are going to an outside bistro down by the boat docks. Want to join us?" Beth asked.

"Shannon glanced over to John and John shrugged, "Sounds good to me. I have a few more stops to make before lunch, so why don't we meet back here around~~~say~~~12:30?"

"Great! See you then," Ben said. "Good to see you kids again!"

As they left, Ben turned to Beth and asked, "What would you like to do until Noon?"

"Does your heel feel good enough for a little walking?"

"Well it does right now, but I don't know how well it will hold up. I guess I'll just have to give it a try and see how it goes. What did you have in mind?"

"I'd like to take you back to one of the shops I went into earlier. It is not very far from here and there are some shirts I want to show to you. I want to see if you like the same one I liked when I was looking through them."

"What sort of shirts are you talking about?"

"They are T-shirts with different scenes on them and I know how you like to wear T-shirts."

"All right my dear~~~lead the way," Ben said as he rose from his bench. Beth took his hand and smiled as she led the way. After they entered, Ben immediately noticed the huge array of souvenirs and keepsakes that the shop offered. Beth led him to a rack that held many T-shirts with various scenes of the island and its many attractions.

"Just look through these shirts, sweetheart and let me know which one you like the best," Beth said, with a hint of excitement in her voice. Not knowing exactly what she was after, he busied himself moving them apart until he found one that he took from the rack, holding it up and examining it more closely.

"I like this one, but I haven't seen them all yet," he reported. It was a scene apparently taken from the perspective of the Grand Hotel overlooking the bay area and the docks. He laid it aside and continued looking through the remaining shirts. The last one then caught his eye and he instantly smiled and stated, "This is the one; I like this one~~~no doubt about it!"

Ben had selected a scene of a flower bed, either around the Grand Hotel, or perhaps the one behind their hotel. It was a bed of daisies in full bloom in bright sunlight, with the centers dark brown and happy looking. The flower bed was surrounded by lush green grass that was so inviting it conjured up a desire to lie down next to the daisies to soak up the warm sunshine.

"This brings back memories~~~beautiful memories," he said as he looked at Beth with eyes that were glistening from the moisture that was suddenly forming in them.

Beth was elated as it was the one she had picked out as well. "It is yours darling; I want to get it for you."

"But honey, I wouldn't be able to wear it or explain where I purchased it."

"Nonsense, you could have purchased it anywhere during your trip; it doesn't indicate it came from here."

"Yes, I guess that's true. I wish we didn't have to be so secretive."

"Are you feeling guilty?" she asked, concerned that he might.

"No, I feel that for the first time in my life I'm doing what is right~~~really right. It's just that I don't want to hurt anybody. We've been all through this before."

"I know dear and neither do I~~~and we won't." She was suddenly sad as she knew the ones who hurt from their relationship are the two of them. Their time together is sweet and fulfilling, but the long absences are so painful. And she is filled with the gnawing angst that they do not have the benefit of time.

"So, do I get to buy it for you?" she asked with the smile returning to her face.

"Yes of course, if it will make you happy."

"It will make me very happy. I want to buy clothes for you."

"Well, let me look around here and see if I can find a garter belt for you and some real sexy black hose," he laughed.

Beth laughed and replied, "Oh I hated those things. We used to have to wear them before pantyhose and I truly hated them."

"Well heck, you wouldn't have to wear it very long~~~just for a few minutes," he winked.

"We don't need any of that~~~besides I doubt they sell any of that here. I better buy this and get you out of here before you get any other ideas like that," she laughed.

While Beth took her selection to the cash register, Ben looked around the rest of the shop. There was a little bit for every taste, but he was glad he had already purchased the bracelet for her. He decided he would give it to her later this evening during dinner.

"Well, did you find any garter belts," she asked as she walked up next to him. Ben laughed and replied, "No, but I asked that clerk over there if they had any. She sent a stock boy back to the warehouse to look for some. It might take a while for him to find them as I doubt if he knows what they look like."

"You did not!"

"Yeah, I did, but I don't think she knew what I was talking about, either."

The look on Beth's face was one of disbelief and amusement. Ben could not keep a straight face or maybe it was his eyes that gave him away. Whatever it was, Beth's face finally broke into a broad smile as she took his arm and said, "Come along dear; time to go."

Grinning broadly as he took her hand, he looked down to her face and said, "I love you! I have so much fun with you! You are a pure delight!"

She returned his smile and replied, "I love you, too. I've never laughed so much before."

They soon returned to the bench they had left earlier, continuing to hold hands as they waited for John and Shannon to return. Beth leaned up to Ben and kissed his cheek. He smiled, then leaned down and kissed her lips. Beth then said, "If somebody sees this, they might think we are in love."

"They will be right!" Ben replied. "They will be right!"

"Well, look at the lovebirds," John said as he and Shannon approached them seeing Ben's arm around Beth's shoulders.

"Hey, you're early," Ben said looking at his watch.

"Yes, I covered a few of the places I wanted to visit, but Shannon wanted to get back and talk with Beth."

"Well John, you'll learn about women as you go along; they love to talk," Ben quipped, feeling an elbow in his ribs. "Ouch! What was that for?"

"Don't pay any attention to him Shannon. They like to talk, too," Beth said with a broad smile on her face.

"Yes, I know they do, especially about cars, fishing, hunting and things that don't much interest me," Shannon replied. "I guess that's normal."

"What do you say we get on over to that eatery where we can all sit down around the table, the ladies can talk and you and I can lie about cars, fishing, hunting and all that stuff," Ben suggested.

"Yes, we might as well get over there and find a good table," John added. "Shall we go, ladies?"

The ladies took the lead as Ben and John fell in behind them. "Is this the way things are after being married for a long time?" John asked.

"Well, no~~~not necessarily. You'll find your marriage will be mostly what *you* make it. I've heard some say it's a 50-50 proposition, but I disagree. I think the woman usually gives more if it is going to last, but the guy has to learn to yield as well. If you have a good woman to start with, she will go over and beyond what has to be done to hold everything together. Just love her, John. Show her all the respect that you do now and *never* take her for granted."

"Is that how Beth has been to you all of these years?"

Ben was quiet before he answered. "Beth and I never married. I've loved her for over 55 years, but we've never married."

"But why not; I don't understand."

"I guess I didn't want to ruin a perfect relationship," Ben said with a chuckle.

John laughed, and was not satisfied with what Ben had told him, but didn't pursue it~~~at least not right now.

Beth and Shannon were still chatting as they entered the patio area of the bistro, while Ben took the lead, guiding them to a table to the side of the patio, offering some shade as well as some broken sunshine. John, being the perfect gentleman, pulled the chair out for Shannon. Ben suddenly felt guilty as he had not been doing that for Beth. Too many years of absent mindedness had led to neglect in that regard. Hurriedly, he rushed over to Beth's chair and grabbed it before she could pull it out from under the table.

"Thank you John," she responded.

Ben was bewildered; what was she thanking John for?

"Uhhh, you're welcome, my dear; I'm Ben."

Beth laughed as she sat down. "I know sweetheart; I was thanking John for reminding you to be the gentleman I know you are."

"Seems like we were talking about that very thing, weren't we John?"

"Actually, you were doing the talking~~~I just listened," he laughed. "It was what you said that reminded me to seat Shannon."

"Oh really; what was that about," asked Beth

"Yes, I think I'd like to know what that was all about, too," replied Shannon.

"I don't know anything about that; we were just talking about showing the ladies how to bait a hook, right John?" Ben winked.

"Yeah, something like that," John smiled. "Speaking of which, do you do much fishing, Ben?"

"No, not so much anymore; I used to when I was younger, but it seemed like time got away from me."

Beth looked at Shannon with a befuddled look on her face. Both women knew that somehow the men had very skillfully avoided the questions. Shannon leaned across to Beth and asked, "What just happened?"

"I think they think they pulled a fast one over on us. But we can get them later when they aren't expecting it~~~one on one," she winked. "You'll catch on in time, dear."

Shannon smiled, feeling her affection for Beth growing stronger as she came to know her more and more. The conversation between Ben and John became more engrossed and the two women found they too were enjoying each other's views and opinions on so many things that only interest women. Both couples were so into their conversations they hardly noticed the waitress approach to take their order.

"Excuse me; would you like to order now?"

"Ohh, I'm sorry. I think we had better stop talking so much and take a look at the menu," Beth replied.

After a quick glance at the menu, Beth ordered a Chicken Caesar Wrap and tomato soup while Ben decided to have the same. Shannon ordered for the two of them and it is doubtful John knew what he was going to get. As soon as the waitress left with their order, the four of them launched back into their respective conversations until their lunches arrived. The conversations continued, but were more a four way now that they were eating. After lunch was over, they continued their conversations until it was time to keep their appointment for the Catamaran sailing.

Ben picked up the tab as they made their departure and John covered the tip. As they made their way to the docking area, Ben walked with Beth this time, holding her hand as they walked. John and Shannon followed behind, John taking his cue and took Shannon's hand in his. Shannon smiled and was very happy that they had met this older couple, still not understanding the seemingly strange relationship they have. She knew they were not married, yet she knew they were very close and their relationship was a long lasting one. She also knew she wanted to know more about them, but didn't quite know how to bring the subject up without appearing nosy.

They arrived at the dock and were helped aboard the Catamaran. Even with the outriggers, Ben felt the small body rock from side to side as he moved to sit down. Soon all were aboard, the captain unfurled the sail and the boat slowly moved away from the dock. Ben was intent on how a sailboat could use the prevailing wind to go where the skipper wanted it to go. He knew nothing about tacking, or coming about, or any of the sailing jargon. He only hoped he would not ask too many questions.

They moved further out into the bay and away from the docks; the wind picked up and Ben noticed that the sail was fully filled and expanded in a peculiar relationship with the axis of the boat.

"It seems like the wind would push us over the way the wind is blowing right now," Ben remarked.

"It might if it wasn't for the keel, a very heavy structure that extends under the boat that resembles a sail," Beth replied. "And the outrigger also helps to prevent us from tipping over. Are you nervous, darling?"

"No~~~John said he'd save me if we go overboard," he laughed. "But that water is pretty cold!"

Ben watched intently as the skipper kept manipulating a small sail in the front of the boat and turning the rudder at the same time.

"Excuse me sir, but what is the little sail in the front used for; the one you keep moving back and forth?" Ben asked the skipper.

"It directs the apparent wind back over the leeward side of the main sail," the skipper replied.

Not wanting to appear too ignorant, he followed with another question, "How do you know when it is doing that correctly?"

"Well, you can generally tell when it stops luffing."

"Ohh, I see," Ben said so as to not seem like he had no idea what the man was talking about. He then turned to Beth and whispered, "Do you know what he's talking about?"

Beth laughed and said, "Yes, the front sail is called a Jib, and it is used to help the boat tack, along with the tiller. Did you notice how it was flapping in the wind when he first let it out?"

"Yes."

"That is called luffing and when that stops, he knows the boat is turning in the direction he wants it to go. He can then pull it back."

"What is tack?" I'm sorry honey; I just never studied anything about sailing."

"That's all right, I don't mind the questions. Tacking is moving the boat at angles against the wind to provide the forward motion we need to go where we want to go. It is sort of like traveling in a zigzag way. Apparent wind is the wind we feel when we are moving our bodies through the air, and it is the wind that the motion of the boat creates to fill the jib. The captain uses that to move the front of the boat in the direction he wants to go."

"Hey John, do you understand this stuff?" Ben asked.

"I know how to make my car move and how to make it go where I want it to go. But I leave sailing to others," John replied.

"My sentiments exactly," Ben chuckled.

They continued farther out into the bay and soon Ben and John engaged in conversation they both knew more about. Beth and Shannon then became engaged in their own chats and soon Shannon asked, "Beth, do you mind if I ask you a personal question?"

"No, you can ask anything you wish, but I retain the option of answering it or not," she laughed.

"Oh, yes of course, I understand. It is just that John and I have really enjoyed meeting the two of you and would like to keep in touch after we leave, but I don't know if that is possible. I'm not sure I understand your living arrangements."

"It isn't necessary that you understand our living arrangements. I can give you my address, but I'm not at liberty to give you Ben's address. Of course, you can give me your address and I would be very happy to correspond with you."

Shannon was still not happy with that answer and she felt she was really pushing the envelope. Changing her tactics slightly, she continued, "How long have you known Ben? I mean~~~"

"We have known each other most all of our lives. Shannon~~~Ben and I met when we were very young. We didn't really know it at the time, but we fell deeply in love with each other. Cupid plays some very dirty tricks on people at times."

Beth was quiet for a while, and Shannon felt it was best to say nothing.

After a short pause, Beth continued, "Circumstances beyond our control separated us and we lost track of each other. I was hurt and sad for a while, but at 15 years old one's heart heals rather quickly and life goes on." Beth paused again, but then went on, "In a few years I met a man and married, raised a daughter and soon my husband and I drifted apart and eventually divorced. I went through a period of time that made me feel like I never wanted anything to do with men again. They always seemed to bring hurt and sadness to me."

Beth looked out over the water as if in deep thought before continuing. "Looking back, I found the only time I ever truly was comfortable in a relationship with a man, was with a boy when I was growing up. Even that brought pain and sadness, but not because of anything we did, but what we couldn't do. I relived those moments many times over during those lonely years."

"What did you do after the divorce?" Shannon asked.

"I went back to school deciding to devote the rest of my life to children, confident I didn't need a man~~~that I could take care of myself and my daughter, Karen. In time I received my doctorate and joined a pediatrics practice."

"How did you meet Ben again?"

"Ohh, that's a long story, but briefly we connected on the Internet. It was like our first kiss when that happened; it was electric! The rest is history."

"How long ago was that?"

"Not very long ago; not nearly long enough! I wish it had been decades ago!"

"What about Ben? What was his life like?"

"Well honey, you would have to ask him about that," Beth laughed. "I still have not found out everything about him, but I know enough to know there has never been anyone like him for me. He is my soul mate; the one that was meant for me. Cupid was mean to bring us together when we were so young!"

Shannon was pleased that Beth had shared this with her. She knew that anyone who observed them together would know what she had just said was true. They were right for each other. They complimented each other like the old fashioned magnets; she was the white Scottie dog, and he was the black one. They stick together like they belong.

The sailing took them to a vantage point where they could nearly view the entire span of the Mackinaw Bridge. "Beth, have you ever been to San Francisco," Ben asked.

"Yes, just briefly as a side trip from Sacramento. It was a long time ago and we were only able to spend one day there. We did take a ride on a cable car and crossed the bay over the Oakland Bay Bridge. We saw the Golden Gate, but only from a distance. While it is a majestic and beautiful bridge, I don't think it has anything over this one. It might be larger and longer, but this one is every bit as beautiful."

"Yes, it is very beautiful," Ben replied.

"I wish we had more time; I would like to go up into the UP with you. There is a museum at Whitefish Point that houses artifacts and history of the Edmund Fitzgerald and a lot of other ships that have sank in that bay."

"Sweetheart, I wish you wouldn't talk about sinking; we're still on this boat," Ben said with a chuckle and a wink. "I'm just kidding; yes I would like to go up there with you, too. It might be cold up there right now. I'd also like to watch those huge freighters move through those locks at Sault Saint Marie."

"Maybe someday we can do that," Beth replied, looking out over the bay with so much doubt filling her head.

"When are you folks leaving," John asked.

"Tomorrow morning. We will drive back to Midland and then Beth flies back to Columbus, Ben replied. "How about you; when will you leave?"

"We have the rest of the week. I think we are going to rent some bicycles and try to ride up to the northern part of the island. It might take the better part of the day."

"That sounds like fun. Where do you work, John?"

"I'm an engineer at Caterpillar Tractor Company, in Peoria, Illinois. We normally do not take vacation at this time of the year, but I managed some time off for our honeymoon."

"Caterpillar, is that where those big yellow tractors are made?"

"Yes, but a lot more than just tractors; a lot of various types of earth moving equipment are developed and produced by Caterpillar."

"Where did you get your engineering degree?"

"Well, it took me a few extra years, but I finally earned it from Bradley University in Peoria. Are you familiar with Bradley?"

"Yes, I remember when I was in high school they used to have terrific basketball teams. I don't follow that stuff much anymore."

"What did you do before you retired, Ben?"

"I worked as a representative for one of the major defense contractors. It was my job to explain some of the advantages of the equipment we produced that would work in the air defense of our country during the Cold War. After the war ended and the Russians magically disappeared, I worked as a consultant for an industrial firm that provided different motion control systems for industry. I traveled a lot and enjoyed it until 9-11. Soon after that I began looking forward to retirement."

"Do you miss working?"

"Ohh sometimes I do, but not often. I miss the relationships I had with the people, and I get bored at times, but there is enough to keep me busy at home."

"Do you have hobbies that keep you busy?'

"Yes, while I mentioned to you that I didn't do any fishing anymore, I never really got into hunting, but have always enjoyed target shooting. That used to keep me busy, but I find I don't get out doing that very often anymore. I think you will find when you retire you'll wonder when you ever had time to work," Ben said with a smile.

As the catamaran rounded a jutting shoreline, they passed by the Round Island Lighthouse making their return trip to Mackinac.

"Ben, have you ever wondered how romantic it must have been to have lived in those lighthouses, keeping the beacon shining and running throughout the nights in all kinds of weather?" Beth asked.

"Uhh no, not exactly; it seems to me that it would be pretty harsh, especially during the winter months and in inclement weather."

"But think how much fun it would be huddling and snuggling up close under the covers to keep warm," Beth said with a hint of excitement in her voice.

Ben frowned and replied, "I think while you would be huddled under those warm covers, I'd be up in the top of that tower working on that light, trying to keep it moving in that frigid environment."

"But I would keep your side of the bed warm for you when you came back down," she chuckled.

"I would feel like an iceberg when I would crawl in beside you, then we would both be cold. I can hear you already~~~'Oh, don't touch me with those cold hands!'"

"Oh darling, I would never say that to you no matter how cold your hands."

Ben laughed heartily and replied, "Yeah you say that now, but I'd bet you would change your tune when it's -40 degrees outside."

"What's so funny up there," Shannon asked.

"Oh Beth just had a very chilling thought, Ben replied. She thinks she would like to live in a lighthouse."

"Ohh, what a neat idea! I think that would be so romantic," Shannon countered.

Ben could only shake his head in bewilderment. "There is no way we will ever fully understand these creatures we lovingly call women," he thought, "but it is very clear we could never live without them."

The skipper of the catamaran skillfully made a clean docking, ending the sailing trip. Ben was the first one out of the boat, turning to help first Beth, then Shannon onto the dock. As John was preparing to disembark, he shook the captain's hand and thanked him for a very enjoyable sailing. Ben then extended his hand to John pulling him up out of the boat. "Well, looks like I didn't have to go in after you," John wink. "You must have had a death grip on the side rails."

Ben laughed as he replied, "You bet I did! I felt that water splash up on me several times, and it was cold! No way did I want to take a dip in that frigid water."

Shannon turned to Beth and asked, "Where are the two of you off to now?"

"I think we are going to go back to our hotel for a nap. We have a late evening planned as it will be our last night here. What about you kids~~~what are you going to do now?"

"I'm not sure what John wants to do next. I could use a nap too, but I'll have to see what he wants to do. I think I could entice him to take a nap with me," she winked.

Beth laughed and replied, "Yes, I'll just bet you can."

"Well darling, I'm ready for that nap you promised we would take this afternoon," Ben addressed Beth as the two men approached them. "That sailing can tire a guy out pretty quickly."

"John, Beth was just telling me that they are going to take a nap this afternoon. I thought that sounded like a great idea," Shannon said as she took John's hand, rubbing her hip against his leg. "What do you think?"

"Uhh, yeah~~~I mean that sounds good to me. Will we see the two of you again before you leave?"

"I don't think so," Ben replied, "we will be leaving pretty early in the morning; right after breakfast."

Shannon reached into her purse and retrieved a small notebook and a pen. She jotted down their address in Illinois and handed it to Beth. "This is our home address for now. We might be moving soon, so I hope we can keep in touch."

Beth sensed the concern in her voice, fearful that she may never hear from them again. "Let me use your notebook, dear; I'll write down my address for you and I promise I will write. Maybe we can exchange email addresses later?"

"Ohh, that's great; we have really enjoyed meeting you both!"

"Thank you; Ben and I have enjoyed our time with you as well."

John and Ben were making their farewells and were starting to make their way over to the two women when Shannon whispered to Beth, "Beth, I hope you and Ben can get together~~~I mean~~~really together. You are so right for each other."

Beth smiled and replied, "Yes, I know we are; that is our hope too. You are very sweet."

"John, Shannon, it's been a lot of fun. Maybe we can meet again on your 25th right here, Ben said with a laugh.

"Do you promise?" John asked.

"Only if the two of you push us around in wheelchairs," Ben replied.

"That's a deal; it would be our pleasure."

Beth then gave Shannon a hug and whispered in her ear, "Be happy dear; never let a day go by without telling him that you love him. Don't ever be afraid to say you are sorry~~~even if the argument isn't your fault."

Shannon felt the tear against her cheek that was from Beth's eye. She knew she was going to miss this lady.

"Goodbye dear." Then turning to John she said, "Goodbye John; take good care of this precious lady."

"I will~~~I promise," he stammered before extending his hand to Ben. "Shannon and I are proud to have met you both. Have a safe trip home~~~and the best to you always."

"Thank you John and the very best to you and Shannon, too."

The couples then turned and walked their separate ways. Ben and Beth were both quiet during the trip back to their hotel, both engrossed in their thoughts~~~about 25 years from now.

CHAPTER XVI
Special Evening

After entering their room, Beth collapsed on the bed. Ben knew she was tired, both physically and mentally, while he felt sweaty and in need of a cool, relaxing shower. He entered the bathroom and stood over the commode as he relieved his bladder, thinking the sound would resemble a running shower. To his surprise, Beth did not enter and he was pleased she had not, as he needed this time to be alone with his thoughts, if only for a short time. He quietly undressed and entered the shower, accepting the water temperature that he never seemed to be able to adjust properly. His thoughts were reeling, envious of the young couple they had just left, beginning their lives together, as Ben knew his own was winding down. He knew he was not fearful of dying, but he dreaded the thought of leaving Beth.

He ended the shower and wrapped a towel around his body before moving into the bedroom. Beth appeared to be asleep, so he gently moved onto the bed so as to not disturb her. She was awake and rolled over on her side to face him. Ben saw that her eyes were wet and knew that she had been crying.

"What is this; why the tears?"

"I don't know; I just feel sad. I hated to see them go~~~and I'm~~~I'm going to hate tomorrow," she said as another tear ran out the corner of her eye.

Ben leaned forward, kissed the tear away and whispered in her ear, "Tomorrow is a whole other day away. Today is now and we have tonight and it will be wonderful. There is no time for sadness now. We are together and it is a time to build memories that will have to last us for a while and that is exactly what we are going to do. I love you Beth Callaway. More than life, I love you."

"I love you too~~~so much it hurts at times," she said as she moved closer to him to kiss his mouth. "How was your shower?"

"Lonesome. And either too hot or too cold. I settled for cold."

"Ohh, snuggle up close to me sweetheart; I'll warm you up."

As she said this, she reached over his chest and began rubbing his back. Ben closed his eyes relishing the feel of her fingers stroking his back. Soon his breathing slowed and became shallow, telling her he had fallen asleep. She smiled, gently kissed his forehead, closed her eyes and joined him in sleep.

The sound of laughter outside their room woke Beth with a start. The sun that had previously flooded the room with light, now slipped low in the sky and the room was considerably darker. She looked at the clock next to the bed and was surprised that she had slept so long. It was already 5:05; time to get up and start the process of presenting herself for their dinner date, as their reservations were for 7:00. She looked at Ben, noticed how peaceful he looked and decided to let him sleep a little longer while she showered. She slipped quietly off the bed and entered the bathroom. Slowly she undressed and appraised her body in the full length mirror mounted on the inside of the bathroom door. Even though the years had taken its toll on her body, she had done well preserving it, keeping it lean and firm with daily exercise and walking. She loved to walk and was now happy that she had continued to do that over the years.

After adjusting the water to her preference, she carefully stepped in, letting the warm water cascade over her body. She closed her eyes and instantly her mind flashed ahead to tomorrow and the sadness that it would bring. She knew she had to put these thoughts aside, or they would ruin the time they had remaining.

"Do you need any help in there? I'm good at doing backs."

Beth laughed as she replied, "Backs are not the only thing you are good with, but I'll take a rain check if that is okay."

"Have you been up very long?"

"No, just a few minutes. I can't believe how long we slept."

"We were both tired; we've been pretty busy the past few days, plus the wind and sun out on the water really sapped me. I feel rested now; ready to chase you around the room later."

"Why do you think you will have to chase me? I won't be running."

"But you don't know what I have in mind," he replied with an evil chuckle.

"It doesn't matter; anything is fine with me~~~as long as it is with you."

Ben smiled as he began dressing. "How did I ever get so lucky," he thought.

As Ben was slipping into his shoes, Beth emerged from the bathroom with her robe wrapped tightly around her body. She had a mischievous grin on her face as she stood before him and slowly started to open her robe. Ben instantly thought she was going to give him a hint of the delights he will be able to enjoy later. Instead, as the robe opened, he found that she had already put on a pair of brief, black lacy panties and a matching black bra. The contrast against her fair alabaster skin took Ben's breath away.

"Wow," he muttered, barely able to speak, "I wasn't ready for that," he mumbled after swallowing hard, "you are stunning!"

He rose up off his chair with one shoe on and one off, taking her into his arms holding her close to him with a hug so tight that Beth could feel his body shaking.

"Hold that thought for later darling; I have to get dressed," she laughed.

He again swallowed hard, finding that his throat suddenly felt restricted. He knew it was going to be hard to keep his mind on dinner.

Turning away from him, she continued dressing as Ben sat down to put his other shoe on, finding it hard to take his eyes off her. Beth could not hold back her laughter.

"What's so funny?" Ben asked with a bewildered look on his face.

"Ohh, just the way you jumped up with one shoe on and one shoe off. You had that same look on your face when I sucked the donut frosting off your thumb when we were in Indianapolis. Do you remember that time?"

Ben laughed, "How could I ever forget? In all my years I had never felt anything so sensuous."

Laughing, she turned to him with her arms outstretched wide to the sides and asked, "How do I look?" Beth had put on a pair of black dress slacks with a black turtle neck sweater and a pair of black pumps. Ben dressed in a pair of dark blue Dockers with a light blue polo shirt and black loafers. As he rose to take her hands in his, he stammered, "You look fabulous, as you always do, even in a gunnysack. Do you think we are over dressed? I feel sort of out of uniform without my jeans."

Smiling she replied, "No sweetheart, we have a long way to go to reach that plateau, but you do look nice. Are you going to do anything to your hair?"

"Ohh yeah, I almost forgot." He raised his hand, stroked it across his head, down both sides and declared, "Okay, I'm all ready!"

He took her hand and headed toward the door~~~Beth following along~~~still laughing.

After a rather brisk walk to the west side of the bay, they arrived at the Iroquois Hotel, which is situated on a point of land that juts out into the bay; the dining room offering a panoramic view of Lake Huron and the Mackinac Bridge. Soon after entering the Carriage Room an attendant greeted them and asked if they had a preference to seating.

"Could we have a table close to the window overlooking the bay?" Ben asked with a wink.

"Yes sir, just this way," as he led the way to a table that was situated between two large windows that presented a gorgeous view of the bay, almost making one feel like they were sitting out on the water. Beth surveyed the room as they approached their table, instantly enjoying the soft, romantic piano music that wafted across the room.

"How is this, sir?" the attendant asked.

"Oh this is perfect! Thank you very much," Ben replied.

A single candle on the table flickered as the attendant seated Beth. "The candle seems to be flirting with you, Ma'am," he said to her in a soft, warm voice as he positioned the chair for her. Ben had to look away to hide the smile he felt tightening his lips, finding it hard to look at Beth at that moment.

"The waitress will soon be over to receive your order."

Beth smiled and thanked him, then looked at Ben and excitedly said, "Oh Ben, the music sounds so much like Ernesto Cortazar; so romantic! And look, the moon is already starting to rise! What are you laughing about?"

He could no longer contain his laughter. "A flirting candle~~~well, can't say I blame it~~~or the attendant either." He was seated with his back to the window, turned and looked to the west and noted the sun was low on the horizon.

"That's the sun, honey," he chuckled.

"No silly; you're looking in the wrong direction. You should sit over here so you can see outside," she said as she touched a chair that was to the side of her.

"No, I would rather look at you; besides, I want to keep an eye on that candle," he said as he turned to the other direction and did indeed see the moon which appeared full and held much promise for later. Turning back around to face her, he reached across the table, took both her hands in his and winked, "There is nothing I would rather look at than just your face."

Before Beth could respond, the waitress appeared and gave them both menus, adding; "We have an 8 ounce top sirloin on special tonight and as usual the prime rib is excellent. Can I get you something to drink?"

Ben smiled and replied, "Instead of studying the menu, I was too busy studying her. Could we have a little time to look at the menu, please?"

"Yes, of course; can I get you something to drink while you decide?"

"Just water for me," Beth replied.

"Yes, that will be fine for me as well; perhaps a small jug of a sweet white wine on the side," Ben added.

The waitress smiled broadly and chuckled quietly to herself and replied, "Thank you; I'll bring a wine chart back shortly with your drinks."

As the waitress left, Ben, embarrassed, looked at Beth and muttered, "Uhh, I guess it ain't called a jug, ya think?"

"Probably not; maybe it's called a schooner?"

"No, I think that is what beer is served in."

"Oh honey, it doesn't matter. I'm the last of the big drinkers to be answering that question," she smiled. "We had better decide what we are going to order for dinner."

Ben opened the menu and his eyes immediately spotted Alaskan Halibut. "Oh, I found it," he announced.

"Already~~~what did you find?"

"Halibut~~~have you ever had halibut?"

"No, I don't think so. Is it anything like salmon?"

"Oh no; nothing at all like salmon. It is a very mild, delicate fish from Alaska. It is the most delicious fish you will ever sink your teeth in."

"It's pricey!"

"But worth every penny," Ben replied.

"Okay, you convinced me. What do we get to go with it?"

"You pick the rest."

"Okay, we will have a small green salad, and what do you think about a bottle of Sauvignon Blanc or Pinot Grigio?"

The surprise on Ben's face was undeniable. "If I had known you knew that much about wine, I would not have shown my ignorance."

"Oh, I don't know much about it; I just know the reds give me a headache, but I can tolerate a little bit of the whites. I won't drink very much."

"Well in that case, we better not get a bottle, just that small jug I mentioned. I don't want you to have to carry me back to the hotel," he laughed.

Beth laughed," I wouldn't be in any shape to carry you after just my glass of wine. Do you like lemon meringue pie?"

"I think so but I haven't had any for so long; I don't really remember."

"Why don't we share one?"

"Can you eat it if I decide I don't like it?"

"We can take it back and have it in the morning if we don't eat it all tonight."

Ben smiled and replied, "You are so resourceful. All those years of saving leftovers are showing. That is something John and Shannon would not even think about today."

"They will after they start their family. I've never asked you; do you mind eating leftovers?"

"Honey, does it look like I ever turned *anything* down? If I never ate leftovers, I wouldn't have eaten very much at all. Come to think of it, maybe I ate too many leftovers." Ben winked.

Beth merely smiled and said nothing. She knew there was no safe way out of the question he posed.

The waitress returned with the wine chart and to take their order. Ben permitted Beth to order for both of them, winked at the waitress and thanked her for the chart. She returned a knowing smile to Ben and departed with their order. Ben turned his chair a bit so he could share the view with Beth. The moon was rising higher in the sky, but the sun had not yet set. The water in the bay looked calm, with just a few gentle waves causing the fading sunlight to flicker and flirt with them.

"It is so beautiful and peaceful here. I forgot to ask you; did you enjoy the sailing this afternoon?"

"Oh yes! I think the best part was docking back up when we returned," he joked.

"Oh seriously~~~did you like it?" She chuckled.

"Yes, it was very interesting. I think it takes a lot of learning and practice to be able to maneuver one of those things. I'll stick to motor boats."

"I like it because it is so quiet and peaceful~~~so serene and alone with nature."

"Have you ever gone out sailing and sunbathed in the nude on one? That would really get you close to nature," Ben said with a sly grin across his face.

Before she could answer, the waitress returned with their wine and water. Ben raised his wine glass to his lips, but merely peered over the top of the glass and said, "Well?"

"Well, what?"

"Have you ever taken it all off outdoors~~~you know~~~close to nature?"

"No, of course not!" Beth paused and then added, "Have you?"

"Yes, many times. Heck, when I was younger I didn't have a pair of swimming trunks, so when I spent the summers on the farm, we just stripped down and jumped in."

"Were there girls there, too?"

"No, not in those days; that came later. There was a group of us once that were holed up in this hotel near Chicago during a convention back in the late sixties. We had been drinking quite a bit and we decided to get in the pool. It was late and the lifeguard was not on duty, so technically no one was supposed to be in the pool. We didn't have swimming gear. We decided if we were very quiet, no one would ever know."

"And there were women with you, too?"

"Oh yes, and they were smashed too."

"Were you married then?"

"Yes."

"Did she join you?"

"Uhh~~~she wasn't there."

"Oh. Well, what happened?"

"Well Sam, this guy that is always the life of the party, suggested we jump in naked, that it would be real refreshing as it was such a hot and humid evening. Besides, it was dark and no one would see anything. So, he stripped down and did a full gainer off the diving board. The rest of us guys got to laughing so hard, we quickly got out of our clothes and joined him; but I did not go off the diving board."

"Well, what did the women do then?"

"They started laughing and gathered close to the pool looking down at us. We were so drunk we hadn't noticed that there were lights on the side of the pool under the water and we were over exposed. Sam told them they had their laughs, so when do we get ours. All but two of them stripped down to their panties, but did not take them off. It didn't matter because after they were wet they became transparent."

"Oh my gosh! What happened next?"

"Well contrary to our plans to remain quiet, we became very loud, laughing and carrying on until we caused a complaint I guess and management made us all get out and leave. Most of us spent the rest of the night in our cars."

Beth laughed so hard she could barely speak, finally saying, "Good! That should teach you a lesson."

"It did! I learned it was a lot of fun," Ben laughed. "It was a little bit criminal, but a whole lot worth it! It was also very enlightening as this one woman really exposed herself in a way I don't think she meant to do. It was amazing how when she took off her bra, her breasts disappeared too." Ben paused and then laughed, "We should do that sometime."

"Only if we have a private pool in our backyard with a 12 foot privacy fence all around the perimeter," she remarked with authority.

Beth smiled and was quiet. Beth took his hand and asked, "Are you reminiscing about that night in the pool?"

"No, not at all; I was just wondering what it would cost to build that fence."

Beth was still laughing when the waitress returned with their dinner.

Ben moved his chair back and prepared the napkin on his lap. The platter with the broiled halibut was placed before them, smelling delicious with the salad as a side dish. There was also a side of roasted baby red potatoes and some hot dinner rolls with real butter.

"Do you wish anything else right now?" the waitress asked.

"No thank you, not right at the moment," Beth replied. "Everything looks wonderful."

"Very well then; enjoy your meal."

Ben took a sip of his wine and found it fine, although he does not usually prefer the whites. He sampled the salad and found it fresh and crisp with a light balsamic house dressing.

Beth could not wait to try the halibut, as she had never eaten it before. Her first bite was a delight, as Ben watched the expression on her face.

Her eyes sparkled as she glanced up to him smiling and said, "Ohh, this is absolutely delicious. It is so light and fresh."

Ben smiled and was pleased that the meal had met with her approval, happy that he had suggested the halibut.

The sun had now set, allowing the colors and hues of twilight, shimmering off the water, to play on her face. Ben was finding it difficult to keep his eyes from her as she busied herself with her meal. She ate in such a dainty way, seemingly enjoying each bite. The more he watched her, the more he was aware that his shoulders were beginning to sag as he felt totally doomed. She was melting him simply by sitting across from him at this table.

Business in the restaurant was picking up as those who dined later were being seated. The overhead lights were dimming down, the atmosphere was becoming cozier and Ben was feeling more and more unsettled. He readjusted his 6 foot, 200 pound frame in the chair, cleared his throat and decided to get a grip on his emotions. "My gosh~~~I'm a grown man~~~senior citizen if you will~~~and I feel like an adolescent," he thought. He then set about the business of devouring the excellent fish before it got cold.

Being a slower eater, Beth was still enjoying her dinner as Ben took his last bite of the halibut. The sun had since slipped below the horizon and the moon took over the heavens; high and bright in a clear sky. The waitress returned to clear the table and delivered their lemon meringue pie.

"Will there be anything else," she asked.

"Yes," Ben replied, "I think we would like to have a couple of snifters of American Fruits Apple Brandy, if you have that brand."

"I will check on that right away, sir."

"Thank you."

As she left, Ben's gaze returned to Beth and he lost his breath. Where the sun earlier had played on Beth's face, the moon, now reflecting off the gentle waves of the bay, cast a soft pale glow. The flickering candle teased Ben, creating mysterious shadows upon her upper body and her hands. Her eyes were gleaming, sending fire out toward Ben in a way he had never seen before. She appeared angelic, so surreal, her smile so inviting. She interlaced her fingers together resting her chin on the back side of her hands, smiling at him, reducing him to pulp.

"Oh my God," he thought, "will I be able to make love to this woman? Could it even be permitted? How can it be me that she wants?" He swallowed hard feeling his heart rate increase, taking in her pure beauty along with what nature was adding

"Beth," he started, his voice weak and scratchy, "you are unbelievably beautiful."

"Oh sweetheart, you are just so biased."

"No~~~ any man that would be sitting here right now would see you the same way I do. I feel like the luckiest man in the world."

Beth smiled and replied, "I love you, too."

Ben reached into his pocket and removed the small box containing the bracelet he had purchased earlier. He handed it to her saying, "I didn't have any way to wrap it for you. I'd buy diamonds, but they didn't have any."

Beth opened the box, her eyes sparkling from the flickering candle and the moonlight, and replied, "Ohh, Ben, where~~~when did you get this?"

"When I caught you looking the other way; here~~~let me put it on you."

She handed it to Ben and he attached it around her left wrist. "It is beautiful," she whispered. "It's a lover's knot. Thank you, sweetheart."

"You're welcome; I wish it was something else. If I could, I would get down on my knees right here in front of God and everyone in this place and ask you to marry me. I don't think I ever really proposed before~~~I think we just sort of took things for granted. But I would now."

"And I would accept; without giving it another thought," she replied.

Ben lowered his mouth to her hand and kissed it. "I love you Beth. I love you with everything that is in me."

"I know you do~~~and I love you with all my heart and soul, my love." Beth paused as she felt her eyes becoming moist, "Let me give you a bite of this pie."

Beth then took her knife and cut out a wedge of the lemon meringue pie, placing it on one of the small dessert plates. She then cut off the tip of the wedge with her fork and carefully placed it in his mouth, her hand shaking as she did. "How is that; is it like you remember?"

"Yum, yes it is very good. It really wakes up the saliva glands in front of my ears," he chuckled.

"Ohh, do you mean it is tart?" she asked before trying a bite on her own.

"No, it is just very sweet and very good. Not as sweet as your lips, though."

Beth smiled as she lifted a bite of the pie to her mouth. "Umm, I see what you mean! It is very rich and sweet. The meringue is not bland, but very sweet, definitely not on my diet."

"I'd say it isn't on my diet either, but I don't seem to have one," he laughed, "I love desserts."

The waitress returned with two snifters of brandy and placed them on the table. "We did not have the brand that you requested, but our bartender thinks you will find this one very satisfactory, if not, just let me know and we will remove it from your tab."

Ben lifted his snifter with his hand under the bowl and swirled the amber liquid around, then held it to his nose to catch the aromas before taking a sip. He rolled it around in his mouth letting the vapors rise up in the back of his mouth into his sinuses before swallowing it. It was warm as it slid down into his stomach, but very pleasant.

"Yes, this is very good; please express my gratitude to your bartender."

"Thank you sir; I'm happy you like it."

As she left, Ben smiled at Beth and said, "Well, it's time for you to try it now. Kinda get a sniff of it first to try to capture the different flavors before taking it into your mouth. Try that first and let me know what you think you can detect."

Beth looked at Ben with a look of 'I don't know about this' but slowly lifted the glass by the short stem, finding it very awkward to handle.

"Hold it like this honey, with your hand cupping the bowl on the bottom. Your hand will give it stability and also tends to warm the brandy. Swirl it around first to wake it up," Ben instructed.

"I didn't know it was sleeping," she laughed.

Ben chuckled, "It's just a figure of speech sweetheart; it sort of stirs up the different scents and flavors."

Beth moved the snifter sharply to the side and nearly sloshed some of the liquid onto her sweater. Ben then placed his hand over hers and guided her in a gentle circular motion that swirled the brandy without tossing it over the side. "Just like this," he said in a low seductive voice, "with the gentle hands I know that you have."

"Ohh, I haven't even tasted it yet and I think I already like brandy," she replied in her own seductive voice.

"Now it is ready for you to take a sniff. This process is called 'getting the nose', if you can imagine that," as he let go of her hand.

As she brought the glass to her nose, she inhaled softly, breathing in the vapors. "I smell apples and alcohol," she said as if she knew he would be disappointed.

"That's good! That means your *sniffer* is working," he laughed. "Now take a little sip and hold it in your mouth and move your tongue through the brandy. If you can, let it get to the back of your mouth without choking and breathe through the back of your nose, it you can understand what I'm trying to say. It's a little tricky, so you might have to practice."

Ben watch as she did as he instructed, her eyes telling him that she was having a little difficulty, but she was very dedicated. "You can swallow it when you are ready and you should feel a warm feeling all the way to your tummy."

She swallowed the sip and her eyes became wider, "Did you say warm? It feels hot!"

Ben laughed, "Only the first sip does, the next ones will be pleasant and warm and is actually good for the digestion." As he said this, he took another sip and smiled at her as he swallowed it. "I think I can detect a flavor of nuts~~~perhaps cashews."

Beth then decided to try it again and concentrated on doing everything the way he had taught her. She was able to swirl the snifter without spilling any, took a sniff, followed by another sip. She then performed the perfunctory task of nearly choking herself by trying to suck the vapors up her nose from inside her mouth. She gathered up her strength and swallowed the hot liquid, surprisingly finding it was warm and pleasant this time, as Ben had said it would.

"Ohh wow, I think I detect the scent of~~~let me see~~~or the flavor of~~~apples and~~~alcohol," she smiled, as it went down much easier this time."

Ben was delighted with her. He instinctively knew she would find some fun in this relatively new adventure, as she was not a drinker. He would be careful with her so she would not drink too much.

"Some folks like to warm brandy before they drink it, but I find it is very good at room temperature by holding it in your hand and sipping it very slowly. While it is not my favorite drink, it is good for an after dinner drink sometimes. Maybe we will try some Drambuie our next time."

Beth looked straight into his eyes and asked, "When will that be, Ben? When will that be?"

Ben sat straight back in his chair as if he was slapped. "I don't know my love~~~I just don't know. But let's not get lost in the 'what ifs' tonight; tonight is for us~~~now. Tonight we drink brandy; tomorrow it's Drambuie."

He then raised his snifter and added, "I drink to you my love, to us, to our love and to our life together."

Holding his glass in front of him, he waited for her to raise her glass as she was just looking at him still digesting what he had said. "Honey, I made a toast," he paused, "you are supposed to raise your glass and then drink a big gulp of your brandy."

"I know sweetheart; it's the big gulp I'm worried about."

"Then just take a sip; it will feel good in your tummy."

"It's starting to feel good in my head, too," she giggled.

"You are delightful, my love. Tonight~~~we let our hair down."

"Well, I can do that tonight, but darling~~~you already have," she laughed.

Loudly emitting a roar of laughter, he sat back relieved that the subject had become lighter and carefree. She loved to tease and he could see she was going to be fun later. His laughter swept across the table to Beth, who ignited an outburst of her own, her eyes sparkling in the candlelight. She loved the fact that he was so easy to play with and that she could say whatever came to mind without fear of hurting his feelings. He loved to be teased and loved to give it back. It was playful with them and she also knew they were going to have fun later.

As the laughter subsided, Beth took another sip of her brandy as she looked across to him with a look of promise in her eyes. She had taken her shoe off and extended her foot under the table, caressing his lower leg with her foot. Ben nearly choked on his drink when he felt her foot.

"I dare you to slump down in your chair a bit," she said to him with a wink.

Chuckling in his deep suggestive way, he replied, "I learned a long time ago to ignore dares."

"What brought you to that conclusion?"

"My friends used to dare me to do things, I guess because they knew I would do them. I always ended up in trouble and they always had a good laugh~~~at my expense. I finally wised up and told them to kiss me where the sun never shines."

An inquisitive smile crossed her face learning of this new revelation. "What kind of trouble did you get into?"

"Oh nothing with the law, but it was very close a couple of times. Mostly in school," he paused and then continued laughing. "One of the best ones was when we found a Baby Ruth candy bar on the ground and the sun had melted it somewhat, coiling it making it look like something that a dog had dropped. I picked it up and mentioned that it would be funny if our teacher were to find this in her desk drawer."

"What does this have to do with a dare?"

"Well, they dared me to do it, so I did."

"Oh! What happened?"

"Nothing for a while; in fact, I had almost forgotten about it until she finally opened her drawer. Then the~~err~~candy bar hit the fan! She pushed her chair back screaming and my friends exploded in laughter.

After she composed herself, she looked at us with a look of complete disgust on her face and asked which one of us put it there. All three of my so called good buddies pointed their fingers at me and proudly stated, "Ben did it!"

"Benjamin, did you put this in here?" she asked me. "Of course I knew I was in deep~~~chocolate when she called me Benjamin. I reluctantly admitted that I did. She told me to come up there and retrieve it and clean up her desk."

Beth was still shaking her head laughing when she asked, "And did you?"

"Oh yes. I didn't know exactly what to do with it, so I picked it up and ate it."

"Oh no; you didn't!"

"Yes, I'm afraid I did. I thought Miss Jones was going to lose her breakfast. After she stopped shrieking, she sent me to the principal's office."

Beth was now having trouble getting words out due to her uncontrollable laughter, but managed to asked, "Ohh honey~~~ what~~~did he do?"

"Well, he asked me if I wanted him to call a doctor. I told him I didn't need a doctor as it was just a candy bar. He said the teacher told him it was dog poop. I insisted it was a Baby Ruth and asked him if he wanted to smell my breath. He declined and turned his back. I was pretty sure he was laughing."

"Did he punish you?"

"No, not directly; he called my folks and told them what had happened. Mom got all excited, but I think Dad thought it was cool. She insisted that I get a spanking and what she wanted she always got. Dad didn't spank me very hard, so I was sure he thought it was funny."

"What grade were you in when you did this?"

"Fourth~~~and that was about when I started to think it was time I stopped accepting those dares. I also decided it was time to find some new friends."

"Yes, I think that was a good idea. They weren't very good friends~~~but I am," she replied as she continued to caress his leg with her foot.

"I know you are, but I'm afraid if I slumped down in this chair, I might not be able to get back out of it. I probably wouldn't even want to the way you are working that foot."

Beth giggled and slumped down a little in her chair, but found that she could not reach up as high as she wanted.

"Naughty girl," he laughed. Your toes are going to get you in trouble."

"That's okay; I can handle that kind of trouble." She then tipped up her snifter and drained the remaining amber liquid that was now warm and felt good moving down to her stomach. She felt good, a little lightheaded, but so relaxed and comfortable. There was only one thing she wanted now and it was sitting across the table from her.

"Are you ready to go to bed with me?" she asked with that look of promise in her eyes again.

"Yes, I am always ready for that. Are you going to use that foot on me some more?"

"Ummmm~~~perhaps some other things as well."

"Well, reel in your foot and put your shoe on then; here comes the waitress."

"Is there anything else, sir?"

"No, I don't believe so; just the check please."

Ben quickly signed the check; he pushed back his chair, stood and moved around the table to help Beth out of her chair. She wobbled as she stood up for a second and his eyes sparkled as he quipped, "Ah ha, your foot chilled and numbed while you had your shoes off, huh?"

"No way", she stammered, "just the brandy and the wine. I'm not used to drinking."

Leaning forward, he kissed her cheek. "Come my dear; Daddy is going to take you home." Smiling broadly, she took his hand and gracefully slipped into step with him.

The evening air was cool, but not cold. They walked slowly hand in hand along the docks until they came to a bench overlooking the bay, the moon high and the light bright, reflecting off the now calm waters.

"Oh Ben, can we sit here for a while? It is so beautiful and peaceful."

"Yes, at lease the gulls are bedded down now and won't try to practice carrier landings on my dome~~~or worse yet~~~a bomb run."

"Silly man," she laughed, "you are funny."

As they sat down on the bench, Ben placed his right arm behind and around her, grasping her shoulder holding her tight against him. She lowered her head against his shoulder and whispered, "Oh honey, I don't ever want to leave this place."

Ben gazed out over the water, watching the silvery moonlight flirting with them as it rode over the gentle waves. He both knew and felt what she was feeling at this special time. He could only imagine what they must look like sitting there in the moonlight, the cool, yet warm balmy breeze gently caressing their faces. Finally he spoke, his voice soft and breaking slightly, "We have to leave this place~~~but we will take the beauty of it and the time we have spent here in our hearts and our memories. This night, this moment, will live with me for the rest of my days~~~it will be among my last thoughts. I love you Beth. I love you more than just this place, but what you have given me while we have been here. I have learned to live and breathe again and that is much more important than any place~~~other than the place that you occupy in my heart. You will never leave that place."

They both sat quietly, silent as tears dropped from Beth's cheeks to her lap. "Why has it taken this long to find this much happiness?" she wondered.

Ben's thoughts raced back to the fifties, remembering as if it was only yesterday when he first kissed this woman, this girl who stole his heart and went away before he knew what had happened to him. Those days turned to weeks, months, then years, wondering what had happened to her; why he could not get the memory of her out of his mind~~~and his heart. Now at last he had found her; they were finally together and he felt complete, like his search had finally ended. But now the time was fast approaching for them to part again, and everything inside of him opposed that, resisted it, feeling the sharp pangs of loneliness already creeping in. Knowing he had to push these feelings aside for now, remembering what he had told her earlier, but finding giving advice was much easier than practicing what he gave.

Beth tilted her head up to kiss his cheek, tasting the salt of his tears. She turned to him kissing him full on the mouth, their tears mingling together and blending with their lips. Their bodies trembled, mixed with the sobs welling up inside them, coupled with the thrill of the kiss; both somehow sensing they would never experience another time like this again, but neither openly expressing those fears. She clung to him, not wanting to move; instead, wanting this moment to last forever.

Soon the chill of the evening was encompassing them and it was time for them to leave this place. Ben removed his arm from behind her and turned his body toward her. He placed both of his hands gently on either side of her face, cupping it between them and softly kissed her lips. "It is time to take you home, my love."

Composing herself, she quickly added, "Oh yes and time for a nice warm shower. Would you like to join me?"

"Yes I would love that," he replied as he took both her hands and helped her to her feet. They then turned hand in hand and continued on their way back to their hotel.

They were almost to the entrance of the hotel when Beth pulled Ben over to a walk that went to the rear of the hotel. "Let's walk back to the flower gardens; I want to see if the daisies are sleeping."

"Sleeping? How can you tell if they are sleeping? I didn't know flowers went to bed; I thought they were always in bed."

Beth laughed, "Oh silly~~~they fold their petals in over the pistils and stamens to keep them warm after the sun is gone."

"Really? I guess that makes sense; I'd want to keep my pistil warm, too. What do they shoot with their pistil?"

"No, not pistol as in a gun; it is the part of the flower that is used in reproduction~~~the part that holds the ovaries."

"Uhh, pistil is female?" Ben asked quizzically.

"Yes; the stamen and the anther hold the pollen that is used to fertilize the flower. They are injected into the pistils."

"How is that done? Do they get together in that bed after dark?"

"No, the bees and sometimes birds do it by extracting nectar from the flower, leaving behind some of the very fine grains from the stamens into the pistils."

"Ohh, I got it now; it's all about the birds and the bees," he laughed.

"Oh Ben," she laughed, "you knew that all along and were putting me on."

"You did well sweetheart. But to be honest, I thought it was the other way around," he chuckled.

"Well maybe it is; you could be right. It's been a long time since high school biology class."

Ben watched as she bent down to touch the drooping daisy that was obviously 'sleeping'.

"Yes, she has a knack for perking things up for sure," he thought. "Must be something they teach in med school."

"There is a lot of dew on them tonight, soon the cold of winter will put them to sleep for a long rest," she said with a note of sadness in her voice."

"But they will be back in the spring, won't they?" Ben asked, without a hint of tease in his voice.

"Some will but I'm not sure about all of the flowers. Plant life was not my specialty; some are annuals and some are not~~~I don't remember which is which anymore."

"Come on darling, let's go inside; you're getting cold," he said as he took her hand and led her back to the front of the hotel.

They were quiet while they made their way through the hotel, arriving at their door. Ben inserted his key opening the door for Beth to enter. She walked a few steps inside, turned and waited for Ben to close and lock the door behind him. Before he could take a step, she rushed to him, her arms around his neck pulling his mouth to hers kissing him with a passion he had not felt previously. His arms went around her waist and her shoulders returning the deep passionate kiss, feeling his pulse increase. His right hand moved down first to her rear, then moved up under her black turtle neck sweater, feeling the cool skin of her back.

"Honey, you are cold," he whispered into her ear as the kiss ended. "Let's get you in the shower to warm up."

Without a word, her hands went to the bottom of his shirt lifting it up to his arms. He lifted them allowing her to raise his shirt up over his head. After tossing the shirt aside, her hands went to his belt buckle while Ben returned his hands under her sweater to the clasps of her bra, quickly unhooking it allowing it to relax around her body. She unfastened his belt and opened the zipper, then put her hands inside the waist of his Dockers, placing both of them flat against his body, sliding them down over his hips, letting them fall to the floor at his feet.

Ben took the opportunity to lift her sweater up over and off her head, taking his breath away viewing her standing in front of him with her black slacks and black bra that was now loose, allowing some cleavage in stark contrast with the white of her skin.

He swallowed hard, his voice weak and raspy as he said, "My God Beth; you are stunning in all that black!"

She smiled as she rolled her shoulders forward allowing the bra to slide down and off her arms. Catching it by its strap in her hand, she handed it to him then unfastened her slacks letting them fall to the floor. She bent over to remove her pumps and lifted the slacks off the floor tossing them over with the sweater. Standing now in front of him with only her black panties, her small pert, pink-tipped breasts jutting out from her chest was a vision Ben was trying to photograph in his mind. He was paralyzed as he stood there, his mouth gaped open unable to speak. Beth took his hand and guided him over to the couch and let him sit while she busied herself removing his loafers, his socks and the crumpled Dockers from around his ankles. Taking both his hands in hers, she helped him up off the couch.

"Now we are even," she said in a low and sultry voice.

Ben took her into his arms, pulling her close to his chest. "You are so beautiful," he paused, "you take my breath away."

Beth kissed him lightly and then took his hand leading him into the bathroom. She adjusted the shower, slid her panties down and stepped inside, turned and held out her hands as an invitation to him to join her. Ben instantly shed his shorts and joined her inside the shower. He again took her into his arms letting the warm water cascade down over their bodies. He lifted his face to the stream, feeling the jets pound against his lips reminding him of the kiss she had given him earlier.

He lowered his face to hers, touching his lips lightly to hers, slowly increasing the intensity until it was hard to distinguish the steam of the water from that of their bodies. Beth handed him the liquid soap without a word. He filled his hands with the thick, rich lotion, and moved his hands to her back away from the water. Holding her chest tightly against his own, he massaged her back with the soap, moving it down to her bottom, loving the feel of his hands moving over the swell and softness of her buttocks, alternately kneading and caressing them. Beth took the soap after Ben had finished, looked directly into his eyes as she repeated the process on him.

There were no words as they bathed each other, just sensuous touching, lavishing in the warm stream of water cascading over their bodies. The rinsing now complete, Beth reached behind her and turned off the water. Reaching out of the shower she retrieved a bath towel and began to dry Ben's body. He closed his eyes as she moved her hands over his body, leaving nothing untouched. When she finished, she handed the towel to him. She preferred to be dried by dabbing her body softly with the towel and he was more than happy to oblige.

As she stepped out of the shower, he kissed her back and shoulders. She turned and smiled at him as she wrapped herself in a terry cloth robe, then left the bathroom. Ben stepped out of the shower, grabbed another dry towel and dried his feet before putting on a pair of leisure shorts without a shirt, turned off the light and left the bathroom. He walked into the bedroom and found Beth in bed with a sheet pulled up to her chin, the terry cloth robe lying across the foot of the bed. As he approached the bed, she reached across her body and pulled the sheet back towards her feet. She held out her arms as an open invitation to him. Ben's eyes blinked and his heart skipped a beat. He removed his shorts and climbed into bed next to her, snaking his body up alongside hers, feeling the warmth of her skin against his.

"Hi. What has kept you so long?" she asked with a wink.

"I was trying to figure out if this is all a dream or if it is all real."

"What did you decide?"

"I haven't made up my mind yet; I still have some experimenting to do."

"Well, the laboratory is now open," she replied as she kissed him.

Ben's head was spinning as he pulled her over on top of him. Their kisses were like a summer storm, a tornado without the rain or cold, but wet heat and wind, breathing through nostrils, their mouths locked together. Hands and fingers were like tentacles, everywhere at once, their bodies melting and fusing together. A thin film of perspiration covered their entwined bodies as their temperatures rose along with their passion.

Their love flowed into each other in ways unknown or felt before~~~both fearing it might very well be the last time. The room became a paradise for two lovers locked together in embraces that neither questioned nor wanted to, without words, only touches, thrusts, kisses that took them to places never visited before. Time was irrelevant and seemed to stand still for this moment. Beth's body began convulsing as she felt Ben shaking and trembling in her arms, their passion building to a crescendo much like an orchestra, hearts beating fortissimo like pounding drums, as the cymbals came together in a loud and thundering finale.

Later, as calm swept over them, Beth sighed and said, "Sweetheart, I feel like a teenager again."

Ben was still feeling subtle spasms sweep through his body, chuckled as he replied, "You may not feel like a teenager in the morning. We might not be able to get out of bed."

"I know," she smiled, adding, "Have you ever made love like this before?"

"No~~~I never have. I've never felt like this before. I've never wanted anyone like this. All evening long I could not take my eyes off you~~~especially the way you surprised me when you opened your robe before we left."

"I know~~~I could see it in your eyes; I was afraid we weren't going to get to the restaurant," she laughed.

'Oh baby, I never thought I could make love again. I'm surprised at what we have just done."

"Why did you think that? We made love in Indianapolis, and you were fine."

"No~~~I wasn't like this. I was so full of fear then, that nothing would work, and it nearly didn't; I wanted so much to please you~~~it had been so ~~~long." As Ben spoke, tears formed in his eyes. "I thought that after so long I had lost the ability to feel passion again~~~but I was wrong~~~I've never felt it like this."

"Oh sweetheart, you have lost nothing! I've never been touched like you touch me, with total love, passion and respect of my body. You take me places I've never been. I want to give you so much."

"You do give me so much. You are so totally uninhibited. You know how to love unashamedly. I feel like what we do together is so open and honest and there is nothing held back. I sense I know what you want and I know you know what pleases me. Everything is just so right and good."

"Yes, it is," she murmured as she nuzzled his neck moving her lips to his chest. "I'll show you just how much you have not lost."

Ben closed his eyes and his thoughts suddenly went back to that day in the woods again and when they sat in her dad's car in the garage. "Funny how things turn out," he thought. How he had felt pain from so much denial of the urgent want he felt for her then. But there would be no denial now. He remembered how she had touched him then, tentatively, unsure of herself. Now she was very sure of herself, her touch gentle and expert, hands and lips all knowing, flowing and removing any hint that there would be any pain this time. She was making love to him in ways he could have only imagined in those early days. Another storm was brewing and he felt himself being swept away with it, higher and higher he soared into the heights until his freefall began and his chute opened letting him down gently into the softness of her embrace. As his heart settled into a more normal cadence, he drew her up to him, sharing a special kiss that would forever bond them together.

Beth placed her head on his shoulder, slid her leg across his belly and combed her fingers through the gray hair on his chest. They lay there until their breathing subsided and sleep overtook them. They knew that tomorrow, today's joy would turn to sadness. For now, Beth was content to listen to his heart beating in his chest, satisfied he was at peace and happy.

How long they slept, Beth did not know. She opened her eyes and found the room still dark except for the light the moon was affording. They had moved while they were asleep; Ben was on his right side, Beth was spooning up against his back, her body formed perfectly and tightly to his. She gently kissed the back of his neck, fearful of wakening him while softly stroking his chest with her left hand.

"That feels good," he said. "I'll give you an hour to quit that!"

"How long have you been awake?" she asked, a tinge of surprise in her voice.

"I don't know; I've been listening to you snore for a while~~~rattling the windows," he teased.

"Ohh, I was not," she laughed. "Can't you sleep?"

"Don't want to~~~morning will come too soon if I sleep."

"I know; I think that is why I woke up. I like lying here like this beside you, and I can't enjoy that if I'm sleeping."

"Beth, I don't quite know how to say this, but I'll try to say it anyhow."

"What is it? You know you can say anything to me~~~anything at all."

"I know that, except I just don't know how to put it in words that can truly convey my feelings. You know I love you, but do you know how much and how much this time means to me?"

"Yes, I think so~~~and it means so much to me, too."

"But, if we never have another time like this again~~~"

"No!" she cut him off, "I don't want to hear that kind of talk!"

"You just said I could tell you anything."

"Yes, you can; but I don't want you to even think those kinds of thoughts. We have more tomorrows and the rest of our lives."

"Yes," he thought, "the rest of our lives~~~but how long is that?"

"We better try to get some sleep; we have a long drive in a bit," he said as he turned to plant a kiss on her cheek.

It was a while before Beth found sleep again as she pondered what he had said~~~and wondered why; wishing she had not cut him off.

CHAPTER XVII
Painful Goodbyes

Ben opened his eyes as the room was just beginning to show the first signs of dawn. Lying still, he listened closely to Beth's breathing, satisfied she was still asleep. Moving carefully to avoid waking her, he slowly rose from the bed and quietly moved to the desk across the room. In the subdued light of the room, he quickly scribbled a note to Beth, attempting to explain what he could not tell her the evening before, placed it in an envelope and slipped it in his luggage. Pleased that he had not disturbed her sleep, he entered the bathroom, started the shower and stepped in.

"Damn," he thought, "how the hell does she adjust this shower?" While the water was cold, it was also invigorating, causing him to hurry before frostbite set in. The sound of running water caused Beth to stir; opening her eyes finding the room was filling with the first rays of sunlight. She stretched, slipped on her robe and padded over to the bathroom, letting the fresh scent of his soap fill her nostrils. She loved the smell of his, but it was too harsh for her skin, preferring instead a non-allergenic soap of her own. When they showered together, Ben shared her soap to avoid any discomfort that his may cause her. She knew that this was probably his time of solitude to contemplate the events of the day that were to come, as she would have her moments alone as well.

"Good morning, sweetheart," she announced, the door slightly ajar.

"Hello, baby~~~I didn't mean to wake you."

"It's okay; I was ready to get up."

Ben shut off the shower and stepped out to towel off. After shaving and brushing his teeth, he pulled on a pair of shorts and a T-shirt and exited the bathroom. Beth was checking the weather report on the TV, still in her robe. "I have the bathroom all warmed up for you, my love."

"You do? Oh thank you. You smell so good," she winked as she rose up to kiss his lips. "You taste good, too! You have me at a disadvantage with my dragon-mouth. Did you have any trouble adjusting the shower?"

"You always taste good~~~even in the morning. I might have stretched the truth a bit~~~about warming up the bathroom for you. It is a bit chilly in there. That shower and I just don't get along!"

"I'm sorry sweetheart. I could have adjusted it for you. If you like, you could run down to the lobby and pick up a newspaper while I shower and get dressed. I thought we could pack our luggage after breakfast, if that is okay."

"You looked too peaceful~~~I didn't want to disturb you. Enjoy your shower sweetheart. Are you sure you don't want me to wash your back?"

"Beth chuckled, "You never miss a chance, do you? Besides, you are dried off now and nearly dressed, so I'll have to rough it."

Ben closed the door as he finished dressing, wondering when he would be able to wash her back again~~~if ever. "No, I have to put those thoughts out of my head," he thought. "No time for that now."

"I'll be back in a jiffy~~~going down after a paper," he yelled through the bathroom door. Making sure he had a room key, he pulled the door shut behind him, checking to see that it locked before proceeding to the lobby. As he reached the elevator, he met a young man already waiting for the car to arrive. "Good morning," Ben greeted the man. The man's reply was merely a low grunting sound, causing Ben to think the man must be a slow riser and not yet fully up to speed. As they entered the elevator car and the door closed, Ben again tried to make conversation with the man. "Looks like another beautiful day on the island."

"It's gonna rain," he snarled.

"Oh really, I must have missed that report," Ben replied.

The man looked straight ahead and offered no response. The elevator reached the lobby, the door opened and the man swiftly exited without a word, quickly walking around the corner and out of sight.

"Must be having a bad day already," Ben thought. "How could it be any worse than what today is going to bring me?"

Ben searched through the newspapers looking for one that had a weather summary for the nation and settled on USA Today. He folded it up under his arm and made his way back to the elevator, wondering if he would see the man again; pleased to find that he did not. He did not need any more negative vibrations today~~~from any quarter.

He opened the door to their room and found Beth already dressed and applying the finishing touches to her hair. Ben could not get over how efficient she was with almost everything she did. He never knew a woman that could be 'fixed' and ready to go as quickly as Beth.

"What took you so long? I've missed you," she winked.

"You are amazing! I thought I was fast, but I can't hold a candle to you."

"Well sweetheart, by now I know where everything is and I know how to take care of it," she chuckled.

Ben shook his head and replied, "I can't argue with that; and I might add, you know how to use it too."

She turned to him and looked up into his eyes and said in a low, soft pleading voice, "Ben~~~hold me~~~just hold me for a while."

He took her into his arms, her head against his chest and his face in her hair. He could feel her body trembling and he knew that inside she was crying. "Dammit!" he thought, "why do we have to part? Why does love have to hurt so damn much? When is enough time, enough?"

There were no words. They held onto each other as if to prevent the other from leaving. Neither wanted to leave, but both knew that they must. Finally Beth pulled back at arm's length, looked up to him, smiled and said, "Let's go get some breakfast; we have to eat darling."

Ben turned and placed his hand on the door handle, "Are you ready?"

"Yes."

Together they left and entered the elevator to the lobby. They silently entered the buffet line and slowly made their way through, neither putting much on their plate; both sticking with fruit, juices and coffee. They did not speak as they moved to a table, rather merely looked at each other occasionally as if they were taking mental photographs. The pain in their eyes clearly expressing more than words could possibly convey. It was clearly going to be a difficult morning.

Dropping her fork to her plate, Beth looked at him and stated with a tone of finality in her voice, "I can't eat anymore; we may as well go pack."

"Yes, I guess so."

Quietly, they left the dining room and returned to their room. Ben decided that he was going to try to do something to break them out of this sullenness.

He closed the door behind them, paused for a moment before asking her, "Do you remember the time I was showing off for you trying to do no-handed flips and fell flat on my rump?"

Beth smiled and replied, "Yes, I remember."

"Remember how I acted so cool as if I had planned it that way until I turned around and you started laughing at me?"

"Yes," Beth replied, starting to chuckle.

"And why were you laughing?"

"Silly~~~because you had ripped the seat of your pants out~~~the whole seam was gone."

"Yes, it was. It took a while before I figured out what you were laughing about until I kept feeling this breeze across the back of my legs. I remember reaching around to feel if there was a hole back there and the whole back of my jeans was wide open."

"You should have seen the look on your face," Beth laughed.

"Oh, I was so embarrassed, I tried walking backwards when I walked you home so you couldn't see that big gaping hole, tripped and fell flat on my back again, with both legs wide open giving you a full, wide open view."

Now Beth was laughing hard, seeing the vision in her mind again. Her laughter excited Ben's laughter, and soon they were holding each other in raucous laughter. "Oh honey that taught me a lesson I never forgot."

"What was that, sweetheart?"

"To quit showing off for you; I always end up showing my ass."

The laughter erupted again. "Oh, sweetheart, how can we walk away from this? I'm going to miss all of this, your humor, the fun we have."

"No you won't; I won't let you. I'll keep sending funnies to you."

"You know it won't be the same," she thought to herself. "You had better get started on your luggage. We have the ferry to catch before long," she reminded him.

Ben hummed a tune while he busied himself putting his things together on the couch, while Beth used the bed. As quickly as he packed his clothes, she still finished before he did.

"How do you do that?" he asked.

"Oh honey, it's not that I'm fast; you are just too slow. Men are always slow packing"

"You are fast in other ways too, like when you are getting ready to go places. I think I figured that one out, though."

"Oh you have; and what have you concluded?"

"You are so beautiful to start with, you don't have to work very long to look good. You are a natural."

"No, no, you are just so biased. It is just that after all these years, I have come to the realization that there is only so much I can do."

"No, I'm not. I noticed that the first time I saw you~~~no makeup at all; just natural beauty. After all these years, I still cannot take my eyes off you."

"I'm going to miss that, too," she mused.

"No baby, you are not going to miss anything. I will be with you every day. I'm never really far from you."

"I will always be there for you too, anytime you need me, I will be there."

"I know that, honey~~~I know that. We better get outa here, if you are all ready."

"Yes, I'm ready~~~but I'm not. I will never be ready; but yes, we had better go now. I think we can leave the bags here and they will take them to the ferry for us."

"Oh yeah, that will be great." As he moved toward the door, Beth surveyed the room one last time as if she might be forgetting something. Ben turned to see if she was coming and wondered if she might be thinking the same thing he was at this moment~~~and hoped that she was not. "Let's go sweetheart; I've checked the place and I'm sure we have everything."

Beth slowly moved to the door taking Ben's hand and replied, "No darling, I think we are leaving something here~~~I just don't know what it is." As she spoke, Ben could see her eyes starting to water, and knew instinctively she was indeed thinking the same thing that had raced through his mind moments before, bringing with them a choking, suffocating feeling much like a panic attack.

"Is my hair straight," he asked with a wink.

Beth looked up to the top of his head and smiled, "What I can see looks okay." She then fell against him, her arms tightly around his waist and her head on his chest. "Please Ben, please kiss me one more time before we leave."

Ben moved his upper body slightly away from her and tilted her face up by placing his index finger under her chin. He slowly lowered his lips to hers lightly, gently kissing her much like the first time 55 years ago. As the kiss ended, Ben started to move his head away when Beth's hands swiftly went to the back of his head pulling him back hard against her mouth kissing him passionately.

"Okay, I'm ready to go now," she said with a smile.

Ben swallowed hard and replied with a raspy voice, "So am I~~~but we don't have enough time."

Beth laughed, "Silly boy, you know what I mean."

Ben shook his head in bewilderment. "You are amazing, just like that you lit my fire."

"And what do you think you did to me?"

"You know, this ain't supposed to happen like this at our age."

"Yes, and it isn't going to last forever. Oh Ben, we are only as old as we think. Besides, we have a lot of time to make up~~~we may never get caught up, but we can try. Ohh darling, let's go before I change my mind," as she took his arm turning him back to face the door.

Ben opened the door, turned and exited the room. Beth followed as they entered the elevator. He pulled her to him, tightly in his arms again finding how perfectly they fused together, as the elevator reached the lobby. They walked together, hand in hand, to the desk to check out. "Are your bags in the room, sir?" the clerk asked.

"Yes, they are; right inside the door."

"Very good sir, we will get them to the dock right away. I hope you've had a pleasant stay and plan to come back and stay with us again."

"Thank you; we would love that," Beth replied.

Ben nodded, took Beth's hand and led them to the entrance. Upon leaving the hotel he felt Beth slow, and fall behind him. She was looking over her shoulder as if something had captured her attention. Ben stopped, turned and took both her hands in his and smiled, "You want to go back to see the flowers again, don't you?"

"No, not really; I just~~~I just hate leaving."

"We can go back; did you remember to pack your daisy?"

"Yes. I wrapped it carefully in a plastic bag and have put it in my carryon bag. It should survive the trip back to Columbus."

"Someday, I'll plant you a whole bed of daisies. Then I'll sit back and watch you bend over to take care of them~~~plotting evil thoughts for later," he chuckled.

"You are such a voyeur, you know."

"Only when I'm with you~~~always have been. I could sit and watch you move for hours. The way you walk and swing your butt, looking over your shoulder to see if I'm watching you."

"I do not swing my~~~my butt; whatever gave you that idea?" she said feigning indignation.

Ben laughed, "Honey, you have never been behind you to see how it flirts with me. Those two buns are like eyes winking at me when you walk. I'm saved by the fact you don't always wear jeans. Otherwise, I could not be responsible for what I might do in public," he chuckled.

"Ohh, you are just silly." Then as an afterthought she added, "Really?"

Ben could not contain his laughter. "Really! I love the way you walk and you still have a nice firm butt, still high and not hanging loose around your legs."

"Oh, how gross! My jeans just make it look that way."

"You forget, I've seen it without your jeans, and it is delectable."

"Well, I'm glad that you like it; it's the only one I have," she laughed.

"Well, here we are. Do we need anything special to board?"

"I have our passes in my purse; I think that is all we need."

They climbed aboard the ferry, Beth opting to sit on top outside so she could see the island again as it faded away~~~into her memory. Soon the ferry pulled away from the dock making a slow turn and got under way. There was no way she could hide the tears that quietly ran down her cheeks~~~and neither could Ben. Holding hands, there were no words needed. They both knew~~~they both felt the terrible pangs of leaving what was so precious to them.

Slowly, the island became smaller and the mainland loomed larger. Beth's heart was heavy while Ben's was breaking. He hated this feeling, this restriction in his throat as if it was constricting, making it harder to breathe. He had felt this before and it scared him. Thoughts were racing through his mind, causing his toes to curl and his fist to clench. Without being aware of it, he was squeezing Beth's hand. "Ouch. Is something wrong Ben?"

"Oh no, I'm sorry. Did I squeeze your hand too tightly?"

"Yes, but it is okay. I just thought something was wrong; you had such a strange look on your face."

"I'm fine, nothing is wrong," he said, hoping he wasn't lying to her. "I just feel bad about leaving, that's all."

"We have a lot of memories to keep us warm this winter. I've been thinking about when we can be together again," Beth murmured quietly, as she gazed back toward the island. She then turned her head to him and asked, "Have you thought about that?"

Ben was quiet, looking out over the water, before answering, "Yes, and the thought is not very comforting. The winter months seem so long and cold. Thanksgiving, Christmas, times I would like to spend with you will be hard to get through. I come alive in the Spring when the flowers are in fresh bloom and I will miss you terribly then. The worst part is," he paused and turned to look into her eyes before continuing, "is that I don't know the answer to your question."

Beth looked away from him to hide the tears that were beginning to well up in her eyes, as she wanted to hear him say something more definitive, to mention a date to meet again. They both knew the call was his to make, as she could work it into her schedule most anytime. Yet she understood his reluctance to obligate himself so early because of his other commitments. While she also understood and respected his devotion to his wife, she knew he would not be the man she loved if he turned his back on her. This was clear to her before entering into this relationship, but never the less hurt it her deeply. Feeling cheated by time and fate, she would take whatever time he could manage; there was no other choice.

Ben felt her thoughts as they both had this uncanny ability to communicate certain things without speaking. "I'm sorry, baby; I just wish I knew when we could be together again. You know I wish things were different, but we just have what we have. Sometimes I feel like I should let you go~~~to be free to find someone that can give you what I cannot. But I'm too selfish and cannot bear the thought of not ever seeing you again, or feeling your love every day."

"Oh Ben, don't be foolish. I have been alone for so many years, knowing there was someone missing in my life, someone I needed for fulfillment. I never actively looked around for that someone and accepted the fact that at my age it was much too late to find the one person I had always needed. But when we found each other," she paused as if she was having trouble finding the words, "my whole world came together as if we had never parted. I can't explain it~~~it just felt right and that it should be~~~that we should be. You were the missing someone. Now I just hope it's not hanging the next time we meet."

"What? "

"My butt."

Ben was silent, but even through the sadness, he felt his lips forming a smile. "She is amazing," he thought.

The ferry was now pulling into the dock on the mainland and the conversation was lost. Ben smiled at her and placed his arm around her shoulder, letting her head fall against his shoulder. "We're back," he whispered to her. "Dammit, we're back".

The gates opened and the passengers began departing. Ben helped Beth to her feet and they walked toward the gate hand in hand. Together they made their way to the station to wait for their luggage; leaving her there while he went to get the car. When he returned, the luggage was with Beth and they loaded it into the trunk of the car. He held the door for Beth as she entered and buckled up. As he seated himself, he found his hand shaking as he inserted the key into the ignition.

"Are you okay?" Beth asked.

"No, I'm not okay. I do not feel that it is right that we are leaving this place. I think we should just disappear somewhere, where no one would ever find us. Crazy, isn't it, thinking like an adolescent again. Maybe lost in Lake Huron. Who would ever know?"

Beth laughed, "Honey, I think they could drag the lake and find our bodies if that happened. But I like the way you think. It's okay sweetheart; we will have our time."

Ben started the engine and proceeded to I-75 and began their trip south to Midland. It would be a long distance, but one that Ben knew would not be nearly as long as the trip north. They were both quiet as Ben navigated through the traffic before entering the Interstate highway. Once he was off the ramp and onto the highway, he set the cruise and sat back to relax. "I think the minimum is 45 on this route, isn't it?" he asked with a chuckle.

"Yes, I think so. Is that what you just set?"

"No, I set it at 55. Will that give us plenty of time to make your flight?"

"Yes, I think so. We don't have to be there until 3:30.

"That's good, I don't want to mess around too long and cause you to miss it~~~or would I?"

"Remember, I have a connection to make at O'Hare, and if we are late it would mess that up too. So we better not tarry too long."

"You can't blame me for trying."

They drove for nearly an hour without another word, each engrossed in their own thoughts. Then Beth lifted the arm rest that separated the two parts of the bench seat, loosened and removed her seat belt and moved over next to Ben.

"Whoa, if a cop drives by and sees you sitting this close, we could get a seat belt violation," Ben said with a wink.

"I'll pay the fine, besides he won't see me if I put my head in your lap, will he?"

"Uhh, no~~~and I probably won't see him either, if you put your head there."

Beth laughed, "I will behave myself. Besides, I don't want to cause you to have an accident."

She adjusted herself and placed her head on his lap with her face away from his body. Ben dropped his right hand to her head and gently stroked the side of her face as he drove. He glanced over to her body that was curled up on the seat next to him, admiring the narrowing of her waist, the swell of her hip, tapering down to her thigh. He knew it was going to be a chore keeping his eyes on the road.

"What you said on the ferry, is what I felt too when we found each other. I had long given up any thought of ever being truly happy again. I figured that any possibility of passion was a distant memory and put it out of my mind. I was floating, kinda hanging around waiting to die. Hell, in so many ways, I was already dead. But when I saw your name, it was like I was reborn or something. I was excited~~~a feeling I hadn't felt in such a long time. All those memories of so many years came flooding back and I knew I wanted you. No matter what would happen,

I knew I would never be the same again." Ben was quiet then and Beth had said nothing. He wondered if she had fallen asleep.

"It did feel right, much like you said; like we should be~~~that we were meant to be together," he continued. "I stumbled around trying to find the way to tell you."

"You didn't have to," she replied, "I already knew. I could tell from the way you expressed yourself and if there was any doubt, it was dissolved after that first phone call. I knew I loved you and it was you I had missed all those years~~~what I always wanted and needed in my life. But I never thought there was any chance of finding happiness again, either. I just gathered myself together and told myself that I didn't need anyone. I did pretty well for a while~~~I thought."

"I thought you went to sleep on me," Ben chuckled.

"No, of course not," she replied. "I was listening to you and enjoying the way your fingers touched my face. Your touch is so soft and gentle~~~and warm. I love the feel of your hamstrings against my face when you shift your foot around. If this is getting uncomfortable for you, let me know and I will sit up."

"No, you're fine; you're making more memories for me."

"Ben, will there be any trouble when you get home?"

"No, I don't think so. Julie checks in on her when I travel, so everything should be okay. I never received any calls, so I'm sure everything is well there. She has everything she needs."

"Is Julie married?"

"Divorced; has been for quite a while now."

"Did you like her husband?"

"No. Nobody is ever good enough for your daughter."

"I wonder what my dad thought about you."

"Well, if he would have caught us in the garage that time, he probably would have wanted to 'take me out'", Ben chuckled.

"Maybe so, but I think he would have liked you in time."

"Perhaps. I liked your mom. She was very pretty~~~like her daughter."

"I loved both of them very much. Dad was very gentle and mom was so knowledgeable about so many things. She made growing up easy for Lynn and me. What about your parents?"

"I was found under a cabbage leaf. Don't know how I got there or who found me."

Beth laughed, "Seriously, how was your relationship with them?"

"I am serious. That's what mom told me when I asked her where I came from and I had no reason to doubt her."

The tone in his voice told Beth to avoid any more questions about that topic. There were times when it was obvious that Ben didn't want to speak about certain things and she knew this was one of them.

They were both quiet again as the miles continued to mount. As the distance grew shorter, the conversation became less, and Beth wondered if she might have said something wrong.

Ben hated the smell around airports; the smell of jet exhaust always filled the air, reminding him of an impending departure. He sensed that it was already filling his nostrils as they neared Midland. Entering the traffic pattern, he instantly became angry and frustrated with the merging drivers. "Damn fools," he muttered to himself, "where the hell did he learn to drive~~~get the hell in your own lane!"

Beth had since sat up and had fastened her seat belt, bewildered by his sudden outburst. She had never seen him behave like this before. The traffic did not seem that congested or give rise for alarm. Clearly, he was upset. She reached across the seat, touched his leg and asked, "Honey, are you okay?"

"No, I'm not okay!" he barked. "Who can be okay in the midst of a bunch of dumbasses that can't drive?"

Beth left her hand on his leg, but did not say anything else, quietly hoping they could get into the airport without any further disturbance. After some grunting, growling, sudden turns and braking, Ben finally pulled into a parking space in the airport parking lot. He turned off the engine, placed both hands on the top of the steering wheel and rested his head on the back of his hands. His body shook, as if he was sobbing. "I'm sorry baby," his voice weak and breaking. "I just," he paused for what seemed to Beth a very long time, "I just don't want~~~to be here."

Beth loosened her seat belt, lifted the center arm rest and slid over next to him. She kneaded the back of his neck with her fingers and kissed his cheek. "I don't want to be here, either. I don't want to get on that plane and leave you, but I must." She paused to see if he would react to what she had just said, but he said nothing.

"Ben~~~don't be angry; it's not like you. Honey, we've had so much more in just three days than most have in a lifetime~~~and we will have more. Anger is not good for you and it scares me when you get angry."

Ben raised his head, leaned back against the seat, took a deep breath and looked into her eyes. "Seems like I've been saying I'm sorry a lot lately. I am sorry Beth; I didn't mean to scare you. I just feel so helpless and inadequate. I hate putting you on an airplane to send you away from me and I wonder why I'm doing this."

"Because you know you must; because that is the way things are right now. I guess it is the price we have to pay for all of this stolen happiness."

"Stolen?" he asked incredulously, "I think it was we who had our lives stolen from us all those years ago. It was cruel wandering around looking for something I couldn't find, not even knowing for sure what it was. No my love, I don't think we are stealing anything. We've given and now it's time we get something back~~~but dammit~~~we're still giving."

"Honey, we can't change the past; we made our way through those years, made choices and commitments we have to live with. How could we know we would find each other again? Neither can we change how we feel, but we can control how we deal with this."

Beth paused and looked out the window trying to gather her thoughts. Ben still maintained a tight grip on the steering wheel, apparently deep in thought. She then continued, "I'm happy with what we have found and what we share. These days have been the most fulfilling days of my life, and I want more days with you. I want to share the rest of my life with you. For whatever reason, fate brought us together and I trust fate will determine what is in store for us. After all, fate has been kind to us so far~~~even if things hurt so much at times. Our love has withstood the test of time and it will endure."

Ben removed his hands from the wheel and took her into his arms. "You are the most together person, man or woman, I have ever known. Everything you have said is so right and true. I just feel it is I who is cheating you. You are free and able to be with me whenever I can get away and that's just not fair to you."

"Honey, fair no longer has anything to do with our lives. Lots of things in life are not fair. What happened to us when we were young was not fair either, but we adapt and go on, and we will again and again. I do not feel you are cheating me in any way. I understand completely your situation and respect you for honoring your commitment. I love you so much Ben, and I will accept every minute I can share with you, anytime; that's just the way it is!"

Ben's eyes filled with tears as he looked into her eyes and listened to what she was saying. "Is it any wonder that he fell in love with this girl all those years ago," he thought, "and why it is so hard to leave her now?"

He spoke, his voice low and soft, "You are a treasure to me, the very spark in my life, the reason I go on. I need you so much, knowing you are there for me. You are like medicine to me. When I'm down, you lift me. My life no longer has any meaning without you."

"I know that darling, and that is exactly how I feel about you. We need each other and we are never any further away than a phone call."

She tilted her head to his mouth and kissed his lips, tasting the salt that had come from his eyes. The kiss was soft and long, tender and pliant, one that seemed to make everything else around them disappear. They were two souls alone in the universe, floating aimlessly among the stars, never wanting to leave this place, hand in hand alone, together for eternity.

But the 'journey' ended as they returned to earth, their lips parting. Beth placed her face against his neck kissing his ear and whispering, "We better go sweetheart."

"Yes, I guess so," he replied as he pecked a light kiss on her lips before turning toward the door. He went around the car, stopping to open the trunk. Beth noticed that he was fumbling around in his luggage for something and he placed what appeared to be an envelope inside his jacket. He continued around to open the door for Beth, something he hadn't become accustomed to in all the years before, and amused it had become important now. Together they went to the rear of the car to retrieve her bags, handing the smaller one to Beth, then picking up the larger one. As they began the walk toward the terminal, Ben spoke, "I hate the smell of these places!"

"I know you do; you've told me that before. But didn't it smell better when you flew to Indianapolis to meet me last year? Or when you met me here a few days ago?"

"Yeah, I guess it probably did, but I was so excited I didn't notice it.

All I could think about was finding you there and seeing you again after so long."

"Well just think, the next time you smell the jet exhaust, we will be seeing each other again."

"Yeah and how flying starts with long walks! I swear it takes longer to get to the terminals than it takes to fly to where ever it is one is going!" Clearly, he was grumbling as he continued, "My feet tell me I almost need a flight to get from these damn parking lots to the terminal."

Beth was silent. She knew he was still having a hard time with this departure. She had never heard him complain so much and that troubled her, sensing there was more than this separation troubling him. Fear about what it might be, troubled her even more.

Finally entering the terminal they found their way to Beth's registration counter. After checking her luggage and obtaining her boarding pass, they found some seats nearby. Ben remained standing after Beth was seated; reached inside his jacket and removed the envelope Beth had seen him place there earlier. He handed it to her, looked into her eyes and said, "This is a letter I put together for you, but I don't want you to read it unless you don't hear from me for more than a day or two. It contains some phone numbers that you can call with instructions for you to follow."

"This sounds awfully sinister; will it self-destruct after I read it? And why can't I open it now?"

He chuckled as he replied, "No, there is nothing covert or sinister~~~it is just something you can use in the event I lose my phone, or have to take Helen somewhere~~~or whatever. The numbers belong to trusted contacts you will be able to reach and I will inform those people about you so they will know who you are. That's why I wanted one of your business cards. I just don't think there is any reason for you to open it now."

"You make it sound like one of those envelopes to be opened only in the event of death."

"No, of course not; it's quite the contrary really. It is just a sort of insurance thing to make sure you can find me and know where I am in case I have to move temporarily. That happens sometimes if I have to take Helen for treatment."

"Okay then; I won't open it. Are you going to be okay~~~I mean after I leave. What are you going to do after my plane leaves?"

"I hadn't thought about it. Maybe I'll go to a pub and drown my sorrows," he winked.

"No don't do that; promise me that you won't do that!"

"I'll go to the park and wait for your call after you land in Columbus."

"I can call you after I land in Chicago if you like. I have some layover time there."

"Yes, I would appreciate that~~~I worry about you when you are in the air."

Beth took his hand, "No, you shouldn't worry about me~~~or anything. I'm an experienced flyer and have done this many times and can take care of myself. Besides, I love to fly. One day we will fly together."

"Heck, I thought that's what we were doing the last few days. It's that landing thing that I don't like!"

Beth laughed, "I don't either, darling~~~I don't either."

Ben held her hand in his left hand, stroked the back of her hand with his other and fondled the love knot bracelet he had given her the night before, with his finger tips. The time passed by very quickly as a voice came over the speakers announcing her flight number.

"I better get through security honey; sometimes it takes a while."

"Those jets don't have a thing on time; it flies too!" Ben mumbled.

"Maybe it will keep flying while we are apart and before long we will be together again," she replied as she stood and picked up her carryon bag."

Ben took the bag from her and placed it back on the chair he had just vacated. He took her into his arms holding her tightly against him. Beth's arms went around him, feeling his body tremble while he held her. The emotion Ben had been feeling now consumed Beth as she found it hard to let go.

"I miss you already," she said, holding back a sob that she felt welling up deep inside her.

Ben was silent, fearful of trying to speak not knowing what his voice would sound like. Instead he whispered into her ear, "I will take you with me in my heart."

They released each other and Beth bent down to pick up her bag.

Tears from both eyes fell to the floor at her feet and streamed down her cheeks. He placed his hands lightly on both sides of her face, using his thumbs to trace the lines the tears had made, then lightly kissed her the way he had that very first time so many years ago.

He dropped his hands to grasp both of her shoulders, looked into her eyes and smiled. "They're still as electric as they were the first time."

They turned and he walked with her to the entrance of the security station. He stood there and watched as their hands slipped apart and she went through the metal detector, removed her shoes and retrieved her carryon bag from the x-ray conveyor. She turned and smiled at him, then disappeared around a corner.

He moved to an area where he could see a part of what he thought might be her aircraft and watched it move away from the gate, and then went outside to find an area where he could see the aircraft lift off the ground and rise up into the heavens. He stood and watched until he was satisfied Beth's jet was airborne and banking into the most favorable winds aloft, staring at it until it was out of sight, tears falling down his cheeks, fearing he may never see her again.

CHAPTER XVIII
An Urgent Call

~~~~*RETURN TO PRESENT DAY*

Beth had settled back on the sofa in Julie's living room and had become silent. Julie had been sitting next to her, but on the edge of the sofa facing Beth and used the break in Beth's dissertation to ask, "Did Dad wait for your call in the park or did he go to a pub to drown his sorrows?"

Beth laughed, "Oh yes, he told me he went to the park, but I could tell by the way he was talking he had made a side trip to get there. I could tell he had been crying; his voice always became very weak after he had been emotionally upset."

"I only remember dad crying once~~~after mom's accident. He was different after that~~~kind of withdrawn. I couldn't tell what he was thinking anymore. I used to be able to look into his eyes and almost read his thoughts~~~but not after that."

"Ben never told me much about the accident. Do you know how it happened?"

"Not entirely, just bits and pieces. I remember it was in the early winter and during one of the season's first snowfalls. It rained before the snow started, creating a terrible road surface. Cars were sliding all over everywhere. Dad always told her she drove too fast, but she ignored him and told him he was a poke ass," she chuckled. "We guessed she was driving too fast for conditions, as well as everyone else that day. It is believed she lost control and slid over in front of a semi-tractor trailer rig and was T-boned. It was a miracle she was not killed, as the car was totally crushed. She nearly died several times during her stay in the hospital."
~~~~

"Was her hospital stay very long?"

"Yes it was and there were many trips afterwards for surgeries to correct shattered bones and plastic surgery on her face. All sorts of complications arose such as infections, spiking temperatures, pneumonia~~~just one thing after another. The medical cost was enormous. Dad looked like he aged a lot during that time."

"Yes, stress does that to us, placing great strain on our entire system. Sometimes the stress of losing a spouse suddenly can cause the death of the other. Did Ben lose much time from work?"

"I know he lost some time, but I don't know how much. He spent a lot of time at the hospital; many times staying overnight for several days. He became pretty rundown during those days. Mom's rehab is never-ending, which added to dad's responsibilities. I helped him as much as I could~~~but I know it~~~wasn't enough."

Beth sensed Julie was suffering from an undeserved feeling of guilt, as if she had failed her dad when he needed her most. She moved to the edge of the sofa and turned to Julie, taking her into her arms. "Nonsense my dear; you were under a tremendous strain as well! You were both hurting and you did all you could. Ben adored you! He spoke of you many times and his eyes sparkled when he mentioned your name. He wondered how you managed so well living alone and admired your resourcefulness. I can tell you~~~your father was very proud of you!"

"I know he was and I was proud of him. It's just that~~~about a year or so later, Dad had a heart attack. If only~~~"

"No Julie~~~no ifs; just put those thoughts out of your mind! You could have done nothing to prevent that. There is a multitude of factors that contribute to heart attacks and stress is only one. Your father knew he had not taken good care of himself long before the events that led up to his heart attack."

"Did he tell you that?"

"Yes he did. He told me about the years he had smoked so heavily, drank too much, didn't exercise like he should have, didn't eat properly; all the things that increase the risks of heart attack and stroke~~~he seemed to relish. Besides, he had genetic predispositions that weigh so heavily. You have his genes too my dear~~~the very reason you should avoid placing so much stress on yourself."

Julie looked into Beth's eyes and smiled, "You are a very good doctor," she sniffed. "Maybe if you would have been here you could have helped him."

Beth shifter her position on the couch as the mere suggestion made her nervous.

"No~~~no one could help him; he was very ill."

"How do you know?"

"I reviewed his medical records. Ben was suffering from congestive heart failure; his heart just was not a strong pump anymore. He would need a transplant, but he was not a candidate for one."

Julie sat up straight and there was a hint of indignation in her voice as she asked, "Who decides that~~~and when did you see his charts?"

Beth had not wanted to go there, but somehow Julie had talked her right into another trap, even though it was inadvertent. She was silent for what seemed like hours before Julie spoke again, "Beth, when did you see his medical records?"

Beth's voice was subdued as she replied, "Before he~~~passed."

"You were here before Dad died?" she asked incredulously.

"Yes."

"How~~~why~~~I mean~~~how did you know?"

"Ben called me~~~told me he wasn't feeling well and that he was going to see his cardiologist. He said he felt out of breath and had no energy. He couldn't walk very far without having to sit down to catch his breath. He said he felt like he did before he suffered the MI. I told him to call 911, but he wanted to drive to the hospital. I became very emphatic and almost yelled at him to get off the phone and call 911 right now! He said I was over reacting, but I told him if he didn't call I would call from here. He said he would, and I wanted him to call me as soon as he was there. He said he would." Beth recited the information as if she had rehearsed it all.

"He must have done that, as the hospital called me and told me that he had been admitted. Did he call you?" Julie asked.

"No, he couldn't due to the oxygen mask. He had his cardio call me instead. I got more information from him than I would have from Ben anyhow and I was on the very next flight to Midland."

"Where did you go? Where did you stay?"

"I stayed in the resident doctor's quarters in the hospital, which enabled me to be close to him and keep in touch with his condition."

"I don't see how I could have missed you," Julie said, shaking her head in disbelief.

"If only you knew how close you came to seeing me," she thought before replying, "I would sit with him during the evenings when visiting hours were over."

"Were you with him when~~~"

"Yes."

Julie raised her voice, almost shouting at her, "Why didn't someone call me? Why didn't *you* call me?"

"I couldn't. Ben wouldn't let me. Let me try to explain," she pleaded, knowing it probably would make no difference. "I entered his room~~~"

~~~~RETURN TO SEPTEMBER 2007

~~~and she found Ben with lines attached to his right arm, electrodes running from his chest to supply the monitor his vitals and a nasal cannula in his nostrils. He smiled and his eyes lit up as soon as he saw her, "Oh, am I glad to see you; I've missed you," he sang out, holding his left arm out to her waiting for her hug.

She rushed to his bedside and bent over him, her upper body across his, kissing his forehead first, then his lips. "Oh honey! How are you feeling? Are you comfortable?"

"Well Doc, I was hoping you could tell me that. And by the way, this doesn't look very professional," he winked.

"It's a new type of therapy, still in the experimental stages. Sometimes it takes multiple doses, sometimes even injections. If you have brushed your teeth this morning, I'll give you a tongue injection?"

"Yeah, I have, but my mouth is very dry."

"The oxygen does that sometimes," she said as she brought his water glass over to give him a sip of water. "I'll be right back."

"Where are you going? You just got here."

"To see if I can find another glass for this," she replied as she held out a large white daisy.

"You and your daisies; do you remember when I gave you the first one?"

"Yes I do. Just hold that thought~~~I'll be right back."

Soon she returned with another water glass, added a bit of water and set the daisy in the glass, placing it on a table to the side where he could see it. She turned and sat down next to his bed saying, "I haven't seen your charts yet, so I need you to tell me how you feel."

"I feel better than when I first got here. They gave me something that made it easier to breathe and of course I guess the oxygen helps. But it seemed like it took a lot of energy to brush my teeth. I had to get that done, 'cause I figured you were coming to see me."

"And just how did you know that?"

"Well, because that was the only prayer I made. I figured I wasn't asking for much, so the ole man upstairs ought to at least grant me that request before I check out."

"Stop that! You're not checking out except for out of here to get well and go home. We have plans together~~~remember?"

"Yes, I remember. I also remember the first time we shared a tongue injection~~~in the park during our school picnic. It was our first French kiss." He smiled as his mind went back to that day. "Do you remember how hot we both became?"

She chuckled adding, "Oh my gosh yes, my heart was pounding and we were both so excited. It was so innocent and sweet. I remember how we both said we loved each other, and then followed it with 'I think'. Do you remember?"

"Yes, I've never forgotten that day and what we said. We had no idea how much those words were so true. How could we know as we had never experienced anything like that before? I sometimes think we should have run away that day."

"We were too young. I've thought about those times so often and realize there was never another time that was so good and innocent," she said as she kissed his hand. "Of course, we could not have run away then; we would have starved to death," she laughed.

Ben stared at the ceiling in thought before adding, "It wasn't long after you left that I knew I really did love you. Hell, I'd been looking for you ever since, just in all the wrong places." He looked back at her before adding, "The search was worth it~~~as I found you and life has never been the same since."

"Sweetheart, have you ever wondered how many times you have thought about me? There were so many times I'd see someone or something that reminded me of those times and of you."

"I'd never be able to venture a guess. There were times I would close my eyes when I was in bed and I'd see your face. It made me feel like a pervert, because I'd see you as a 14 year old girl and here I was, a 40 year old man. But I loved that little girl; knew I always would."

"How do you see me now?"

"The same~~~I see the little girl all grown up into the beautiful woman that is right beside me now. You have not changed~~~not even a little bit. You have the same eyes that look at me with so much love. While the blond in your hair has changed to silver and gold, it is still the hair I loved to brush against my face. Your lips are still the soft sweet lips that knocked me off my feet all those years before~~~and still do. The basic goodness that emanated from you then is still there and glows in your face." Ben paused to suck in great volumes of air through his open mouth before continuing. "No honey, you have not changed at all~~~not a bit. You are still the little girl I fell in love with!" He paused again and a tear formed in his eyes before asking. "How do you see me now?"

"I still see you as the boy who led me by the hand into that little clearing and taught me about love and emotions which I had never felt before or since. It was just so right and felt so good. I remember after our very first kiss, I went into the bathroom and looked in the mirror to see if my lips looked any different~~~because they felt so different. Of course they still looked the same, but the gentle way you kissed me, without any demands; the way you touched me as if I was someone very special, made me feel very different and unique. You were always so tender and gentle with me; today you are the loving and caring man that was the boy who held my heart all those years without me knowing what had happened. Yes, you are the same, except you are a little wounded now, but we are going to get you back on your feet right away and get you out of here."

Ben smiled and replied, "Whatever you say, doc."

"Honey, I better be scarce for a while, as visiting time is about to start and you'll be getting company." She softly kissed him saying, "I'll be back later and spend the evening with you."

"Okay baby, I'll see you later." He reached for her hand before she turned to leave; the look in his eyes spoke more than his words, "I'm so glad you're here!"

She smiled, squeezed his hand, turned and left to return to the nurse's station to go over his charts. She felt her heart sink as she read over test results, nurse remarks and his physician's notes, realizing he was very ill. His heart was badly damaged and not able to pump blood very efficiently and would soon cause him to drown on his own fluids. She knew he could be given drugs to make him more comfortable, but she also knew he would not want those and neither did she. The instructions he left in the letter he had given her at the airport the day she left, made it pretty clear he would want to stay alert and be aware of every minute; it would be up to her to see that his wishes were carried out, and she was totally committed to fulfilling his wishes.

She left a note for Dr. Collins to get in touch with her as soon as possible to discuss his treatment. Having only spoken with him by phone, she was anxious to talk with him in person. Her mind was going over the things she wished to converse with him as she approached the elevator and pushed the down button on her way to the cafeteria to grab a bite to eat. Her heart nearly stopped as the elevator door opened and without warning, she was face to face with a young woman accompanied by an older woman in a wheelchair preparing to exit. Instantly, she recognized them from the pictures Ben had shown her of Julie and Helen. With her heart racing and nearly out of breath, she managed a meek smile and a head nod, as Julie navigated the wheelchair toward her and returned her salutation. After they passed, Beth entered the elevator, turned and watched them enter Ben's room. Suddenly, she felt a chill and her eyes began to burn, feeling much older than she felt just moments before.

By the time she reached the cafeteria, she was convinced that it would be difficult to spend much time with Ben. Beth's mind was far from wanting something to eat, so she settled on just a small salad. She was just finishing it when her cell phone rang. It was Dr. Collins; he was in the ICU and was about to check in on Ben. He would be available to converse with her considering his condition and treatment options. Beth knew that she could not meet with him while Julie and Helen were there.

"I was hoping I could talk to you alone first; there are some things I wish to discuss with you in private."

"Of course, I will be in the ICU for the next hour or so as I have some other patients to look in on. I'll be happy to talk to you then."

"Thank you Doctor. I'll see you shortly."

Beth had another cup of decaf coffee to let some time pass before heading back to the ICU. As she entered the area, she went to the nurses' station again finding Ben's chart returned to the files, so she knew he had either finished with Ben or had not yet started. Soon he returned and approached the counter.

"Hello, are you Dr. Callaway?"

Beth stood up and extended her hand, "Yes, I'm Dr. Elizabeth Callaway. You must be Dr. Collins?"

"Yes, I am. I'm so happy to meet you. Benjamin has told me much about you and how dedicated you are to the children in Columbus. I know he thinks a great deal of you and values your expertise."

"Thank you. As you know, I am not a cardiologist and am not here to question your judgment. I am only here to comfort Ben and see that his wishes are carried out."

"I understand~~~probably more than you realize. I've been Benjamin's doctor for over 20 years and have come to know him quite well. He is a good man and I have assured him I will honor your requests. He has already indicated to me this is to be kept very confidential and as you know, the patient's wishes and privacy are our prime concern as physicians."

"Yes of course it is and that is Ben's most emphatic wish. Ben and I go back a long~~~"

"Yes I know, he has explained this to me in great detail and I fully understand. Like I said before, I've known him for a very long time and am aware of his~~~circumstances. You can rest assured I will take every precaution to protect his privacy~~~and yours."

"Thank you, I appreciate that. Going over his charts I can see his prognosis is not very promising. I hear the rattling in his chest from the fluid accumulation in his lungs. Do you feel there is anything that can be done to alleviate or reduce the fluid buildup?"

"No, I'm afraid not. We have done everything to rid his body of as much fluid that can be done without dialysis, as his kidneys are beginning to fail. I don't feel that is a viable option due to his overall condition. His cardiac function is just so very poor and is not putting enough blood into general circulation; therefore dialysis would not help him. As you know, the heart has to move the fluid out of the lungs and into circulation and that is not being done. We can administer medication that would ease his symptoms, but he has indicated he does not want that."

"No he doesn't, but he may change his mind as his condition worsens."

"That probably will not be long; these things accelerate pretty rapidly."

Those words struck Beth like a sledge hammer. She did not want to hear those dreaded words and suddenly felt an overwhelming urge to hurry back to Ben's bedside, as time was now becoming a premium.

Her voice was shaking and weak as she replied, "Thank you Dr. Collins, I appreciate all you have done and are doing for Ben."

"You are very welcome. If there is anything I can do to make him more comfortable at any time, you can reach me at this number," he stated as he handed Beth a card that included an emergency pager number he had highlighted.

"Thank you. It is so good to have met you."

"You're welcome. I will be talking to you later."

Suddenly what Dr. Collins had said set in~~~Ben was dying and there was nothing anyone could do to prevent it. She grew increasingly nervous as she waited for the visiting period to end. She felt precious time for them was quickly vanishing, knowing inside that Ben was failing faster than she had first thought. From her location at the nurses' station, she could see the opening into Ben's unit. Finally, she saw Julie and her mother leave and slowly move toward the elevator. After the elevator door closed, she hurried to Ben's room.

Walking into his unit, she could see his condition had deteriorated rapidly from when she had left him earlier. His monitor revealed an increased pulse rate, and the EKG tracing had changed. His heart was working harder and the nasal cannula had been replaced with a mask covering his mouth and nose. His eyes were closed, so she quietly moved the chair nearer his bed and gently held his hand in hers.

"Ben. Darling, are you awake?"

His eyes opened and a smile crossed his lips. "Yes, I'm awake~~~playing possum, waiting for you. Take this damn mask off~~~so I can kiss you," he gasped.

"Oh honey~~~you need more oxygen than what that tubing could provide."

"Bull shit!" He paused to get his breath, as the last exclamation sapped all his reserve. Finally, he continued, "You know better than~~~Doc," he paused. "I need your~~~medicine more than oxygen." Beth was perplexed by his behavior. "Now please get this~~~thing off my face~~~so I can kiss you."

Beth smiled meekly then stood up and lifted the mask up off his face. Leaning over him, she touched his lips with hers very lightly.

"That's better. That's the ~~~medicine I need. Still takes~~~ my breath away"

"No it is not the kiss that took your breath away, it is the lack of oxygen that took your breath away," she retorted as she placed the mask back over his face. Ben knew from her tone that she was not going to take any more nonsense from him.

"How did the visit with your family go?"

"Are you going to stay with me?"

"You know I will, if you behave yourself and keep that mask on."

Ben did not reply right away, and Beth wondered why he had ignored her question. Finally he looked at her and meekly said, "I don't want you to leave me."

"I'm not going to leave you, sweetheart. Do you want to sleep, honey?" she asked.

"Oh no, I don't want to sleep," he paused again, "I want to hold you close. Climb up here with me."

"No honey, I can't. Just let me put my head on your chest," she replied as she sat back down on her chair and placed her head on his chest.

Ben placed his hand on her head, running his fingers through her soft hair. He felt his eyes burning, but no tears would flow as the oxygen had dried his eyes. He knew he was dying and the only thing that bothered him about that knowledge was the fact he was going to leave her. "Damn!" he thought, "All my life spent looking for her, I finally find her and it's all over. Not fair, just not fair." Soon his breathing slowed and Beth knew he had fallen asleep, even though he did not want to sleep. She settled back in the recliner and eventually found sleep after staring at his monitor for what seemed like hours.

The activity in the ICU unit picked up along with the noise. Beth looked at her watch and discovered she had slept for nearly 5 hours. Ben was still sleeping, although it appeared he had moved, or had been moved. The tracings on the monitor seemed unchanged as she lowered her head to his chest. Finally, he stirred and placed his hand on the side of her face, slowly stroking it gently.

"You're still here."

"Of course I am. I'm not going anywhere without you."

His mouth was fairly covered by the mask preventing her from seeing his smile, but his eyes gave him away. It was clear he was pleased she was there with him. Tears formed in her eyes feeling the love he was projecting to her through his eyes.

Beth jumped to her feet as she heard the nurse greet Helen and Julie as they approached the room. Beth quickly moved out of the room and moved in a direction away from the visitors, tears running down her face, fearful to look back toward them. "Please God, let him hang on a while longer," she silently prayed as she continued to walk away. "Don't let him think I abandoned him."

The hours passed slowly until finally Helen and Julie left. She hurried back to his unit and found him with his eyes closed, but the monitor still actively showing ragged traces of his pulse.

She again lowered her head to his chest to listen to the inrush of air to his lungs, the breathing very irregular and the horrible rattle of fluid in his lungs. The heart she loved to listen to thump along so happily, now struggled to make another beat. "It isn't fair," she thought, "just not fair." Unlike Ben, her eyes were full of tears and they ran down her cheeks onto his chest. She reached across his body and interlinked her fingers with his, feeling his grip a mere hint of what it used to be.

"Don't cry baby~~~just be happy we found~~~each other," he whispered so low Beth could barely hear him with the mask covering his face. "If I died before~~~found you," he paused and moved his head from side to side before continuing, "think what we~~~missed." She nodded her head against his face in the affirmative, fearful her voice would give her away.

"You're awake. I thought you were sleeping. I love you," her voice broke and strained.

Beth did not move for several hours, stroking his chest, her fingers combing through the gray hair, as Ben apparently drifted off to sleep. Suddenly his chest surged upwards in a desperate gasp for air that shook Beth, causing her to raise her head to glance at the monitor. His pulse had increased dramatically, indicating he was in distress. She ran her hand over his bare head, finding it wet with perspiration. Standing up, she leaned over him and gently kissed his forehead. His eyes opened and in spite of his stress, a smile crossed his lips.

The nurse entered with a syringe and approached his bed. "What is that," Beth asked.

"It is a sedative that will ease his breathing and make him more comfortable."

"I asked you what it is; what is the drug?" Beth asked sternly.

"It is a combination of morphine and adrenaline, I believe. Dr. Collins ordered it."

"Dr. Collins knows that Ben has the option to refuse that injection. Morphine puts him to sleep, and he doesn't want to sleep now; perhaps later."

The nurse shrugged her shoulders, turned and left the unit. Beth then looked back at Ben's face and found him smiling broadly, his breathing slowed considerably. "You did good, sweetheart," he whispered, "you did good."

She lifted his mask briefly and softly kissed his lips. While he didn't say anything, she could tell he was pleased. "I think I know you better than that nurse and know what you need," she said with a smile. Ben nodded his head and managed a wink.

"Thank you," he murmured weakly, "for loving me."

Beth could only shake her head from side to side. "No," she thought, "It should be me thanking you." She fell forward and placed her head next to his, holding him as close to her as she possibly could. He found the strength to raise his right arm placing it over her shoulders. She listened to his lungs rattling, working hard to clear the fluid to allow more air.

Gathering as much air as he could he whispered, "I've loved you all my life~~~and missed you~~~most of it."

Beth could see that he was trying to say something more. She remained silent, stroking his head and neck, smiling at him, their eyes locked. She could always look inside him through his eyes; it was like a window to his soul. He then continued, "My heart is broken~~~only room for you now." He paused again, longer this time, his eyes still searching hers. "I'm taking you with me~~~in my heart," clearly struggling now, "not going to miss you anymore."

"Don't speak, sweetheart," Beth replied, her voice trembling violently, tears now streaming down her face, "Yes, I'm going with you~~~I won't be long."

"Yes I know~~~I love you~~~"

She placed her head back on his chest again and said "I love you, too," and listened to the heart that had given her so much love, struggle one more time and then go silent. She heard his last breath escape his lips forming her name, "~~~Beth."

Fear and loneliness suddenly gripped her as she realized he was gone and with him, a very big part of her as well. She was frozen, not wanting to move; holding him and wishing desperately to hear his heart beat again. Finally, she rose and removed the mask from his face. She leaned down and kissed his lips before moving to the lavatory to wet a washcloth with warm water to wipe his face. Tenderly, she wiped the dried tears from his face and straightened the hair that ringed his head. Once more she kissed his forehead and whispered to him, "I will take you with me in my heart~~~you will never leave me

CHAPTER XIX
The Last Daisy

~~~~*RETURN TO PRESENT DAY*

Julie leaped to her feet, so angry the words all ran together almost incoherently. "How could you not have called me~~~us? You~~~you knew~~~knew he was dying and~~~and you didn't call us!" She gathered her thoughts together and continued, almost screaming, "How could you be so damn selfish and not call us?"

Beth's eyes filled with tears and streamed down her face. "I wanted to let you know~~~I felt you should be there~~~but, but Ben would not let me."

"How could he stop you? No, nooo, you just did not want us to know about your little secret!"

"I'm so sorry Julie. I know how you must feel. I just could not go against his wishes. And yes~~~I was selfish too; I did not want to leave him. I'm so sorry I hurt you!"

"I cannot believe this! How could I have been taken in by you like this? I should have known~~~I should have known! Those~~~those daisies on his grave, the one in dad's room~~~ohhh, how could I have been so damn stupid? Is this the kind of web you spun around my father?" Julie paused, her pulse racing, and glared for what seemed like hours. Beth knew there was nothing more she could say that would quell Julie's anger. Finally she spoke again, her voice projecting a tone of finality. "I think you should leave~~~now! I don't ever want to see you again."

Beth slowly stood to leave, feeling like she had failed Ben. She had felt a bond forming with Julie and wanted to pursue it and nurture it, but
~~~~

now it looked like any chance of that was shattered. She reached into her purse and removed the letter Ben had given her.

Her hand was shaking violently and her voice quivered as she extended it out to Julie. "Julie, this is the letter Ben gave me at the airport before I returned to Columbus. I want you to have it."

"I don't want it! I don't want anything you have! I just want you to leave!"

Beth felt her heart sinking; her legs weak and trembling as she slowly turned and moved toward the door. Everything she had hoped would come to pass with the two of them seemed lost and hopeless. Her vision was blurred when she reached for the door handle, her hands weak and shaking as she opened the door. Without realizing, a strong blast of air entered the room, taking the letter from her hand and swiftly blew it underneath a small table adjacent to the door. Her legs were like rubber bands as she walked to the car, suddenly feeling much older and wishing she could die. "Oh Ben, how could I have done this~~~I hurt her so much," she thought. "Oh why did I tell her?"

Her hand was still shaking, finding it difficult to place the key into the ignition switch. Finally, the engine came to life and she felt her stomach churn as the car moved away from the curb and into the traffic. Her tear-filled eyes blurred her vision, making her keenly aware she no longer cared what happened to her, as if all her bridges were being burned forever. She wanted to lie down somewhere and die.

Upon entering her hotel room, she rushed into the bathroom and immediately lost the contents of her stomach. Huge sobs pulled at her diaphragm between spasms of stomach upheavals, causing her to nearly choke. Feeling her life was now over, as if there was no longer anything left to live for, she pulled herself up off the floor, threw her body across the bed and wept uncontrollably. Tears would not come anymore; just jerking sobs that ripped at her gut, shaking her to the core. The sorrow of Ben's passing came rushing back, more hurtful now feeling that she could never visit his grave again. The beautiful memories they shared together escaped her now, when she needed them most.

Soon after Beth had left, the anger Julie had felt hearing the revelations from Beth overwhelmed her. Tears that never seemed to flow when her father died now flooded her eyes causing sobs that coursed through her body. There had always been a mystery about her dad she never quite understood; something that made him seem distant from her. Without being fully aware of it, she always felt a subtle resentment toward him, as if he was keeping something from her~~~something she felt was very special to him, yet he would not share it with her. Many times she would see him staring at the ceiling with a smile on his face~~~somewhere else~~~certainly not home with her mother and her. That resentment held back the tears when he died, coupled with the fact he died alone, without them. Now it all came to the surface and she cried until there were no tears left. Now she could blame someone else for the resentment she felt toward her father; it was Beth's fault!

Completely exhausted from the distress and emotion, she collapsed on the sofa. As her head reached the pillow, her swollen eyes spotted something under the end table near the door. Fearing she might fall asleep, she got up to lock the door, and then stooped down to retrieve whatever was under the table. Instantly, it was clear to her that it was the envelope that Beth had wanted to give to her. Her first impulse was to throw it away, but she recognized her father's scrawl that read: *Beth. Only to be opened if you haven't heard from me for a day or two.*

Not really caring that it was addressed to Beth, she was curious as to what her father had said before he died, even if it was something he had written to Beth. Opening the envelope, she slowly began to read the hand scribbled words of her dad.

My darling,

If you are reading this, it means I'm probably incapacitated and not able to call you. I've enclosed these telephone numbers for you to call and I have already informed these "colleagues" of yours to obey your every command. They have been instructed to keep you informed of what is going on with me and you are to be treated as one of my medical team members. They have your card, so they already know who you are. I have told my cardiologist he is supposed to grant your wishes, as I have appointed you my guardian in case I'm not able to convey my wishes to them. I trust you implicitly! I've told you before~~~I trust you with my life.

I have suspected for some time now that there is something going on in my chest. I hope I have not waited too long to check it out. Hopefully, that is all that is going on now. Whatever, there are some things I want you to know and I trust you will carry them out for me, if I am not able.

I've told you many times I want to spend my last days with you and you alone. I have spent the bulk of my life without you, instead giving myself to my family, who I also love very much. We both knew and understood why that should be. Fate was very cruel to us, taking you away from me when we were too young to do anything about it. It should have been us from the beginning, but life just didn't work out that way. Somehow, we found each other after too many years, and the ember that smoldered all those years became an inferno. I owe you the rest of my time. We owe it to each other. I hope that we can sometime read this together lying next to each other with your head on my shoulder, then throw it on the floor and enjoy another sweet kiss. However, if that is not possible, then I want to spend the time I have left with you, exclusively. I'll try my best to hold out for that to happen, so that we can be alone. I know this is a hell of a way to say all this and it seems so macabre,(is that a word, Doc) but it has to be said. See why I didn't want you to open this earlier?

I hope you never take any flak for doing this. Julie might be angry with you, but if so, show her this letter, as I don't want her to be angry with you. It has always been my hope that someday you could meet Julie and learn to love her as I do. The two of you are so much alike. I had always hoped to meet Karen; who knows, maybe all of this has already happened as you read this~~~but I don't think so. I hope I am wrong as there is so much more I want to share with you.

If I can't wait for you to get to me, always remember, you are the love of my life. I love you with every fiber of my being and soul. No matter where I'm going, I'm taking you with me in this breaking heart of mine. You will always dwell in my heart and soul.

I love you, my precious sweetheart. That first kiss has lasted a lifetime! Wow! What a trip! Thank you for the most joyous time of my life.

Forever in my heart and soul,

Ben

Julie was frozen as she read the letter. It was almost like her dad had known how she would react and was talking to her from the grave. He knew her so well and Julie felt she had let him down. She read it again and again; especially the part about her father's wish that Beth will not receive any flak for carrying out his wishes. Now she knew where her father was during those times he seemed so distant, and why he couldn't share those thoughts with her. How could he? "Ohhh, how stupid of me~~~what have I done?" she murmured to herself. Quickly she fixed her hair and makeup. Suddenly a thought crossed her mind and without pausing, she crossed to her library and removed the dictionary. She removed a flattened daisy she had found in her father's room after he had died, had taken it home and preserved it inside the dictionary.

"Oh, I have one more stop to make before I get to Beth's hotel," she thought. "I just hope I can make it in time," she murmured as she rushed out of her home. Hoping she could make her stop and get to Beth before she leaves for the airport, she weaved through traffic at a hellish rate. Finally, she arrived at the hotel, her heart racing, hoping she wasn't too late and wondering what she was going to say. She parked her car, made her way into the hotel and nervously approached Beth's room.

Beth had just finished attempting to hide her swollen eyes with makeup and was preparing to leave for the airport when there was a knock on her door. Opening it, she found Julie standing there holding the envelope in one hand; her other hand behind her back.

"This belongs to you," her voice weak and shaking, "you must have dropped it on the floor before you left."

Beth was startled to see Julie and immediately thought she had not vented all her anger. "What was in her other hand~~~a gun; was she planning to shoot me?" she wondered. She realized she didn't care as she took the envelope from her and with a quivering voice said, "Thank you, Julie. I'm so~~~"

Julie cut her off, extending her other hand from behind her back which held a single daisy and a small elongated package, "I think this belongs to you too."

Beth took the daisy and the package that contained the pressed and dried daisy. The bewilderment she displayed on her face spoke more than her words, as she stammered, "What is~~~where~~~where did you find this? How~~~"

"I found this one in dad's ICU unit when mother and I visited him. It was in a glass of water and I wondered who might have placed it there. I was drawn to it because it was so vibrant when I first saw it, but after dad died, it drooped and appeared like it had died, too. After everything you told me about the times you spent with dad and how the daisies were always popping up with you, I realized where the daisy in his room had come from~~~and when it was put there. You were there early, weren't you?"

"Yes, I came as soon as I talked to Ben's cardiologist. I tried to stay out of you and your mother's way during the day hours. I looked in from time to time to see how you were doing. I just tried to find the times when you were home to spend with Ben. I didn't want to interfere with your time with him"

"I know that now."

"Julie, please come in."

Julie entered the room, stared at the floor and said, "I read the letter. I understand now and feel terrible about the things I said to you. Thank you for being with my dad when his time came. I know now that is how he wanted it to be and he was happy when he left us."

Raising her face to look Beth directly into her eyes, she continued, "Oh, and this one is for you~~~sort of a peace offering," she sheepishly said, handing the fresh daisy to Beth.

"Oh thank God~~~Julie!" Beth took her into her arms and tears that both had thought were gone filled their eyes again. But they were different tears now; ones of relief instead of sadness. They embraced each other for what seemed like hours, feeling their bodies tremble and jerk, until Beth held Julie at arm's length and looked into her eyes. "Your father knew you very well~~~he knew both of us very well. You were the apple of his eye and I know he wanted the two of us to spend time together. He wanted us to know each other. Maybe tomorrow we can both take this daisy to him, together."

"Isn't your plane due to leave soon?"

"Yes, but maybe you could call that friend of yours that works for the airline," Beth winked through the tears.

"Oh yes, I will. And together we can check on some properties that are for sale in the area."

"I would love that. I would truly love that. Ohh please Julie, sit down while I put this daisy in some water before it dries out any more."

"Okay. I better call my friend at the airport and see if we can change your reservations," Julie replied as she was seated and entered the number in her cell phone.

Beth entered the bathroom with the daisy to place it in a glass of water. She looked into the mirror seeing her reflection holding the daisy tightly in her hand, her swollen eyes and the fresh makeup running down her face. She held it to her lips and kissed it gently. She felt her chest swell as the first breath of sweet relief filled her lungs. She could again feel his presence, seeing his smiling face in the daisy, knowing he would always be present in her heart. She carefully placed the daisy in the glass, gently cupping it with her hands, adjusting it perfectly in front of the mirror. Seeing it from the front, the back of it reflecting in the mirror, told her that while he had left, he was still here. A broad smile crossed her face as she joined Julie, knowing there will be many bright days ahead, and many daisies to cultivate~~~together.